Library VERSION ONLY

Ebook Cover: Pretty in ink creations
Editing & Formatting: Little Tailfeather Publishing
Editing, Proofing, backgrounds, & Formatting: Dirty Sexy Words/ Storm shield Editing/Little Tailfeather Publishing
Cassandra's logos: Pretty in Ink Creations/Artlogo
Goosebusters Alpha team: Kat Silver, Becky Ross, Erica Taryn
Sensitivity Readers: Brit Mason, Gail Jericho
Translation Consultant: Mo Jacobs
Legal Services: Joshua Farley, esq.
Agent: Laura Pink at SBR Media
Images/Fonts: Depositphotos, Shutterstock, Canva, & Photoshop

No GenAI was used within this book. All errors and greatness are by an adhd muppet.

SIGNATURE PAGE

CASSANDRA FEATHERSTONE

CONTENT WARNINGS

This is a *whychoose contemporary romance with poly elements*—our FMC, Remy, will not have to choose between love interests.

There are many situations included that are intended for mature audiences (18+).

In this book, there may be instances/references that could trigger some individuals such as:

- *HACKING*
- *SMUGGLING*
- *DECAPITATION*
- *DECOMPOSITION*
- PAST TRAUMA (PHYSICAL & EMOTIONAL)
- VIOLENCE
- EMOTIONAL ABUSE
- ALCOHOL ABUSE
- PTSD
- BLOOD
- DOMESTIC VIOLENCE
- FOUL LANGUAGE- LOTS OF IT.

- GRAPHIC VIOLENCE
- UNHEALTHY COPING MECHANISMS
- DEATH
- BODY MODIFICATIONS
- FANCY PIERCINGS
- EXPLICIT TORTURE/RENDITION METHODS (BRIEF, BUT THERE)
- ELECTROCUTION
- WATERBOARDING
- DENTAL EXTRACTION
- CUTTING
- BEATINGS
- STARVATION
- SOUND TORTURE
- SLEEP DEPRIVATION
- SENSORY DEPRIVATION- NON SEXUAL
- RESTRAINTS
- GUN VIOLENCE
- KNIFE VIOLENCE
- DANGEROUS FEATS THAT SHOULD NOT BE ATTEMPTED AT HOME
- RAW SEX
- A SHADOW DOUCHE
- WIRE PLAY
- INAPPROPRIATE USE OF GUITAR STRINGS
- LOTS AND LOTS OF SNARK
- POP CULTURE REFERENCES
- EASTER EGG APPEARANCES OF CHARACTERS FROM OTHER SERIES IN THIS UNIVERSE
- *THEFT*
- *ASSASSINATIONS*
- *HEISTS*
- *EMOTIONAL MANIPULATION*
- *SEXUAL COERCION (USED AS A WEAPON BY MCS BUT NO CHEATING)*
- *BAD DECISIONS MADE BY ALL AT TIMES*

- ROUGH SEX
- PUBLIC SEX
- BDSM
- *BODY PARTS USED AS A MESSAGE*
- *HUMAN TRAFFICKING (MC)*
- *KIDNAPPING (SOME MCS, SOME OUTSIDE MAIN GROUP)*
- *THREATS OF SEXUAL ABUSE—BUT DOES NOT HAPPEN ON OR OFF PAGE*
- *DRUG USE*
- *DRUG SALES*
- *POOR TREATMENT OF SUBORDINATES*
- *FORCED VOYEURISM (NOT NON-CON)*
- *EXPLOSIONS*

No sexual practices in this book should be taken as safe or appropriate for real life application.

Content warnings are important and I don't ever want to harm a reader.

STALK CASSANDRA FEATHERSTONE IN THE DARK CORNERS OF THE WEB

JOIN MY FACEBOOK GROUP AND FOLLOW ME EVERYWHERE!

WANT MORE?

SIGN UP FOR MY
BI-WEEKLY MANIFESTO FOR A FREE
SERIES SAMPLER:

AUTHOR RAMBLINGS

FEATHERSTONE

Readers,

This year has been a crazy and I am so grateful to you for sticking it out with me.

I was light years ahead with my writing—including this book—until the little skirmish in June, followed by my grandma's passing. It was a lot in terms of my mental health, but also in dealing with my family. Once I got everything settled, I was behind on IPWT, but I was also gliding into preparation for the WOTR con in July. That put me further behind, and well, it just snowballed from there.

However, I am proud as hell to have put out IPWT after all that time and adversity and now... I'm fluffing my feathers over getting Ruthless out without too much postponement.

Remy is a fantastic FMC to follow Dolly in that, while our bunny is finding her way, the assassin knows exactly who she is and why. Her singular focus in this book made the spice level lower, but it's showcased a massive amount of character development and world-building. My alphas have been salivating over the new information they've gotten from this book, including the glimpses of how some characters became who they are now.

Keep in mind, there are three more books, so you're not gonna get everything just yet.

Whereas Dolly is finding out her convictions, Remy—no matter what her alias is at the time—knows exactly what is beyond her boundaries and acts upon it without fail. She's fully in her 'villain era' and unashamed, which I adore.

I'm headed into this place myself, and it's like waking up from amnesia to remember who I am.

Hopefully, you will love seeing the growth, friendship, ferocity, and thrills this book has in store. I'm excited for the next book on my docket and the cover reveal for Wicked.

Remember: I'm only placing preorders on my site from now on (except for co-writes/collections) and doing so will ensure your copy of that book comes before it gets loaded to the Zon. I won't have to fight tight deadlines that can cripple us and it allows me to produce more content, more often because I can jump around.

As always, I am eternally grateful for all of your support and kindness. My readers are a special community of their own, be it on FB, IG, Ream, or even in person. I love hearing from you and appreciate all your amazing reviews and posts.

Blood and guts,

Cassandra Featherstone
QUEEN OF SMART. SASSY SPICE

READER'S NOTE
A FEW THINGS YOU SHOULD KNOW...

Bloodthirsty should be read *before* this book.

I would consider the series a medium burn, slow build family group.

___This particular book is a slower burn due to specific plot circumstances.___

The series will get spicier in the following books. If you're looking for porn with little to no plot, no judgment, but this isn't the series for you. It's also not closed door or FTB, so I believe the spice will be worth the wait. I realize spice scales are subjective and everyone has different opinions on it, so forgive me if mine and yours aren't totally aligned.

This is a multi-book series, so *everything will not be revealed in the first book*. Some plot lines will continue through series in a larger arc and not get resolved in the first or even the next book.

I write lengthy books with intricate world building, strong character development, and *lots* of tiny threads that stretch throughout a series that may not always seem important at first glance. However, I promise nothing I put to paper and leave in the book is unimportant; it may simply become *more* important later on. There is no 'throwaway' detail in my worlds, so every scene will mean something eventually.

I promise it will all get tied up and have a HEA; don't worry!

Ruthless is a why choose/poly romance, which means our FMC will not have to choose. It is part of a larger universe called the *Legends of the Ouroboros*, but you do not have to read other series to enjoy this book. You may miss an Easter egg or two, but you won't be lost.

There are some words that are slang, jargon, or foreign that may seem to be spelled wrong—*please email the author or find her on social media rather than report to Amazon* if you find a typo. This has been proofed and edited *several* times since release; if you believe you found errors, you may not be correct. It could be a stylistic choice or a dialect choice. Please do not assume the two ARC teams, betas, alphas, and several proofers missed everything you believe is incorrect.

Please do not email critical feedback that is not a simple typo or formatting issue—this book is written and released. It will not be changed after publication to suit personal editing opinions or requests.

If you see this book *anywhere besides Kindle Unlimited in ebook format,* please reach out to me via social media or email. Pirating kills my ability to write full time and I am so grateful for your help.

Contact my team for typos or to report piracy: teamcassan drafeatherstone@cassandrafeatherstone.com

A NOTE TO MY LOVING FAMILY MEMBERS AND FRIENDS...

THANK YOU FOR SUPPORTING ME BY BUYING MY WORK.

NO, REALLY, I APPRECIATE YOU ALL HELPING ME MAKE MY CHILDHOOD DREAMS COME TRUE.

HOWEVER, I'M NEVER GOING TO ALLOW A REPEAT OF THE ILL-FATED PARTY OF 2021. I CANNOT DO IT. IT'S JUST TOO CRINGE.

THEREFORE, YOU ARE HEREBY WARNED NOT TO READ THIS BOOK UNLESS YOU'RE PREPARED TO DEAL WITH THE DESTRUCTION OF YOUR ALGORITHMS THAT HAPPENS WHEN YOU GOOGLE THIS SHIT INSTEAD OF ASKING ME.

BOILERPLATE CAVEAT: IF YOU CHOOSE TO KEEP READING, KNOW THAT AT NO TIME WILL I EXPLAIN TERMS, POSITIONS, THEMES, TROPES, OR ANY OTHER PART OF THIS NOVEL AT FAMILY EVENTS, IN GROUP CHATS, OR ON SOCIAL MEDIA.

DON'T ASK.

To the women out there working to shatter glass ceilings and break down walls put there by insecure men, The Guillotine suggests letting your crazy out…once.

Just so they know who they're messing with.

RUTHLESS PLAYLISTS

CHAPTER TITLE SONGS

Ruthless Chapter Playlist

BONUS PLAYLIST

Take 'Em Out Playlist

WAIT!

A FINAL REMINDER BEFORE YOU READ...

My series typically have prequels, gap novellas/novels, and bonus material that are integral to your having a satisfying reading experience.

If you have not read the other pieces in this series, you may feel as though you have missed critical details, developments, plot points, and other information. This will cause the book to appear to have continuity gaps that it does not have.

If you have not read the bonus material for this series, it is available online here, in audio versions (if applicable), and in print special editions (if applicable).

I highly recommend consulting the bonus page prior to reading this new title so you're up to speed on all the things going on in this world.

Happy reading!

PREVIOUSLY ON BLOODTHIRSTY...

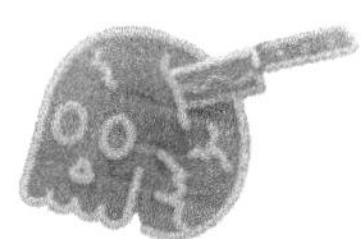

Remy Arsine Benoit has secrets—ones that keep her alive. The rumors of her death were widely exaggerated, as the saying goes.

Since that fateful night at the *Les Invisibles* training academy, she clawed her way from the depths using every skill and ruthless instinct she had to eventually claw her way to the top of her intended profession while hiding behind the mantle of The Guillotine. No one knows the feared assassin is a woman, much less that it's a silver haired girl who supposedly died in an explosion while trying to escape the criminal organization that raised her to be a bloodthirsty killer.

After she took her revenge on her ex-mentor, she went on a rampage that solidified her reputation and since built a thriving business based on her cold, efficient handling of the contracts she accepts. Remy is a shadow in the dark—she keeps crash pads and home bases, not a home. She has caches of equipment and supplies all over the world to help her complete missions. The Guillotine works alone because no one can be trusted.

That is a lesson she learned when the five men she called her team and her first loves betrayed her—an action that led to her 'death' in a fiery explosion on the water.

Unfortunately, Remy's past became her present when she decided to celebrate in a tourist bar in Paris after a successful job. Against her better judgment, she rescues international rock star and member of The Five, Coda Ramone from a group of drunken frat boys. From that moment on, her expertly planned life is completely up-ended.

The Guillotine is contacted by a mysterious client she calls 'Shadow Douche' who offers her a contract to kill the infamous hacker *La Arana*. She accepts despite knowing that is the code name for another one of her exes, Raz Miranda. Obtaining the intel necessary to track the most secretive hacker in the world takes her on a merry chase around Europe where she runs into the rest of The Five while in various disguises. None of them recognize one another—a fact made possible by professional disguises, body augmentations, and the changes in appearance as they all grew up.

Remy breaks all of her rules with them—including sleeping with Jinx and Dwyn—and finally ends up at a party where everyone gets taken hostage by odd criminals who refuse to give up their employer before they die. Recognition sparks on her end and with the help of a colleague from past jobs, Remy decides to meet up with the guys in London to lay everything on the table.

After all, someone is clearly trying to kill them or her and she's tired of playing games.

Read the prologue to refresh yourself on what happens in the final chapter of *Bloodthirsty*.

HEY, YOU!

PROLOGUE (FROM BLOODTHIRSTY)

REMY

The barrel on my forehead doesn't bother me. It's not the first gun pointed at me, nor is it the first time I've had one to my forehead like this.

But the man in front of me is well aware of that.

I should have known Raz would put the pieces together. He's always been the most brilliant and best multi-step thinker in the group. His IQ trumps mine, and that's nothing to shake your finger at. Now he's looking at me as if he'd truly love to finish the job that Professor Arnaud and the fuckwits at *l'Académie* started all those years ago. It's a wee bit sad, but I can understand why.

As much as I mourned them—and myself—they had to mourn me and their part in my death.

"If it was going to be anyone, I should have known it would be you," I mumble. Slowly, I reach up and pull the wig off of my head. Next, I unzip the hoodie to reveal the tiny, backless crop top that will allow them to search for the marks they will need to confirm Raz's theory. Then I remove the wig caps one by one and let the waterfall of white hair fall to my waist. Last, I put my finger in each eye and pop out the contacts masking my unique eye color. When I'm done, I look up at them, tossing the UV light I crammed in my pants pocket at Coda. "Go on, then. Do what you must."

He fumbles for a second, but I assume that has to be because he can't process what he's seeing. When it takes too long, Mo strides over and grabs the device from him, clicking it on and pointing it at me. The light crawls over my body and I turn slowly so they can see the tattoos running over me until they get to what they're looking for.

Just below my right breast on my ribcage, the brand of *Les Invisibles* is still raised. I've had UV ink swirled around it to distract from the symbol, but in the middle, shining like a beacon, is the mark of The Six. I never had it removed, just augmented my work around it so it didn't appear to be the mark of an organization.

"Mother. Fucker," Dwyn breathes as his eyes widen. "It's… It's…"

"The rumors of my death were greatly exaggerated," I snark as I look at Jinx. The curve of his lips gives me hope and I turn my gaze to the man holding the light on me.

"I'll say," Coda mutters. "This is some Elvis level bullshit right here."

"Thank you very much." I do my best impression of The King, but it doesn't get the laughs I wanted.

"Look…"

"We carried a casket," Raz snarls as he yanks the gun away and turns on his heel. "We had to bargain with that old bastard to get them to call it an accident. Do you know what price we paid for your bullshit?!"

That sends me over the edge. *How fucking dare he talk about the price they paid?* Nothing that happened to them could remotely compare to the ordeal I went through escaping that hellhole, reinventing myself, and starting out on my own for the first time in my entire life.

"Look, you sanctimonious twat. I didn't come here to rehash the past, but since you opened that steaming pile of shit; take a big, nutty bite." I look at each of them one by one before I continue. "You may have hurt and you may have gotten punished for whatever you did after I was gone. But none of that compares with what I had to do to get away from there without anyone knowing."

Raz opens his mouth, but I hold up my hand. "No, sir. You don't get to snark at me about your poor wittle feelings. I had to do things I never imagined, even growing up in *LI*. Once I'd swum the thirty miles to shore while injured, dehydrated and ducking fucking sharks, I had to do things I will never speak of again. Once I had enough money, I got out of the country. It took months to make my way to Europe and the entire time, I took on the jobs almost no one will take. I had nightmares for the first five years; I still sleep less than most humans."

Mo frowns, and even Coda rubs the back of his neck, but they stay quiet.

"When I finally got to Europe, it was almost a year after the explosion. Things had healed wrong. I had no identity, and Remy was dead. I'd never in my life been on my own with no support before, but I knew what to do to establish myself. So I did more horrible things to fund that. And little by little, I built a reputation as a bloodthirsty, ruthless villain they began to call 'The Guillotine'. It suited me and I let it ride, even though no one seemed to realize I was a female. After a while, I purposely allowed the legend to be devoid of any identifying information—it helped me work in the shadows."

"I tracked Arnaud down in my second year. He'd left the safety of *l'Academie*—something I'm sure you all had a part in—and I made him pay for swaying you all to betray me. That didn't fix me and I went on a famous bender they called '*La Revolution de Guillotine*'. I never liked the stupid naming thing, but man, did that blood and gore fest get me clients. *Et voila*, I was established."

Jinx clears his throat and looks around before asking, "Why didn't you come for us? I mean, even for revenge if you hated us so much."

My smile is bitter as I pull the pocket wire out and fiddle with it to quell my anxiety. "Because I never healed from your bullshit. I thought about sneaking into rooms and slicing every one of your heads off repeatedly… But I couldn't even plan your deaths without plunging myself into the darkness. When I let the darkness in, I ceased to exist. So, eventually, I pretended you all died instead of me."

"Your solution was to play 'if you can't see me, I can't see you' like when we were kids?" Dwyn gives me a tiny smirk and I feel one knot in my chest loosen.

"Sort of?" I shrug my shoulders. "I got the UV ink over time to cover the mark. I covered all the scars from training. I created my network, all on my own, and by the time I finished that, revenge didn't seem important anymore. The life I had with you in it ended when that bomb went off on the boat and I didn't look back."

"We grieved for you. We mourned. Hell, none of us has had a serious relationship with anyone outside of this group for over a decade, Remy." The quiet statement comes from Coda, and he lifts his beautiful sapphire eyes to mine. "The number of times one of us has bailed another out of some semi-suicidal mission or bender is more than I'd prefer to admit."

"Especially him," Mo grumbles as he crosses his arms over his chest.

I sigh, sliding the garrote open and closed, letting the familiar motion soothe me. "Would it help to say that I haven't helped myself to round two with a person since the boat? The first time I even considered it was…"

"With us." Dwyn's face lights up when he realizes what it took me far longer to figure out.

I nod silently, not looking any of them in the eyes. "Yes."

"Why?" Raz whirls around and glares at me. "Why did you leave them bullshit clues and take off?"

Letting my weapon snap back into place, I wrap my arms around myself. "Hell if I know. I did it with Dwyn before I slipped out to my real compartment to hide. I was shocked at myself all day afterward. Then that fucking party happened, and I was trying to leave, and Jinx stopped me. I did it again, and I had no idea why."

"You know why," Mo growls. "Just admit it."

Tears prick behind my eyes and I refuse to let anyone see that. "Look, asshole. I'm broken; I'm so fucking broken that the three therapists I saw all couldn't even figure out where to begin before I killed them. I quit trying after that. I've lived like an unattached vagabond ever since. I don't have an actual home—only crash-pads and storage units—and Lys is the first almost-friend I've ever had. And I kind of only did that three days ago. Don't ask me to tell you why in the hell I do anything right now, because I do. not. Know."

BEFORE ANYONE else can interrogate me, a loud alarm sounds from what seems to be Raz's pocket. His eyes widen and he pulls the device out, looking at the screen with a perturbed expression. "Fuck. Fuck, fuck, fuck... How in the goddamn hell is this possible?" he yells.

"RAZ!" Jinx walks over and puts his hand on his arm. "Slow down and tell us what's wrong."

He whirls on me and snarls, "Did you do this? Is this your ultimate revenge?"

"Is what my ultimate revenge, you twatwaffle? I have no idea what you're even talking about!" I scream back.

This kind of shit is why I stayed alone and unencumbered all of those years. All men do is cause fucking problems and then blame them on you simply because you don't have a dick to swing back at them.

Newsflash for these motherfuckers: I *will not* let them treat me like shit again.

"I set up cams and shit earlier. Because I remember what it looked like in Berlin, I also set up sensors and a few other things. Nothing —not one thing—has tripped any of it all afternoon or I would not have let us walk in here. But…"

Mo sucks in a deep breath and lets it out slowly. "But what, Raz?"

"The alarms are going off. Not for now, while we're here, but they're alerting me from the fucking past." He glares at me again, and I throw my hands up.

"I didn't even know we were coming here until, like, an hour beforehand! You fuckers hid it from me!"

"Plenty of time to—"

"Raz, what timestamps do those messages have on them?" Jinx tilts his head as he asks, looking hopeful.

He frowns and scrolls for a moment, then sighs. "Earlier than when we told her. Fuck."

"Unless I'm a goddamned psychic, it wasn't me!" I point at him, my expression mutinous. "Why would I do something to this place and walk into it? That's fucking bad tradecraft and you know it!"

"I wasn't really thinking about—"

Another loud sound interrupts his retort, this time a computerized voice that booms through the room. "Execute. Three, two, one…"

"Out, out, out!" Mo shouts as his eyes widen. "Go!"

They drop all pretense as we drop our bullshit and run for the door like the hounds of Hades are on our heels. Cramming our way through the doorway, we burst into the hall leading to the classroom and every one of us sprints towards the entrance we came in through. I look over my shoulder, seeing the boys I loved in the men I'm running with, and in that moment, the world explodes.

I knew saving that dick in Paris was going to get me killed.

Then everything goes black.

DOWN WITH THE SICKNESS

REMY

The metal music is blaring at top volume—as it has for twenty-four hours a day for the past two weeks.

I tune it out easily; the CapRes training on the island always included sound deprivation and overstimulation. After the first couple times, you find rest while sirens or metal music or sounds of battle are on blast. You have to learn to go somewhere else in your head. I can say the same for torture, and there's been plenty of that during my time here, too.

Wigs, makeup, and prosthetics are long gone at this point in my stay. My long silver hair is matted and filthy, but since I'm so careful not to let anyone see the real me, it hasn't triggered recognition. My captors still don't know who I am—not even one of my many aliases, much less my real name. I'm covered in dirt, dried blood, bruises, scrapes, and various injuries from their 'hospitality', but beyond my trademark snark, they've gotten nothing out of me.

That's how it will stay until I'm ready.

"Tell us who you work for, girl." The gap-toothed asshole takes a big bite of the sandwich he's holding, relishing it in front of me.

They haven't fed me more than scraps since I've been here and they assume that means I haven't eaten. I guess they think waving a sandwich in front of a hungry woman will work when physical torture hasn't, but these guys are not the brains of this outfit. I've only heard the smooth British educated tones of the man I assume is their boss a few times as they passed the door to my cell. I never see him when they bring me into this room and he hasn't once tried to question me. Honestly, I might have to let go of this lead soon because Lys is probably losing her goddamn mind listening to the tapes for clues.

My cracked lips curve as I spit on the floor, taunting the smelly idiot eating in front of me. Silence is a powerful weapon and I've used it to keep control of the situation often since someone hustled here me in a black hood like I was in a B action flick. If they thought that would keep me disoriented, again, they underestimate the depth of my training. The drive here was long and bumpy—off-road—and they didn't put me in a plane or helo. It's unlikely we crossed a border because I would have heard telltale signs of hiding me as they crossed it.

We're still in Somalia; that's all I need to know.

The impact of a fist on my jaw makes my head fly backward, but it's not nearly as hard as it could have been. Whoever punched me isn't a trained fighter, or he would have clocked me hard enough to make ducks circle my skull. I spit again, this time tasting blood as I arch a brow and smirk. Part of my resistance is ensuring that physical torture *never* gets them a sound, not even a whimper. I'll shoot back a taunt in a little bit, but I want them to realize the pain makes me even quieter. It helps manage the methods they choose to force me to talk.

"You *will* talk, girl. We're only the appetizer, you understand. Your reluctance to give us what we want is only fueling the fire for later. The pain you feel now is but a whisper of what will happen when he joins us." The clown actually grins at me with lettuce hanging out of his mouth. "You don't want him to come, do you?"

Yes, actually, I do. I'm tired of glaring at minions.

I don't respond, though. I merely continue giving him a smug expression as I lean back in the rickety chair. The bindings they use are rudimentary and the throwaway fuckers they have trying to pry information out of me are stooges. To get what I came for, I need someone *much* higher up the food chain. This rogue outfit was born of a more serious organization, so while they don't mind beating or waterboarding me, none of them has threatened sexual assault.

Truth be told, that might save their lives—emphasis on might.

Allowing myself to be captured was part of my plan from the start. Lys wasn't happy about it, but they did not train her skill set for shit like this. She's not a survivor of *Les Invisibles* and their special brand of recruit molding, so she can't possibly understand why I decided on this course of action. After months of tracking down leads that were dead ends, we needed to take risks, or we'd never find them. I refuse to allow failure to be an option, especially in this mission.

A speaker crackles, and I frown as my eyes dart around the room. The music is still blaring, but that noise tells me something is about to happen. Satisfaction courses through my tired limbs and I feel adrenaline kick in as I wait to see what my continued obstinance is going to get me. Perhaps I finally broke the dickwad in charge and he'll send these goons packing so the actual show can begin.

Of course, that means I have to be prepared for the pain to amp up significantly.

"*Otvedite yeye obratno v kameru. Ya yeshche ne gotov.*[1]"

The voice is dark and cold, not at all like the soft, clipped tone of the British man I've heard speaking in the hallway. I don't know if this is the true leader or yet another lackey, but it sounds like they have plans for me later. I make a show of rolling my eyes and letting my head drop back on my shoulders as if I'm bored. If the disembodied Russki is watching, he'll see that his threat isn't affecting me. That should loosen his tongue up when he finally makes an appearance.

"Oh, little girl. You've made a mistake," the sandwich dude cackles. "The boss is letting *Mangust* have a crack at you. No one survives his special brand of… attention."

My smile widens and I purposely let a whiff of my personal brand of crazy out. It's so rare that the people I'm going to kill actually see me beforehand that I don't get to play with my food as much as I'd like. "Cobras kill mongooses and even they die, eventually."

"Such brave words for a woman bound to a chair. You won't be so flip when you're sitting with the executioner," he replies before striding over. "In fact, I shall enjoy hearing your screams echo off the walls of this place. I may even record it for later."

"Everyone has kinks, man." I shrug and widen my eyes until I know I look unhinged. Being disturbing was—*is*—one of Dwyn's favorite methods of distraction and using his tricks makes my stomach clench, but I can't show it. When I get out of this filthy hellhole, I can let all of my fear and grief out, but not until I get what I need out of these morons.

My captor snorts as he undoes the ropes and cuffs holding me, then presses the barrel of a gun to my spine. "Try anything and you'll be eating from a tube for the rest of your life—if you survive."

"You'll have to work harder than that to scare me," I sing-song. "You're not the first man to hold a gun to my back; hell, you're not even the first one this month, jackass."

"But I may well be the last."

We'll see about that, Stinky.

I've been lying on the concrete floor for what feels like hours. There's a messy, gross pallet in the corner of my prison, but I never use it. I can only assume from the condition of everything in this place that it's crawling with bugs or lice. I'd prefer the backache that comes with sleeping on the hard rock to that every day of the week. So when they leave me in here, I lie here and let my mind wander to other places to pass the time. I must look like a zombie when my eyes go hazy and my jaw is slack, but I don't move around until the darkness descends at night.

That's when I do stretches and yoga, keeping my muscles fresh and ready for the time when I'll need them. It's when I capture the extra food I've been keeping myself strong by choking down. This isn't the first time I've eaten insects and rodents to stay alive, and I imagine it won't be the last. Such is the life of someone raised to kill or be killed by a bunch of psychopaths on a remote island. Societal norms are non-existent in the world I grew up in.

My mind wanders as my body relaxes, allowing me to remember another time when I had to sleep on a stone floor and eat rats. Much like this time, I was calm but aware, biding my time until I could make my escape.

"This is bullshit. How the fuck did I end up here? This is all fucking Mo's fault. I'm going to beat his ass when I get out of here!"

Sighing, I lifted my head from my knees. I knew I'd been in this dark corner for days—maybe even a week. Time didn't flow linearly when they left us in the cavern. I learned that the first year I was thrown in here and four years later, I still had to remind myself the entire time. They used it to break us before we got dumped into the jungle for the rest of CapRes. It never worked on me, but I'd seen people give in before.

This was the first time they'd put someone in the same hole as me, though. I wondered if those sadists were trying to force someone to take me out because they'd never been able to get me to crack. If so, they were destined for disappointment; I'd kill someone without a second thought if it meant I'd survive. That was part of why I shied away from making friends or socializing at l'Academie—my life would always come first and they built this place for playing us against one another.

Except them…

The guys I saved in years past have been part of my life little by little, but I tried to keep them at arm's length. I knew their loyalty was to one another and I couldn't risk getting dependent on people who would never choose me if it came down to it. The appeal of each of them was hard to deny: Coda with his soulful lyrics, Jinx teaching me to mimic emotions so I can fool people, Raz showing me how to code, and Mo sparring with me in secret. It took a lot of restraint not to get used to having them around, but I managed so far.

"Hello? I hear you breathing, asshole. Who are you? Show yourself!"

Fuck.

I uncurled my body from the protective ball I liked to stay in while down here, scooting on my butt to the edge of the shadows. My vision cleared slowly as I took in the guy pacing back and forth manically. He looked familiar, but I wasn't entirely sure, so I stayed just shy of the light when I answered. "I'm no one. Just another person locked up down here. I won't bother you."

The sounds of feet moving stopped and I could almost hear the wheels turning in his head. "You're a girl."

"Excellent deduction, Dr. Watson."

That got me a snort, followed by a chuckle. "Okay. A wise-ass girl. Got it. How long have you been down here?"

Eyes narrowing in suspicion, I shrugged, though I knew he couldn't see it. "Long enough. Time is immaterial in the hole; you should know that."

"Fuck," he muttered and the pacing starts again. "What the hell is their game putting us together? Do they think I'll kill you? I would if I had to, but that's not my game. Are they messing with my head? They have to be messing with my head. Christ knows this is the worst part, and this is a scheme to finally get

me. That old bastard thinks he'll crack me, but he's wrong. I won't let them win…"

Oh, boy. This guy isn't made for captivity.

He probably wasn't wrong about their intentions and I wasn't eager to see what would happen after minutes stretch into hours if he was this agitated this quickly. The amount of food and water they provided for the stay down here wouldn't cover this much energy being spent constantly, especially if the sound of his steps accurately depicts his size. My fellow detainee would give in within days if he didn't slow the hell down.

"Um, you might calm down. You're burning a lot of energy," I offered quietly.

That earned me another scoff. "Thanks. I never thought of that, Sherlock. Good thing I have you here to give me such sterling advice."

Asshole.

"Fine. Make yourself weak and let them win. See if I care."

Mystery dickhead paused in his movement again, and the crunching of loose debris on the ground told me he was coming closer to the safety of my shadows. I scooted back, but that didn't deter him. He bent down, squatting in front of my hiding place, and lowered his voice. "I'm sorry; that was rude. I'm not Mo and I rarely act like this big of a jackass to people."

Mo? Holy shit, is this the elusive fifth member of their group?

"Who's Mo?" I asked carefully. For all I knew, this guy was a plant, and if my instructors realized I had any connections to other recruits, they would use it against me for certain. I had to be very cautious about what information I gave until I was sure.

"How the fuck do you not know who Mauricio is? That asshole stomps his way all over campus like the god of the mountain!" He paused and I could feel his grin in the darkness when he clapped his hands. "I can't wait to tell that fucker someone doesn't know who he is! Wait. Does that mean you don't know who I am?"

Definitely the one guy I hadn't met yet from their crew. No one else would have dared to talk about the fearsome leader in such a familiar fashion.

"I know of him, I guess," I mumbled carefully. "Now that you described him."

"You can come out, you know. I won't hurt you. I meant it when I said that's not my thing. I'm a creeper, not a head knocker or snake."

He held a hand out and though I felt a little better at his admission; I ignored it to scoot out on my own. "Don't knock snakes. We're very useful in keeping people alive when we want to be."

"Oh, shit! You're her!*"*

Uh-oh. What the hell does that mean?

"I'm who?" I asked as I combed my hair with my fingers self-consciously. The last member of that gang of boys that ruled this place was even more hand-some than the others and I looked like Cousin It at this point.

He rose to his feet, bouncing in excitement as he started pacing again. His hands ran through his hair as he replied in a giddy voice. "Her. You're her. I'm the only one who hasn't met her yet. And now I have. They've been tight-lipped assholes for years and I couldn't figure out why. Like, they get with chicks all the time, and we share or swap stories, but no one would tell me about this mysterious chick. I've been so fucking jealous and now you're here!"

What the shit is he talking about?

So I took a deep breath and tried again, ignoring the odd pinch in my chest when he talked about the guys being with other girls on the island. "Who do you think I am?"

"You're the unicorn; I know it!" He stopped his frenetic movement for a moment to give me a lop-sided grin. "Every year since they started sending us to CapRes, one of my dickhead brothers comes back to camp with a story about this wild chick who saved their life. That always made it sound like a fairy tale because we're the best fucking recruits in this hellhole, so what chick is saving any of us from anything? But from year one until now, a different one of those fuckers comes back with this tale of an unbelievable rescue. I thought they were all conspiring to fuck with me!"

I blink. The guys had always been so insistent that I couldn't tell anyone about their visits. After I saved each of them, the visits got a little more crowded— except Mo. He always came alone, and I figured there was a reason, but I didn't ask for fear he'd stop coming. "They told you they were…rescued?"

"Like fucking damsels every time! I cannot believe *you're real!" The hyper pre-teen drops to the ground, sitting in front of me with bright, happy eyes. "I'm Dwyn, by the way. Since those dicks never told me your name, I have to introduce myself."*

It took me a moment, but I pushed down my mistrust and crawled out into the light a little further to look at him. "I'm Remy. I'm sorry you thought I was a prank."

"Don't be sorry! Dumping me down here with you means I won't lose my goddamn mind. I'll have you to talk to until they fish us out!"

Oh, no. They must not have told him I'm not the best conversationalist. I stayed alone more often than not and I had the social skills of a shut-in. "That… will be… awesome?"

"Hell yes, it will! Now, tell me about the first time you saved one of my bros. I bet your story is so different…"

The scene playing in my mind cuts off immediately when I hear a shout outside of my door and it opens to reveal the stinky asshole from earlier. He gives me a smug grin as he says, "Come, little girl. *Mangust* will see you now."

Here we go…

---

1. Take her back to her cell. I'm not ready yet.

ARE YOU READY FOR IT?

REMY

T̲H̲E̲ ̲G̲U̲A̲R̲D̲S̲ ̲H̲U̲S̲T̲L̲E̲ ̲M̲E̲ ̲I̲N̲T̲O̲ ̲A̲ ̲L̲A̲R̲G̲E̲ ̲C̲I̲N̲D̲E̲R̲ ̲B̲L̲O̲C̲K̲ ̲R̲O̲O̲M̲ ̲W̲I̲T̲H̲ a stainless steel chair in the middle. It looks like a dental chair, but far less comfortable. My eyes scan my surroundings as they drag me by armpits, taking in the various racks of scary looking implements on the walls. Everything about this space is meant to intimidate, so I know it was designed by someone with a background in psy ops. Luckily, it all looks clean, which means I don't have to worry about someone examining my fluids when I'm gone. You'd think it would be the last of my worries, but as a graduate of *LI*, they have trained me to ensure I don't leave a trace.

There's an excellent reason for that.

My 'escorts' slam me down onto the chair and buckle me in, strapping my limbs down with bindings they believe will keep me in place. I don't make a sound; instead, I keep my mirth to myself. Their equipment is so standard that it's laughable and I'm not worried about it in the slightest. I'm not even concerned about whether their sharp tools are cleaned appropriately or simply washed—the experimentation *LI* did on us as children wasn't as basic as changing our appearance or sterilizing the girls. We're damn near immune to pathogens and poisons; that's yet another grueling part of the inhuman training we went through year after year.

A switch is flipped on the side of the chair and they lean me back, leaving my eyes blinded by a bright light above me as I stare vacantly. My focus is on the bright corona of light as the surrounding voices speak in Arabic until heavy boots sound on the floor. The chatter stops when the stomping person enters and I know this means *Mangust* has arrived. Silence descends, leaving only the footsteps of their interrogator as they walk in a circle around the chair. I don't move or even flick my gaze to the person looking at me—they derive their power from fear and not looking at them steals it.

"A ty govorish' po Russki?[1]"

His voice is like liquid fire, smooth and dark. I detect a hint of an accent that I can't place without further dialogue, but I'm certain he's ex-GRU, or a mercenary born of the fall of the Iron Curtain. I lock my expression in place and I don't even blink while he waits for me to respond. Forcing him to talk first means I've won the first power play, but this will be a long game, and I have to conserve my energy and focus. Once he gets to work, I'll need every ounce of my strength to survive the pain without giving in.

I know this from experience.

"Perhaps I should switch to English, then?" The man steps closer and I feel the excitement in his tone. He enjoys his work and those are the ones you have to look out for—the sociopaths who *only* feel good when they are causing others pain.

"She won't talk," the stinky man who questioned me for the first few weeks interrupts our standoff with a snort. "We even used the battery, comrade."

Mangust snorts in disgust. "Idiots. Beatings and car batteries are for amateurs."

"The water did not work, either. Someone has trained this one. You will need to speed up your process."

The air shifts as my new captor walks away and I hear a scuffle followed by choking. On a low growl, *Mangust* says, "You do not tell me what to do, Ali. I answer only to our boss and you'd do well to remember it before I decide to strap *you* to my chair."

Christ, I hate internal power struggles. This is why I've always worked alone.

The door opens and closes, letting me know Ali retreated like the coward I knew he was. Footsteps signal the return of my new torture buddy, and I mentally prepare myself for what is coming next. I have to keep my mouth shut and float away so the pain from whatever instrument he chooses is outside of my consciousness. Metal scrapes and the fuck head hums under his breath as places various items on what sounds like a metal tray. It's so cliche, but he must be lining up a tool on a surgical tray to bring it close while he works.

Like most purveyors of physical rendition, he's using the silence and the wait to put me on edge. A burst of adrenaline will make all of my nerves more sensitive and he's hoping to amp me up before he even begins. Unfortunately, much like my statement about the gun yesterday, this dumbs hit is not the first person to try this bullshit and he won't be the last. My history and profession have prepared me for a situation like this.

He's going to be very disappointed.

"Now, *malen'kiy vor,*[2] you will tell me the answers I seek or we will see how much you can tolerate when a true artisan plies his trade."

It takes every ounce of restraint in my body not to roll my eyes. If he thinks cuts and slices will motivate me more than electrocution and fists, he's deluded. But I can't get saucy with him—not yet. I have to stoke his frustration until he gets chatty, so I work the information I want out of him rather than the opposite. Running my mouth won't help me until he's lost his temper. So I stay silent and still, gazing blankly into the bright light.

Clucking his tongue, he slides the tray over and picks up one of the tools on it. I can hear every single move he makes like it's in stereo when I'm like this. Blinding my eyes is making my other senses sharper, and I wait for the first cut to come. When it does, my brain has drifted far enough that it's little more than a burning sensation on my bicep. The scent of blood fills my nostrils, but my breaths don't speed up.

I'm deep in the zone—disassociating to a tattoo parlor where I got my ink when I got to Europe.

"No reaction? How sad. I'll have to try harder."

Time seems like it's stopped as he uses various blades, pliers, and even a small kitchen torch on the soft parts of my frame. I don't make a sound or move a centimeter and with every failed attempt; the frustration radiating off him in waves grows stronger. I'll be sore and crusted with blood and gore when they throw me back into my cell, but I'll survive. I'm here for a reason and everything that's happened since I arrived is a means to an end.

All I have to do is survive it until they let what I need slip.

The tray clatters when he loses his temper, knocking all the dirty instruments on the ground. I hear him stomping around the room, cursing in Russian as he tries to figure out what he can do to get a rise out of me. Hot breath comes close when he snarls down at me. "You are not a mere thief. The resistance to my methods tells me you are much more than we believed. I am certain you are part of something larger and I will get it out of you if I have to bring you back to life over and over until you squeal."

I arch a single brow, letting it be the only response he gets.

A roar echoes in the steel and tile room. I struggle not to smile as he stomps away with a string of curses once again. This guy pretends to be a consummate professional, but he's not. Truly professional torturers never get emotional; they only get more creative. Whoever *Mangust* is, he's not what he makes himself out to be. If I were to guess, he simply enjoys causing pain, and that's allowed him to hang his shingle to various criminals and syndicates as a rendition specialist. That just makes him a sadist and knowing that makes my job even easier.

"Ali!"

His shout makes the door swing open, the telltale creak of its hinges letting me know there are guards waiting right outside. That's also good to know; when I decide to end this charade, I need to have every detail imprinted on my brain so I can hurry and get out. After a few moments of scuffling, they tilt the chair up and my eyes blink as they adjust from staring into the bright light for so long. Spots dance in front of me as rough hands undo the bindings one by one and I'm yanked to the floor. My legs are like jelly from being in the chair, so I hear my first jailer yell for help when I crumple to the ground.

Good. I want them to continue underestimating me and they're making it easy for me.

My face stays impassive as two people haul me by the armpits out of the room and down the hall. The door to my cage swings open with another creak, and I'm tossed in like a sack of potatoes before it slams again. Keeping still until I hear their footsteps fade away, I finally smirk to myself under the curtain of my filthy hair. Yet again, I've foiled their efforts and the longer I do so, the more likely they are to give me what I can here for.

The lights in my cell turn off suddenly and the sound of death metal starts up again. I crawl to my favorite spot in the corner and prop my body against the wall with a sigh of relief. Now that visibility is limited, I can finally close my eyes and let the waves of pain loose. Once they finish rippling through me, I'll be ready for round two. I take one more deep breath to prepare myself, then I unlock the gates mentally.

I'll black out in three… two… one…

WHEN I COME TO, I stretch my legs out and shake them. *Mangust* didn't focus nearly as much on my lower half as he did above the waist, so they feel much less sore and crusty. The amount of 'cut, cut, deep slice' he did means I'll have to have my tats fixed once the scars settle and for that alone, I'm definitely taking his fucking head. I don't care what I have to get my hands on. The car battery was less expensive to deal with in comparison.

That motherfucker is going to pay for screwing with my ink.

I'm not sure what he'll try next, but I have to steel myself for whatever it is. It will certainly be more painful; I'm not naïve. I can't worry about it, though. The information I need about their boss will allow me to track the son of a bitch, and then it will be my turn to twist the screws. Lys found a tiny, almost inscrutable clue connected to the leader of this bullshit outfit last month, and I'm going to pull that thread until it unravels. If I'm lucky, it will be the first real hint of finding my missing men.

My eyes might leak if I weren't so damned dehydrated. The thought of locating even *one* of them after the explosion racked that building four months ago makes my heart jump in my chest. From the moment I awakened in Lys' car, speeding away from the zoo as if our asses were on fire, I've been working every contact, every criminal, and every corner of the web for hints about them. I thought they were dead for the first couple of weeks, and that sent me on yet another rampage of blood and gore. I tore through Europe with the precision of a military drone, trying to satiate my need for vengeance. Every job was a bloodbath, and every contract netted me a small fortune.

Until one day, I ran into an odd woman in Prague. The rainbow haired chick stopped in the middle of a busy street, staring at me like I was a ghost and my alarm bells went off. I ducked into an alley and tore a path through the city that rivaled a certain thief in a Disney cartoon. At the end of my run, I paused, leaning against a tree in the park and when I opened my eyes, there she fucking was. She just stared at me again and I pulled the knife from the small of my back, preparing to gut her like a trout, but then she spoke.

"Aye. They said I'd see ye, and I did. I'll be buggered." The lilting Irish accent made me rifle through the jobs I did in that country, hoping to place the face before one of us had to die. "Listen up, ye Smurf. I'm supposed to tell ye they're not dead. Follow the trail and find the treasure."

My first thought was, *what in Lucky Charms bullshit is this*? Spinning my blade on my palm like Dwyn taught me, I studied the women for a moment. Something about her was otherworldly, and it unnerved me. I don't believe in shit like that, but it was almost like she could see right through me. Finally, I broke the silence to say something snarky in response, and she just shrugged.

"Not my bloody job to convince you. I've done my bit. The rest is up to you." That said, she turned on her heel and walked away as if nothing had happened.

Honestly, I thought I might be losing my marbles. I didn't even tell Lys for a couple of days. She was already worried I was going off the deep end of grief and imagining some weird fortune telling an Irish unicorn woman wouldn't have made her feel any better. But wondering about it got the best of me and she looked excited— that's when I found out my thieving bestie definitely believed in shit like this. The weirdo's word sent her into overdrive and I reluctantly followed, setting up new protocols, spiders, and networks online to search for information.

Two weeks later, she happened upon the whispers of this group and for a second, I considered stepping into some house of worship for a reason that *wasn't* death. That instinct passed, of course, because I don't believe in that anymore that I do rainbow leprechauns, but for a moment…

Despite all of our prep for this mission, I know Lys is on the other end of the tech freaking out. The implant allowing her to hear recordings of everything going on around me doesn't work two ways, so all she knows is the sound of what's being said or done to me. As someone who's been on the other end of that, she'll never be the same, especially once *Mangust* ramps up his efforts. But if this gives us even a whiff of the trail leading to one or more of The Five? I'd suffer through all of it again without batting a lash. After all, it's what they trained me to do.

I've always been a weapon of mass destruction.

Too bad these morons won't find that out until it's too late.

---

1. And do you speak Russian?
2. little thief

SCARS

REMY

The voices in the hall wake me up. I allow myself small naps in my corner because I know sleep deprivation is one of the best ways to catch a subject off guard. Between that and my inconsistent sustenance, I'm aware they've been trying their damndest to get me in a suggestible state. No one has used drugs…yet. I'd bet that will be *Mangust*'s next move. My cracked, dry lips curve in the darkness as I imagine the tirade he'll launch into when he discovers his gambit isn't working.

I love when they underestimate me.

The door flies open with a bang and Ali stomps in with a smug smile on his filthy face. "Don't hide, little girl. You had to know this was coming. Today, you will talk and the pain will end. I have one hundred thousand shillings on you breaking."

I arch a brow as he comes over and jerks me out of the shadows roughly. My body stays limp—something I do specifically to keep him thinking I'm too weak to stand on my own. Ali curses and yells for another guard; once the next goon gets my other side, they heft me out of the room together. I tailor every minor detail of my behavior toward making them think they have me beat, and what I do in the room will be much the same. I need to lead *Mangust* on a little to keep him from giving up, but I also have to make sure I get him talking. I'm tired of stale bread and fucking bugs for dinner; I want out of this hellhole.

"This bitch better give up her secrets today. The boss is getting impatient and I don't want to see what that psycho will do if he's allowed to go whole hog. I heard it's a bloodbath," the second guy mutters to Ali.

"She will! There's no way she can resist the things he has in store for her," Ali replies as they drag me down the hall. "When she does, you will owe me, my friend."

"If you say so. I've never seen a woman survive like she has so far. Whoever she is, the boss was right to keep her for questioning instead of letting you kill her."

I'm spared their 'bad guy prattle' when we enter the sterile white environment of *Mangust*'s room. Just like last time, they hoist me onto the chair and methodically strap me in, grinning like morons the entire time. It's hard not to laugh—even the disposable minions *LI* uses for suicide missions aren't stupid as these motherfuckers. Whoever the 'boss' is, they don't understand the value of having cannon fodder that can at least tie their goddamned shoes.

"Just wait, princess. He's going to make you scream so beautifully."

My eyes find the bright light, training on it again so I can dive into the place in my head where I go to disassociate. I'm aware of the door opening again as they leave and the heavy footsteps of the *Mangust* entering, but I don't move.

"Ah! What a beautiful morning it is, *malen'kiy vor*[1]. It will be perfect for your submission." He walks away from the chair and the sound of the tray rolling over follows him back. "It does not matter in the end, but I assure you, the equipment I am using today is all sterile. If not for what the hypodermic contains, it would be quite safe."

I don't react as he laughs at his own joke, but I listen closely to what he's doing. The tools he picks up don't make a clinking sound like the scalpel and torch from the other day. After a few moments of silence, I hear a faint squeezing sound that has to be a hypodermic being prepped. *Thank fuck.* If his next round of torture is chemical and toxin based, it might hurt a bit, but I'll make it through without needing more ink repaired.

When I find those assholes, I'm making them pay for my scar cover-ups.

The pinch of the needle going in barely registers, but I feel a tingle as the drugs work their way through my veins. Staying still isn't hard—I focus on the light and the thoughts in my head instead of the external stimuli. Two more pricks tell me he's mixed up a truth serum cocktail—probably sodium thiopental, scopolamine, and amobarbital. The barbiturates are geared towards relaxing me while the devil's breath is aimed at putting me in a hypnotic, suggestible state of mind. He doesn't know this is a complete waste of his time, but I do.

Les Invisibles used scopolamine on us from the minute we started CapRes at eight.

"I'll give you a few minutes for this to set in, *malen'kiy vor*, and then we will have a *real* chat."

I sink into my mind further, letting the haze settle over my vision and my thoughts. The trick to mastering this shit is to both let it ride and force your mind to work at its speed. If you fight the effects, everything gets even cloudier, and control slips from your fingers like feathers. My limbs get heavy and my body feels like it's melting into the chair after a few moments. I purposely slow my breaths, making him think I'm further along in the process so I can guide this interview.

Hot breath hits my face as he leans in and spreads my eyelids to look at me closely. "Ah, yes. It's working quickly. We will have this over with before lunch; I'm certain of it."

Fat chance, cocksucker.

The world spins when he tilts the chair upward until I'm completely upright but strapped down. I let the spots dance in front of my eyes, knowing that it will help me keep from getting nauseous if I don't fight the vertigo. His voice sounds farther away as the drugs really kick in and I can't help but snicker. Giggles are part of my plan, as is laughter when strategically used to rankle his pride. Everything is going to plan…so far. If I can keep it up, I'll push him enough to make mistakes.

"That sound tells me you are almost there. Why don't we start with something easy, eh? What is your name, girl?"

His face is fuzzy, but I look at it as I grin. "I'm Batman."

My head whips to the side as his fist crashes into my jaw before I can blink. I let the giggles tumble from my lips as I feel blood trickle down my chin. It wasn't a love tap, but it didn't break anything. The bruise will heal eventually. I'm gonna look like a fucking stunt double when I get out of here, but as the QB in the movie said 'pain fades, chicks dig scars, glory lasts forever'. The reward I'm here to claim is well worth the pain I've been suffering for the past few weeks. It's not the worst I've felt and it won't be the last time some jackhole beats the shit out of me, either. Such is the nature of my profession.

"You think you're funny, eh? The first words you say in over a week and you're cracking jokes. We will see about that," he snarls as he stomps over to the door. Yanking it open, *Mangust* shouts into the hallway. "Come! We move her to the room with the buckets."

Oh, that's not good.

I withstood the waterboarding and electricity fine when they were separate. Now that this dick filled me full of drugs, adding in juice and sluice might actually stop my goddamned heart if he's not careful. If those fuckers amp it up and don't stay below the waist, it will go from a sexy tingle I used to enjoy with Dwyn to a dangerous situation quickly. Since I've mostly taunted them silently, using my words now will only speed up their plan. I have to keep to my original timeline and hope *Mangust* knows enough about this to keep Ali and his idiots from frying my brain pan.

Remy, you can work with this. He's off the rails sooner than expected; that means you're close.

"She's off her rocker. You'll have her spilling her guts within moments," Ali says as he and his buddy get me untangled from the chair and drag me to the door again.

Mangust simply grunts, and I feel his eyes on me as they let my feet scrape over the rocky floor. "I brought along some extra encouragement—just in case."

That gets my attention and I whisper memory mantras in my mind to help me stay focused. Adding more drugs and harder torture is going to test my abilities. I wouldn't have expected a ragtag bunch of clowns like this to have a guy with knowledge like this grunting Russian, but *c'est la vie*. More detailed research is a footnote. I'll have to go over with Lys when I get out of here. I wouldn't have missed extra contacts, but she's not used to profiling the people rather than the entry/exit points for thefts.

Within moments, I'm slammed into the rickety ass chair I was in previously and they zip tie me down. *Mistake number one, cockwaffles.* I let my head loll back, continuing to pretend I'm off my ass on the pharmaceuticals he pumped into me. *Mangust* walks over and plunges the needle he's carrying into my arm hard, making me grit my teeth behind my crazy smile. He's lucky he didn't break the fucking tip off; that would have definitely been a problem.

"Get the bucket, Ali," he growls, as he glares at me. "We'll start with water."

Drowning is low on my fear scale because of CapRes   this will be cake.

The goons bring the side table over and place the large trough full of dirty water on it before scooting it back behind my head. Ali hands a piece of cloth to my new torture buddy and he grins evilly as he lowers it over my face. My eyes focus on the ceiling as I prepare myself mentally for what's coming next.

"Tell me who you work for and this will end," *Mangust* says before using the cloth to push my head below the water and hold it.

My lungs expand, and I keep staring at the point above, even through the water. I've slowed my heart rate and kept my mouth closed, but eventually, it won't be a choice. Physiologically, I can only hold it for so long—three minutes is my record—and my body will force me to struggle for air. Once it does, the effect will cause my system to panic until he lifts me out.

The haze around my vision gets more intense as the need for air burns and I sputter when my ability to hold it fails. Water fills me and panic rushes through me, but I keep counting in my head, knowing I can do this if I don't let it consume me. Finally, they pull my head out by my hair and I spit out water in gurgling bursts. Sucking in slow, deep breaths, I don't make a face or say anything. That earns me another dunking, and another, until I can't separate them.

"Who do you work for?" He repeats himself calmly each time, but the tension in the air is palpable.

On the next round, my brain starts to unfuzz—my body is rejecting the barbiturates now and I almost smile. It takes a massive amount of control not to allow them to know, but as soon as that victory comes, an intense burning crawls through my veins. Clamping my jaw down to prevent a gasp, I realize the last drug has taken effect.

Fuck. This complicates things. I need a distraction.

My mind wanders to the past and I remember why I'm enduring this shit. I see me teaching Dwyn how to meditate so he can focus his hyper mind when he needs to be still. The sounds of Coda making up songs to distract himself from pain training. Raz, Mo, Dwyn, and I all squinting at Jinx's laptop when he paused it during movies or clips so we could learn to read micro-expressions. My frustration as Raz taught me to code line by line patiently. *This shit is why I have to get through this.*

When *Mangust* pulls me up the next time, I smirk, finally croaking an answer. "She's a real bitch, my boss. Kills people like you fools before breakfast; just you wait."

His eyes widen, and I can tell he's struggling to contain his glee. "Very good, girl. You're making a wise decision. Tell me more."

A hand pushes me under again and the fire in my veins makes it hard to focus on not drowning, but I manage. This time when they lift me out, I spit water at Ali, who curses as he backs away. The satisfaction from my act of rebellion fuels me, so I look *Mangust* dead in the eye and say, "She's big on loyalty. I'd never betray her; you're wasting your time, motherfucker."

Oh, that got him.

"You will or you will die, cunt!"

The big man finally loses his temper, and it's hard not to grin like a cat that caught the canary. I don't even care that he used my least favorite insult on the planet—I've won. Emotions are the enemy of true pros and his have bubbled over. He'll make stupid mistakes now and I know I can get him to talk.

Knocking the water off the table, he whirls towards Ali and the goons. They're looking at him in surprise, but *Mangust* doesn't notice as he screams. *"Get the battery! Set it up now!"*

Moment of truth, Remy. He's lost it.

---

1. Little thief

BODIES

REMY

The number one rule of dealing with a narcissistic sociopath is not to give them what they want. No matter what it is, what it costs you, or how badly it hurts, withhold the thing they crave the most—your emotions. They're incapable of it and they feed from you like an emotional vampire, bleeding you dry until you have nothing left to give.

Most people in the circles I travel in are some variation of psychopath or sociopath, but the truly damaged ones seek to destroy not only their targets, but everything around them in fits of impotent rage. Even if you aren't the most confident individual on the planet, your belief in your self-worth trumps their real opinion of themselves, but you'd never know it by how they strut around waving their superiority in the air like a Superbowl trophy.

That's why despite the lingering fog in my brain from *Mangust's* fucked up cocktail of mind-altering drugs, I'm pushing the limits of my trained abilities to keep him from seeing my feelings. The minute I give him my pain, he'll have what he needs and it will allow him to kill me 'by mistake' even if I haven't given him the info he wants.

I've dealt with this type before—ones far more experienced and talented than this pissant—and I survived with minimal scarring. I'll come out of this as well and when I'm done flogging the remains of his corpse, he'll be as inconsequential as the dude who polished Shakespeare's shoes.

"Up again!" he shouts and I have to lock my limbs so I don't wince.

If he goes above twenty-five amps below the waist or ten above, we're going to have a problem.

My torturer is infuriated because I pushed him just far enough to enlist his low rent goons to assist with my 'interrogation.' Not giving into him when he damn near drowned me forced him to take more drastic measures and now he doesn't have many options left that won't summarily kill me. The fucking additional drug he injected me with burns in my veins, but it could be one of a thousand things, from pharmaceuticals to a virus or bacteria aimed at my death in the next few hours or days. I'm less worried about that—*Les Invisibles* had an entire wing devoted to modifying our genes to resist a laundry list of things—than I am his temper.

Another jolt rockets over me and my teeth grip the wooden stick they kindly placed there. Electrics won't break me; they couldn't know Dwyn and I played with them for years prepping for the final year of CapRes on the island. In fact, the one time one of the guys almost got sexy with me before the debacle—

Shit! That was definitely more than recommended amperage.

I open my eyes, letting the smallest of smirks grace my lips around the bit. It keeps me from speaking, but I make sure my expression is taunting. I want him to hear 'is that all you got?' in his head.

"*Mangust*, perhaps she has had enough for today. If we kill her before we get the name of her employer, the boss will—"

"*Tishina! Voz'mite shchiptsy dlya izvlecheniya.*[1]"

Well, fuck. The guys' rescue bill is going up by the minute.

Ali scrambles to do his bidding and the others move the leads and wires, then the table and the rest of their shit. My captor is done with electricity for today, and now he's moved on to something a lot less pleasant. I sigh quietly in my mind when they remove the stick, deciding this is the time to be strategic.

"You realize I speak Russian, right?" I give him a bored look as he paces around me. "My boss is a stickler for training."

He snorts. "Your boss will be missing an asset when I'm done. Whether it's from my attention or the injection, your time on this planet is limited. You should give me what I want, and I'll make it far less painful."

Virus or bacteria, then. Too bad The Company nano-particles will take care of it.

"If you had any idea what *real* professionals do in training, you'd realize that was wasted effort, man."

A frown creases his brow, and he stalks over, eyes narrowing. "What do you mean?"

"I've had the fucking plague more times than you've had a cold, bro. This is amateur hour shit." With that, I shut my mouth and close my eyes, cutting off his means of communication.

The ensuing howl of anger gives me a warm feeling in my stomach, but I keep the mask of indifference on. Depriving him of satisfaction and glee works well—my experience is serving me well. *Of course, I'm gonna have a fuckton of explaining to do when I get out here.* Lys will have every bit of this on tape and I haven't given her more than my Duchess legend. A legend I spent over a decade building up that is now *ruined* thanks to the Shadowy Douche who started this goddamn bullshit, by the way.

I'll get him, too, before this is all over. The Guillotine never forgets, nor does she forgive.

My brain reminds me of the very guys I'm here taking this torture in order to find, but the rattling of a metal tray cuts the thought off. I know what's on it; the last few tools this dick is ever going to use on me. I have to get him babbling now before I'm gumming my food for weeks.

"Your boss is too chickenshit to be here while you work. Must suck," I throw out before the minions place the equivalent of a gag spreader between my lips.

"Ha! *Il Tasso* would not lower themself to be present for a lowlife." His grin widens as he brandishes the extractor. "But I'll send your regards."

Jesus, criminals are reaching these days. The Badger and The Mongoose? A good exterminator would defeat those furry dipshits.

I can snort with the spreader in, so I do. That makes him growl low and shove the tool into my mouth, grasping a back molar hard. *Here it comes…* I brace myself mentally and when he yanks it out, I'm able to suppress the wail that threatens to escape. Instead, I arch a brow at the smirking sadist and shrug as best I can in the restraints. He knows I can't speak with the spreader in and he hasn't moved it, so I'm fairly certain I'm going to need more than one implant when I get the hell out of here.

The second tooth hurts less than the first because I've slipped into a safe space in my head. At least it's on the opposite side—that was kind of him. *Mangust* is muttering to himself as blood pours down my chin and I simply sit still, waiting for him to ask me a question I can use to press for more information. When he finally lowers the extractor and gestures for Ali to pull the gag, I meet his eyes and he tilts his head. "Are you ready to give me what I want now?"

"Why in the hell did you morons pick the mongoose and the badger? Who's afraid of rodents?" My reply makes his expression tighten, so I continue despite the trail of saliva and blood still dribbling from my injured mouth. "My boss thinks you're pussies, guaranteed."

Since my boss is me, I can say that with confidence, just as I could say I'm going to take two of his teeth for every one of mine he yanks.

His response is a derisive snort. "Your boss isn't here, little girl. *Il Tasso* is everywhere."

"Doubtful. I've never heard of either of you fucking knobs and I've been around," I reply before purposefully spitting on the floor.

"Such brave words for one living on borrowed time. You'll never meet my boss, but I can guarantee *Il Tasso* will find yours. Maybe he'll even let me negotiate with her as I have with you."

I can't help it—a laugh drops from my lips. *Man, this guy is an idiot.* "Again, I beg to differ."

Mangust advances, stepping closer and pushing the tray of implements that Ali brought him to my side. "All you have to do is tell me where I can find her and I'll end your pain. Think of how good it will feel."

Oh, I have been.

My fingers wiggle in the ties, and I carefully move them to get the feeling back. Slowly, I press my back flush to it so I don't draw attention to my movements. I'll only have a few seconds after their initial reaction to pull this off—my life depends on it. Placing my feet on the front legs next, I sneer at *Mangust* as he holds up various metal tools tauntingly. "I would rather slit my wrists and swim in a shark tank, asshole."

"Perhaps that can be arranged."

He turns away and I see my moment. Taking a deep breath, I throw my weight backwards, toppling the chair to the ground with a clang. Using the soles of my feet and backward momentum, I push upward and swing my zip tied wrists over my head in one motion. *Hooray for hyper mobility!* Ali rushes toward me and I spin, slamming the chair still attached to one ankle into him hard.

Mangust's angry roar interrupts *his* howl of pain, and I laugh. I only have two more restraints to get out of before he dies.

"You little *bitch!*" he growls, striding over with a large knife in his hand.

That'll do, pig.

Clasping my hands together in a prayer formation, I raise my hands above my head and bring them down in a hard arc. My palms push outward and the zip tie breaks like it's made of sand. Every single part of my body aches with the injuries and effects of the drugs they gave me, but I'm running on pure adrenaline now. Hands curl into fists and despite the weight I'm dragging on one foot, I drop into a defensive position as the Russian comes closer.

"You're nothing but a cheesy stereotype, moron. Unfortunately for you, I earned the moniker I bear. You and your loser boss may have branded yourselves in order to seem more powerful than you are, but you'll be forgotten before your corpse hits the floor. It's a shame, really."

The flash of a knife swiping past my cheek pauses my chatter, and he laughs. "Oh? Why is that?"

"You'd be much more famous if you knew my true identity and survived." My elbow connects with his ribs and when he doubles over, my other hand meets his jaw in a vicious right hook. That rings his bell hard enough for him to drop the blade, and I scramble across the floor to grab it. Grasping it, I free my foot just in time to tuck and roll away from the enormous hands reaching for me. I lost the damn knife as I moved, but that's okay. All I needed was to have full control of my body to deal with these idiots.

The shadow approaching behind me has me bouncing to my feet and instinct takes over. A hard spin kick to the chest of Ali sends him flying and when my eyes lift to *Mangust,* he's coming at me directly. I purposely back up, knowing it will get me within range of weapons should I need them. Every bruise, scab, and throbbing burn on my body is screaming, but I ignore it in favor of the thrill of the fight. They fashioned me into the person I am through agony and suffering; kill or be killed is in my DNA.

Winning is not an option as much as a foregone conclusion.

"Tell me where to find *Il Tasso* and I might let you live," I taunt, flipping the script on him as I watch him study me.

His grimace tells me he's onto my game, so it's unlikely I'm getting any more intel out of him. The supposed infamous interrogator has accepted that he may die for his arrogance and he's determined not to give me any quarter before it happens. That's a shame, as it would cut down on my detective work, but I can work with it. Dropping my stance lower, I eye his center of gravity; his size is an advantage and a hindrance depending on who he's fighting. I plan for it to be the latter.

Pushing off, I run at him like a linebacker, using the momentum and my good shoulder to hit my target as hard as possible. He stumbles backwards, his limbs flying as he's knocked off-balance, and I use that shock. Sweeping my leg out, I take him down entirely and climb onto his back. My arms encircle his neck, putting me in prime position to squeeze. His shouted curses fade as I put more pressure on the carotid and he struggles to throw me off. Holding on like a fucking spider monkey, I keep tightening my grip until I feel the familiar deflation that comes with a mark losing blood pressure to their head. Finally, his body goes limp, and he falls flat underneath me.

I have to give it to him—the motherfucker was a fighter.

I stay still for a few moments, sucking in deep breaths as my body shivers with the amount of chemicals and shit rocketing through my system. Between his drugs and my body's natural hormones, I feel like I mixed a Red Bull and heroin and they're duking it out in my limbic regions. But I only have so much time before someone figures out I'm free and that means I have to get my shit together. Opening my eyes wide and blinking until my vision clears, I give

Mangust a hard kick in the ribs, then lean down to check his pulse. He's gone, but I'm not done with him *or* his passed out cohort on the other side of the room.

The room is silent as I walk over to their trays of horrors and pick up the glimmering amputation surgical knife with a dark grin.

Yes, this will do nicely for the message I intend to leave.

Nothing says '*The Guillotine is alive and coming for you*' like a facility full of rotting corpses with no heads.

If I can just find a bag to carry the damn things when I leave, I'll be set.

---

1. Silence! Use the extraction tongs.

YOU SHOULD SEE ME IN A CROWN

REMY

I'm not sure how long it took me to slice my way through the halls to the room from the first day they brought me to this compound. Truthfully, when I'm in the zone, time seems to flow like water and I don't even have to think—I simply eliminate the obstacles. The sense of satisfaction that fills me helps me ignore the aches and pains; it's all mind over matter with that.

Looking around, I spot my favorite boots and let out a sigh of relief. Thank *fuck* none of those idiots stole or bartered them for booze yet. They're sitting in a corner by the waning fire where someone was cooking before I went feral downstairs. Picking them up, I put them on the single table in the middle of the room while I sort through the rest of my former disguise. The wig is fucked up, but I can probably make do with it. I can use the socks for something besides my feet and the long shirt is torn, but I can use it as well.

My eyes scan the room, knowing I need a bag or I won't be able to execute the second part of my message to *Il Tasso*. A snort escapes my lips when I see the blue and yellow handle of the

IKEA bag everyone in the world seems to own—even desert terrorists.

Yes, this will do nicely.

I sling it over my shoulder and plop on the chair, wincing as I force my battered feet into the boots. The first 'interrogation' tactic was the feet caning and they're still swollen and bruised. I avoided stepping in the mess I made downstairs as I headed up here, but I'll need tools from *Mangust's* special room to finish. I'd rather get entrails on my boots than my feet, so I have to squeeze my broken toes in whether it hurts or not. Once I get them tied, I walk over to pick up one of the cooled coals in the fireplace, stuffing it in my pocket for later.

Inhaling the infinitely fresher air for a moment, I let my heart slow as I take the shirt, wig, bag, and socks in one hand. The surgical knife is caked in… everything… but I'm not tucking it away until I'm one hundred percent certain no other fuckwits are coming out of the woodwork. My eyes catch on a jacket hanging on the back of the door and though a leather motor-cycle jacket will not match my haphazard outfit, it screams trophy.

I deserve a trophy, and I've never been one to pass on treating myself.

After I snatch it off the hook, I head back to the basement to do what I have to so I can get the fuck out of here. The bodies litter the hall in grotesque positions, but I whistle a jaunty dwarf tune as I hop over them. I'd prefer to do shit more cleanly than this, but death is my job and I'm in my element.

Don't judge me.

I pull the door to the torture room open and walk inside with a grin. It doesn't matter that I'm covered in grime, blood, and gore —sand and dirt will join it soon enough. Dropping the clothes on the chair, I turn to the wall of instruments, finding what I'm looking for. The Stryker bone saw gleams in the clean, well-lit room, calling to me like a siren at sea.

Pushing the button once to hear it buzz, I close my eyes with a sigh of pleasure. It's not my wire, but this will have to do.

The bag hangs off my arm as I go into the hall, and one by one, I use the Stryker to separate my captors' heads from their necks. They fill the big ass IKEA bag to the brim, but I think I have a solution for that. If I can't secure them, I'm in for a shitty ride across the desert to the closest town. I tap my fingers against my lips as I stride into *Mangust's* room. But luckily, I see what I need. An industrial staple gun—which I'm now very glad they didn't get to use on me—is hanging on one of the pegs. It takes a ton of staples and some dedication, but I get the bag closed well enough to travel.

That's step one, Remy. Now for step two.

I tug on the jacket, then comb the wig until I can shape it into a fat raven colored braid. It's too damaged to wear down, plus that wouldn't work well for my trip. Squinting, I look around until I see a pile of the zip ties they'd used on me. I grab one and slip it around the end of the braid, pulling it tight. Once that's secured, I use another to get my hair tied back and then cut the bottom of one of the socks off. Stretching it until it gives, I push it over my head and use it as a shitty wig cap. Hopefully, it will keep wispies from escaping. If not, it's the best I got and I'll be damned if I'm not already Macgyver-ing the *shit* out of this stuff.

Struggling with the wig until my silver locks disappear, I sigh when I get it on. I probably look like hell in a handbasket, but that's what the shirt is for. A few rips and several wraps around my head form a very crappy *niqab*, but I can't quite get it to stay in place. A frustrated growl escapes my lips and I stomp over the sink, yanking drawers open until I see something that might help. This is risky, but fuck if I know what else to do. I'm locked in a death basement with seven headless bodies and I have to navigate through an unfamiliar desert to get to civilization.

So I break off several of the hypodermics and use the needles to pin the fabric over my face carefully. The only thing I'll need to worry about now is my eyes, but I'm going to go dig in these fuck-ers' pockets until I find a pair of shades. It's not like they're going to be needing them; they don't have fucking heads anymore.

I should take money out of the wallets, too. I'll need it if I have to stop along the way or bribe anyone.

That settled, I sit down on the chair. I'll need to do one more thing to make this ridiculous bullshit look a bit more authentic. Taking the coal out of my pocket, I slam it on the arm of the chair, watching it break into powder and pieces. I wipe the knife clean on my pants and look into the mirrored edge as I use a finger to rim my eyes with the powdery coal. Not only will this help with the glare, but it will seem much more natural and distract people when I arrive in town.

It's not perfect, but very little in life is. This will do long enough to get to the rathole I'd rented and contact Lys with the beacon. Groaning, I stand up and criss-cross the straps of the IKEA head bag, putting it on my back like a backpack. My entire body is one walking throb of pain, but I can't focus on that now—not when I finally got what I came for and I'm within striking distance of getting home.

I kick both Ali and *Mangust's* bodies as I head back to the stairs and up towards the light.

And miles to go before I sleep…

I SHOULD'VE KNOWN when I found that damn jacket it was a harbinger of doom.

Every bump and pothole in this godforsaken road from the waste-land to the city has made my bones jar and my injuries scream as I push the motorbike as hard as I can. Luckily, night fell not long after my escape from the poor man's Manson ranch and, by the look of the stars, I'm headed southeast from a disputed border region towards the capital. That's a helluva ride on this fucking thing and I doubt I'd survive it given the upheaval in the country. I'll have to cross the disputed zones to get to the southwest coast where Mogadishu is located. As far as I know, Al Shabaab controls much of that territory at this point, and while my Arabic is solid, I don't have access to everything I'll need to buy my way through the enclaves.

Unfortunately, I have to get to the capital to activate the rest of my fucking plan to get home, so I'm going to have to be creative.

I swear to hell and back. If those motherfuckers don't kiss my goddamned feet when I find them, I'm going to chop off their balls.

My memory of the geography of this part of Africa is a little fuzzy—though that could be the goddamn drugs I haven't worked completely out of my system—but if I hit Beledweyne, I can stow away on a cargo plane to Mogadishu. Worst case, I can steal a car and take the whole six-hour drive, but I'd like to avoid it. Hiding on the plane is likely to be far safer than the open road. I don't mind killing people, but I have the feeling I'm going to need to sleep eventually. There won't be an option for that if I have to drive.

Revving the engine, I speed up even though it's going to make my ass and every other part of my body ache like I'm being disarticulated. I have to get to town before it gets really dark and I lose the ability to bribe someone at the airstrip for my passage.

WHEN I PULL into the small city, I look for a good place to find food and a bathroom. The bag of heads on my back is doing pretty well, but I'm gonna need some ice or this will get smelly soon. I don't want to lose the efficacy of my statement, so I'll have to take care of that right after I piss in a place that isn't going to get sand in uncomfortable locations.

I slow down until I see more buildings that look like businesses scouting for a bar or restaurant. When I find what I'm looking for, I pull the bike into an adjacent alley. It could get stolen and that will make things more difficult, but since it looks like it belongs to bad guys, I'm hoping that won't happen.

Ducking out of the alley with my IKEA bag on my back, I walk down the street, looking at the various shops. My eyes widen when I see a sign that pronounces one small building the police station —I definitely missed that on the way in. I need some fucking tech, and I need it soon. I'm running around like a goddamn nomad from the Bible and it's dangerous. Luckily, I spot an open market just past the cop shop, so I walk faster until I can get inside.

Of course, now I have to get as much as I can with the money I swiped from the assholes who were holding me captive. I don't know exactly what the exchange rate is these days, but it's probably somewhere in the one dollar equals five hundred shilling range. That may be overestimating, but if I'm right, it means I have nearly fifty thousand in their money and I should be able to get food, drink, and ice. I might have to swipe the phone and it won't be great, but it'll do until Mogadishu.

That's doubly true if I get Lys on the line before I arrive. She'll make sure there's a drop somewhere and I'll be able to get cleaned up before I smuggle myself out of the country.

At least I'm still here to have these troubles. It's more than I can verify right now about my guys.

SURVIVOR

REMY

MY MAKESHIFT HEADING COVERING HELPS ME KEEP THE YOUNG GUY at the counter from looking at me too closely. You'd think the gigantic bag on back would draw suspicion, but he's much more focused on the tiny TV with a soccer game blaring from it. Smiling to myself, I creep around the store as if I'm browsing, but my quick fingers are disappearing things into my pockets, bag, and coat for later. He won't catch me stealing—Dwyn was a harsh taskmaster with teaching all of us the curriculum to the school of the seven bells.

He could pick the pocket of the Queen Mum without the palace guards notic-ing… even as a kid.

My heart aches in my chest; the worry is a raw wound that makes me dip my head and look at the floor until I get it locked down again. Those assholes have a lot of explaining and groveling to do before I can trust them again, but I refuse to allow some shadowy douche nugget to auction them to the highest bidder before I get my due. Of course, the jury is still out on whether or not I can actually heal enough to fully trust anyone again, much less those guys. Every dead therapist I've had thought I'd need intensive work before that was possible and I sure as fuck didn't stick around for that nonsense.

"Ohhhhhhhhh!"

I turn my head at the loud shout, watching the cashier carefully. The ref probably did something he didn't agree with and, like every armchair sports guy, he's yelling at the screen as if someone can hear him. Shaking my head, I walk to the where I see the burner phones, keeping my guard up as I study nearby products. They're in a locked case, so I have to get into this thing without him noticing.

Son of a bitch, nothing is ever easy.

Moving back into the aisle with toiletries, I squat down and pretend to look at shampoos while I open packages of bobby and safety pins. Tucking the empty plastic and cardboard behind the other shit, I put the entire contents in the zipper pocket of the motorcycle jacket except one of each. *Waste not, want not, Remy,* I think to myself. Without my favorite lock picking kit along, these should help me on my journey home. The soccer guy is yelling again, but I ignore it to walk over to the case with the phones and start working the flimsy lock.

It doesn't take me more than a few minutes to get it open and as soon as the cashier shouts again; I slip a decent phone out to shove it in my gross head bag. Picking the case closed to prevent after heist consequences, I walk over to the counter and place a few energy bars and water on it. I need to buy something to make it seem like I have a legit reason to be here. I don't want the dude figuring out merch is missing and start looking through security cam footage before I get the hell out of this town.

Over the years, I've learned that even distracted dipshits like this can be more observant than you expect.

"*Nabadeey nabadgelyo*[1]," the soccer guy says, only taking his eyes off the TV long enough to ring me up and give me back my change.

I duck my head, murmuring softly, "*Maalin wanaagsan.*[2]"

He doesn't acknowledge that I've said 'have a good day' and it's evening, but I honestly don't have a lot of Somali in my tool bag. If he'd spoken to me in Arabic, we would have been fine; hell, if he'd spoken in over twenty major languages, I would have been more fluent. But this is my first time in Somalia and I only had a few weeks to prepare for this mission. I didn't have time to do my usual work-up on the country, customs, languages, and geography that is my normal routine for a long job.

Walking out the door, I look up and down the street, making sure I'm not being watched. I highly doubt my captors have anyone left, but I'm thorough. What I need now is some fucking ice and a place to sneak into, where I can use a landline to call the number for Lys. She can remotely activate this phone and set up my ex-fill in Mogadishu once I arrive. Then I can rest my fucking weary ass for a little while before I make my way to the airport before I drop in exhaustion.

The café I saw when I rolled in is a good choice for rest, but I highly doubt I'll convince anyone working in the food biz to let me use a phone. Squinting as I walk down the street at a medium pace, I note a building that appears to be a small hotel. That will work, even if it's really a by the hour rental. Walking in, I look around the modest lobby, realizing it was likely apartments at one point, but it's been turned into short-term rentals instead. Whether it's for prostitution or stop over lodging for the more nefarious groups in this region, I'm not sure, but it'll work for me.

I look at the young girl working at a desk in the back corner, hoping it's the second option and not the first—she doesn't look older than fourteen. "*Kam thaman alghurfati?*[3]"

"*Thamaniat eashar 'alf shalan ya sayidati,*[4]" she replies, looking up at me through her lashes, then back down at the desk quickly.

I frown. Best math I can do says that's about thirty dollars an hour and now I know for sure this isn't a pit stop for terrorists and villains—at least, not for sleeping. I'm not a fan of this bullshit and if I could, I'd spend time here hunting down the pigs who set this place up, but I can't right every wrong in the world. There are a few people in my line of work who moonlight as semi-vigilantes—*Le Voleur de Sang*'s consorts seem to be some of them—but I don't have the luxury. Lys can send an anonymous tip through *Mercatus*, though.

Reluctantly, I nod and slap shillings on the counter to cover four hours. I'm using bigger bills on purpose, hoping that will force her to walk away from her desk and the phone I need so badly. Once she carefully counts them, her brow furrows. The slight girl looks at the bills again and shakes her head, holding up a finger to me. I nod, as if I understand what she didn't say, and watch her head to the back room with the cash clutched in her fist.

Score.

As soon as she's gone, I pick up the old style phone, dialing in a long series of numbers that will connect me to my new and closest friend. Each ring makes me feel more nervous until finally, a robotic voice message answers the line. Looking around, I whisper into the handset in French. "*Texte reçu. Pique-nique à Mogadiscio. Envoyez des oiseaux. Sentier pavé jusqu'au joueur de flûte. Soirée pyjama à Beledweyne. Nombre de nouvelles boîtes de conserve à suivre.*[5]"

Before the girl comes back, I type in a series of numbers on the keypad that Lys will use tones to identify. That will give her what she needs to activate my new phone and I'll be able to open more dialogue with her as I travel. *Of course, it will all have to be in code because this thing will have zero security, but it'll do.* Hanging up, I clasp my hands in front of me, smiling as the desk worker finally returns with my change. She seems to have a red mark on her face and the rage bubbles up inside of me, but I know I can't draw attention to myself by dealing with it.

But I know people who will and I'll make sure they come for her.

"Shukran sidti. Ghurfatuk thalathat wasitat eashar. Hadha hu miftahiki[6]," she whispers as she hands me the money and a heavy key.

"Shukran.[7]" I dip my head and head up the stairs, hefting my stinky bag onto my back until I get up to the third floor.

When I get inside my room, I drop the bag and grab a bucket that is clearly meant for ice, heading for the hallway to fill the bathtub so I can get these damn heads chilled. It takes a bazillion trips with the small thing, but when I get it full of ice, I place the bag in it with a sigh of relief. Now that I've taken care of the tools of my message, I flop on the bed, closing my eyes. I'm so fucking sore and tired that I can't even *feel* the pain I should be in. It's probably shock, which means a really rude awakening is coming, but I have so much to do before that happens.

I have to get proper food—not the stolen snacks I'll take with me on the road tomorrow—and I need to get cleaner. For the love of all that's holy, I *really* need a fucking drink.

"Will this badger asshole really lead me to Coda?" I whisper to myself. "I would have thought people would notice his absence, but Charice covered it up with rehab. He has to be going insane."

Out of everyone, Dwyn and Coda do the worst when locked up with nothing specific to occupy their minds. They won't break, but it will damage the hell out of them and it will be hard to get either out of their specific mental hole afterward. Dwyn will go off the deep end—he'll take riskier jobs and do crazier shit until something blows up in his face. Coda's method of handling it is not quite as outwardly destructive, but he'll burn through booze and drugs like he's trying to rival a seventies icon.

I don't want that for either of them; there's only so many times you gamble with that shit before you get a bad hand.

Keeping his disappearance a secret will only last so long—even with the reach of *Les Invisibles*. I have to get my ass out of this country, debrief with Lys, and track down the idiot who has Coda before this mess gets worse. The longer The Five stay MIA or underground, the more repercussions there will be, both in the public eye and behind the scenes at that viper nest they call HQ. I can only imagine how many secret factions within *LI* there are just waiting for the mighty to fall.

There's always a Brutus waiting in the wings, hoping to catch Caesar unaware.

I sigh heavily, still shunting the agony of my weeks of torture and malnourishment to its mental box to deal with later, and roll to my feet. No one is going to attempt a fucking coup on my watch. My boys spent over a decade climbing the ranks of that treacherous organization for a reason—I may not know what the fuck it is yet, but I'll be damned if I'm going to have their sacrifices go to waste.

Stomping into the bathroom, I clean the stink off of me so I can show my battered face in public without drawing the attention of the authorities. I unpin the makeshift *niqab* first, dunking my hair and face under the running water in the sink.

Truthfully, I need a full-on shower, not a brief rub down, but since I filled my tub with ice and severed heads, this will have to do. I don't bother trying to untangle my long silver locks; that will require hours of conditioning. The crappy soap and water sting in every cut, scrape, burn, and mark as I use the cheap, rough cloth and towel on them. Gritting my teeth, I breathe through my mouth and endure until I'm mostly presentable.

Sadly, I barely even notice the lingering stench of body parts; it's just part of who I am now.

The Guillotine revels in the deaths of her enemies, even when she's beaten to a pulp.

---

1. Peace be with you.
2. Good day.
3. How much is my room?

4. Eighteen thousand shillings, my lady
5. Text received. Picnic in Mogadishu. Send birds. Paved trail to the Pied Piper. Pajama party in Beledweyne. Number of new cans to follow.
6. Thank you Madame. Your room is three ten. This is your key.
7. Thank you.

WHAT'S THE FREQUENCY, KENNETH?

CODA

FOUR MONTHS.

At least, I think it's been four months. The ashy tic marks I've been making when I think the day changes add up to around that length of time. It's hard to know if I'm right, though, because I have to keep them hidden behind the hard metal bed frame and some get smudged, plus there's no fucking windows in this damned hole.

When I woke up after the blast, they covered my head in a black bag like some stupid spy movie and I was in a vehicle traveling over *much* rougher roads than downtown London. It didn't take me long to suss out that either the bad guy who'd been trying to kill our girl had me—which would have been shitty, but possibly information—or I'd already been sold out to a bidder because they didn't need me.

Admitting that helped me decide how I was going to play it whenever we stopped.

Obviously, I could have kicked up a fuss and tried to escape from the damn transport, but with my eyes covered and no one talking,

I had no idea what weapons they had. Worse than that, I had no clue how long it was since I got knocked out or what terrain we were in. I could have broken free to find myself in a goddamned snow storm in a tee shirt, so letting my temper rule would have been a stupid idea. Being cautious wasn't my normal MO, but since I had zero intel and no way to gather it, I knew I had to be patient like our fearless team leader would.

Reining in my hyperactivity became a problem within hours of waking—thank fuck for Mo's insistence on all the damn meditation practice.

The minute the vehicle stopped, I tensed up, waiting for some sort of painful beating, but it didn't come. Hands grabbed my arms, holding on tightly enough to bruise as they guided me into some sort of building silently. Then they dumped me in this cell, leaving me to rot most days. Food comes three times a day, though if they're smart interrogators, meals come at the wrong times to make my internal clock stayed fucked up. It's shoved through a slot in the door and no one ever says anything.

One morning I woke up with a sting in my right arm and I figured out they had to have injected me with something. A quick inspection told me they'd bathed, shaved, and dressed me, but everything else was undisturbed. I have no idea who the hell did it, but they made damn sure I wouldn't see *or* hear anything that went on while they did so.

Fucking weird.

I spend most of my days struggling to keep my ADHD from going insane and trying to figure out who and where I am. Even when I try to speak to the food delivery person on the other side of the heavy steel doors, I get nothing. My captors can only be traffickers—they're waiting for the hype to die down from my disappearance to move me. Some demented fuck out there will pay top dollar for a hot motherfucker with a famous face like me and the assholes holding me know they can't sell me off until the news cycles change.

Sadly, I probably have a better chance of escaping once I'm sold than I do now.

Running a frustrated hand through my hair, I wonder for the millionth time where my team and the girl we thought we lost are. Were they captured, too? Killed? Sold to the highest bidder? I have no idea, and it makes every cell in my body itch all day long. My nights are full of dark images representing the possibilities, so I usually manage a small amount of physical activity to keep my muscles sharp before I tire out.

Good news is the party time withdrawal faded in the first two weeks. Sucked ass, but I'm clean as a nun's panties now.

"Not that being here and not knowing if the rest of them are dead isn't making me *wish* for some kind of chemical relief," I mutter to myself. Talking to the walls is another one of my favorite pastimes at the moment and while it's not the same as talking to a person, at least it keeps my chords from getting rusty. "That way I can sing for my new master from my gilded cage wherever the fuck these scum bags are auctioning me off."

Shaking my head, I drop to the floor and start a round of push ups. It's part of my morning routine and I'll be damned if my melancholy is going to keep me from using the routine to settle myself. Doing the same things in a dependable pattern is the only way I'm keeping my brain from short circuiting with the lack of stimulation. Clearly, these bastards had no idea some of my medication was actually needed, not just part of being a wild rockstar.

I'm amazed I've managed this for so long, but the deep-seated need to know what in the holy hell happened that allowed Remy Benoit to live is driving me.

"Even if she died in the damn blast, I have to find out. Someone, somewhere, will spill the beans when I get out of this mess," I grumble as I continue my exercises. "No fucking way I'm going to the grave without understanding how the devil's greatest trick was convincing everyone he didn't exist."

When I'm done with push-ups, I start the sets of crunches. My abs burn as I move through each type, but the pain is grounding. I had a lot of cuts, bruises, scrapes and two sets of stitches when I could check myself out for the first time after I woke up in the truck. Some of them have scarred and one was a deep fucking gash in my stomach that took for damn ever to heal. As I touch my elbows to my knees, I wonder for a moment if they were drugging me every time they fed me at first so they could tend to my wound.

That would explain why the detox was so heinous—they were using heavier shit than I normally partake in and my body got used to it.

My lip curls as I eye the vomit bucket in the corner. I made good use of it during the dry out spell. I'm still not sure how they're getting clothes changes and cleaning done in here, but I can only hope it's through a much less addictive gas or some shit. I never want to go through a forced rehab like the one I went through here. It was a damn good thing there's absolutely nothing in this place to pick apart or use to harm myself—that's how bad it was.

"What's the point of all this, though? Whoever kept trying to blow Remy up didn't seem to aim at The Six as much as taking us off the board. They had no compunction shipping me off to this nightmare, so they're not law enforcement. If they had a vendetta against *LI*, I'd be dead, not being imprisoned and kept healthy. What do these fuckers want?"

No one answers, of course, and I flop back on the ground. My fingers tap on the ground as if I'm playing a piano and the act of pretending to play one of my songs on the keys helps me focus. I have to be ready; when I get away from my captors, the hunt for my team begins. Working out what we missed is the only way I'll know where to start. There has to be something both the guys and Remy missed when we set up the meet, and I'll be damned if I know what it is. Raz does most of the recon, and he's not here to help me sort through the nest of bullshit in my noggin.

"Could they be after one of her aliases, not Remy? Jinxy and Dwyn outed her as The Duchess and she flat out told us she's The Guillotine. But what if she has *more* big name criminal covers?" I ponder that for a moment, trying to decide if it seems like it's legit. Unfortunately, Remy is one of the smartest people I've ever met, so it really is. *So who else could she have been running under on Mercatus?*

Anyone in attendance at that damn shitty party is off the table. She wouldn't bother having a body double attend just to pretend to be another criminal. Hell, no one knew Duchess and Guillotine were the same, so it has to be the same for other possibilities. Their skill sets are disparate enough that they wouldn't be expected to bid on the same jobs. Theft and assassination are Dwyn and Mo's influences. Could she be hiding aliases under Raz or Jinx's specialties?

No one would expect a hacker to be a hands-on thief, but a grifter could travel in the same circles.

I wrinkle my nose. She can't have a public face like me; it would be far too risky to show herself all the time and keep up an underworld presence in more than one group of criminals.

Unless…

I rub my hand over my face, trying to work out how being a fixer would work. *Maybe she's one of those background people who keep everything they do out of camera range?* Pausing, I mutter, "Politics. If she's running grifter cons that lead to fixer needs, she could play both ends against the middle. She wouldn't have to show her face anywhere but sleazy back rooms and secret meet-ups."

It could definitely get you hunted—marks with that much clout get vicious.

"Jinx hasn't mentioned another major player running around, though. And no one warned me about a competitor undercutting my marks, so…"

It takes a lot to shock me, but the thought that Remy might run a solo version of The Six completely on her own makes my entire body tense up. The list of people who'd want one or more of her alter egos wiped off the planet might even dwarf ours. Anyone with any sense would know simply killing her wouldn't solve all of their problems—no professional in any of our fields works without leaving hair triggers on their misdeeds if they end up dead. Whether it's a person, their info passes to on death or even a tech tripwire that will activate if their DNA gets uploaded, we all have various ways of keeping our clients honest.

Rolling up to sitting, I put my forearms on my knees. "So they wouldn't want her dead. But killing us—*if* they know who we are to her—would certainly start another Guillotine-style rampage."

Holy fuck.

Hurting people who have no attachments is complex. Someone as used to death as Remy would mourn, take vengeance, and likely go back to work. If you really wanted to take her off the board without killing her, you'd have to damage her so much she wouldn't be able to shrug it off. My eyes widen as I look at the wall, realization spiking in my veins as I get what's going on.

Remy is almost certainly alive and so are the rest of my team. Whoever is after her, for whatever reason, is playing a very dangerous long game. They left her alive and absolutely no trace of what happened to us. Even if she hates our guts for the betrayal, there's no way she's not looking for us. In fact, the girl I knew would spend the rest of all time hunting to the ends of the Earth just so she could bitch us out.

We're scattered to the winds, alive, but unable to contact the world, so she spins her wheels indefinitely.

"What does that get this asshole, though?" I whisper as I rise to my feet. "How could fucking with one criminal or even six possibly benefit them?"

I don't know, but luckily, I have plenty of time on my hands to figure it out.

PARANOID

REMY

Once I'm clean, I gather my shit and make certain my new headscarf is secured. Depending on the city, there are some extremely conservative folks and I don't want to start a war over not observing the correct customs. I need to stay under the radar so I can get through tonight, race to Mogadishu, and get to Lys. My intel may not hold for long and I have to get on the trail before it's cold.

I jog downstairs, ignoring the girl at the counter as she talks to a couple that are *not* here for a vacation stay. Keeping my eye on the prize is my highest priority, so I can't get involved with the sordid shit going on in this dump. I exit the hotel quietly, heading for the restaurant I saw on my way in. It's on a corner and if I choose my seat carefully, I'll have a full view of the traffic on either side of the open air café.

The city is busy, even for one of the smaller areas in this region, and I blend into the crowd seamlessly until I get to my destination. When I step inside, very few people look up and I pat myself on the back for my good instincts. It's clearly a local spot and the people there are uninterested in random tourists who pass through. Eyeing the open tables, I find one where I can place my back against the wall and look out at everyone. The kitchen is kitty-corner to the spot, so I walk over and seat myself quickly.

"*Soo dhawoow*, miss. *Sideen kuugu adeegi karaa?*[1]"

I blink at the girl, who appeared out of thin air clutching a tray and a piece of paper. She doesn't look older than twelve, but I'd bet she's helping to support her family. "*Ma heli karaa bariis iskukaris iyo shaah chai?*[2]"

Her face lights up when I order the national dish and a favored drink. I did enough research before I came to know what I would and wouldn't eat because you can't depend on the Internet in some countries. The last thing I wanted to do was end up eating something I hate—though, I guess after weeks of eating bugs and rats, anything would be an improvement. Charred ashes would probably taste good in comparison.

"*Haa! Haa, seegay. Isla markiiba waan keeni doonaa.*[3]"

I watch her take off towards the kitchen, then I slump back in my chair to monitor the comings and goings around me. There are two men at the bar who have eyes that say 'criminal,' but I'd wager they're small timers. Their weapons aren't hidden artfully and the rest of the people aren't staying too far away. Likely they're minions of a bigger bad and low enough level that the locals don't worry about them invading their space.

My server approaches with a tray full of delicious smelling food, setting it down, along with my drink. I thank her and only after she's gone, do I lean in to scent the dish. The spices I expect to smell—garlic, cumin, turmeric, coriander, paprika and more—are present, but no stray scents catch my nose. It's always prudent to be careful as a woman traveling alone and, despite my young server's exuberance, she could be a tool for unsavory assholes. *Khaad* being used to kidnap women is not unheard of and I just got out of captivity, so it doesn't hurt to be suspicious.

When I'm satisfied my food isn't spiked, I dig in with fervor. The meat they used is camel and its flavor is distinctive enough from lean beef that I recognize it. The *baris isukukaris* could have been made with lamb, goat, chicken, or beef, but this is a delicacy in this part of the world. I'd surmise my chai has camel milk in it as well—not that it doesn't smell absolutely delicious. Rusty water for weeks will take away your inhibitions about drinking whatever is handy, just like eating bugs will.

As my stomach gets warmer, I ponder the turn of events since I left Lys. I'm not sure how the group who had me is linked to the Shadow Douche, but they're definitely linked to finding Coda. It feels like I'm missing something in the bigger picture because putting a hit on Raz and kidnapping the guys after the bomb is so… anticlimactic. Someone who's tried to blow us into bitty pieces twice wouldn't keep any of us alive—though I only have a glimmer of hope Coda is and zero intel to back up the wellbeing of the others.

It doesn't fit and there has to be more than one player in this game.

I frown at my plate as I eat, working out the chess moves I'll have to make after Mogadishu. Lys and I need to go through the offerings on *Mercatus* under my various aliases so we know what's going on in each sector of the criminal world. Clues to the guys' whereabouts—if they're alive—might show up there now that a couple months have passed. There might also be a trail for these morons I'm tracking; hopefully, I can use the bits and pieces I picked up to lead me to the next step in locating Coda. I'll have to take at least a week to heal up the damage *Mangust* and his fuckwits did, so it doesn't affect my ability to switch between aliases as I creep through the underworld. Right now, I have far too many scabs and bruises to fool anyone. Covering all this shit with makeup would be a damn nightmare, so staying put while we trawl the dark web isn't a choice.

Being in Somalia didn't burn many of my IDs for once, so I should be able to hit my storage unit in Paris and start ordering refills for the ones I burned on my adventures after seeing Coda at that stupid bar. I'll need to send packages to all my drop spots with the clothes and accessories first, then create all the personas from my databases of shelf identities. I've been designing thirty to forty a year since I escaped the island, so it's only a matter of actually making the documents for them and packing the kits.

That's a task for future Remy because I don't have time to slip back to all the countries I've been to recently.

It would be a hell of a lot easier if I had random assistants all over, but that leaves me open to betrayal. After the guys, I haven't truly trusted anyone to have my back. Everything I do is all on my own and even now, my gut is churning because I'm working with Lys. She's been a suitable partner since the bar in London and I have zero reason to think she'll turn, but I'm a damaged motherfucker. It's hard to unlearn the trauma patterns of the past—painful, in fact. I'm trying, though.

"Wax kale ma ku heli karaa, seego?[4]*"*

Looking up at the smiling girl, I shake my head, and she wanders away to another table. The food is delicious, and the chai is on point. Overloading myself after weeks of almost nothing won't help me. If I throw it all up when I get back to my room, I won't have helped a damn thing. I need to ease myself back into a non-starvation diet. Sucking in a slow breath, I finish the rest of my meal while I continue to run the list of shit to do in my head.

The life of a major criminal isn't nearly as glamorous as people think.

When I'm done, I toss some of the money I stole from my dead captors on the table. I'm leaving a tip but not one so generous that the girl will remember me and tell others. Making my way past the low level jackasses at the bar, I lift their wallets without a hitch, grinning to myself. Sometimes, little shit like this amuses the hell out of me. It's only a bonus that it will give me more funds for my trip across the country with my bag full of rotting heads. Besides, guaranteed, these assholes deserve to be knocked down a peg or two.

I'm halfway down the block before I hear the faint sounds of a scuffle behind me and I smirk, knowing it's probably them discovering their wallets are MIA. Hopefully, they aim at all the other ne'er-do-wells in the bar and not the staff, but I can't worry about it. My outlook has been far too soft in the part of my journey as it is and I wonder if finding my ex-friends then losing them is cracking my armor. That's a consequence I can't afford and I have to shore my walls up now.

Nothing about this journey to locate The Five or mete out vengeance for their deaths is going to be gentle.

With that in mind, I enter my hotel and pay not an iota of attention to what's going on in the lobby. I trudge up the stairs carefully, watching the corners and listening for anyone following. Something doesn't feel right now that I shut my emotions off again and I'll be damned if I'm getting jumped because I forgot who I was for a few hours. Deciding not to exit on my own floors, I go one up and across, then descend.

My eyes narrow as I look at the hallway, trying to find out if anything seems out of place. It looks clear, but I still have the feeling in my gut. I place my back against the wall, creeping down the poorly lit corridor silently. When I get to my door, I slide the key in the lock, unlocking it, then listening for a response inside. I hear nothing, so I swing the door open and stay behind it so any gunshots will bury in the wall facing it. Nothing comes and I burst into the frame in a fighting stance.

No one's here, but my gut is never wrong.

I enter slowly, cross-crossing my steps as I look at every nook and crevice of the room for someone lurking. When I don't find anyone, I let out a frustrated breath. I know something is wrong, but I can't put my finger on it. I'll have to check all of my makeshift surveillance traps one by one to see where the intruder was. They may not be here now, but I am certain someone was in my room. There's a scent of tobacco that wasn't here before and though I haven't located their purpose yet, I will eventually.

"Come on, Remy. What the fuck would someone want in your room? You showed up with no luggage besides the heads and didn't look like a rich tourist." I squint as I check the bathroom—nope, heads still there, exactly as I left them.

Is it possible someone has already found Mangust and his men?

Doubtful. They never had visitors while I was there; I memorized every voice, and I killed them all. There wasn't a damn phone or computer in the whole place, so they couldn't have talked to anyone before my personal massacre. This has to be something else—something less major bad guy and more local moron.

Narrowing my eyes, I pull out the burner and turn the flashlight on, then turn off the lights. Slowly, I walk around the room, flashing it over things until I hit pay dirt. The glare of a tiny lens catches the beam of light from my phone. It's positioned in a corner of the bedroom near the ceiling and aimed right where it could see me disrobe. Teeth clenched, I stride back to the bathroom and, sure as shit, I find another one aimed at the shower.

"Perverted motherfuckers want to use me to get their rocks off or sell as a peeping vid online—or both. I'll skin them alive and enjoy their screams," I growl under my breath. "And they say *I'm* a monster for killing people without a qualm. Sex traders are the absolute *scum* of the Earth."

I planned on letting the bullshit going on at this place go because it's not the hill to die on today, but nope.

---

1. Welcome, miss. How can I serve you?
2. Can I have steamed rice and chai tea?
3. Yes! Yep, missed it. I will bring it right away.
4. Can I get you something else, miss?

CONTROL

REMY

My innate fury didn't want to wait for nightfall, but I forced myself to tend to my heads and plot without acting rashly. I don't have a lot of lines, but sex trafficking and involving innocent families are the two big ones. The lifestyle I lead and the people in it have made their own choices, even if there weren't many things to choose from. There's always a way out at some point and plenty of *LI* operatives have found less unsavory 'retirement' opportunities, I'd wager. Not every mission related death is real—look at my escape. I can't be the only person to ever figure out how to disappear; they teach us to do it, for fuck's sake.

But selling humans for profit is beyond my acceptance levels—sue me, I'm a fucking complicated bitch.

It flitters through my head that any of the guys could be caught up in one of those rings and I have to swallow back the evidence of my earlier meal to keep from vomiting on the floor. They're all unreasonably hot in adulthood, and the price they'd fetch in those types of auctions, especially with Coda's fame, is shudder-worthy. You could buy small countries for the amount that man would command in a super elite online auction—guaranteed.

"They can't be selling them all. Maybe not even any of them. This could be *their* enemies, not yours, and that would make them valuable for reasons besides luring you out, Remy," I mutter to myself. I've gotten good at talking myself off ledges over the years; I had to. I don't have partners or sidekicks, it's just me and my metric asston of identities against the world.

I guess Lys is here for now, but I can't call her again to settle my ire about the pigs running this hotel.

A quick glance at the clock tells me it's late enough to start creeping, so I gather what little I have to keep myself disguised and out of sight, then slip out the door of my room. This side quest will put me behind by an hour or so, but it needs to be done. As I make my way downstairs, I keep my ears open, listening for sounds of any security or bumps in the night that might give me away. When I get to the main floor, I slip out of the stairwell, waiting to see if there's a night person at the counter.

After a few moments, it becomes clear that this place isn't monitored at night. There's probably another location they run their girls out of at night and as gross as that is, I don't have time for it. I do have time to let myself into the back office and royally fuck up their operation if they have their shit online. It will have to do for now because I need to get my ass back on the bike and head for Mogadishu to catch my ride.

Once I leave my message in the most public place possible, of course.

Looking around the front desk, I locate a few items I can use to pick the lock. I doubt it will require much Macgyver-ing because this place isn't exactly the Ritz. A paperclip, a stiff piece of plastic and the scissors should do in a pinch. Worst case, I can shoulder it open, but that will make way more noise than I want. I pause to look at the reservation book, committing every name and date on it to memory. While I may not have time at the moment, I'll circle back to these motherfuckers later.

Jimmying the crappy lock only takes a moment—and not even all of the makeshift tools—and I slip into the office. It's small, but filled with monitors that flicker between the bedrooms of the hotel. There's a laptop on the desk and the video feed is obviously going to a rack of hard drives sitting on top of the server. *Son of a bitch.* I rummage around until I find something to wrap the lot of them and the laptop up because I'm taking *all* of it.

I didn't come here to be a goddamn bleeding heart hero, but such is life sometimes.

Once I've secured the stuff I'm taking along for the ride, I disconnect everything, using the scissors to cut the cords to the recorder. It won't stop them, but it'll take time to get them replaced. A quick check in one of the drawers nets me a screwdriver, so I open the back of the DVR and pull out the memory and the motherboard, grinding them under the heel of my boots. That should do it for now. If the assholes watching were here, I'd leave a much more stringent message, but that's not to be this evening.

Stepping out of the office after I put what little I used back in place, I move to the front desk again, sighing in relief when I find an extra trash bag underneath the one being used. The bundle of electronics goes inside and I tie off carefully. I'll need this to keep head juice from seeping in as I ride for the capital. I'm not making another stop after this unless it's for gas. If I have to fucking hold my bladder for the entire time, I will.

Wouldn't be the first or the last time.

I'm satisfied with my vendetta as I head up to my room to pack the bag and get the hell out of here. Now that I've destroyed shit, I can't risk being here much longer. Someone will eventually arrive to work, and I want to be long gone when that happens. The patrons of this place aren't the type to go after their disgusting sideline, so it won't be a stretch for them to accuse a dirty, foreign woman traveling alone with a suspicious bag. I wasn't very stealthy when I checked in other than the fake name, but I didn't need to be.

Now, I have enough shit to get me through until I reach my destination and can wash the stink of dead people off.

Time to hit the road, Remy.

FOR THE FIRST HALF HOUR, I'm following the *Wadada Iridda Aamin.* There's not a lot for me to consider pausing at, but I'm determined to get as far away from Beledweyne as possible before I stop. I left more of a trail than normal, but I lost my temper. I despise that kind of shit and I'll have to make certain I have contractors working to ensure my face is wiped clean if it shows up anywhere. It's not only creepy, but dangerous and those motherfuckers are only at the beginning of my wrath.

"That's for future Remy. What current Remy needs to do is figure out who the hell this *Il Tasso* moron is and follow him to whatever auction they've got Coda slated in. It doesn't matter what *kind* of trafficking it's supporting—he's too valuable to have sold without a ramp up. They'd have to set it up, open the bidding, and let a war start. If it's about intel, it will move faster because his disappearance won't stay secret for long. But if it's about sex, they'll draw it out until some panting fuckwit drops a fortune to get their hands on him. I hate to root for the latter, but it gives me more time."

Of course, no one answers because I'm talking to myself on a lonely desert road.

Shaking my head to clear it, I move on to the next mystery. I've been locked up for weeks chasing this lead, but when I get to Mogadishu, I'll hop the plane to meet Lys in Paris. We'll hunt down this new dipshit, but I'm anxious to hear how tracing the movements on the dark web might take us to hot tips on the other guys. The bot net I built has been running the entire time I was gone. Hopefully, it's tracked some hints of Raz online or whispers about Dwyn, Jinx, or Mo. Their trails have been ice cold since the bomb, but if there's a chance Coda got out, they did, too.

"Keep telling yourself that, Remy. Faint hope isn't your M.O., but until you have confirmation, they're alive. They wouldn't dare die before you could let them have it for their fucking childish, asshole behavior on the island. You might be past it, but telling them off is your right."

The balance between wanting to make sure the idiots who broke my heart as a teen aren't dead and needing to kick them all the balls for it is a tricky tightrope to walk. Some days, I considered giving up and letting them deal with their fucking mess; some days I woke up vowing revenge on the Shadow Douche who *has* to be connected to this somehow. I've never been so torn in my entire life, but at least it kept me going. Having my indecisiveness about the men of The Five was a big motivator while I was locked in that stupid cell munching on bugs.

I owe them an asskicking for my ink being fucked up now, too.

Oddly, I haven't noticed the pain from all the injuries I'm ignoring. I suppose it's my ingrained ability to compartmentalize partnering with my training at the island. We were constantly injured and there was no one to coddle us if we ached. You had to learn to set it aside, rise above, and lick your wounds later on or you'd die. I haven't cleaned them as well as I'd prefer, though, so I want to hit up another drug store in Mogadishu so I can scrub the burns, scrapes, and gashes. I won't die, but it'll scar and I hate that shit.

By the time I reach the next leg of my trip, I've decided to rescue the guys, *then* berate them. Whether that will last or not, who knows, but at least I'm considering more than killing them myself.

That has to count for something, right?

THE DRIVE down *Wadada Buulebarde* is long as fuck. I stopped three hours in for gas, a few snacks, and then hit the road as fast as possible. The less witnesses I leave the better off I am. I've spent a lot of time and effort keeping my true countenance off of video surveillance and tech, but I don't have access to the fancy shit in the middle of the damn desert. The *hijab* and the kohl are the best I can do to alter myself. Lucky for me, people on the road aren't interested in looking at a random person speeding along with a mysterious bag strapped to them. If that doesn't say something about this part of the world, I don't know what does.

I finally make the turn at *Wadada Wadnaha* right before dusk. That's good for me because the city will be less crowded as I make my way towards *Aden Adde International Airport*. I know they have plenty of flights out of the country on any given day, but the major carriers won't go direct to France. I'd have to stop in Istanbul or Frankfurt, so cargo flights are key.

Weaving in and out of traffic in the main part of town, I head for the underbelly first. Once it's dark, I'll divest myself of the smelly heads in a public place, leaving the message for those who should receive it. Then I'm going to clean myself up, text Lys to let her know I'm here, and wait for the info about what flight I'm shipping myself on.

Not that much longer and I'm home.

The idea of being in a real bathroom, clothes that don't stink, and finding a goddamn dentist is so appealing that I groan. I'm prone to luxury because I can afford it, but I never thought of myself as dependent on it until now. It's been a long time since I did shit like allow myself to be captured and tortured—my status as The Guillotine elevates me enough to ignore jobs that might require this sort of thing. I did a lot of them when I first escaped the island, but in recent years, I'm as much a luxury assassin as the places I haunt while I'm on jobs.

Again, my life's a fucking disaster because of those same five fucking dudes.

"That's it. Stop whining like a little bitch, Remy," I whisper to myself. "Get your shit together, get home, and teach this shadowy cocklicker a lesson. If his people are behind this, you know it won't end with finding The Five. That will only kick start another round of bullshit as you figure out why he took a hit out on Raz and possibly the rest of the team. There's no time to bemoan your circumstances, only act."

Pulling onto a side street, I make my way out of the main part of the city, looking for clues to lead me to the seedy underbelly. It takes me a bit to find the right person to tail, but once I get a lock on my target, I'm able to follow along. The night falls as we navigate into a darker area, street lights getting more sparse as we head into the bad part of Mogadishu. When the car finally stops, I see a raucous looking bar that is obviously rocking. My lips curve as I pause, watching the people flock into it with barely contained glee. They're from various walks of life, but it's obvious none of them have ever been called a good guy.

Perfect.

I park the bike, slinking into the shadows of boarded up buildings as I make my way down the block. There's an iron fence around the outside patio and it continues past the front door along the face of the building. The spikes at the top will display my message beautifully, even if no one notices it until long after my flight takes off. Hefting the bag, I creep up to the small den of ne'er-do-wells and walk past the doors. A group of men veer off to enter behind me, but they pay me no mind. Once they're inside, I head to the last post to start my squishy, disgusting work.

The Guillotine cannot afford to squeamish.

After my gory mission, I sped out of the red light district until I found a store open. I walked around it casually for as long as I could force myself to wait, making certain the guy at the counter was engrossed in yet another soccer match. Since I ditched my trusty blue bag full of ick, I had the hard drive tucked inside my stolen jacket. That didn't leave a lot of room for theft, but I stuffed what supplies I could in pockets and my clothes. I got a few first aid supplies, some food, a knife, and thank fuck, a pack of wipes.

Now that I'm no longer covered in smelly decomp, I head for the airport. I used the burner I lifted earlier to text Lys one more time, getting the information on the guy she's paid to smuggle me on board this flight. It's about sixteen hours and he was told to prepare a space for that, but who knows if he listened. Minions for hire aren't known for being loyal or even smart enough to realize they might have been hired by a much bigger fish than they knew.

As long as he has water and a space big enough to curl up in, I'll survive another half a day in discomfort.

Sleeping through long trips isn't my usual fare, but given the circumstances of this particular voyage, I should be safe enough. The switchblade I helped myself to will be clutched in my palm and someone will have to make an awful lot of noise to get to me. That will give me time to wake up and gut any intruder—guaranteed. This method of getting out of the country is low rent, low profile, and won't raise alarms anywhere it shouldn't. Lys will be at our predetermined spot when I get to Paris and she'll escort me to yet another safe house.

"Going back to where it started is the best way to prepare for your next steps." Talking to myself is second nature, but it's not like I have another cheerleader to push me through the next eighteen hours. I've learned over the years that voicing things out loud helps me think and outside of doing searches on the idiotic monikers of my ex-kidnappers, I'm not sure what direction I'll have to take to find Coda. "Perhaps it's time to pull Mack out of the drawer."

Grinning to myself, I nod as I turn onto the back road to the cargo section. I pulled out a map while I was in the store, studying the best routes to get around as part of my dicking around in the store earlier. The clerk glared at me occasionally, rightfully surmising I was using the product for free, but it must be fairly common. The one in front was well creased and definitely had been opened before. His attention went back to his small TV quickly, dismissing me as a freeloader without another thought.

Double win for me because it made it easier to steal the things I needed.

The signs lead me to the area Lys described and I park the bike for the last time. Hopping off, I look around, squinting until I see a tall, thin man gesturing animatedly at me. I stride over, keeping a close eye on his hands to make certain this isn't an ambush. "*Ma waxaad tahay albaabka ilaaliye?*[1]"

"*Haa Ma tahay maamulaha furaha?*[2]"

I snort, covering my mouth. Lys thinks she's *so* fucking funny with this shit. "*Haa I geeya iridda aan ka soo galo.*[3]"

The guy nods, ushering me over to the fence to sneak me through a large hole in it. Clearly, I'm not the first person he's done this for, nor will I be the last. Security in bigger countries would shit a brick at a perimeter breach, but here, we sneak in and head for the back of the huge plane without a single soul approaching. When we're inside, he shows me the large crate, pointing to the pillows and supplies inside proudly. I give him a curt nod, climbing in and waiting.

The last thing I hear before it goes dark in my space is the side of the crate being nailed shut, closing me in until we arrive in France.

---

1. Are you a gatekeeper?
2. Yes. Are you the key master?
3. Yes, take me to the entrance.

OUTSIDE

CODA

For the past seven days, I've been trying to unravel the larger web in my head. There's enough dirt and debris in this cramped room for me to sketch out a small brain cloud in symbols like Raz does when he's looking at the chessboard. I'm not nearly as good at it because I get hung up on small details or hyper focus on a single angle, but luckily, I've got nothing but fucking time to recover if I go off on a tangent for a couple hours. So far, I've got the past: Remy's escape, her faked death, whatever she did to survive once off the island, and her eventual transformation into The Guillotine. A lot of that is a question mark because I don't have a fucking clue how she didn't die or what she did to get to land, much less to Europe.

Another corner is based on my life with The Five after she was gone: how we rose to the top, what jobs we did, enemies we made, allies we *think* we have, and the power we amassed during that time. I have symbols for all the *LI* victories that weren't ours, but propelled the organization higher as well. It's a big bucket; *Les Invisibles* has an army of operatives at all levels and fingers in more pies than a bakery. The person pulling the strings could be aiming for the largest target using the smaller ones and I'm not discounting it.

Below that, I have my public cover activities as well as Jinx's. The rest of them operate with much less visibility so their exploits stay in the previous section, but Jinxy and I draw enough attention in our personas that we have special considerations. Friends, lovers, enemies, marks, and targets using these known identities need different scrutiny than shadowy corners of the web. It's a smaller burst of info, but still relevant, I think.

The opposite end of that line is Remy's shit, both suspected and confirmed. Her known kills and heists as The Guillotine and The Duchess, plus the ones attributed to her that have never been claimed. The unclaimed ones are much lower profile and my theory is they had some sort of personal meaning to her that wasn't about money. Her high paying gigs are all panache—they occur in the open, with no evidence other than calling cards. If she hadn't left those signatures, they could have been claimed by anyone in the world because she's been taught to leave zero trace like us. Conversely, the small time shit is similarly untraceable, but not signed. They have the hallmarks of her criminal personas, but no telltale mark to make her involvement definitive.

Just outside of that bubble, I have a list of random high profile jobs and events that people have surmised were done by The Five that I *know* none of us were involved in. Thefts, deaths, plots, schemes, cons, hacks, and other ripples in the global criminal pond that would take a very skilled operative to complete without being caught, but also were never attributed to anyone but lowly braggarts who could not have possibly been the culprit. Over the years, Mo and Raz have spoken of some of these well known occurrences, wondering who is picking up the contracts and successfully working them without credit. There's always bullshit hanger-on fuckers who *want* to say they did it, but the proof never appears and the community ignores their bluster.

But what if they're being done by someone's alternate identity?

If Remy has been operating as *two* well known and respected criminals without being outed, who's to say she isn't running an entire team of them? I had that thought at the beginning of the week and it seemed silly. But honestly? For a woman as smart as she was, it's not actually impossible. She's been setting up the same kind of network the guys and I have for just as long. Remy will have hundreds of burnable IDs, personas, back stops, dead drops, HQs, and bolt holes. She could have created any number of *Mercatus* accounts based on them and be working anything from computer crimes to assassinations.

We taught her everything we knew and she's had time to learn even more, just like us.

I rub my hands over my face, frustration screaming in my veins. If she has been playing the entire board for all this time, the list of people who'd like to take her out is unfathomable. I'd need Raz and his damn supercomputer shit to parse all that data and he's obviously not coming to the rescue. In this damn room, all I have is my non chemically enhanced brain and a bunch of dust to scribble notes with. Of course, given that I have no fucking clue how long I'll be waiting for the motherfuckers holding me to sell my ass, it might not matter.

"This whole scenario only works if some fucknut has been plan-ning this for a really long time," I mutter to myself. "They'd have to build up contacts and resources, plus gather a metric asston of data on her and us. And it wouldn't just be general gossip stuff—they'd need insider info from spies in *LI* and *Mercatus* to start."

But what moron would have the sack to go up against The Guillotine and The Five?

I blink when it comes to me. "The jackholes would *have* to know about our history, which means they'd have to know who Remy really is."

Again, my brain whirls with questions. How in the fuck would some rando discover her true self when she's done such a bang-up job of hiding even from *LI*? It seems almost impossible for the connection to be made by a third party; hell, Jinx and Dwyn *fucked* her and didn't realize! You can't get much goddamned closer than that and neither of them had a *clue* until she showed up at the zoo. Mo fought her, she saved me… Everyone but Razzie had an up close and personal encounter with her but we didn't see it. I suppose it could have been because we weren't looking, but I doubt it. The skill Remy Benoit puts into her fake personas is outstanding and I absolutely believe that's why we didn't figure it out.

The amount of physical alteration to our bodies and faces fooled her—that's Les Invisibles pride and joy.

"But Remy's changes are all true tradecraft. She doesn't go under the knife all the time, I bet. She's learned to do it all old school." My heart thumps a little, impressed with her cunning and abilities even more the longer I think about how incredibly good the girl we lost has become. "She'd be ruling our asses if she'd stayed in The Six. No question about it."

I scoot over, selecting a new spot to work in. This list needs to be about the people at *LI* and in the bigger criminal community that I can remember who might have the money or reach to be involved. It's possible the money source and the leader aren't the same; in fact, it's even possible the money, the leader, and the general for the foot soldiers aren't the same. If they operate as well as *LI*, they would insulate all their pieces like a terror cell so one part getting caught wouldn't take down the others.

Holy fuck. Could there be a silent, major player like Les Invisibles, The Company or Il Noche?

Even considering that blows my damn mind. The power wielded by the three major syndicates is legendary and surmising that there's another one hiding in plain sight is hard to swallow. There are plenty of smaller, less effective groups and scads of independent contractors. But there's only three huge organizations… right?

"This shit makes my brain ache," I grumble as I lean back against the wall. "I wish Raz or Jinxy were here. I'm not as good as them when it comes to organizing and cataloging information. They'd have this sorted in seconds."

Minutes tick by as I stare at the drawings, hoping something jumps out at me and I can continue down the path of discovery. When it doesn't, I push to my feet and head for the cot. Stretching out on it, I stare at the ceiling until my eyes lose focus. My fingers tap against my stomach in random chords and my brain floats along, playing snippets of music and lyrics in my head.

This is how I typically create and I've been ignoring it to work like the others.

If I can give my mind space, creativity will flow again even if I'm hungry, bruised, tired, and frustrated. Eventually, I can't help myself and maybe, just maybe, some wild solution will come out of daydreaming. It's a stretch, but I've had worse ideas that worked out, so I'm going to give it a whirl.

My lips curve as I go back, remembering the girl, the island, and then the time right after she was gone. I let pictures and sounds drift through my consciousness, plucking a little at images and sounds made by people who approached the five of us afterward. The interrogation we all faced from the Commandant and the other leaders was fairly standard—if not painful and scarring—but nothing they did is tripping a wire for me. But some of the High Legion has changed since then because old farts retire and new idiots replace them. Outside of the Commandant, most of those people are now off to their retirement hiding spots or dead. So maybe the clue is in the people who were coming up during that time.

"*The Comtessa* retired two years after. *Le Renard* was killed in a plane crash in the Indian Ocean the year after that. Stupid snooty git didn't even get to his bolt hole when he left. *Caminhante das Sombras* was the next to go after that and he runs some ex-spook criminal resort thing in the Maldives. He's probably safe. Lady Volkov and The Raptor replaced the first two, and *Il Dolce* took the place of the last one." I frown, pushing myself to remember if any other Legion members turned within the decade we were making our way as The Five. A small, niggling sensation is prodding me, saying I've missed someone important, but even I'm not so distracted that I'd miss a fucking Legion member getting replaced.

I hate when I'm sober enough to realize how unmanageable my own head is.

"Okay, so Lady Volkov hates us. But she wouldn't do all this for just The Five. I mean, she could figure out better ways to take us out from her seat. The Raptor doesn't give a fuck about anything but money and we make him money. "

Humming to myself, I allow my brain to go back into drift mode as I strum along with my fingers. This might be the only way I can get myself in the zone and if that's the case, I need to do it.

The fates of my brothers and the girl we once loved might depend on it.

I'M GONNA SHOW YOU CRAZY

REMY

THE PLAN LANDING JOSTLES ME AWAKE AND I CLUTCH MY KNIFE hard as my eyes fly open. I know Lys paid the handler on this end well, but I don't trust people as far as I can spit. Whoever opens my crate could have a weapon or demand more money and I have to be prepared to defend myself. After all, the guy has *no idea* who's stowing away in this box; it's not like Lys told the contractors a famous killer was hopping a ride. That'd be dangerous for more reasons than I can count. So I'll sit here and wait patiently, hoping I don't have to gut a fool.

I'm not opposed; it's just messy.

Gathering what little I have that I'm taking with me, I wait for the plane to taxi across the runway and into place. The cargo doors are loud as fuck when they open and I stay silent as footsteps approach. The person knocks three times on the top of the crate —a predetermined signal—so I use my free hand to cover my eyes as the crowbar tears into the wood. Light comes streaming in as the side falls off, blinding me a little so I hold the knife up where it can be seen. I hear a muttered curse, then a rough voice.

"Up and out, stowaway. We don't have much time."

I scramble out, still adjusting to the bright sun as I stretch my cramped muscles. The pause earns me another huff from the crooked worker, but I can't hobble across the tarmac. Once I can see his scruffy face, I glare as I crack my neck. "Watch your tongue. I speak enough Dutch to know what you said. Luckily for you, I have a more pressing engagement than your death."

He gapes at me as I tuck the knife at the small of my back and wrap the scarf I stole from the bodega over my silver hair. "I-I…"

"Shut up and get me to my transport. We don't have time for this."

The handler swallows hard and turns on his heel, leading me to the exit slowly. When we get to the bottom, he looks around, then motions me to follow. I stride out behind him, holding my head high and walking with purpose. One of the great truths I've found out over the years of being a criminal is that if you walk as if you belong and have a destination, very few people will stop you. Humans simply assume that if you look busy, you are. It makes for easy access to *lots* of places if you know how to fake the 'can't be bothered' busy walk.

"Keep up," my accomplice mutters. "I will get you to the employee area and you should exit with other staff. It will take you to the employee parking lot. What you do from there is your business."

"Understood."

I knew this was the plan, of course. There's a car waiting for me with keys hidden underneath in an unobtrusive spot. I'll leave from the lot and head straight to one of my off-site warehouses to slip into a burner I.D. before I rendezvous with Lys. I don't want my real face captured on CCTV because I don't have time for clean-up. Hence, the scarf I've wrapped to cover myself in the style of a *niqab* versus a hijab.

Our journey takes a few more minutes, lengthened by his pausing to speak with other employees while I lurked behind. By the time we got to the exit, I threw an infuriated glare his way before melting into the crowd of people leaving as the first shift let out. We could have missed this crowd with his obvious distractions and I would have reconsidered my stance on not slitting his throat. I needed to blend until everyone split to head for their vehicles.

Non-professionals never understand that their awkward attempts at disguising behavior only draw more attention, not less.

The sun is bright as I look over the gleaming cars, scanning until I find a very plain looking burgundy sedan in the middle of the pack. It doesn't stand out in any way—except that it's parked between two glistening new cars that are upper mid-tier brands. Lys mentioned the rough in the diamonds, a play on words that tells me I've found the right car. I walk over quickly, not even glancing at anyone else as I mimic someone glad to be out of work for the day.

Bending down, I find the key in a magnetic container tucked far enough back that no one would look. I sigh in relief, clicking the fob and hop in.

Now it's time to shed my skin like a snake and get down to business.

THE DRIVE to my storage unit in Porte de Châtillion takes less time than I would have expected. After the explosion, I waffled over whether we should stay in the city or get the hell out of Dodge, but it seemed prudent to stay while we searched. We might have located one of the guys in a hospital or some roach motel hiding, so it was the best plan. But the longer I waited to hear from them, the more comfortable I got with being in the house Lys and I were in. Paris was close enough to most of Europe and had a large airport with access to trains going everywhere.

I didn't take our location for granted, though, given we almost got blown up there to start. Lys and I both wear disguises everywhere and have been burning through stock more often than we're used to in order to keep from being identified by Shadow Douche or any of his minions. That's why I'm headed to my *second* warehouse, not the one I used when I saved Coda's ass.

Comfort is the enemy of caution.

My unit here isn't tucked in a *Les Invisibles* block, which means I can head straight for the one I want, get inside, and pack my shit. I pull up to the keypad, inputting my entry code, and drive down the lane until I reach the back of the facility. I'm in the furthest east corner at the end, which gives me the advantage of being close enough to the fences around this place to shimmy my ass up and out if someone comes looking. I'd prefer not, but knowing when to fight and when to observe is a skill I've been honing since childhood.

"Come to mama," I mumble as I dismantle my added security measures on the unit and walk inside. Pulling the door closed, I breathe deeply, enjoying the clean, sanitized smell of my workspace. After sucking down sand and dirt for weeks in that fucking compound, this feels like Heaven in concrete walls to my lungs.

Flinging open the first cabinet, I start pulling kits out one by one. I'll need one for today, but at least five more to hold me over while we dig into *Il Tasso*. If I have to scurry off to another place to track him, I can arrange to stop by another storage city along the way. Squinting, I pick *Moira Adelle Bancroft of London, England* off the shelf. The card says she's an assistant to some undersecretary of something or other—which means she comes with a lot of extra docs and identity shit. It might be useful; who knows?

I toss the other four bags into a huge rolling suitcase nearby, then grab the accessory and shoe kits that coordinate with my choices. At one point, I thought about putting pictures on the outside of the kits, but truthfully, I shouldn't choose by what look I feel like sporting. It will lead to non-random adoption. The name, profession, and style of clothes is good enough. I only added the last one so I'd know if the identity had fancy clothes or normal shit— something I absolutely needed to know for my Duchess outings.

Is The Duchess truly burned?

Lys will know. I could also be The Cat if I need to steal, but that's a low level moniker. It doesn't command attention on *Mercatus* like The Guillotine, The Duchess, *Te Atarangi*, or *Dançarina do fogo*. Those are my most developed criminal personas and I'd hate to lose any of them, especially to that douche-y motherfucker. It took almost a decade to make myself stand out in all five disciplines while nurturing low- level personas in the lesser skill sets. I've infiltrated damn near every part of the criminal marketplace in some way and I refuse to lose that advantage. Hopefully,. Lys confirms The Duchess is still able to accept bids and I won't have to tear down that entire network.

Shaking my head, I zip up the case and head for the computer set-up. I want to do a little dark web surfing before I head out to meet my friend. I trust her as much as I can, but there are things I've never told anyone. That caution has kept me alive this long, so I don't see a reason to change. I'm sure she's not revealed everything about herself to me yet, either.

This world is harsh with people who don't use their damn brains, especially women.

"Okay, Shadow asshole. I'm looking for you and this weasel fucker. Get ready."

THE ALARM on my screen goes off when it's time to change into Moira, so I click out of the forums and chats I was monitoring. Grabbing the mobile tech I need, I add it to another smaller case nearby, carefully packing enough burners and 'leave behind'

equipment so I won't have to fetch it again. I pause by the weapons case, leaning in to scan my retinas, and grin broadly as I take the array in the first cabinet.

Knife, knife, gun, plastic gun, four wires, brass knuckles, boom stick, baton…

Once I'm satisfied, I dump it all in with my tech and close that as well. I probably don't need *all* the things I snatched, but after being locked up like an animal in the desert, I want as much fire-power as I can handle.

Moira's clothes bag has a pair of high-waisted black dress pants, a silk halter in a purple, and a short bolero jacket. I pop the brown contacts in, blinking until they settle, and then fit the wig cap on. The honey blond wig falls mid back, but I wrap it up in a stylish chignon so it doesn't get caught in the baggage I have to lug outside. A quick addition of flats and some conservative jewelry almost completes the look. It only takes a little foundation, lipstick, and some winged eyeliner to bring the whole effect together. It's not quite French, but it's very chic and definitely continental.

"Pleasure to meet you," I murmur to myself a couple of times to test exactly how I want her accent and intonation to land. When I nail it, I recite a couple sonnets quickly, getting my mouth to fit around normal and unusual words with Moira's voice.

Got it.

The last thing I grab is the oversized purse with a crossbody strap, securing the IDs, phone, and makeup in it before I take the handles of the rolling cases. I'm ready now; all I need to do is drive to Montmartre to meet Lys in the tiny bar she set as the meet location.

"Almost home, Remy. Just a little farther and you can rest."

Famous last words if there ever were any.

WALK THROUGH THE FIRE

MO

Squinting in the sunlight, I raise the binoculars to my eyes so I can surveil the cars coming down the dirt road. The compound I'm living at is deep in the hills of Colombia, and unannounced vehicles usually aren't a good sign. I find the drug trade tedious as hell —it's mostly criminals killing other criminals so they can supply other criminals. If I wasn't following protocol after the explosion in Paris, I wouldn't get caught dead doing this shit.

"Not a lot of elegant choices to be had when you're looking for last minute, long-term work in my field," I mutter under my breath. The humvees swerve around the mines laid into the driveway and I groan. "Great. Another fucking mole to ferret out and torture until I find out how they got turned. It's like the back of a goddamn shampoo bottle in this hellhole."

Dealers and cartel hangers-on are about as loyal as a rabid dog next to a bloody steak.

Pushing the button on my comm, I push my irritation down

before alerting my team. *"Dos humvees. Trampas sobrevividas. Rata en la cocina. Activa la respuesta alfa.*[1]*"*

My notification seems to fall on deaf ears for a few moments and I curse under my breath again. The lazy assed, untrained cartel soldiers I command frequently fuck off to shoot tequila or sample their boss' product if they can get away with it. Worse yet, they wander off to terrorize the female house or cut staff. That shit doesn't fucking fly with me and I've had to recruit more than one new member in order to replace ones I taught a lesson in consent. However, at this moment, I need those ridiculous clowns to answer me before these damn transports get past my next barrier.

Of course they'd all be dicking around when there's an invasion when El Jefe and his familia are in residence.

"Gilipollas! Vayan a sus lugares antes de que el jefe nos castre a todos. Han traspasado el primer perímetro.[2]*"*

Barking into the mic, I toss the binoculars aside and rise from the ground. I often take the high ground when on guard duty because none of the idiots here can hit the broad side of a barn door. They're spoiled by only needing to spray large bursts of automatic weapon fire into their targets, so no one has taken the time to teach them that if you can hit your target from a distance, your survival rate skyrockets. Some of the most elite marksmen in the world trained me; fuck if I'm going to pretend to Rambo and risk my ass if I don't have to.

"General Mortimer, los hombres informan de la brecha en el segundo perímetro.[3]*"*

I snort, shaking my head as I detach the Tac 50 from the stand and striding down the hill quickly. Someone will get the rest of my shit later, but right now, my job is to find a perch and take out the engine block of those vehicles before they get closer to *la casa.* "Fucking Mortimer. What a stupid ass identity. I sound like a squat old git living in a village in Britain, not an internationally feared member of The Five."

To be fair, I'm doing *exactly* what we agreed to do if anything went sideways in a big way. I'd say that our ex-friend coming back from the dead and almost getting blown to bits is about as upside-down, backwards, and sideways as any mission could go. So when I woke up in a damn elephant exhibit, thrown a hundred feet from the building, I scraped all the elephant shit off of me and limped away with my tail between my legs.

Note To Self #213: Murder Jinx and Raz for their failure to scout the location properly and the ability to say 'scraped all the elephant shit off of me' with a straight face.

When I reach the crest that I want to use, I find a good place to lie down before looking through the Smith & Bender scope. I see them coming over the section that will put them in range, so I lick my finger, putting it in the air briefly so I can account for the wind. Once I've adjusted, I relax my body and my breathing slows until all I can see is the target coming closer. The sound of a lone warbler—I do not know which one—is all I hear as my breath comes in and out. As they cross my field, I squeeze the trigger in sharp succession, then lift my face away from the scope to see the damage.

Both vehicles veer off the road, tires squealing as they crash into the trees surrounding the road that leads to the interior of the compound.

Excellent.

"General! General! Eras tú?[4]*"*

My eyes roll to the sky as I rub my face in frustration. *Of course it was me. Who the fuck else would it have been, Batman?* Rolling to my feet, I grab my rifle and stomp down over the ridge, through the oasis, and across the back garden to the house. There are plenty of family members of *El Jefe* lounging around on the grounds, from children to older adults. I'd like to think if they understood how woefully incompetent his soldiers are, they'd get the fuck away from this death trap, but I know better. His money promises a much better life than they would have away from him and none of them want to go back to living a less glamorous lifestyle.

I shouldn't be so judgmental, but there are *children* here—another button that sends me off the deep end. None of my *real* brothers would be happy about that shit, either. I suppose it's why the five of us—plus the living dead girl—have always gotten along. We don't have a lot of morals, but innocent women and children aren't in our acceptable loss columns.

There are plenty at *LI* who don't share those small boundaries and, though I despise being in the same room as the slimy fuckers, I have to keep my feelings to myself. Criminal empires are vast webs of various lines of business and the uglier and more taboo the trade is, the more money it brings in. The Five planned to deep-six the human trafficking wing of *LI* once we got control, but that grumpy old fuck, The Commandant, never fucking ages, much less dies. It's looking more and more like he'll be retiring well after we're past the age to do so ourselves.

"Not the point right now, Mo," I grumble as I head for the barracks. My goal at the moment is interrogating the intruders. I'm sure the dumb fucks have finally gotten their hands on them on now that I shot out their transportation. "Get your head in the game."

That's been asking a lot since the explosion. I'm normally laser focused on my jobs, but lying low for a minimum of six months before I try to contact my brothers hasn't been easy. Since we got inducted and named The Six, the protocol has always been to get as far from where the incident occurred and stay down until the cooling time has passed. I'm sure it's what the others are doing, but the ghost of Remy Arsine Benoit added to the mix has me on edge.

Is it possible we lost her again just as she got back? I don't even know how to feel about that.

I've turned this crap over and over in my head for the past four months, but I haven't been able to decide what I think. She could be a fake—a smart grifter would have gotten close to someone who knew her. With the knowledge of her connection to The Five, they could have used a ghost to throw off our game and take us out. And if she's not a fake, then I can't fathom what in the hell she's been doing for damn near a decade while she was building up the persona of The Guillotine.

"That's not true. I know exactly what she's been doing if she's for real. She's been killing everything in her path without fail for thirteen years." My lips twist as I grimace, knowing we played a part in her complete divorce from humanity when we betrayed her. The tears I saw before we had to run spoke volumes about how hard starting that life was and I'm not sure I'll ever get answers about the time after the boat blew now.

Anger at myself floods me and when I reach the door to the shack we use for interrogations, I'm pulsing with the need to take my rage out on someone. I can't very well punish myself here, but I can make sure this idiot they have tied to a chair suffers for his stupidity. My glare cuts through the men in the room, conveying how I feel about being the only thing standing between *El Jefe* and death—*again*.

This isn't the first ill-planned incursion this month and it won't be the last. Our drug lord boss unseated a revered predecessor, and he hasn't gotten his army or the rest of the cartels to respect his authority as yet. It's why I got hired—clean up his ranks, protect his home and family, and most of all, instill the fear of *El Santa Muerte* in the competition. His youth and education overseas should be assets—and they are in how he's re-vamping the business, I can tell—but among the ranks of soldiers, lieutenants, killers, and the rest, it makes him soft. Even killing his predecessor on a live feed didn't earn him the cred it should have.

If he wasn't using kids as mules, look-outs, and scouts, I'd probably respect him a little.

Unfortunately for him, he's as scummy as every other dealer and kingpin I've met in this line of business. So I do my job, but I'm sure as fuck not giving him any advice. However, this dumbshit in the ropes doesn't know I dislike my boss, nor do the nervous-looking soldiers standing around waiting for me to unleash. In their eyes, I'm the consummate professional and killer they should aim to be.

"What is your name?" I bark at the dirty, bloody twenty-something looking at me with fake bravery in his eyes. "Tell me and perhaps this will be merciful."

He spits over his shoulder; the liquid hitting the ground as we stare. I don't know if he was smart enough to realize spitting *at* me would *guarantee* his death, but if so, he's more intelligent than I expected. The silence hangs heavy in the air as I wait, watching him for the tells that will help me get the information I need without resorting to torture. I don't *care* about doing it—though I don't enjoy it like Dwyn or the ghostly woman in our life do.

However, I know intel retrieved through those means is only reliable about thirty percent of the time, which makes it inefficient.

"*Dije, dime tu nombre o sufre las consecuencias.*[5]" He might not speak enough English to explain, though I find in the cartel regions, it is far more common to speak broken English than they would have you believe. They've been taught how, but choose not to so they can feign ignorance when a non-Spanish speaker confronts them.

The guy just glares, notching his chin up defiantly. I groan internally as the men around hoot and holler in excitement. They're treating this like a fucking pay-per-view event and if I don't get rid of them while I question the lone survivor, I'll get nothing from him. He'll die before he loses face in front of all these assholes.

Just fucking peachy.

"*Dejar. Me encargaré de esto solo. Castigo por tu incompetencia.*[6]"

One man looks like he's going to protest and I give him a feral grin, hoping he realizes doing so will cause me to add him to the ticket. He swallows hard, motioning for the others to follow him out of the room. Once the door closes, I turn back to my hostage.

"Where were we? Ah. Your name or a finger. Your choice, *amigo*."

---

1. Two humvees. Traps survived. Rat in the kitchen. Activates the alpha response.
2. Douchebag! Go to your places before the boss castrates us all. They have crossed the first perimeter.
3. General Mortimer, the men report the breach in the second perimeter!
4. General! General! Was that you?
5. I said, tell me your name or suffer the consequences.
6. Leave. I'll take care of this alone. Punishment for your incompetence.

TAKE A HINT

REMY

The café/bar is a hole in the wall in the artsy district of Paris, close to the more touristy section. I'm sure Lys picked it because there's enough people spilling over from the travelers to make it busy, but not so busy we'd stick out like sore thumbs. Neither of us is a stranger to this locale and speaking fluently won't draw attention in this cross-section of Parisian traffic.

That's why I would have picked this place, and I assume her skill level in setting meets is at least close to mine.

I parked several blocks away from my destination and made sure my Moira persona was rock solid before I got out of the car. Taking only my crossbody and messenger, I left the cases in the car's trunk; I knew we'd grab them and ditch it after we ate. Lys will have her vehicle and we don't need the one I left the airport with now that I'm Moira. Someone will find it with the keys inside and they'll have a lucky day—or so they'll think.

For the moment, I'm watching the ingress and egress of people at the location. I haven't seen Lys yet, but that doesn't mean she's not here. Before I got myself captured, I was teaching her some of the finer points of hiding in plain sight. Thieves know how to meld into shadows and sneak into places they don't belong, but they don't often peacock in public when they're working solo. In order to keep my survival secret, she needed to tighten up her skills in that area. Since she's had several weeks, I fervently hope that she almost fools me.

I wouldn't expect her to totally snow me in such a short time, but if she makes me look twice, I'll be pleased.

Squinting, I examine the patrons sitting on the sidewalk and just inside the bistro. If I discount the ones not seated alone, it leaves five. Two appear male and three present as female, but I won't use that to rule anyone out. I've taken on a male persona many times if it suited me and Lys might well have today. One of the easiest ways to complete an objective is to choose the path everyone dismisses as unfeasible. They'll never look in that direction because they wrote it off in their head.

It's hard to gauge height when your targets are seated, but one woman's feet barely brush the bottom rung of the stool she's on. That's *definitely* not my friend; she's tall enough to touch the ground. Now I'm down to four, so I tilt my head to study their frames. The guy on the east end is far too big unless she stuffed her clothes, so he's out. She could be the bookish dude in the middle, but I'm going to go with the redhead playing on her phone. It's so self-absorbed looking that it's probably masking her surveilling the whole room.

I stride across the street, walking up to the table occupied by my choice, and grin when I see my friend under the hipster glasses. *Score.* "*Bonne soirée mon amie. Je suis désolé, je suis en retard.*[1]"

"Oh, stop it." Lys eyes me carefully, taking me in carefully. "I assume all your remnants of the trip are covered by copious blender?"

Groaning, I nod. "Yes. I have a lot to heal and I'll need to book some appointments to address a few unexpected consequences as well."

"Unexpected?"

"We'll need a dentist to start." I arch a brow, shrugging. "Low level pricks with an ax to grind are hard to plan around."

Lys shakes her head and sighs. "We could have done this another way. I told you that."

"Ahhh, but a few weeks to get intel on our next move rather than months? It's worth it. I don't have many original chompers, anyway. It's nothing new." I reach into my bag and pull out the drive for a second, then stuff it back in. "I have an extra assignment to deal with while we're working on it."

"Are you *kidding*? You took a job in the middle of the goddamn desert?"

Rolling my eyes at her disbelief, I pause when the server comes up to the table for an order. Since I'm hungry and tired as hell, I order a sandwich and a triple espresso. Once he leaves, I give her a pointed look. "I did not. But I also have a code—it's my own and it may not make sense, but some shit doesn't pass if I'm around. So I have an actual slave trader to destroy from afar and a trail to a middleman to follow. Is that an issue?"

"Nope," she says, drawing out the word ridiculously. "Far be it for me to question the all powerful Guillotine."

"Shhhh," I hiss. It doesn't seem like anyone is paying attention, but the last thing I want is that name caught on some camera or cell phone recording. "More cautious, Lys. Your identity isn't nearly as secret as all mine are."

"Sorry." My friend winces and pretends to stretch, checking out the surrounding room. "I did a sweep when I got here. But you're right, we don't know who we're up against in some cases."

"Shadow Douche could have spies or equipment or hackers any and everywhere. That I haven't received a message since the bomb is very suspicious. I doubt he believes I'm dead, but he's gone to ground. It's unnerving."

"I agree." She frowns, looking uncomfortable for a moment before she finally says, "Is it possible he believes the two targets are dead, so he's leaving you alone?"

I've considered that, especially because we've had such trouble trying to track the guys down.

"Maybe. But… My gut seems to think they aren't. Otherwise, I wouldn't be focusing only on them. If I truly had a…feeling… I'd keep looking but focus on the Douche instead." Our food comes and I frown at my plate before plucking the pickle off of mine to crunch. "It's not in my nature to be an optimist, Lys. My childhood didn't raise someone who looks for sunshine. If my instincts are telling me to hunt, that's what I have to do."

Slouching in her chair, my friend sips her Vieux Carré slowly, then nods. "I guess those same instincts have kept you alive longer than most solo artists in your field. Trusting them is not likely to be a mistake. I trust mine when I think a job has gone astray, so I understand."

I chew the rest of the salty delight, then look at her seriously. "I appreciate it. You're seeing more of me than I usually allow since we met up in London. Those dipshits we're looking for have seen the most, but you're right behind them. I'm not sure how I feel about that. It's unsettling."

Lys blinks, her expression amused. "Aw, Remy. You terrifying, awkward turnip—that's like winning a stamp of approval from you. I feel like I should have Christmas cards made for us now."

Narrowing my eyes, I snatch the knife by my plate and plant it between her fingers, burying it in the wood. "Not funny."

She winces, leaving her splayed fingers on the table in a challenge. "Hit a nerve, did I? You have to admit you give a shit about someone, eventually. Those guys are going to grovel, I'm sure, but they'll expect you to actually express emotions afterward."

"I'll burn that building when I come to it," I mutter as I let go of the knife handle. "First, we have to *find* them. Then they need to fucking explain themselves and if I can deal with the answers, maybe *I'll* let them in. Lots of 'ifs' there, Lys."

"But Re—" She stops when I glare at her, ducking her chin before whispering, "What the hell do I call you then?"

My lips curve up as I tap on the table. *Dashdash dashdashdash dot dot dot dotdashdot dotdash.* Arching a brow, I wait quietly.

"Okay, *Moira*, I get it. My spy shit needs work when I'm not in thief mode. Speaking of which, how did I do for today?" Her lashes bat as she mimics a coquette, and I laugh.

"Passable. I had to narrow the lone people down when I was watching. Your outward disguise looks nothing like you—which is good. But you need to learn to adopt an actual persona, Lys. I know you might do that sometimes when you work, but if you're traveling with me, it has to be *all the time*. If people can see you, it cannot be the real you. Understand?"

I can tell she's mulling it over. Then she sighs. "Got it. Being a top tier assassin is a royal pain in the ass."

You have no *idea.*

"I don't know anything else. From a very young age, the guys and I got conditioned for this life in ways even many of our colleagues would shudder to learn. It's not for the faint of heart, nor for anyone with much conscience, but it's who I am." I smile a little, feeling exposed again. My time on the island is not something I want to delve into with her, especially in this setting. "But that is a topic for later."

"Knowing you, that means never." I shrug and she chuckles as she sips her drink again. "Did you fill up on the way here, *Moira*?"

"Yes. It may not last the duration of our stay, but it's enough for us to track the moron in charge of my former host." Delight at the message I left for the nebulous gangster we're now hunting flows through me. "I'm certain we will hear whispers soon. I was not subtle."

She snorts, reaching over to steal a piece of fruit from my plate. "I imagine you weren't. That mission took two weeks longer than you expected."

"And I had to eat vermin again. That always makes me angry."

The look of horror on her face is palpable. "I don't want to know. No, wait, I do. Maybe I don't. Hell, I haven't decided yet. It may require a great deal of alcohol before I know for sure."

My eyes light up and wipe my mouth with a napkin. "That sounds perfect. Shall we?"

Lys stands, dropping bills on the table for the check, her eyes dancing. "Let's grab your gear and we'll head back to base."

I nod, slinging my bag over my shoulder as I rise. We're halfway across the patio when a piercing whistle sounds behind us. I ignore it, not willing to give attention to anyone who calls out to women like dogs. Lys rolls her eyes at me and we both chuckle as we keep moving. Before we get to the street, a rough hand grabs my elbow, jerking me back. I spin on my heel, turning to look at the moron as I work to hold my temper. Moira wouldn't throat punch this asshole, but I want to.

"Too good to speak to us, eh?" The drunken idiot leers at me and his friend just smirks. "You bitches are all the same. Right, Pierre?"

Oh, did you pick the wrong girls for this *shit.*

"I don't know you, but I imagine the 'bitches' object to your rancid B.O. and terrible breath." I sniff, jerking my chin up haughtily. "But it could be your basement level I.Q.—I haven't decided yet."

Lys snorts and the friend steps into her space, trying to box her in. My light-fingered friend doesn't back down; she simply stares at the smelly dipshit as if he's something she scraped off her shoe. "I vote for odor, Moira. They stink of cheap wine and onions."

I'm not wrong about how stupid these twits are, though, because Stinky number one crowds me as he snarls, "You think you're better than us because of what's in your pants."

"Uh, yeah," I reply with an incredulous look. "Duh."

His friend reaches for Lys, but she ducks away with a grin. "You don't even *know* what we have in our pants, dumbfuck. It could be a total shocker."

"Oh, shit, Alain. We've got some of those weirdos. Maybe we should expose them so everyone can see what freaks they are!"

Now they've done it. Homophobia and transphobia are no-nos in Remy-land, too.

"Are you boys asking nicely to see what I've got in my pants? I can make that happen." I smile sweetly, batting my lashes.

"Ha! No, we don't want to see, freak. But we're going to show everyone else."

"I get the feeling you really, really *don't* want to see what's in there," Lys mutters as she backs away from Pierre, watching me carefully.

They ignore her, joining to advance on me, and I reach into the handy pockets, pulling out twin switchblades. Flicking them open with a broad grin, I spin one on my palm like Dwyn taught. "You see, boys, what I have in pants is… knives. Still want a peek?"

Time stands still for about twenty seconds as they gape, then take off across the street without another word. I click the blades shut, tucking them away before anyone else notices I'm standing there like a fucking Avenger. "You told them they didn't want to know."

"Girl, let's get out of here before we get arrested. I swear to fuck, I can't take you anywhere."

She's not wrong.

---

1. Good evening my friend. I'm sorry, I'm late.

MOST GIRLS

REMY

"Like you actually taunted the dude who had you hooked up to a car battery?" Lys' eyes are glassy from the absinthe as she asks, and I shrug.

"My mouth will forever be my downfall, I'm afraid. When he lost his temper, I was millimeters from saying 'Oh, hey, buddy! Big feelings!' like people do to toddlers." Tossing back another hit of the Green Fairy, I lean against the couch, enjoying the buzz.

I wouldn't be if I didn't know we'd quintuple backtracked for two hours when leaving the cafe with my shit and Lys fortified this safe house like a goddamn bunker while I was away. It was a condition of her staying and she showed me the new security when we finally trudged into the house after ensuring we weren't tailed. Those things made me feel comfortable enough to let loose and I have to say, it's a fucking relief. We have mounds of food that aren't bugs and rats, good booze, comfortable clothes, and I'm clean. It's like the *Ritz* compared to my cage, so I'm a happy assassin.

At least, as happy as I can be without retrieving the guys and gutting those who deserve it like halibut.

"B-big…f-feelings…," she gasps as she howls with laughter. "For fuck's sake, Remy."

Plucking a berry off the plate of fresh fruit, I smirk. "Most men are particularly easy to manipulate, even without using my body. If you hit them where it hurts emotionally, they lose control. I think it's how they're raised, to be honest. All testosterone and no ability to process shit that isn't violence."

Her brow arches and she pours herself another drink as she ponders that statement. "A bit bottom of the ocean for absinthe night, but yeah. I find women *much* more difficult unless they're like, damaged. You know? Working a male mark or partner for a heist is usually a snap. Chicks think so much; you have to sell it more."

I nod and shrug. "Operating on my own for thirteen years has made that simpler. I don't have to do anything if it doesn't help me complete the job, nor do I have to explain myself. Hence feeling like that idiot who thought he was some badass torturer was having a tantrum. Life is chaos and no one should expect to get their way all the time, no matter what it's about. That's the mark of a fucking narcissist."

Lys closes her eyes and holds up a hand. "Testify, woman. I did a job with *Ape Regina* once and that bitch was so rigid about everything that it seemed like she had the Eiffel Tower shoved up her ass. And trust me… her methods were absolute trash. Like, she's dumb as a post and expects everyone else to be as well. How she's risen to the top is baffling and infuriating."

I'm going to blow her mind, but my reach is much broader than hers and I know the players as if they're characters in the TV show I live in.

"She wasn't big when I started, Lys. I mean, she had some minions and a small support crew, but it wasn't anything to write home about." I take another shot, letting out a belch that makes her giggle like a cartoon character, and go on. "*Regina* has always been a legend in her own mind, but her strength doesn't lie where she thinks it does. When she wasn't advancing in the *Mercatus* ratings like she wanted, she consulted with a well-connected mid-tier architect. The architect took her plans and mocked up a job that would make people take her seriously."

My friend frowns and picks up a buttery croissant, taking a big bite before she responds. "*Regina* tells *everyone* she does all the construction and shit on her own. It's like a badge of honor for her. If you mean that Russian affair, she crows about constantly if you work with her. The bitch acts like it was on par with D.B. Cooper."

"Oh, I know. This gem fell into my lap when I had a falling out with her over a job she tried to snake out from under me. Are you ready for the punchline?" I've never told anyone this; it's a piece of information I've kept under wraps to use when the time came and telling Lys means she could steal my leverage. But I'm trying to be a normal human with her, so I have to go out on a limb sometime.

Might as well be about this, not shit with the guys.

"Hit me, babe."

"Soooo… She fired the architect, saying she could do better. Didn't even pay a consulting fee. Then she took the entire plan, put a spin on it, and launched her career in public without once mentioning she had help with creating it. By the time she was bragging, it was too late and too dangerous for her consultant to make their side of the story known. They let it go and ever since, *Regina* has been riding that wave to more and more customers believing she has skills she doesn't have."

Her purple braids cascade over her shoulders as she flops out on the floor, flat on her back, and looks up at the ceiling. "Holy. Shit. Remy. Her career is a lie based on stealing shit from her crews. Like, I wondered why she watched them do all the work, but I figured it was an ego thing."

"Fuck, no. The cunt knows how to do some basic shit, but not the way she says and definitely not without a serious amount of backup propping her up. It's all…" I gesture vaguely, waving my hands in the air. "… man behind the curtain shit. Hysterical part is, she fucking believes it. If people could see the shit I have, they'd run for the hills when she walks into a room—even a chat room."

"Man, us lowly middle tier people are completely out of the loop, even in our own skill sets." Her head lolls on the floor as she looks over at me. "What other crazy shit do you have to share? I'm boring in comparison, but I love hearing your tea."

Frowning, I look at the bottom of my glass. I can't give her everything and I feel shitty about it. I'm not ready for that kind of leap and I don't want to ruin our night. So I pick something I can share, though I shouldn't, because neither of us wants to die.

Death is preferable to emotions any day.

"There's a process to this hunt we're on. I learned it from hacking files less than ten people on earth are aware of. The faces may change over the years, but the number does not. I shouldn't know many, many things I know, and it's why I survived thirteen years ago."

Lys sits, her expression bleary as she grabs the bottle and pours another glass for both of us. "Tell me. I don't care if I end up on double secret probation or whatever."

Leaning against the couch, I suck in a deep breath and look at the ceiling for a moment before I let it out. "There's protocol for situations going **FUBAR** like it did at the zoo. Both at an institutional level and a team level, especially teams like The Five who have been working together since childhood."

"Protocol for getting blown up? Like an escape hatch?"

I shake my head. "No. It's not about escape as much as regrouping. *LI* has policies at an organization level for how to handle a team or individuals going dark. There's no 'retirement' in their ranks—not unless you sit far enough up to be in the High Legion or their echelon. So agents with missions that end poorly need to be accounted for, both as assets and liabilities."

"Ugh!" she groans and shakes her glass at me. "There had better not be math involved in this shit. I'm too drunk for fucking equations, you bitch."

I've been too sober to admit it before, so we're even.

"Sort of?" I admit with a wince. "But we don't have to do it. I just have to explain how it relates to what we've been doing and why. Then you'll get why I made the moves I have since we drove away."

Lys holds her glass out and we clink them together, then she gives me a thumbs up, squinting at her digit comically. "You have been very '*Taken*' about your pursuit. Like, I get you have that particular set of skills, Rem, but your dedication is… insane."

Chuckling at her movie reference, I take another gulp of absinthe, enjoying the burn before I go on. "When operatives get brought in, they inspect them from head to toe. Everything gets tested, weighed, measured, and entered in their matrix for future agents. Physical stats, I.Q., genetics, DNA, psychological tests—the whole goddamn enchilada. They take five-year-olds with no idea what is happening and predict their future value to *LI* on the spot."

"What? How?"

"The files I had access to have gotten doctored, I assume, because they go back, like, *centuries*, which can't be accurate. Must be some sort of code, but I didn't bother to check that because what I wanted to know was if anyone had ever escaped that life. Outside of granted retirement, the answer was no—until me." I rub my temples, remembering how hard I sobbed when I figured out that tidbit. It made me determined in the end, but at first, I lost my mind. I wasn't planning to get one person; no, I needed six.

It was depressing as fuck, but I knew even as a teen we'd be dead if we didn't get out.

"How does that even apply? Obviously, no one ever escapes a crew that kills people for saying their name out loud. You had to realize you were looking for a unicorn, even as a kid."

"Hope springs eternal when you're young, eh? Also, ego and hormones." I chuckle derisively. "What I found out instead was what my overlords do when a mission is compromised and assets go dark. It was… logical, but incredibly eye-opening."

"Spill, woman. We're getting sober."

"Okay, okay. They have an advisory panel who assesses the data that comes out of that actuarial equation. Together, an accountant, a physician, a shrink, an ops tech, and a trainer assign the recruit a value that increases over time as more data gets dumped into their profile. By the time they start missions or join a team, this number informs *every* decision they make about the operative. They can prevent them from joining a HVT, keep them out of the field, force them into the classroom—whatever they want because their monetary value to *LI* is all that matters."

Lys' eyes narrow and she growls, "They put an *actual* price on your future… at five?"

"Yup." I shrug, unbothered by that aspect. It's logical and makes good business sense, so it doesn't bother me. That's probably how my asshole superiors raised me, but it's hard to argue with science. *LI* isn't making that decision based on fluffy bullshit; no, they do the work and I see how it makes them continue to reign supreme. "They have protocols, and those are based on the value of both the team and the individuals. The numbers define the time they spend hunting down the missing, the amount of resources they assign to it, and the urgency of confirming death, capture, or escape. *LI* would never let anyone go—unless they've confirmed death—but they also won't spend frivolously. They can be patient if the asset isn't worth a serious investment."

She frowns. "Why didn't they come after you?"

"That's a story for another night. But I've been pushing so hard because I *know* what The Five's numbers were when I escaped. They've only increased their profile and their reach since. I'd estimate in the mid nine figures by now, so *LI* will be lying low for a longer rest period. The guys themselves will have a bug-out timeframe that is lengthy, so whether they're dead, captured, or hiding? That's up in the air still and could be for a couple months. We *have* to find them before *LI* gets serious about searching."

The thief sighs and swirls her drink, looking at the bright green liquid. "You need to either confirm their death or rescue them before they go from asset to liability."

"Yes. And since I know what their value to *LI* is, I have a very good idea of what they'd go for on various open markets for anything from intel extraction to sex trafficking to revenge killing. It's fuzzy, but ten million plus isn't out of pocket. Raz for sure, because of his skills, and maybe Coda for the right pervert. If they're captured and anyone decodes the mark of The Five, they'll go for close to a billion."

"Great," Lys breathes as she gives me a look full of resignation. "We're hunting prey that knows how to hide and might do so while half the criminals on the planet would spend enough to buy a fucking island to get their hands on them. Plus, their old employers think they're worth the GDP of Antigua individually, so they'll be in the way soon. That about it?"

"Yep. That covers it," I grin as I toss back my drink. "Aren't you glad we're friends now?"

"I didn't mention they got you killed," she mutters. "You attract psychos like a fucking Addams."

Tell me about it, sister.

WARRIOR

REMY

The incessant beeping of the computers set up in the open air living room wakes me from a drunken slumber for the second time since I joined forces with Lys. She might actually be the devil because I'd never admit it out loud, but her influence is worse on me than mine is on her. I never fuck off in the middle of missions or crises like this—yet here I am, hungover like a frat bro again. The descent from the highs of the Fairy isn't as bad as hitting the ground face first after our tequila binge.

Thank fucking Christ.

"Remy, you have a knife, right?"

My body freezes in place and my hand slips under my pillow to grip the weapon there. "Yes."

"Can you please cut my fucking eyeballs out of my head to relieve the pressure? I'm *dying*."

I swear under my breath, letting go of the switchblade as I flop onto my back. "Lys, you have to be careful with that shit. I was ready to bleed a motherfucker."

It's quiet for a second, then she bursts into giggles. "I know it's not funny, but it's fucking amazing that you're as achy as me, but you were ready to hop up to give an intruder a big, red Chicago smile."

"It's the training," I mumble. "I popped a guy's head like a pimple with a vise after he broke my arm one time. Doing it fucked up the break even worse, but hearing him scream until it crushed his skull was beautiful."

"You have an interesting idea of beauty."

I grin a little, closing my eyes. "You have *no* idea."

"Do you think we should see why your fucking equipment is blaring like we're going to be invaded?"

Her voice is wistful, and I know she wishes all this shit was over so we could just… hang. This kind of shit is not normal for a grab and go thief, but it's commonplace for me. "I think that sound is killing me and even if it's not important, I want it to stop."

"Bugger."

Grunting as I roll over and pull myself to a sitting position, I make certain I won't feel sick like I did last time. Nausea doesn't follow, so I crawl over to the desk and pull myself into the big command center chair. It takes a moment for my vision to focus on various screens until I find where the alert is coming from.

Oh, goddamn it.

The windows monitoring *Mercatus* are lit with a big announcement from a patron. Closer inspection tells me it's been posted on the forums I'd visit as every single one of my A-list identities. Whatever the anonymous customer is planning, they want to be sure that criminals from every corner of the dark web are aware. I've seen something like it before, but it's been over a year since anyone said 'fuck an open market' and blitzed the whole underground.

I don't like this one fucking bit.

"Lys… someone has orchestrated a blitzkrieg."

"*Shit,*" she hisses as I hear her fumbling to get up and over to the screens. By the time she's sorted, I've got the forums open on all six screens, showing the message blinking at the top of them. "I shouldn't ask, but *how* do you have access to six sectors of *Mercatus?*"

My smug grin and wink make her groan. "Technically, I have access to seven. But I rarely visit the ones I'd prefer not to see the contents or shouldn't have been able to get into. Trafficking and customer chats are fairly disgusting on every possible level, so I stay out unless I'm hunting for something."

"I am *way* too hungover to even ask how the fiddle playing shit you got into all this." Her hands come up to rub her temples and she pauses for a moment, like it's taking her time to form coherent sentences. "A blitzkrieg is bad news because it means the customer has so many components to their job that it can't get completed without forming cells. The damn boards will accept the requisite amount of pros for each component in a cell, then instructions will go out to all the spokes on the wheels."

I snort, giving her an amused look. "That's quite a few metaphors in one statement."

"Shut up. I'm not afraid of you."

She probably should be, but we're past that, it seems.

"They'll run this shit like planning a terrorist attack; I knew what you meant. The problem lies in figuring out what the actual fuck the whole chessboard looks like. People don't run these because rarely is something so huge you can't just form a pro team to accomplish it. Six to twelve people should be enough to get damn near anything done," I mutter. "Blitzes usually form six to eight teams of five. What is going on for someone to tap thirty plus criminals high enough on the ladder to be using *Mercatus?*"

Her expression turns to concern. "They might be setting up a *Forum Romanum*. That would require wheels from the major sectors to accomplish. You'd need thieves to acquire the highest value items, assassins to kill if desired, grifters to run a game on marks, hitters to kidnap or subdue, and hackers steal, program, or obtain information. There hasn't been one in…"

"Thirteen years," I croak.

"That's when you—"

"Yes. It's after I died." I raise my hand to pinch the bridge of my nose. "I've always believed my former employers arranged it to establish their new golden boys' among the top level criminals."

Lys winces and tilts her head at me. "Are you upset it worked, or that it wasn't to locate you?"

"Neither," I reply. "I didn't want anyone looking and at that point, I certainly didn't give a rat's ass if those guys were climbing the bad guy ladder. All I cared about was surviving. That was the worst year of my life, which is saying a fucking lot, given my childhood."

"We could find the tequila and use the 'hair of the dog' method to deal with this?" Lys says with a lopsided grin.

"Hell, no. One hangover a quarter is enough for me. Plus, this timing is not a coincidence. Even if I believed in them—which I don't—it would explain why that shadowy asshole has been quiet for months. Planning this announcement and it all entails would take that long."

"But why now? If he thinks you and the guys are dead—he's got what he wanted. *More* than what he wanted, in fact. So this is… what? A brag?"

I shake my head, tapping my fingers on my lips. "Doubtful. He hid behind a voice changer, shadows, and underground exchanges. If that motherfucker was ready to come into the light, he'd simply announce himself. This is a trap, I think. He's baiting the hook and watching from above. Maybe he knows I'm alive? Or maybe he knows more?"

My eyes slide over the screen, and I watch as my contemporaries bid on the spots. I'd love to believe that I'm right—Shadow Douche is organizing this, and he knows the guys are alive. That's far more optimistic than I'm comfortable being, and it's not likely. However, the only way I'll know what the hell is up with this shit is to find out for myself.

That means giving up more secrets to my new friend.

Pressing my hands over my face until I can argue myself into submission, I spin the chair to face Lys. I remove my palms and look at her seriously, trying to fight off the deep gut feeling of unease. Suspicion is ingrained in my soul after so many years alone and I gave her so much truth last night. Alcohol helped, but I have no intention of imbibing again so soon. I have to woman up and share this whether I want to or not.

"I can't allow myself to have too much hope for things I lost once before. But the only way I'll be able to focus on the search for *Il Tasso* is if I embed myself in this mess so I can figure out what's going on. And yes, I have the cred needed to get chosen in all six fields, not just two."

Lys snorts, giving me a knowing smile. "I'm not stupid, Remy. You have access to the gamut, and that means you earned it. Outside of the two you *don't* take part in unless forced, your admission told me you take part in the others willingly. But you don't have to do it all; I can take the thieves' forum. No one can do it all, even if you've convinced yourself you can."

I blink at her, digesting her words slowly. *Depend on someone else to do work I can do on my own?* It's not in my nature, nor in my history since the island. Remy Arsine Benoit is The Guillotine, and The Guillotine doesn't need anyone. How in the hell am I supposed to deal with all the shit going *and* give up control to someone else?

She might as well have asked if I wanted to move into a suburb and start baking cookies for the PTA.

"I-I don't know if…"

Her purple brow arches. "Did I *ask* for permission? You may be the big dog in this friendship, Remy, but I only take orders I agree with. I'll bid if I want to and you'll just have to deal with it when I beat you."

"Beat me?" I chuckle, my lips curving as I parry back. "Lys, The Duchess has dark web fan pages. You will not beat me for the thief position."

"The Duchess may be too 'high brow' for their plans. We don't know what in the hell these assholes are asking for. The bid posts don't say a damn thing about what the bidders are being asked to work on," Lys counters, as she finally rises to her feet. "I'm going to get a water and when I get back, you're going to have thought over my *kind offer* and be willing to *let someone help you* because you sat here for over a month waiting to see how badly you got *tortured. Capiche?*"

My jaw drops as I watch her hobble away. Elysium, my new associate, just attempted to *blackmail* me with guilt. And *she* called my identity too hoity-toity for this job. I've taken people's kidneys for less than that. Worse than all that put together is the weirdly proud feeling in my gut. Like… I'm impressed she's standing up to me and I want to encourage it.

What in the name of Jack the Ripper is happening to me?

My eyes flip to the forums for assassins, grifters, hitters, and fixers. It couldn't hurt to bid for those now and enter the ring as The Duchess later. *Right?* Cursing under my breath, I start with fixers, typing furiously so I can get the bid in and move on to the next one. This whole 'being a normal human' thing is for the goddamn birds and I *hate* it. Maybe.

I make a frustrated sound as I finish the first bid and move on to the next. Lys comes back in, giving me an expectant look as she hands me a bottle of water. "What?"

"Come to your senses, then?"

Rolling my eyes, I make an irritated face. "Fine. Bid for the thief one. Maybe it's better if I avoid doing a bunch of bullshit, flip-trick climbing until after I've gotten my tattoos and teeth fixed. I did just get renditioned for over a month."

"*Purposefully*," she reminds me with a smirk. "Don't forget that part."

"Yes, *purposely*," I reply. "Letting them think they could break me was a strategic gambit intended to make the morons let their guard down."

"Hmmph. One that was unnecessary in my opinion, but fair enough. I'll handle the vastly more physical thievery. I *have* done shit like this before, you know."

"We'll see what happens when you apply." My grumble is begrudging. I know she's talented and sought after, but I dislike adding variables I need to be concerned about in my plans. Once I was reborn, I've placed people in three categories: don't care, victims, and targets. Most of the world lives in 'don't care' which can lead to death, indifference, or a multitude of reactions. The other two are obvious, and I always know how to handle those.

Unfortunately, this spunky thief and the reappearance of my guys are forcing me to consider a new category: 'not enemies.' At least, I *think* that's the new bucket and it's confusing as fucking hell. I'm not thrilled with those in it being in the middle of all this fucking bullshit and that's new as well.

The Guillotine does not like change.

ANGEL WITH A SHOTGUN

DWYN

I cannot fucking stress enough how hard it is to twiddle my thumbs for six *minutes*, much less six *months*.

Keeping myself busy when my brain is going a million miles at a time is usually something I accomplish by taking the most impossible jobs available. But I *can't* because then the bloody psycho who blew up that damn building might know I'm alive. I don't have Mo to yell at me or even Jinxy to be soothing. And I *definitely* don't have the girl I've been holding a candle for throughout my entire adulthood, although she's fucking come back from the dead.

Everything about my life is severely fucked and there's not enough alcohol in Tokyo to make up for it.

My personal magical mystery tour started out by waking up in some freaking hospital with my head stitched up, a broken arm, and 'John Doe' on a chart. It didn't take me long to suss out someone in security found me stuck in a motherfucking *tree* in the *tiger* habitat. I was lucky no one fancied a midnight snack, but not lucky enough to escape unscathed. I stayed there, pretending to have amnesia until the break was well enough healed to stealthily go AWOL. I followed protocol to the letter—not that I'll get any kudos from Mo—and hopped a boat across the channel, then a train. Once I was at the edge of the continent, I stowed away in a cargo plane and ended up here.

It's not a bad place, really, and there's enough shit happening to help control my ADHD, but I *hate* being sidelined. Stealing is in my blood and the penny ante shit I've been doing to slake my thirst isn't cutting it anymore. The adrenaline from scaling a building or popping a military grade safe is addictive to someone like me. I haven't had a 'hit' since the damn building blew up and I'm jonesing.

Not to mention I have no idea who survived and who didn't.

"If some asswad took Remy away again, I swear to hell, I'll burn the entire continent down to find him," I grumble under my breath. I've never cared much about lying low or keeping the heat off of us, so I'm serious when I say I'll go on an unsanctioned rampage. "But that's why she and I work so well together."

Remy always knew how to soothe me or rile me up, depending on which one served us best. Despite her calculating exterior, she has a raging fury inside, just like me. The cool, removed Remy who can hang with Jinx and Mo did not orchestrate that little tour across Europe that earned her the 'Guillotine' moniker. No, that was the girl who could out-drink Coda and I before a huge assessment and still hit a target like she's an extension of the weapon. It was the girl who has no problem killing any obstacles in her path without compunction, but worried about keeping that thief she was working with unharmed.

When she lived on the island with us, she found a balance between those two parts of her. The woman who stood in front of us in the zoo didn't seem to have that anymore. It made me sad to realize she'd shut away the part of her that found joy in the worst place on earth with us. The Five weren't happy, per se, but we found fun together or pleasure in shit occasionally. Not in the healthiest of ways, granted, but it happened.

The Remy bitching us out had every right to do so, but she felt like a shell of the girl who would have lit us up as teens.

"No more of that shit, then. If she's alive, I'll tie her up and fuck her until she sparkles again." A lady on the bus bench I pass looks at me with wide eyes and I wave my hand at her. "Figure of speech. Nothing to see here, move along."

Scratching my chin, I lift a piece of the fruit I'm peeling with my knife to my lips. I should probably be more careful when I'm talking to myself in public. I don't have Razzie to wipe cams or Jinxy to coax someone out of reporting me to the fuzz. *But normies are so fucking nosy, you know?* It's not like I was even *looking* at the chick; why was she even listening to me dialogue with myself? Judgy fucking losers, that's what the non-criminal humans on this planet are. I've got zero use for them; it's boring.

Shit. I've gone on a tangent again. Back to focusing.

I'm on the street for a reason, actually. That building houses the Tokyo branch of a *huge* tech firm and I want access to their servers. I'm not stealing anything as much as borrowing their computing power. And maybe one of their nerds—but only for like, maybe an hour. All I want is one of their keyboard warriors to log into a Tor network and let me do some sifting through Mercatus for signs of my brothers or my girl.

Obviously, I could do it somewhere else with a stolen laptop and an internet cafe Wi-Fi, but doing it *here* will make it damn near impossible to identify who accessed the damn market. I guarantee the nerd will cover his or her tracks because their company would fire them for hitting the unstable, unsafe dark web on their network. That makes it safe from cops or whatever. If any thugs show up, the entire place will go on lockdown and fear of breach will protect me from my unsavory brethren from finding out I'm alive.

It's genius, really.

I have to focus long enough to get inside without being detected first. That's been the challenge. I have a good disguise I snatched from a mega mart place, but I don't have I.D. Not letting people know I didn't get turned into soup prevents me from accessing the *LI* storage units in the city and I haven't been stealing anything big enough to afford fake creds that will pass scrutiny at a big ass tech company. Unless…

Heaving a sigh, I scratch my ear as I admit what I'll have to do. I need to make enough to get a mildly passable identification and then get a damn job for some janitorial company or some such. Day jobs often require me to become employed as a delivery guy, technician, or custodial staff member briefly, so I know the drill. Once I have *real* creds I can use to walk into the building, I can scope out which geek to squeeze, and then I'll get a look at the market to see who might be left in one piece.

Fuck, I wish I'd thought of this a month ago.

Of course, the first month after the blast was the hospital, then my trip, and embarrassingly, during the first couple of weeks, everything Pokémon distracted me until I got my brain under control again. I am pretty highly ranked in most of the battle gyms, though, so I guess it wasn't *that* much of a waste of my time. What the hell else was I going to do, anyway? Dwyn O'Shanahan hasn't been on his own since he was a kid unless during a job and this 'exile protocol' shit was never supposed to happen!

"Stop wigging out," I mutter to myself as I peel and watch the front of my target building. "You'll attract attention and you know that won't help. You'll have a job by the weekend if you say the right things and you always say the right things."

I have no idea how I'm going to survive another month and a half of 'no contact,' but the end can't come soon enough.

THE UNIFORM HANGS off me loosely as I trudge toward the front door of *Yokohama Industries*. It's not some big social media giant like Meta or an innovation station like Google, but this place will have the right computers and power to help me get what I want. Plus, it won't have nearly the tight fucking security those big name companies will, even for staff that's contracted out. I don't need some asshole in chinos running a background check on me when my job is supposed to be cleaning toilets.

"They'd be right to do so, I guess, since I'm not *Aaron Jackson*, but I'm not after their corporate design plans, either." I ponder for a moment, shrugging when it hits me. "Today, anyway."

The badge beeps at the gates, and the guards wave at the group of us who cleared the scanners, herding us towards the elevators. My assignment from the staffing company has me starting on the eleventh floor and working my way up, but I won't follow it. Using the skills Jinx has drilled into me, I could charm info out of the other applicants in the waiting room of the staffing place. Some of them had worked temp jobs at my chosen target before, and it took little encouragement to get them to spill about the layout and the people who work there.

That's how I know I should get off on eleven as my assignment says, but find the side stairs, climb to eighteen, and corner one of the Oracle database admins in their break room. They're the least socialized and barely respond when spoken to, according to my eager sources. It won't take much to threaten, cajole, and instruct them so I get what I want.

"If I'm lucky, not a single toilet to deal with."

One man in the elevator gives me an odd look and I huff. *What is with the fucking rudeness? Did I ask this fucker?* Shaking my head, I go back to watching the lighted buttons on the panel, feeling antsy and trapped in the small, crowded space. I don't ride *in* elevators as much as *on* them and it's a very different experience. For one thing, I'd rather smell grease and motors than the amount of cheap cologne filling this damn car. The sheep really want to bathe in their shit, it seems.

Sheep.

I grin to myself—that makes me remember something. That almost distracts me enough to make it to my floor without saying anything when some idiot *sneezes* on my fucking *neck*. My fist clench and I whirl around to look at the sniveling shit with barely contained rage. "Are you fucking kidding me?"

The haughty jackass in a knock-off suit looks at me like I'm something he scraped off of his shoe. "I doubt it was any worse than what you'll be dealing with as you clean up the filth left behind tonight."

Gritting my teeth, I search out the badge on his lapel, disappointed to note he's not the nerd I'm looking for. Would have been nice to put the fear of Buddha or God or who-the-fuck-ever into him while I was accomplishing my mission, but alas, it's not to be. So I tip the corners of my lips up as I raise manic eyes to his, making certain he can see the promise of pain in his future. "You shouldn't look down on the people who are doing jobs you don't want to do yourself. It's not only rude, but stupid. If zombies attacked tomorrow, your skill at filling out spreadsheets wouldn't keep your snooty ass alive. Being good at disinfecting shit might."

Satisfied with my logic, I turn away from him, aware he's probably on his phone, figuring out a way to report me to someone as we speak. Pity for him; I won't be here longer than the next hour and after that, Aaron disappears into the ether. His revenge plot will fall as flat as his cock probably is when he tries to get it up.

I whistle as I exit on floor eleven.

That's not a problem I have in the slightest.

BATTLEFIELD

REMY

Lys goes out the next day, hoping to pal around with some of her thief friends and get the lowdown on what their community is saying about the blitz. I let her go, but I highly doubt random lifters and cat burglars will have useful information about an event as big as this. Not that I told her that; I don't want her to get pissy again about contributing. My control issues made her mad once this week; I refuse to do it again.

While she's gone, I'm poking around the hacker section of *Mercatus*. *Te Atarangi* isn't as lauded as *La Araña*, but the reputation I've built allows me to surf around the jobs and chats here without being laughed out of the room. Before I went after the group that landed me in the desert, I spent hours sifting through the commentary in each part of *Mercatus*, hoping to find a whiff of the guys doing jobs under other names. Nothing stood out, and I was disappointed, but not surprised.

Out of all the professions supported in this criminal marketplace, the one for computer geeks is the hardest to navigate. Hackers are typically reclusive, introverted beings who turn into brash braggarts in their comfort zone online. Entry level knobheads run around, taking credit for jobs that they didn't take part in, and the bigger fish have to smack them around to clear the air. They talk in riddles, codes, and equations as if it's normal for everyone around them to understand. It's infuriating sometimes, but my time with Raz gave me the tools to wade through it without too much effort.

The buzz seems to be about the blitz here, too, and I examine every posted bid carefully. I know exactly how my ex-team member presented himself when he was amongst his peers and I'm pretty sure I could tell if one of them was him. I growl with irritation when I comb through the posts with no luck. The current bidders couldn't carry his mouse with a forklift; they won't get chosen for the tech cell. It's odd to see something this huge without comments from the heavy weights, though.

Are they avoiding it? Do they know something the baby hackers don't?

Frowning, I continue poking around the chat rooms until I'm satisfied. There's absolutely nothing about Raz in here and not a single hint about why the blitz isn't being descended on like locusts in a new crop field. I chew on my lip, deciding if I want to get bolder or let it be. If Raz is alive, he might see the hook and get curious. Maybe it will lure him out and I'll be able to track him down. Hell, if I'm good enough, he might even know it's me.

Te Atarangi: Seeking input.

X-Factor: Port?

Te Atarangi: Dual. GPS and Memory.

4v35: Coordinates?

Te Atarangi: Unknown.

X-Factor: Casing?

Te Atarangi: Arachnid.

. . .

THE CHATTER STOPS COLD, and I curse under my breath. I do not know who these green hats are, but I won't get anywhere if I don't attract attention. Pursing my lips, I think about it for a moment and forge ahead, consequences be damned. Raz and Mo have been the most elusive of The Five, which is no surprise, but we can't keep spinning our wheels. This damn *Forum Romanum* has me on edge and I can't put my finger on why.

Te Atarangi: Memory input?

Nyx: Sound off.

Te Atarangi: Suspecting a zero click?

Ph0b14: Flame, flame.

Te Atarangi: Lossage?

Cr0w: Major. No reds.

THAT'S FUCKING WEIRD.

It takes a while to pick up the mono-syllabic, oddly constructed hacker jargon, but the newbs in this room just told me no one thinks there's something *wrong* with the post for the *Forum*. The red hats have simply chosen to ignore it for the moment. It might be because the people who know better have more information than the script kiddies in here, but I will not get what I need from the prospects hanging about. They're as clueless as I am.I thank them and go dark in the hacker forums, leaving the screen up for messages. They know I'm AFK, but my logging program will catch everything while I move to another section.

I take a minute to decide if I want to hit up the hitter area or the grifter zone. I'm purposely leaving the Guillotine's home for last because I want to ensure I'm not recognized. *Mercatus* programmed very specific protocols for the assassin forums so we're able to peruse the open requests without being swamped by people demanding our services who can't afford us and new players looking for mentors. We're a less friendly profession and the last thing they want is us thinning our own ranks over squabbles.

"Definitely hitters. They're blunt and to the point, so if no one knows anything, I can escape quickly."

Turning one screen to the left, I log in as my rarely used alias and scour the current posts. The blitz is a hot topic here as well and the bidders are top tier. The men and women who find jobs here don't seem concerned that this is a set-up. In fact, I see names near Mo's level of competency responding eagerly.

How very bizarre.

I can't figure out why the hackers seem to have gone dark and the hitters are all but having a brawl over spots in their cell. After I do a little digging in their rooms, I set myself to away there as well. I didn't see a hint of Mo and no one had a bad word to say about the blitz. They're all ready to fight for positions, no matter what the cost.

My brow furrows as I turn to the screen on the right side of the hackers, curious to see what the grifters have to say. To my surprise, their blitz post is even more packed than the hitters and the chats are a buzz with speculation. I'm not surprised they're chatty; that's why they're good at what they do. But their eager speculation about what the bigger picture is might give me clues, so I keep scrolling until something catches my eye.

> WagtheDog: I heard they need a group who can fill a Zanzibar.

> CanadaBill: I'm in. Finishing a monte job, but it's almost over.

> Soapy: High competition in Skagway. Might shuffle along.

I CLOSE MY EYES, knowing there's something in my brain about this. Everything in that last comment sounds familiar, but the memory isn't recent. I stare into space, trying to let my conscious mind go until it comes to me. When it hits me, my eyes pop open and I gasp. Soapy Smith was a con artist in America in the late 1800s. He worked in *Skagway*, Alaska, and they named a con called the Skagway Shuffle after him.

Jinx told me that story when he made me memorize the finer points of the big, named cons.

"Is that motherfucker alive and trying to let me know?" I grumble as I search through the forum for more evidence. The Soapy person doesn't talk much, but the account isn't new. It's a seasoned log-in, just not a very active one. That points towards being a burner handle and I bite my lower lip, trying not to get hopeful.

> Dançarina do fogo: I plan to bid. My unit is full and a Zanzibar will net returns.

> Soapy: Below your stature. Wait for another Open Market.

How in the fuck would this gomer know that?

Dançarina do fogo: Prices fluctuate.

Soapy: Not enough.

"Okay, I'm going to hunt this asshole down. They either know more about the blitz than anyone else, or it really is Jinx. Either way, I have to know."

Dançarina do fogo: Are you in the market?

Soapy: Not a chance.

Rubbing my hands over my face, I groan when the mouthy grifter logs off immediately. Now I'll have to run all the programs I have to crack through the encryption, and I still haven't checked the assassin guild. Sighing, I slide down to another screen that's only running code as it trawls the dark web for signs of the guys or the Douche. I add parameters for this Soapy character into my code, putting in the few clues I saw from his scant posts.

Once I finish, I head back to the final forum. It's quiet and sober, with little movement in the chat rooms. Hackers and assassins share introversion as a personality trait, but we rarely come alive online like they do. The dark web has the shadows we prefer in real life and we stay in them here as well. Some of us—like myself and *Le Voleur*—stick to them religiously to protect our true faces.

The blitz post here has a few cautious responses guarded by the identity shield as all bids are. I think I see someone who represents The Company; their robotic language and stilted yet vague language are a dead giveaway. Unfortunately, their specialty is this type of job and the bid might be any of hundreds of operatives they field. They could tempt me to take part for real if I thought my bloody colleague and his interesting wife would be involved, but that's not guaranteed.

"Why do none of the blitz posts list what skills the contractors need? It seems like the host is going to get a fucking huge amount of responses with little opportunity to sift through them?"

I'm still scrolling through the assassin calls when Lys slams into the house, making me turn to look at her grumpily. She snorts at my dirty look, flopping onto the couch with a gleeful expression. I wait, but she just keeps grinning maniacally until I give in. "What?!"

"The thieves think this whole thing is a mousetrap."

Now I get why the hackers are hiding.

"The hackers are skeptical, too. Hitters and grifters are all in." I pause, watching her as I finish. "And the killers are likewise quiet."

Lys beams, her braids shaking as she nods. "Exactly what I'd presume, given what my friends are saying. They think someone is trying to get everyone to attend a Zanzibar in order to round up as many contractors as possible. Think about the shit that went down at the last two events you were at. My people believe there's a force trying to thin the ranks and you know what that means."

"It means there's a war coming."

"Yep. Big players are going to war and they want all the foot soldiers off the board." Lys smirks as she tilts her head. "You still want me to bid? Because I noticed you didn't mention bidding in your arenas yet."

"That's because I didn't bid yet. I felt like something was off and hadn't been able to identify why yet." My nose wrinkles and I sigh. "I also thought maybe I got a lead on Jinx. I had to add stuff to the spiders we've had running, but who knows if it's just wishful thinking,"

"It's okay to want to find them, Remy. It's okay to care, even if they hurt you. You're allowed to be human."

I snort. "Absolutely not. Humans are weak and gullible and boring. Don't be ridiculous."

Lys gets up, heading over to the sideboard and pouring two scotches. She stops to hand me one, then heads for the couch again. "I've never gotten why you top tier folks, especially in the blood and death skills, act as though you're from another species. 'Humans' this and 'normies' that—is so you can divorce your-selves from emotions enough to do your jobs? If so, it makes sense, but most of you never shed the skin. But you never look happy, either, so maybe that makes sense as well."

My eyes narrow and I sip the mossy whiskey, swirling my glass thoughtfully. "I suppose that's right. But truthfully, none of us think like normal people, much less act like them. So it's easier to look at them as something other than ourselves—both to help us work and to accept our differences."

"Well, I'm not letting you act like a robot when I'm around Remy Benoit. You're going to enjoy some shit that isn't killing and I'm going to learn to do serious shit, so I climb the ladder like you have. Together, we're unstoppable. And we will find those idiots, even if it's just so you can kick them all in the balls for not letting you finish your lecture at the zoo. Deal?"

My grin spreads slowly as I take in the woman who I barely knew a couple months ago, but would definitely shank someone over now. "Sounds delightful."

SOLDIER

JINX

"No one will believe this. Your gambit will not work."

The masked idiot standing behind me at the computer with a Desert Eagle pressed to the base of my skull doesn't respond. I know nothing gets a rise out of them; I've tried to get one of them to react for four long months. The amount of drugs they pump into me so I can't use my skill set varies and sometimes, I feel good enough to give it a go. Other times, I'm not sure if I believe their tale about how I got here or the images in my head. Neither is appealing because my gut, one of my greatest assets, doesn't accept them.

Sighing as I see the lingering grifters drop out of the room, I wait for my captors to instruct me. I don't have any option but to appease them. They have far too much intel on my employers to be bit players, and I haven't gotten one glimpse of a real face the entire time. Even if I could break out, I don't know where I am or who has me, only that they're well funded and connected. Escape would allow me to regroup and prepare for The Five's protocol to end, but that will only matter if any of them are alive.

If she's *alive.*

They've never mentioned the status of my team, much less the girl who rose from the grave. At least, not in current times—they've mentioned the past frequently in their written notes that tell me what I'm required to do. It's not enough information to determine whether they gathered this first hand or through a very skilled mole, but it is enough to take their threats seriously. They have details of missions and jobs no one should know—except *LI* and clients. It spans decades, so I could pin no one client for the leak, and not even hacking *Mercatus* would grant them this amount of detail.

No, this is the work of someone delving into the past exploits of LI with malicious intent.

My hand raises to rub my face, tired of coming in and out of fuzzy periods as they adjust the dosage on the drugs. As a grifter, I have always kept my mind sharp and my instincts right at the edge of consciousness. Otherwise, the requirements of my profession would get me killed. I didn't rise to the top of the heap by over-imbibing or partying too hard while I worked like Coda. Though, to be fair, his cover demands he do much of the shit that gets him in trouble even if he wasn't still mourning our girl.

The barrel of the hand cannon pokes at my skull, bringing me out of my thoughts, and I turn to the masked fuck. "What? There isn't anyone to convince in here. They're off to lives or jobs or whatever. I can't make them appear out of thin air to convince them to go along with this charade your boss has orchestrated."

GoblinFace #1 snorts, then turns, gesturing at Goblinface #2 at the door. The second one leaves, probably to get more instructions. It's weird how none of them speak, even with a voice modulator. I know they can hear, and I'm certain they're not mute. But in my presence, there's nary a sound like I'm some fucking X-man that can use his powers to persuade or absorb their voices. My only guess why they behave this way is they think being deprived of social interaction will make an extrovert like me more pliable.

Too bad we can literally talk to ourselves for hours and stay amused; I don't need them.

I admit, it's wearing thin after this long, but if I survived CapRes, I can survive these morons. They're not putting me through rendition, nor are they doing anything truly scarring. It's bizarre; they seem to want to use me for their aims, but not harm me. I'm not sure why and trying to puzzle out why in the mental state they keep me in is a bitch.

As I muse the reasons why kidnappers would behave this way, Goblinface #2 comes back, handing their cohort a piece of paper. When I see the typed words, I sigh heavily. I'm good at what I do —maybe one of the best in the world—but I'm uncertain I can convince other criminal communities I'm one of them. Perhaps with enough preparation and research, I could whip out a believable alias, but they aren't giving me that. No, they want me to hop into the other forums one by one and fake out seasoned operatives and skilled contractors.

"This won't work. Perhaps I can mimic a hitter or a trafficker since they are very diverse and disparate. *Maybe* I can successfully imitate a thief. I don't know the lingo for an intensely guarded group like the hackers, nor do I have the protocols the assassins use to verify one another. No one will fall for the ruse. "

The goon with the gun waves it at me menacingly, but I shake my head. *No amount of threatening will make this successful. My* captor doesn't relent, so I turn back to the screen in front of me, waiting for the right thing to pop up so I can do as they ask. Luckily, whoever is working the controls picks the hitter forum first and I'm able to watch the discourse for a bit before I'm nudged to begin. I play along with their chatter, learning speech patterns and behaviors as I go, and when I feel confident enough, I work on persuading them to sign up for the job.

I still don't get why they're doing this, but if I'm part of the problem, maybe I can be part of the solution, too.

After they pushed me to rile up every single board in *Mercatus*, the masked men walk me back to the cell I live in. It's basic, but clean and serviceable. I've been in worse places and certainly witnessed worse than that. There's a bed with linens, a table to eat or write at… even an actual toilet versus a bucket. Again, it's not the type of lock up people who intend to kill their captive provide. But there's no way they will let me go once I've served my purpose; I'm too valuable to many groups or buyers for that to happen.

"Maybe I'll end up bought by *LI* to prevent all my inside knowledge from getting out. If this *Forum Romanum* is a ruse to sell off high-value operatives rather than objects, maybe I'm headed for the auction block as well."

There's no one to answer me, so I continue to turn the possibilities over in my head.

When the bomb went off, we were all booking ass to the doors to get clear. I *think* Remy got there first because she was hauling ass like a sprinter. Unfortunately, my memory of the events after haven't ever gotten clearer and I don't trust what the goblins have told me. Their version of the events leans towards everyone but me dying in the blast. I don't believe that in the slightest; I trained with The Five most of life. They don't go down that easily.

Especially Mo and Dwyn—those fuckers are damn near immortal.

"But why are they trying to convince me my team is dead? Wouldn't they be better off saying they'll harm the people I care about rather than taking away all hope?"

I suppose telling me everyone is dead might keep me from trying to escape. If they knew me well enough before they grabbed me, it would make sense to manipulate me in that fashion. However, even that is risky because I might decide there's nothing left for me but vengeance. You can predict human behavior, but it's always a gamble. The variables involved mean you need layers and layers of back-up plans in case the others fail.

Pacing back and forth across my room, I try to recall the actual sequence of events that occurred after the blast. It's mostly shadows and vague blurs, so I've determined I must have hit my head. I probably didn't wake up for several days after they grabbed me. If that's the case, I believe they had to have brought in medical care, including a CT scan. Maybe that's why they keep me fuzzy so often? They're giving me continual follow-ups for a head injury and they don't want me to know.

How very Lost. I could very well be in an asylum somewhere.

"Don't be ridiculous, Jinx," I mutter to myself. "You're not in a nuthouse."

I guess I can't be sure, but my gut says I'm right. They're holding me, using me, and definitely gaslighting me, but… I don't think I'm imagining all of this. Rubbing my eyes, I drop onto the bed and put my elbows on my knees. I've never had such a difficult time figuring out what's reality and what isn't. Even running thousands of cons, playing hundreds of roles, I've never been so damned disconnected from myself.

It's fucking scary.

"Not having anyone speak back doesn't fucking help. I'm muttering to myself like a psych patient all the time and it reinforces the worry that I'm losing it."

Truthfully, I don't understand what any of this is going to accomplish. If my captors had the entire Five or even most of us, they would be much more successful in commanding a premium. I blink, tilting my head as the wheels finally turn. What if the purpose of the *Romanum* is to find out where the rest of my brothers are? If this group got me, perhaps they intended to capture *all* of us. An event as big as they've announced would tie up many of the major and minor players in all the skill sets, plus bring out heavy hitters hiding products and items they might normally sit on for long periods of time.

Including hostages.

"If they get the lower echelons to buy in, bringing in enough stolen shit, the major players will have no choice but to reveal what they've squirreled away. It would be prudent to sit on captives that are HVTs until protocols run out. Declaring the *Romanum* will drive prices higher and create a demand for that sort of auction lot."

It's very possible my kidnappers are looking to complete their set. They're hoping this will bring the sellers out of hiding and allow them to purchase the members of my team like rare fucking Beanie Babies. And if any of them *are* hiding because of our protocols, they'll come to a similar conclusion about this stupid event. That's why they have me stumping for it across the skill boards. The goblins want me to attract the attention of survivors who may not have been captured.

"This is a *lot* of effort and work to assemble us. Death must not be the endgame. But what is? Operatives at our level will not rat out their organizations; they have trained us to resist torture since we were young." Turning on the bed, I lie back, stacking my hands under my head as I look at the ceiling.

What does a 'full set' grant them?

The answer is elusive. I can't think of any codes or gates or anything that requires all five of us to unlock its secrets. Nothing on the island is protected by a single team's prints or DNA; that would be stupid. *Les Invisibles* hasn't reigned for decades by being fools, so I can't imagine they'd do something like that even without informing us. I'm not saying The Commandant doesn't hide shit from our team and probably most of the High Legion, but he also wouldn't do something so… corny kids' movie villain-ish.

"I have to figure out what their true target is before this damn marketplace. If I don't, my gut says more than just my brothers and our zombie ex-team member are at stake."

Remy's face flits through my mind—both from when she called me Casanova and further back, when we were all inseparable.

I can't allow these fuckers to take her away from us again—even if it means losing myself in the process.

PRETTY GIRL

REMY

After her declaration, Lys and I spent the next couple of hours putting in cautious bids for all the cells in *Mercatus*. My gut still thinks there's something off about it and some people who are bidding. I suppose there are folks just as paranoid as me who might post under lesser identities until they see how this shakes out. *Regina* might not be bright enough, but some of my serious contemporaries would be. You wouldn't catch *Le Voleur*, but Horseman might. Even *Alqatu* tends toward a measured approach, so I think the weird little randos chattering in the groups might be Trojan Horses.

We didn't get a response to any of our hard work for four days, so I spent that time helping Lys build up a more well-rounded stash of criminal materials. She was resistant at first, but I reminded her I've been hiding in plain sight for over a decade and my childhood best friends never once suspected I was alive. That got her to relent, and I could breathe easier.

This morning, I'm out with Lys scoping the first task they gave her as an audition for the thieves' group. Stealing a priceless old tome from a museum display isn't the assignment I would expect for such a complex position, but whatever. It's possible the system defending it relates to the penultimate job or perhaps it's simply something the organizer wants to sell in the Zanzibar auctions during the *Forum*. I rarely think this hard about *why* I'm being sent to snatch or kill something unless I feel like the client is hiding something dangerous to my safety.

That is most definitely the case with everything the fucks running this ask of the recruits.

"Moira," Lys asks as she pretends to peruse the guidebook for the museum. "I think we should see the ancient world first. It looks positively *fascinating*."

The girl doesn't let grass grow on her, I'll give her that. We've been working on burner identities for my new friend, but the kind I use take time to create. I snuck out to purchase a few 'good enough for now' kits and disguise pieces in the middle of the night. It did not thrill her that I used my stealth mojo to get in and out without tripping an alarm, but *c'est la vie*. I can't change overnight and doing shit on my own has been my life for a long time.

Plus, I did not burn Moira until now, so I could maximize the lifespan of this identity.

I nod in response to her statement, tilting my head as I look at the map in my hand. "Absolutely, Brittany. I've always loved the Roman Empire; I think about it often."

Lys snorts, then covers her mouth. I'm sure she's amused by my sly reference to our current employers, but the topical pop culture side to my words is likely why she's laughing. She knows I rarely bother with shit like social media, but it kept coming up when I was trawling the Tor layers for hints about the stupid event. I didn't seek it out on purpose or anything.

"You know, I'm not sure if you're scarier when you're completely unaware of the normie world or when you actually pay atten-tion," she says as I point to the path we should take.

Baring my teeth in a grin, I shrug. "Considering I can kill you fifteen ways without breaking a sweat, I'd say I'm terrifying either way."

"Good point. I'll keep that in mind."

We walk through the main lobby casually, stopping to look at signs as if we give a fuck what's going on here outside of the ancient alchemy exhibit. The 'Brittany' persona is a hoot—I amused the shit out of myself, dressing Lys in muted colors, a cardigan, and her braids tucked in a severe bun. The glasses give her a Clark Kent effect and the lack of wild makeup just underlines the bookish historian look. Her cover is a grad student from the Oxford history department and though I realize they could easily be as wild as my companion now, people dismiss what they expect to see.

I press my lips together as we stroll along, feeling weird about casing a job with another person, but also enjoying it. My emotions are closer to my skin than they've been in years since I saved Coda in Paris and Elysium's continued presence is keeping them right there. She hasn't seen what happens when I'm working yet, which concerns me a little. Giving a shit what anyone thinks is fucking strange, too, but I'm ignoring it. But the change between Remy and The Guillotine is stark and I'm not sure how she'll handle it.

Dwyn didn't mind at the ball, but he's seen it before, as have the others.

"No elevators," I mutter as she steers us towards the fancy panels ahead. "I never trap myself in a metal cage unless there's a damn good reason. The stairs suck, but the cardio is good for you, and they often have fewer cameras or security"

Lys snorts and rolls her eyes. "I *have* completed jobs without The Duchess before. But a couple of fancy pants chicks like us aren't likely to take the stairs, even to get steps in, and it will make people look twice. Just follow me and stop being so paranoid."

Not happening, but I'll concede the stupid elevators to make her happy.

"We'll change into a sportier version when we get back. I feel I need to force you to join me on runs in the mornings to make sure your endurance is on par with the shit we may face." The doors open as I smirk and she lets out a soft groan.

Her reaction surprises me; Mo and Dwyn were the most insistent about fitness training. Their professions end up running more than any other, including my own. A good assassin rarely gets trapped in such close calls they need to take off at Mach Five. If they're very good, they're gone before anyone knows what's happened. Thieves have so many variables in their jobs; running is entirely commonplace as far as I know.

"Don't judge, *Moira*," she breathes as the lift jostles and moves upward towards the fifth floor. "I guarantee I can bend in ways you only wish your body moved. Besides, I don't fuck up badly enough to be forced to sprint; I'm that good."

I arch a brow. "D is one of the top five in the world and I'm certain he has to occasionally."

"Uh, that's because The Ghost is a ridiculously talented yet reckless operative who takes retrievals no one else in their right mind would even consider." She shrugs and leans back against the walls. "His psychotic glee at risking his ass on every damn job is well documented."

Warmth spreads through my chest at that statement, and I wrinkle my nose. I'm not sure why knowing Dwyn is infamous among his colleagues for the brash confidence I grew up adoring makes me happy. It's not like I haven't been digging into all their pasts as I searched for them. The Shadow Douche aiming for Raz with single-minded focus told me I had to catch myself up on their exploits. Obviously, Dwyn wasn't on his radar, nor were the others, until I helped them save Jinx at the ball. But I'm still weirdly pleased about Lys' comment, and it makes me irritable.

The Guillotine does not fangirl.

I almost sigh in relief when the elevator stops and the doors open, effectively cutting that conversation short. We have work to do, so I shove the fuzzy feelings away to stride into the atrium where the exhibit halls branch off. Our plan is to peruse the one we're interested in—ancient alchemy—in the middle of our tour through this floor. It won't seem important if it's not at the beginning or end, plus we can shuffle the order to suit the amount of people visiting when we enter. I'd prefer not to be one of the few visitors in the room where our target lives, especially given the camera system in this place. It's too obvious.

"We're taking the Romans first, then?" Lys says, pointing like a true tourist.

Snickering, I nod and follow her as she leads me down the hallway to the displays. I'm not usually this flashy with my initial surveillance, nor do I interact with more people than necessary. My thieving friend, however, smiles at other visitors, coos at a baby in a stroller, and chatters animatedly as we walk to the first exhibit. I guess she has more grifter in her than I thought. By the time we're viewing relics with some rather racy depictions of ancient life, she's giggling and elbowing an elderly woman who's fallen into step with us.

"Look at that thing! It's *not* a 'personal hygiene item.' That's a freaking dildo," she stage-whispers and the woman titters like Lys is doing stand-up.

I'm never *taking to her on a job somewhere like that damned 'Sex Museum' from Prague.*

"It's rather impressive, isn't it? My Wilbur looked like that, and I can tell you, I thought he'd brought something from the zoo on our wedding night…"

Lys collapses in laughter as the woman goes on in horrifying detail about losing her virginity before the first fucking *World War*, and I have to move on before my eye twitching gets too noticeable. I'm no prude, but that a *lot* more information that I ever wanted about old lady sex. I blink as I try in vain to wipe her diatribe out of my brain banks, pretending to squint at different objects as I move far enough away to mute their conversation.

Coda would die on the spot if he was here… I think. He used to love embarrassing me with sex shit when we were kids and teens. The guys weren't exactly inexperienced for long and once I met them all; I blended into their group easily. They didn't hold back because I was around and I didn't let them act like fucking tools about women, either. I kept my shit as quiet as possible because they were stupidly protective, considering I could best everyone of them in the rings. I chalked it up to 'dude shit' and threatened the first guy I fucked with instant death if anyone found out.

No fucking thank you. My vagina was a taboo conversation in my presence, and I didn't fuck around about enforcing that rule.

"Moira, settle this. Do you think the Greeks or the Romans were dirtier?"

I turn, looking at Lys with an owlish expression. "Uh… I suppose equal, depending on what period you're looking at?"

She grins easily, giving the old woman a little wave. "Well, Elmira thought Romans, but I vote for Greeks. So we're going to let her ogle Roman dickfests while we head out for the Greeks."

"Okay. Sounds good," I say as Elmira waves back. Once we're walking past the post-Christian era artifacts, I lean in and hiss, "What the hell was that?!"

"Cover, my dear Moira. That woman comes here twice a week, and she has a mind like a steel trap. If someone ever shows her a video of us walking through, she'll remember our *delightful* conversation and respectful manner, not that we walked around like snooty assholes. It will never occur to her that we could be involved in a theft now; in fact, she'll likely scoff if it's suggested."

Pulling a face, I sigh. "You're right. I just *hate* shit like that. I'd prefer to creep in, do my thing, and leave my imprint in a public message that cannot be ignored."

"Oh, like eight rotting heads stuck to spikes in front of the local miscreant bar? That's what you'd prefer?"

I give her a look as if she's lost her marble. "Yes. That's *exactly* what I'd prefer. Who wouldn't?"

"People who aren't so used to the smell of decomp that they can ride around for eight hours in the heat without retching."

She's got me there.

MONSTER

MO

I̲t̲ ̲d̲i̲d̲n̲'̲t̲ ̲t̲a̲k̲e̲ ̲v̲e̲r̲y̲ ̲l̲o̲n̲g̲ to convince the idiot in the chair to give up who he was working for. To be honest, it rarely happens down here. Cartels only send their expendable members on suicide missions. Getting a challenging captive is almost like seeing a unicorn; their structures simply aren't set up to allow anyone with useful knowledge to be on the front lines. Working for mobs and rich assholes gives me a lot more satisfaction in my work.

But I can't take jobs that would give away who I really am, so I'm stuck in amateur-hour.

Cracking my neck as I sip my morning coffee, I sigh heavily. The coffee is amazing—the one benefit of being here, if you ask me— but it can't make up for being the head clown in the circus. Yes, it's my ego talking, but this is the kind of position I stopped taking *years* ago. Playing at being a general to an army of over-equipped children for a spoiled despot loses its luster after you rise to the top of your profession, no matter how good the money is. At the risk of sounding like an old man, I prefer organizations with a bit more… loyalty.

"Though, who knows how that will change with the shit going on now?"

Society is changing and so are the people coming up in the ranks of every institution—criminal or legit. Not being able to adapt is why both the Sicilians and big corporations alike are struggling to recruit employees who will remain true. Money is a major factor, but also the concept of what workers will accept is changing. That will not affect shit like *Les Invisibles* who snatch orphans and raise brainwashed agents or cartels who are the only option to feed your family, but it sure as fuck does other industries. Even PMCs offer comprehensive shit to get their rosters filled since the damn virus.

I'm usually not so philosophical anymore; that's Jinx or Raz's bailiwick. Giving a shit about why the world works the way it does or how it changes was a wonder I lost on the island. My focus is more on the present—what is happening *now* and how to address it most efficiently. The past can't be amended and the future can't be predicted, so why bother? I think Remy turning up alive and not eating brains pretty much proved my point on that account. Not a single one of us even considered she got out of that explosion alive and we've never looked for her because of that belief.

A fact I assume she'll address in great detail if she made it out alive a second time.

"Maybe she is fucking indestructible—it would explain a goddamn lot."

That's ridiculous, of course. But Remy was reborn like a phoenix into a life that's even bigger than the one she would have had with The Five. She's sitting on top of her skill set behind an impenetrable mask of secrecy that no one has penetrated in over a decade. Not to mention her Duchess persona is pretty high in the thieves' hierarchy—she's not at Dwyn's level, but that could have been a calculated choice. I wouldn't put it past her to make certain they sought only the assassin like blood diamonds. It would keep her from getting discovered—specifically, by The Five and *LI*.

"She was always the smartest of us all."

Stop that, Mo. Stop thinking about her as if she's gone again. You don't know that.

Even if she isn't gone, I can't imagine what the fuck we're going to do once we've all come out of hiding. The night she supposedly died, we betrayed her. I can remember the look on her face when Arnaud showed up to rendezvous with the five of us in tow. Her expression was so shattered, so utterly defeated, that I can't believe she's ever going to forgive us. And maybe she shouldn't, regardless of *why* we did it. Some things are sacred and no amount of begging or groveling evens the score.

"Boss?"

I glare at my coffee for a moment, forcing myself not to snarl at the minion interrupting my morning brood. "*Que?*"

"The men… they want to know what to do with the prisoner. He's been hanging there for four days."

"And he'll hang there until I'm ready."

There's a shuffling sound and I know the man is trying to decide how to respond. Finally, he speaks. "They want to know why we're keeping him alive, General."

The disgust I'm feeling at my actions in the past wells up and I stand, knocking my chair to the ground as I whirl to face him. "Because I *fucking* said so. If they'd been competent enough to keep that shitty group of intruders from breaching the first barrier, we wouldn't *need* to interrogate anyone."

"But, but… General. You have gotten nothing but a name and…"

Stalking closer, I reach out and grip his throat, lifting him off the ground. "A name may lead us to the source of the attack. Did *you tontos* get anything from him before I arrived? Have you elicited more information since I got that name?"

His panicked gasping breaks through the haze in my head, and I lower him to the ground so he can respond. "No, General."

"Then I suggest you take my response to the men and make one of your own: train *harder* and fuck around less before they end up in the shack with the prisoner." I shove him to the door and turn my back on him in dismissal. A slight sound trips my instinct and my eyes narrow.

I turn just in time to see the cowardly moron coming towards me with a bowie knife. Scoffing, I grab his wrist, twisting it before he can get close enough to touch me. He squeals as I continue wrenching it until it snaps, then lean in, using my shoulder to flip him over my shoulder. The second his back hits the ground, I take the knife and press it against his carotid as I stare into his eyes.

"Pitiful. I haven't even finished my coffee this morning and you could be dead by my hand." Shaking my head, I look down at the prone goon in disappointment. "I'll never be able to whip this army of baboons into shape for *El Jefe*. None of you have the requisite skill or temperament. Anyone with fucking sense wouldn't have attacked me while wearing motherfucking *flip-flops*."

The dipshit just gurgles and flails.

Jesus Christ.

I should kill him for even dreaming he could kill me, but then I'd have to train another lieutenant and listen to *El Jefe* bitch about losing a cousin. He's constantly forcing his coked up relatives into my leadership positions and so far, it hasn't worked out for him. In the four months I've been here, he's lost two cousins, a brother-in-law, and three nephews. I didn't kill them all, but I didn't save any of the lazy fuckers, either. I'm a fan of Darwinian theory and *El Jefe*'s gene pool needs draining.

Ignoring the moron as he writhes on the floor, I sit down to look at the screen of my tablet. I spend the blissfully quiet first hours of my mornings scanning through local papers for a hint of my brothers. They might not be taking jobs or making waves, but if you know men as well as I know the other members of The Five, it's easy to spot the little clues.

A priceless artifact in a small town goes missing, but doesn't make national news. Drunken riot in a college town known for bars and partying. Random flips in support for legislation that appear meaningless on the surface but will probably ripple further. That's not to mention looking for shit on video games or e-Sports that would signal a hacker taking interest in his boredom.

Good leaders know how their men deal with loss or failure.

The idiot on my floor finally gets up and stumbles out as I sip my coffee in irritation. "I have no fucking clue what Remy would do in this situation besides disappear for thirteen years."

I flick through the various feeds I've set up by country, hoping to catch a whiff of anyone. By the time I'm working my way through Asia, I hit pay dirt. There's a mention of a security blip at a major software company in Tokyo that forced them to audit their servers to prove no data got stolen. Scratching my chin, I ponder that for a moment. Raz would have taken something, though he might not leave a trail. He blathers on about his prowess a lot and I usually ignore him, but his work is flawless.

They wouldn't have known he'd been there. He's too good.

But the event is suspiciously under-reported and my gut is churning. I've stayed alive in some hairy places by listening to my gut. I'll have to toss out the bait to see if I'm right. If not, I won't hear anything and if I am, I may confirm one of my team is above ground.

I tap out a quick encoded ad for the personals and place it in several Tokyo papers. It's short, to the point, and hopefully, my Japanese isn't as rusty as I think.

"TELL me who gave your boss the order." The guy stares at me, his arms flopping at his sides from the dislocation while hanging. He's playing dumb and though I don't want to do anything rash to appease the jackasses watching, I admit it's tiresome. *"Dime quién le dio la orden a tu jefe.*[1]*"*

When he doesn't respond, I stomp over, pressing the poker against his bare side until he screams in agony. The smell of burned flesh isn't one of my favorites, but it beats the infected ooze on his legs, and definitely beats decomp. My years in this line of work have desensitized me to scent; being the head muscle typically comes with blood, gore, and waste, like thievery comes with gymnastics and rope burns.

"Give me the bolt cutters," I bark at one of the minions hanging about to watch the torture with glee. "He's got fingers and toes left."

"Sí, general. Un honor poder ayudarle, General.[2]*"*

Gag, as Coda would say. These rats would dime me out for a keg of beer and I know it. They fear me, so there has been no mutiny, but not a single one would back me up if needed. They won't die for *El Jefe*, either, and that's why he's stuck in this compound with more family than any sane person can stand. They hired me to train his shitty army, but I think the real reason was to get them skilled enough for him to venture off the property safely.

That's an occasion which has yet to happen because you cannot buy loyalty.

I take the bolt cutters, snapping the mechanism as I walk around the chair slowly. The fear practically emanates from his pores when I finally stop to face my captive. "Tell me something that will make me stop—anything useful."

My request gets his attention, and he stops moaning for a moment to study me through the one eye he can open. "Anything useful?"

"Yes, you fool! I want information useful to *El Jefe*, and if you give it to me, perhaps the pain can end. Don't repeat what I say like a fucking parrot; give me something."

A faintly drunken look comes over his face as I loom closer and I wonder if he's having a stroke until he gasps, "The Bull is sending one of his crews to take part in a big event. He hoped to auction *El Jefe* off to the enemies of his father—or the supporters hiding in the shadows. That is why we came to the compound."

I frown, deciding whether or not I believe him. Torture isn't always a reliable method of interrogation, but in the jungle, you don't have a lot of room to run long cons or be convincing. "He's sending a crew to where to do what? Where is this auction?"

"No one knows yet." The guy whimpers and shakes his head. "Not even the Bull. But he has men and women bidding for jobs, so they will get accepted. If they are, they will be part of the big event. He will come again, so he has someone to sell."

The men behind me whisper to one another and I whirl, flinging the bolt cutters at the loudest one. It knocks him out clean and I sneer at them. "Clean that shit up and get the fuck out. Jose and I have much to talk about." Our prisoner looks at me fearfully as I give him a slow, satisfied smile. "Tell me everything you heard about this auction—*now*."

Even a hitter recognizes when something big is going down in the criminal world and I'll be damned if this doesn't sound like a Forum Romanum.

If it is, I know exactly what I need to do.

---

1. Tell me who gave the order to your boss.
2. Yes, general. An honor to be able to help you, General.

ME AGAINST THE MUSIC

REMY

We finished our tour of the museum without a hitch.

Lys befriended everyone, from the guests to the pimply-faced docents to the ancient security guards with a wink and smile. It was bizarre to watch her be as obvious as possible in her persona while I strive to be almost invisible when I'm prepping for a job, even as The Duchess. It's likely why they call her The Fox—her cunning and guile draw in even the crankiest, standoffish individuals. I watched her quietly, thinking about how artfully Jinx does his thing even when it was seducing me in exactly the way I needed.

I can be charming and delightful, but it doesn't come naturally like it does for them or Coda.

Looking over at my friend, I tilt my head. "Did you get the nighttime footage?"

"Yep. That's what I've been studying while you monitor all that shit for the audition jobs for your other personalities." Her grin is lop-sided, and she winks at me playfully. "The entry alarms are high end but not worrisome. The inside is what I'm muddling through."

"Oh?" I stop working on the hacker forums, stretching my arms above my head as I turn the chair to face her. "How so?"

"They have multiple rotating, pulsating lattice grids, pressure plates, and heat sensors." Her nose wrinkles and she grimaces at the laptop screen. "The effect is an absolute bitch. Do-able solo, but fucking risky."

Giving her a puzzled expression, I rise from my chair and head over to join her on the floor. "So you don't do it solo. Problem solved."

"Uh, Remy, I don't think you get how this works. I know you do shit as The Duchess, but…"

My gaze narrows. "Are you suggesting I can't follow your lead?"

"Multiple. Rotating. Pulsating. Lattice. Grids." She shakes her head, obviously trying to figure out how to say what she means without being mean. "It will take serious flexibility and tumbling skills. Shit that takes years to learn, not days."

I snort. "I know their methods are secretive. That's the *only* reason I'm not laughing at you outright. *LI* training is no joke, Lys. Show me the video and tell me how you plan to approach this. I can follow along without weighing you down; I promise."

Sighing, she sits her chin in her hand. "You realize if you can't, we'll have to book ass or get caught?"

"I do. But quit worrying about me and let me absorb."

"If you say so…"

WE ENDED up compromising on several tactics, which is why three days later, we're both crouched inside of shipping crates, getting jostled around as they're loaded onto a truck bound for the museum. Lys wanted to screw around with window lasers and bars, but if we're going to do this efficiently, the plan can't include more than one ridiculous element. In that respect, she's more like Dwyn than she thinks because he would have insisted on the flashiest steps at every turn, just as she did.

It's the psyche of the thief, I suppose.

Unfortunately for her, an assassin is more concerned with execution—in both senses of the word—and getting away clean. I'm an exception to the flashy rule because of my signature, but that's more about my branding than anything else. The heads are proof of completion for employers and warnings to future targets. Plus, I enjoy the fuck out of my work.

My box lurches and slams back into another one—careless loading of boxes that might contain priceless art irritates as I realize the truck is leaving the docks. According to our research, it should only take a half hour to get from here to the docks in the back of the museum. We measured traffic patterns at night and accounted for variables, so the small breathers we have will cover if there's a delay. I didn't have to do this on the plane from Somalia because my crooked worker made certain my pine box had tiny air holes. That's not a luxury I could plan for this time because the museum shit sits in customs until pick up.

Fucking terrorists and drug dealers ruin shit for everyone.

Once we get inside, Lys gets to run the show. I took entry and exit to make certain they were simple, but the way we handle the extensive inner security was all her plan. Blowing out a breath, I review what she outlined in my head a couple times, then grin to myself. I think the guys would be proud of me—or at least, the teen versions of them would have.

Mo and I fought for control a lot, but it was good-natured. The rest of them always encouraged me to learn to let others help and not be so hyper-independent. It was hard for them to comprehend that I'd been on my own until I got slowly assimilated into their group. I survived the years before them by only trusting myself and learning to do it all solo. Since the explosion, I've returned to that mindset so completely that I rarely take jobs involving more than one person.

I'm relearning how to deal with humans I don't see as a means to an end.

I don't know if my friend understands that or if she's just damn good at reading me, but I appreciate her letting me fumble through this as best I can. She's not a pushover, but she doesn't dig her heels in on every tiny detail, either. We're at opposite ends of the spectrum in terms of personality and approaches to work, but at the moment, I'm not feeling edgy about everything going awry. It's oddly comforting, yet scary at the same time.

Leaning against the back of the crate, I close my eyes, picturing the videos we watched until I thought we'd need to *Clockwork Orange* our lids open.

We're ready—I think.

LUCKILY, the museum didn't have any auditory sensors, nor do their cameras have audio. When I pry open my crate in the darkness of their processing area, the splintering of wood is loud, but quick. I toss the breather in a large garbage bin, watching it sink into the mess of light packing materials before I walk over to Lys' prison. It only takes a second to get her out and we dispose of her mask as well. She shakes out her limbs, eyeing me as I do the same.

"Are you sure you're up to this? You wouldn't do a run-through and I never do jobs without a full rehearsal."

My lips quirk as I nod. "The way my mind works is strange, I know. After watching that video enough, I promise I have the layout down. Your method of putting the timing to a song is new to me, but I like it. I can match my internal visuals to the beat and I'll have a perfect vision of our obstacles without doing a low-risk version. Trust me."

She looks doubtful, but I'm not lying. I have perfect visual recall, near eidetic, and rehearsing will only fuck up my flow. "Okay, but I'm not listening to any gripes if you get stuck."

"Deal."

We bump fists and head for the door to the storage area. It opens into a long hallway shrouded in darkness. The cameras here are *not* infrared, nor do they seem to have night vision based on our perusal of footage for the past couple of days. That seems like a big fucking hole in their net, but even expert designers ignore employee areas when they shouldn't. Not upgrading the equipment there gives them more money to max out the places where valuable stuff lives, but it also opens a gaping hole for people like us.

That's why I won entry and exit—I figured out we could cut out a shit ton of camera dancing.

It only takes a few minutes to navigate our way to the double doors that lead to the museum floor. Security isn't as tight in every corner of the place, only in the most valuable exhibits. The damn book Lys has to steal has more complex measures than the gem department, and I voiced my suspicions about it several times over the past few days. There are lots of priceless first editions and shit that have survived volcanoes, but I couldn't find a damn thing about why this stupid thing is guarded so heavily.

"Still think it's a trap," I mutter under my breath.

Lys wiggles her brows at me, moving along the shadows in front of me as we head to the stairwell. "Can't refuse the audition," she sing-songs just as quietly.

Fuck. Never joining anything has kept me from having to do idiotic junk like this…dollars to donuts.

The stairs don't take long to creep up and when we're on the fifth floor, I slip out the wire cutters to go to work on the door alarm. Lys pushes it open slowly, entering the room carefully. We mapped the camera angles here, so we split up to move in-between frames until we reach the opening of the path to the ancient magic exhibit. She pulls out the spray, illuminating where the grid begins with a quick mist. I nod, popping my headphones in at the same time as her. Her plan involves using the music to time the pulses and rotation of the beams, so we have to be on the same page.

Here we go.

At the first words, I leap forward, springing over the first set of beams in a front handspring. Pausing for the next beats, I drop to a squat, then rise to flip my legs over another one in a one-handed cartwheel. By the time it says 'floor,' I'm wiggling through a grid of calf high lasers like a damn snake. A barrel roll, then kipping to my feet, has me a quarter of the way across the stupid field. I'm able to look over at Lys, confirming she's making progress before I have to duck under a rotation, then do a backbend to avoid the next one.

"Hold steady," I hear in my ear as I kick my feet up to handstand and hold again. The sweep goes by and I walkover, landing just before the chest-high laser pulses behind me.

My snort is soft, but she's not looking back at me as I crouch to slip under more lattice, balancing on my toes as I lift one leg up so far I'm almost in a yoga pose. "I'm doing fine. Concentrate on your own land mines, woman."

Doing this along to a Brittany Spears song and making sure I hit the exact beats isn't a cakewalk, but I enjoy a challenge.

Crossing the rest of the grid takes three repeats of the song, but once we're both there, I let out a breath. "This is *not* a task for an amateur. Just saying."

"You don't think all the snatch and grab newbs will finish their assignments, then?" Lys arches as brow as I pull out the equipment we'll need to divert the more straightforward lasers crisscrossing the room where the book is housed.

"Um, no." I shake my head emphatically, then frown. "Unless you have the hardest fucking one on the list. If so, then maybe? I dislike their method of taking bids then giving the people they deem skilled enough secret auditions via encrypted email. If it smells like decomp, there's a dead body, Lys. And there's one hell of a rotting corpse hiding amongst the bullshit about this *Forum*."

"Could it be your old nemesis from *Les Invisibles* trying to lure his boys out? Rumors of The Commandant's cruelty aren't kind."

That gets a huff of laughter. "Fuck, no. Protocols after a mass fuck-up are there for a reason. He wouldn't spend the time needed to arrange all this, even if he farmed it out. He'd just send sweeper teams everywhere until he got what he wanted—dead or alive."

"I don't want to play 'my dad is a bigger asshole than yours' with you," Lys says with a knowing look. "You win hands down,"

"Unless yours branded you in a public ceremony or used a blowtorch on you, you'd be right."

Not to mention leaving you alone without supplies or weapons in a jungle filled with enemies for months every year.

THE AUDACITY

REMY

"MOVE," I MUMBLE AROUND THE TOOLS IN MY MOUTH. I'M working to disable the temperature sensor by overloading it with activated hand warmers. They'll stay hot enough to mimic what we need as we replace the crusty looking book on the pressure sensor, then cool down while we close the case again. It's a stretch, but we were on a tight timeframe to snatch this thing for the assignment. I didn't have time to source more sophisticated equipment.

Hopefully, the Macgyver-esque crap I pulled together will hold up long enough for us to haul ass to our exit on the loading dock.

Lys huffs as she moves her fingers a bit to the right so I can affix the last one to the glass. It takes a few seconds to cut the hole we need, so I prepare the balloon, tongs, and the water. It takes both of us to manipulate the weight transfer, and I'm certain we're going to fuck it up. But the water inflates the balloon and I ease it onto the plate as she slips the book off with her pair.

"This is the jankiest lift I've ever done and I feel like we're in an episode of the Librarians," I whisper.

"Agreed. The worst part is, I won't be able to tell this damn story to get drinks later on. Those dickwads made me sign an NDA in the assignment portfolio."

I pause, looking at my friend as if she's lost her mind. "Who the fuck is going to enforce that? I'm not saying blab tomorrow, but you socially adept thieves have some 'fish story' drinks hierarchy… use it. I highly doubt the secret organizers of this stuff are going to take you to court."

"True." Her smile is mischievous as she returns to pulling the book out of the case. "I'll edit out your name to protect the innocent. Cross my heart."

Making a grumpy sound as we complete the transfer, I wait until she's got the book tucked into the tactical crossbody she has strapped to her back. Sealing the balloon is a bitch and I'm counting the seconds until it's safely closed. I reach into my pocket and use the same adhesive I did on the hand warmers to replace the glass in the case. This isn't the best method for accomplishing the task and like much of what we just did, I'm concerned as hell it won't hold until we're out.

"Time to go."

We follow the path we took into, pausing to stay off camera each time they move, and I remove the mirrors she used to divert the stationery beams. The stupidly intricate laser grid hallway looms in front of us and I reach down to hover my finger over the 'play button.' Lys nods when she's ready and we take off, reversing our gymnastics until we're safe at the other end. The music stops and a soft sound catches my attention.

Motherfucker.

"Go," I hiss as I take off, sprinting for the door to the stairs as the sound gets closer. Even running the soles of our shoes are quiet, but it means we aren't able to duck the cameras in that main atrium. There's nothing to be done for now and we're well disguised, but I hate coming out of a job unclean.

Lys yanks open the door to the stairs and we scramble down them so quickly we narrowly avoid doing a head first tumble. I leap over the last landing, hitting the ground with a tooth jarring slap before we rush to the employee area.

"What… the hell…?"

I hear her grunting in my earpieces as we slip into the processing area, but I don't respond. I predicated option one for our exit on leaving the fifth floor without tripping alarms. They aren't blaring, but there's no way the person up there didn't hear us tear off into the darkness. If it was an errant guard doing their rounds at the wrong time, they'll rouse the whole place soon. If they haven't pushed a silent alarm button at the guard station, we should be able to use option two. Gesturing at my friend, I open a door at the back of the room.

It's a closet, but it has access to the ventilation system.

"You can climb, right? Free climb?" She snorts as if I've offended her, and I sigh in relief. "Good. We need to take this shaft up twenty feet, then fifty feet across due east, and up another thirty. That will bring us to another room close to the secondary dock. We can't speak in the vent because I'm pretty fucking sure it will echo. Got it?"

"Aye, aye," is her response, and I roll my eyes.

This is going to be a long fucking night.

CRAWLING through the vents silently took longer than expected, but the schematics I found were older than I would have preferred. We had to go around a few internal traps not listed on the security specs and by the time we emerged from the museum; I was ready to murder someone. This 'audition' was definitely a set-up—no question about it. I don't know if *all* the first round jobs were meant to weed people out or if it was aimed at Lys specifically.

Note to self: Figure out if Lys has enemies we need to know about.

I blink when that thought reminds me of Mo, sucking in a deep breath and blowing it out as I follow my friend down the street. We're taking the long route back to our base, leaving enough room between us that people don't assume we're together. At the next corner, we'll split up entirely and regroup once we've made sure we're not being tracked. Too many things went wrong this evening and my internal spider sense is screaming that they weren't all due to lack of prep time.

We hit the corner, and she peels off, heading west while I maintain my course. I reach up and click the earpiece off so there's no signal tying us together, especially since she's got the damn book strapped innocuously to her back. Nothing I found on the thing gave me a clue why the *Forum* runner wanted it so badly, or why the surrounding security was tighter than in rooms filled with diamonds. Other than its age and historical value, *Historia Obscurae de Ouroboros et Eorum Monstris*[1] is no different than any other crackpot book about weird mythical shit. There's no hint of anyone famous or infamous owning it, nor was it part of some memorable incident.

It's hinky, and I don't like shit that has no logical basis.

Grumbling under my breath as I stride down the side streets of Paris, I pull out my phone to give the impression I'm just another woman headed home at a late hour. This detour will add a good chunk of time to my journey back to our headquarters, but we agreed ensuring we weren't being surveilled was paramount. Normally, I'd switch to a new safe house after a disaster like tonight, but we don't have everything we need for Lys, so I can't pick up and move on.

"You survived this long by doing what was necessary without question, and now you're letting all these…*feelings*… fuck up your tradecraft," I chastise myself. "You should cut her loose until the heat dies down. She can take care of herself."

"Who can take care of herself, pretty lady?" The gravelly voice and chuckles that accompany it make me pause, looking up at the Parisian sky with a plea that I misheard.

I'm not in the mood for some penny ante street gang to force me to move them between the three categories I put people in: 'don't care,' 'target,' or 'victim.'

Confronting me when I'm fresh off a buggered mission is a sure way to land yourself in 'victim' without so much as a word. I gather my fury into a ball in my chest to keep from lashing out immediately, then lower my gaze to meet that of the man who spoke. "Me. I suggest you fuck off until you hit the English Channel and then continue fucking off until you hit the ends of the earth. Now, *move*."

He throws his head back and laughs, white teeth flashing at me as he does so. The hyenas behind him follow suit, chorusing rough laughter as they eye me threateningly. "*Je ne pense pas que nous le ferons, ma belle.*[2]"

My eyes roam over the six men slowly, looking for weaknesses and clues alike. Perfect white teeth don't belong on a street gang member, and one of his minions is wearing the Prada combat boots with the stupid pouch. These are not random thugs, nor are they high enough on the food chain to know how to disguise themselves for a hit. Disdain for their lack of skills curls my lip. I didn't work myself to the bone, building a reputation for excellence, to let clowns like this make my profession look stupid.

I'm more offended by how badly they suck than I am about them being here to kill me—or attempt it, anyway.

"I have places to be, gentleman. No time to waste on morons, I'm afraid. Scurry back into the shadows like good little roaches."

Giving them the most condescending smile I'm able to, I step off the curb and walk around their cluster of dipshits. "Ta-ta."

The growl behind me sets off alarm bells and I whirl around, shoving a hand in my pocket as they stalk closer. My favorite weapon slips into my hand as easily as a pen for a poet and the blanket of nothingness that is The Guillotine drapes over my mind. Smirking, I arch a brow at them as they get close enough for me to smell the cognac on their leader's breath. This dumbshit isn't trained well enough to maintain a clear head while imbibing; he'll be slower and clumsier than he thinks.

"You're dead, you little bitch. *Il Tasso* has a message of his own."

The fucking Badger? *How in Lucifer's name does that asshole know where I went?*

I give them a blank look, pretending I have no idea what they're referring to before I mock a yawn. "Sorry, boys. You're bothering the wrong bitch. Doesn't ring a bell."

"I told you it wasn't her, mate! No one who could kill *Mangust* is that small. The boss has bad intel again. He needs to stop listening to—"

"Shut it, Nigel," he roars.

It takes real skill not to laugh in his face; he doesn't even have control of his goon squad, much less this situation.

"Look, if you fellas are having a love spat, I'll be on my way."

His laugh is dark. "I don't think so. The boss will kill us if we don't complete this job. You're the one he wants and when it's done, he can focus on the rest of his tasks."

"I'm not really into group projects, so you'll have to earn your stripes some other way."

Flipping the dirtbag off, I turn and stride away. If they follow this time, I can't let it slide in the name of keeping a low profile. The heads on the fence should have warned this wanna-be crime lord and instead, it made him intent on proving himself. This will have to be nipped in the bud without mercy or he'll simply keep coming. I don't need the distraction or the attention while I'm hunting my prey.

"Get her," he growls.

Sigh.

The first idiot to reach me takes a jab to the throat that sends him reeling, gasping for breath as he stumbles. My elbow flies to the right, slamming into the next one's solar plexus hard. He flies backward and I spin to the left, my foot making contact with his stomach before his arms can reach. The rattling wheezes amuse me, but I don't have time to waste when the largest one barrels towards me with a snarl. He looks like a rhino with his head down, so I side-step the charge and jump onto his back. My thighs hold on tightly as I stretch the cord, hearing the *schink* of my favored weapon with a joy that's almost orgasmic.

"Big mistake. *Huge!*" I lean forward, looping the wire around his neck and use his own momentum as he tries to buck me off to slice his throat almost to the vertebrae.

The gurgling sound is music to my ears, and I pull my faithful weapon free as I jump off the big man. He tumbles to the ground in a heap, allowing me to look at the injured men and their leader with a positively bloodthirsty grin. "Who's next? Mama's got two hands and thirty-two weapons hidden on her. I can go all night."

Horror floods their expressions when I crack my knuckles and drop into a fighting pose.

Really, it has been too long since I killed someone—I feel much better now.

---

1. The Dark History of Ouroboros and Their Monsters
2. I don't think we will, sweetheart.

LITTLE POOR ME

CODA

Something is going on.

The people holding me say little, but the activity level outside of my cell has increased. There are more of them and I hear hushed conversations, but can't make out the words. I figured they were getting ready to move me, but that hasn't happened yet. Instead, they've provided mostly edible food and more water, plus a new set of drab scrubs to wear. I'm hoping for a fucking shower and shave soon; that would be better than anything else.

I fucking stink, and it's not my damn fault.

My current circumstances have highlighted how incredibly privileged my role in The Five is. I've never thought about it like this before, but being the 'fixer' with a famous face allows me to wallow in luxury. I don't have a clue how many times any of the others have had to hunker down in shit holes for extended stays, but I guarantee it was more often than I knew. Smelly vans, dirty gangs, or cramped crawl spaces are probably like second homes to Raz, Mo, and Dwyn. I'm not sure about Jinxy because grifting is pretty high society at his level. But maybe when we first graduated and were still making a name for ourselves   that seems possible.

I, however, got placed in a position of fame and fortune from the beginning. I didn't have to earn a record contract, my accommodations were never sub-par, and everything I needed to be successful got handed to me because *LI* financed it. My sharp glare has always shut others in the industry up when they suggested I was a nepotism baby, but I can see why they'd say it now. All they saw was someone dropped into success, not the boy who barely survived a grueling life on the fucking *LOST* island.

The drawing I've been working on beckons my eyes. After several days of turning it over in my mind, I decided I don't think *Il Dolce* is trying to unseat anyone. Honestly, I don't think *any* of the High Legion are working to take down The Commandant. Piss him off or make him look bad, maybe; Lady Volkov wanted her pet team to be at the top of the heap and she didn't get her way. The Five squashed them like bugs in every category of the trials, so she couldn't whine about the results.

Doesn't stop her from fucking with us, but this is beyond her petty garbage.

Retribution for killing the heirs apparent to the Legion seats would be swift and brutal. The Commandant would have everyone associated with or her team executed after his Crows spent months breaking them for every piece of intel they have. He'd have to raid every orphanage *LI* deals with on every continent to replenish the ranks, and it wouldn't bother him in the slightest. I remember what he ordered them to do to Rinna Hallow.

My eyes close as a burst of memory floods me. "We all had to watch the videos every day until she was gone. The newer Legion members were on teams then—no way they'd risk being at the mercy of the Crows."

Rinna Hallow's screams are part of how Arnaud convinced us to betray Remy. When he ran across our preparations for escape, he used the trauma of those years to convince most of us that Remy would suffer her fate first. The Commandant would find it amusing to make us watch her die slowly and in agony before he started on the rest of us. Dwyn never believed him despite his frequent mentorship of our team. I never understood why the craziest member of our team fought so hard against protecting her, but maybe… maybe he sensed something the rest of us couldn't?

Remy said she killed him, so we can't ever ask him—unless she did.

Thunking my head against the wall, I groan. If I get sold to some weirdo overseas as a personal sex slave or a never-ending concert giver, I'll never know. I've been hoping that *some* of my team is alive, especially Remy. She's been unkillable so far, but what if she took off to save her ass? We'd deserve her desertion, but I'll be forever ruined if that's why I'm still here in this stupid cell.

"Get the prisoner!"

My eyes pop open, and I sit up, moving to hang the blanket so it drapes over my diagram. I don't want these dicks to see my scribbling, but I'm still working out what the fuck might have happened. They haven't gotten me out of this stupid cell since they put me here. There is absolutely something going on; I was right.

THEY TOOK me to another room and gave me supplies to do the very thing I'd been hoping for: shower. I didn't get a lengthy amount of time, but I could scrub the dirt, grime, and ash off me for the first time in months. It was fucking orgasmic—something I never thought I'd say about hot water and cheap hotel soap. I need a shave, too, but the lack of razor wasn't nearly as shocking. They will not give me anything that could get modified to be a weapon.

Afterward, I got escorted back to my prison without a word to explain why they gave me privileges or what might be happening.

I tried speaking to the four guards who walked with, turning on my legendary rockstar charm, but no amount of jokes, grins, or curious questions got a response. I resigned myself to memorize my surroundings instead, tucking the knowledge away for a day when escape seems possible. No amount of random perks can convince me the assholes in masks aren't packing, and despite how much I want free, I don't have the advantage.

Dwyn wouldn't be so cautious, but I'm trying to channel our strategic leader, not the reckless psycho.

Pacing across the room, I consider what I saw on the way to the shower. The structure they're holding me in is clean, bright, and sterile outside of my chamber. It's not some disgusting dungeon; no, it feels more like a hospital or dormitory of some sort. They've kept me woozy much of the time, so there's probably someone with medical training. If I'd only been here a short time, it might not be required, but it's been months and not overdosing me takes a practiced hand.

"Not an inexperienced crew looking to make a buck, but someone who's been around the block at the helm. The ham-fisted twits who took me to get clean had discipline. They didn't react to me at all, and fresh meat would have. No one tried to question me or extract information—not once. I'm here for re-sale, not a pump and dump."

I tap my fingers on my lips as I walk back and forth. If someone would just *speak* to me, it would help untangle the threads in my head. Being by myself with no other input than the ramblings of my mind is making me edgy. Even when I was on tour, there was never a time when I didn't have a cadre of people to listen to me. I knew not to trust them—rock stars don't engender loyalty, only fawning—but it helped me to say it out loud. Doing it with no one around isn't nearly as satisfying, nor does it spark my creativity.

Walking to the door, I bang on it. "Hey, you masked fuckers! I feel sick. Is this fucking food rotten? Do you hear me?"

No one answers and I growl under my breath, turning to slump against the door, sliding down to the floor. I didn't see anyone else besides the goons, so I don't know if I'm their only captive or if they have some sort of Collector-esque menagerie of people gathered to sell off. Looking up, I squint at the bright lights, trying to see if there are hidden cameras, but like the last time I checked, I see nothing. Someone had to be watching me the first few weeks I was detoxing, but fuck if I know how.

This place is like a fucking asylum or a black site.

"Huh." I ponder for a moment, tilting my head. "Maybe it is an asylum. If it's owned by some crooked arm of their business, guards and a skeleton crew of medically trained aides may be the only people allowed in. It wouldn't take a lot of skill to forge that kind of paperwork and they'd be able to keep anyone they kidnap isolated without being questioned."

Blowing a frustrated breath out, I look up at the ceiling. I don't know what else I can do to keep myself sane if this lasts too much longer. Whatever they're cleaning me up for can't come soon enough, even if it is some sick auction. I'd rather fight off a crazed fan than be cooped up in this room with no contact for much longer. If I had my guitar, it wouldn't be so bad, but they haven't given me a single thing to help occupy my mind and I don't expect that to change.

"Think, Coda. You could get through the hole for long periods. You can get through this." There's no one to answer me, of course, and I groan.

I hate the silence and hate being alone…finding the guys when we first arrived at the island was my saving grace.

My eyes close as I think back to that day, remembering how we first met.

The horn on the large cargo ship blew, waking me up. I couldn't see in the dark hold they crammed me into with nearly a hundred other children, but even as a child, I knew it meant we must be close to shore. We'd stopped so many times I did not know how long it was since I was 'adopted' from the orphanage in Brazil. This nightmare boat added more and more children at every stop, making the space get crowded and smelly. They didn't take more than me at my home, but at some stops, they brought in multiple kids.

No one told us who they were or why we were being sent away—only to behave or we'd pay the price.

It was obvious the men corralling us were not to be trifled with, but one boy made a fuss. We watched as they beat him to death, then threw his body over-board. No one tried to fight them after that; it only took one example of their cruelty to keep everyone in line.

I was six when the orphanage sold me to this crew of giant, angry men, but I felt older by the time we reached our final destination.

"Why are you twitching so much?"

The voice came from a boy with a pinched expression and dark eyes. He had the look of someone who got punished a lot before he joined us. There were bruises all over his arms and legs, and his eyes had that look kids get when they're kicked around a lot. It was part suspicious, part angry, and part disconnected from the world. I'd seen it on others, though beatings weren't the only reason they had that expression. The other reasons made me shiver to think about.

"I have trouble sitting still. What's it to you?"

I didn't mean to be nasty, but I couldn't know if this boy was trustworthy or if, being a few years older, he might be as bad as those who'd hurt him now.

"Nothing. It makes you look weak. You don't want to look weak when they take us wherever we're going. That's how they know which ones to pick first."

Mo was always the planner, even then, and when he continued to tell me how to survive, I listened. He was right, and from the second we stepped onto that cursed island, he had my loyalty. No matter how fucked up things got, I could still see that serious kid explaining to me what I needed to do. He could have ignored me, kept that info to himself, but I like to believe it was fate that made me unable to control my focus.

Some people would call my ADHD a curse, but it's led me to my family over and over.

That could never be a curse.

DARKSIDE

REMY

"Look at you. You made me *promise* not to draw attention. Stay under the radar. Make sure no one notices me." Lys stands in the living room with her hands on her hips, glaring at me in irritation.

I rub the back of my neck, my mouth twisted into a half smirk, half sheepish expression. "They accosted me, you know."

I'm not accustomed to having to explain myself to someone.

"You're *covered* in blood."

Pulling the dark auburn wig off, I drop it onto the plastic sheeting she laid out when I showed up at the door. "Hard not to be when your job is sending people to the choir invisible."

My friend arches her brow. She's been home for at least an hour, which gave her time to peel off her alias and set up the disposal materials. "Your job tonight was to help me steal a dusty ass old book. How did a simple walk home turn into a murder party?"

"There's a reason they call me The Guillotine, Lys." I deadpan as I toss the wig caps on the fire pile and start removing weapons.

"No one has ever accused me of solving my problems by handing out puppies."

"Ugh!" she growls, tapping her foot as I unsheathe four knives one by one, placing them on the hall table. "I'm not saying you're not allowed to be yourself; I'm asking how the fuck you got drenched with enough blood to stain your face red like an acolyte in *Queen of the Damned* on a stroll back to the house."

I blink. "Oh. You're not judging me; you're actually curious."

"Yes, you fucking weirdo. I'd like to file this data in my hard drive for future reference."

My chin dips as I remove the ice pick, a retractable baton, and another dagger. "It's odd for me to hear someone planning to continue breathing around me for an unspecified amount of time."

"Remy, if no one's told you before, you turn into a goddamn robot when you take all your weapons off. It's like you're trying to distance yourself from only having your own wiles to rely on." I give her a blank look and she rolls her eyes. "Go on, then."

"A group of assholes pretending to be street thugs cornered me. I was content to tell them to get bent until the leader mentioned our friend the Badger by name. That's when I lost Remy and The Guillotine took over." I shrug, tossing three spring-loaded Guillotine wires in various casings that were on my belt.

Lys tilts her head at the pile growing on the table. "You and The Guillotine are as much the same person as every other persona you've cultivated, including the throw away ones. I dated a shrink once, and she'd say it's what you call your periods of disassociation that allow you to separate your work from your true self. You don't have DID, but you absolutely make use of the training you received from *LI* to mimic it."

Sucking a breath in through my nose, I narrow my eyes. "I fucking hate shrinks. How the hell did you survive fucking one for any length of time?" The noise of three thin daggers hitting the wooden table echoes in the air before she giggles. "I'd rather skin myself alive than listen to someone dissect my brain while they're railing me."

"Don't be ridiculous, Remy. You have to gag headshrinkers or they'll ruin all the fun." Bobbing her brows, she looks at me so seriously that I actually bark a laugh. "There we go. HumanRemy for the win!"

I pause my weapon stripping for a moment, scrubbing my hand over my face. "I probably have quite a few unhealthy habits I've formed while I lived on my own. There wasn't anyone to criticize or call me out on it, so you might end up feeling like a nanny goat. I was raised to be a fucking weapon of mass destruction by a bunch of psychos, you know."

"I'm aware. Honestly, I can't wait to see what happens when we locate one of your fellow lunatics and I have to watch you try to navigate being human in the same space. I'm going to need popcorn like it's a Discovery channel special."

Wincing at her bald honesty, I tug my soaked shirt over my head and throw it in the disposal pile on the floor. Once I'm down to a Kevlar threaded tank, I pull another wire ejector from between my boobs and unstrap the five weapons in their sheathes built into my bra band. "Glad to hear I'll be entertaining you as I sort through thirteen years of trauma and adult hormones while we look for missing team members, duck random hitmen, investigate a shadowy puppet master, and try not to reveal who any of us are to the criminal community at large. Being your personal reality show is the most fulfilling thing I've done in *ages*," I snark.

"You're only at nineteen," she says absently as she looks at me. "Thirteen more? Jesus fucking Christ, Benoit. Do you have a stiletto in your ass?"

My eyes widen, then I laugh again. *Shit, she's good.* "I mean, I probably have weapons meant to look like sex toys in one of my units. I've had to infiltrate clubs before for jobs. Not tonight, though."

"Thank fuck. I wasn't looking forward to putting such a thing in the damn dishwasher."

Ladies and gentleman, Elysium is on a roll.

LYS BANISHED me to the upstairs to get clean an hour ago. The blood staining my skin took longer than I would have expected to wash clean, but it had almost dried by the time I got to the safe house. My path home was long, as I detoured and doubled back many times before I felt certain there were no other surprises trailing along behind me. We'll likely have to move now, but until tomorrow, that's not my immediate concern.

That Il Tasso knew I was in the country, *much less specifically where I was, is much more pressing.*

I jog downstairs clad in yoga pants and a tank, finishing the braid I'm winding my long hair into as I walk. "I don't think he knows who I am still. If he had, one of those douches would have used the name, especially since no one but you knows I'm female."

"Then why is he so *obsessed* with you?" Her voice gets higher pitched and I groan.

One of my new friend's greatest joys is introducing me to movies and shows I never took the time to bother with. My life has been about honing my craft and completing my jobs, not lazing about watching the boob tube. I read, though rarely and mostly trade related non-fiction, but since I escaped the island media hasn't been one of my vices. The only things I paid attention to were news and internet forums that might assist me—a fact that Lys is determined to rectify.

Winding a tie around the end of my braid, I walk into the main room to join her. "I don't know. He's never met me, nor was he at the damn compound. I'm fairly certain there weren't cameras in my cell, so my only theory is his minions sent videos of my interrogations."

"Oh, good! You've attracted a psycho stalker that *isn't* the one we're looking for. Isn't that handy?"

Her reference to Dwyn makes a knot form in my chest, and I huff. "How would you know if he's a stalker?"

Lys snorts, her eyes dancing. "How the man looked at you when you two stormed the castle was positively indecent."

"Of course it was. Sex and blood will do that to us crazy folk." I roll my eyes and stride over to the command center, plopping in my chair to check my alternate *Mercatus* boards. "Have you looked at the damn book yet? We have to drop it in the morning."

"It's a dusty old book with fake magic spells and shit. I even took a picture of it and I have it running through a Tor browser, but nothing that comes up differs from what we found before we snatched it." She shrugs and points to it, sitting on the end table like a toad. "It's a bust. No clue why the dicks running this thing want it."

Fucking great. All that for nothing.

"You can do the hand-off in the morning and I'm going to find a new headquarters. I don't care if they didn't follow me here; Paris is burned." I click into the hitter forum and see the bright notification, the flashing making excitement churning in my gut. "Perhaps this task will lead us to our new landing zone."

"Then shut up and open it. If it's out of town, we need to plan as soon as possible. I *refuse* to fly somewhere nailed into a goddamn crate."

Ignoring her jibe, I click on the message. It outlines a protection detail for a gala charity event in New York City. *Shit.* We're definitely not traveling to the States in wooden boxes. Scanning through the rest of the email, I see the date and time. The shindig is only six days from now, which means we can only travel by air —everything else will take too much of our precious time. "We're headed to New York, Moneypenny."

"Ooh! The clubs there are always packed and I *adore* the clueless people milling about. Some of my friends call it 'Thief Heaven,' you know." Her braids swing as she jumps up and shimmies her ass in excitement. "What's the mission, 007?"

"Guard duty for some spoiled brat socialite. Again, just a name from the news, not anyone connected or even advantageous for politics or business. I suppose her family might be important, but we're not kidnapping her," I say with a frown. "Why the shit is *this* the audition? It's amateur hour. At least your job was challenging."

"We haven't met this chick yet, Remy." Lys peers at me as if I'm quite slow. "Have you ever actually spent time with rich American socialites? Like more than a few minutes?"

I shake my head. "No. Mo taught me about this as part of cross-training, but it was over a decade ago, and I've never actually taken that sort of job as *Dançarina do fogo*. I purposely select the ones more geared towards making targets understand the error of their ways."

"You mean you choose shit where you get to beat the shit out of someone for the client? No surprise there—Loki forbid you take shit where someone might get to know you, even beneath an alias." Her laugh is full of smug glee and I ponder punching her before turning back to my screen. "You're going to *hate* this job with the fire of a thousand suns."

Finishing my response, I hit send and whirl around again. "How do you know? You creep in at night and lift shit, then disappear."

"I do, and I'm fucking baller at it, Rem. But I also interact with normies a fuck ton more than you—both inside and outside of work." She pauses, then her face lights up. "I know what to do. We're going to watch TV tonight and I'm going to show you *all about* what this girl is going to be like."

"Lys, there's not enough alcohol in Ireland for me to watch reality TV. I won't do it." Stomping over to the sofa, I tuck myself into the cushions with a look some might call a pout. *Obviously, it's not; The Guillotine does not pout, she merely glowers.* "You won't convince me."

"No, no, no." She grabs the remote, climbing up next to me and switching on the screen. "Not reality shows. I don't want to wake up with a wire wrapped around my throat. We're going to watch *Gossip Girl.*"

My eyes move between her and the menu for the streaming service she's flicking through.

What kind of fresh hell is that going to be?

PANIC ROOM

REMY

Tapping my fingers on the tray in front of me, I dart my eyes around the darkened interior of the plane. Nothing about this makes me comfortable, but I didn't have enough time to secure better options. From the second I left the burlesque bar and stepped into that damn bar where I saved Coda, I've been forced to do things on timetables not my own. My work has always been flawless because I take the time and patience necessary to construct foolproof plans with multiple fail safes. It's the cornerstone of good work in my field, but as I study every person I can see from my seat, it occurs to me that perhaps I've been purposefully kept running.

I am not infallible when I can examine the board and visualize all the permutations, but my win percentage is enviable.

Being forced to move from Paris to Germany to Austria to London and so on means I never quite get the time to analyze everything thoroughly. Lys and I did many breakdowns while we were hunting The Five after the explosion, but our focus was more about finding them than figuring out how might be pushing the pieces into place. I've thought of little else since we boarded, except that as soon as the door sealed, we were trapped in a flying bomb held aloft by physics over the deepest pits on the earth.

I'm not afraid to fly—I've HALO-dropped before—but I am uncomfortable being in a public space with a meager amount of concealed weapons when there are multiple fuckwits hunting me. The amount of defense items I was able to get 3D printed within two days was impressive, but not enough for me to feel completely at ease. My body might be a weapon but the space in here is limited and the variables immense.

Just imagine what kind of fucking field day the media would have if I had to kill everyone on a goddamn plane… again.

My eyes narrow and I huff. That job was a smaller, private plane and there weren't women and children as far as the eye can see. I could fly this goddamn thing if I had to, but the last time I only had to worry if I would survive, not fucking infants. A shudder runs through me as a baby cries on cue and I can almost feel my ovaries shrinking into my body like they're hiding. They're useless thanks to the doctors on the island, but that noise makes me consider cutting them out just in case.

A snore gets my attention and I press my thumbs into my eyes. The great Elysium, cat burglar extraordinaire, is out like a light beside me. Never mind *Il Tasso* hunting us, The Five missing, or the Shadow Douche… nope, Lys is having a lovely nappy time while we hurtle through space surrounded by strangers who could be anyone. It's a goddamn Christmas miracle this girl has stayed on this side of dirt for this long.

I intend to keep it that way, so the minute she dropped that book, I included her in the planning.

First, we went back to the house and disposed of anything that could be replaced with little effort. Then we wiped down every surface, vacuumed every carpet, and threw away any linens that could give her away. I packed all the equipment and weapons in my cases, called us a ride share, and reluctantly took her to the third and smallest storage unit I keep in Paris. She was like a kid in a candy store when all the supply cabinets were opened, rushing to pick out the tools she'd like to take with us. Her pout was hysterical when I reminded her that we'd be traveling commercial and almost none of it would make it onto the plane.

We picked out five identities for me and packed the three remaining she had from my stock up. After a bit of haggling over leaving her usual tech here, turned off, so we couldn't be traced, we loaded up on enough to tide us over until I can visit one of the five places I have in New York. We left the unit after dark, driving to a ratty motel where we laid low while I waited for the carbon fiber weapons and a suitable passport for Lys to be finished. When we boarded yesterday, I was *Lizbet Montague of Paris, France* and she became *Rosalyn Fairchild of New York, New York*—college roommates during our years at The Sorbonne.

Rosalyn needs to learn not to drool on my shoulder or I'm going to throat punch her and we'll both get arrested.

"Psst. Psst. Rosalyn. Rosalyn," I hiss as I push her off my shoulder. "You're slobbering like a St. Bernard, for fuck's sake."

Lys sits up quickly, her eyes popping open as she looks around in fear. "Wha?"

"Well, if I was here to kill you, you'd be dead. But if I was allergic to drool, we'd be at a draw." I glare at her as she re-orients herself, looking chagrined.

"Fuck, R-Lizzzbettt," she slurs clumsily and I roll my eyes.

This is why you don't pick up strays, I can almost hear Mo laughing in my head. *Smug bastard. I was a stray once.*

"Lesson: If you are dumb enough to fall asleep in a very unpro-tected, yet public space such a fucking airplane, do *not* speak until you have your wits about you. Sleep talking is a great way to fuck up a cover story."

"Got it," she mumbles. "Where's the water? This air is killing me, *Lizbet*."

I hand her the water bottle the air hostess left for her while she was napping. Biting my lip, I wonder if I'm being too harsh; she's not been trained to go long periods of time with little to no sleep. She didn't go through CapRes for eleven years; Lys doesn't have permanent scars from learning how to be nothing more than a tool for the greater glory of a criminal organization. Then I remember Rinna, and the countless colleagues I've seen die over the years because they didn't have that torturous training.

Nope. Not too harsh. Just realistic.

"You need to be a better profiler than anything you've shown me on that chatterbox to survive in the big leagues." Tilting my head, I give her a sheepish grin. "Honestly, that was the only thing I picked up from those ridiculous girls on that show you insisted I watch. Women like that are either full blows psychopaths or very close—they can spot a weakness or flaw from across a room. They immediately know how to exploit it and what levers will push their prey to capitulate. This is what you have to learn."

Lys doesn't look pleased. "That sounds lonely and cynical."

"It is, but you could turn it off if you choose. I don't, but I like breathing most days." My smug smile makes her huff back. "Now, look out into this plane and tell me about the people. You can start a row at a time. This is a reading *and* memory exercise."

I don't mention this is a game Jinx used to help me learn to grift.

"I don't get how this is going to—"

"Humor me, Rosalyn. I don't do shit to hear my own voice."

Sighing, the thief rubs her eyes, then looks across the aisle. She's quiet for a moment, then she turns back to me. "The guy on my end is ex-military. Don't know which one, but his posture says it all. He favors his right leg; he's been moving it a lot. Possibly injured and retired."

Not bad.

"What about the woman next to him?"

"She was in Paris on a business trip but obviously, not a very big business. They flew her coach in crowded seats for a long international flight. Definitely not C-Suite material, so maybe sales? She's bilingual, but pretends she doesn't speak French so she can listen in around her. Maybe the gossipy shit kept her from getting higher in the company?"

I smile a little. She's doing pretty well for someone who took a five hour snooze. "Good catch. I often fake people out by not letting them know I speak the language they're conversing in. Picking when I clue them in is a strategic advantage."

"And how many do you speak exactly?"

"Enough to get by nearly anywhere, but some are stronger than others. I have a facility for learning them on the fly, which was nurtured young. I haven't a damn clue what my native tongue was. I was taken young; my real life slipped out of the hard drive fairly quickly." That admission makes me shift in my seat, coming far too close to putting her in further danger with my former employers for knowing too much. I've already made that mistake once; I don't need to compound it.

"Tell me about those girls two rows back," Lys suggests. "I can't quite make out what the hell is wrong with them. I know something's off, though."

Waiting for a few moments so my stretch isn't obvious, I cut my eyes to the two pretty twenty-somethings sitting at five o'clock. One is chewing her thumbnail, but the manicure she's sporting tells me that's not her usual behavior. Her friend is pretending to be engrossed in a book, but she's really staring at the page. Shifting my gaze to the activity surrounding them, I spot the problem quickly.

Fuck, if they screw this up, there will be issues when we land.

"They're smuggling something," I mutter to her. "Drugs, jewels, perhaps a small exotic? I don't know what, but they're terrible at it and their handler has noticed. This is why I fly in crates, you know. Less chance of a random idiot bringing heat where there is none."

She groans, putting her hand over her eyes. "I *knew* something was up. Christ, Lizbet. If it's internal and it busts... or if it's live and it gets out..."

"I know. I'm glad you asked because the woman watching them is definitely *not* an amateur. She's an experienced shepherd; I can tell by the way she's watching them without seeming to do so. Her position on the plane keeps them from getting off without her knowing and prevents them from reaching a bathroom alone."

"What are we going to do?" she whispers.

"Not a damn thing. Compared to some of the other concerns I have about people on this plane, they're small fries. We keep to ourselves, even if something happens." I glance at them again, frowning as I pick up my water. Of all the rotten luck, our stupid trans-Atlantic flight has smugglers, a few spooks, and a group of men escorting someone in first class. The latter are the least of my concern; they're likely just bodyguards with military training.

The idiot girls are my biggest worry; they don't have a fucking clue and that could be bad news.

"I hope it's not live shit," Lys says with a shiver. She gives the girls one backward glance and then looks at me with a sheepish grin. "Because if there are snakes on this motherfucking plane, *I'm* going to be the one making the scene."

The reference catches me off guard and I snort loud enough that an ex-military guy glares at me from across the aisle. I arch a brow at him, giving him a smile that's more baring my teeth than it is friendly. He finally turns around and I look at my new friend. "You mean to tell me that you don't bat a lash at me showing up stained in blood and gore, but you'll flip your wig over a reptile?"

"I don't like them. They don't have legs, but they don't have fins. It's unnatural." Her arms cross over her chest and I have to bite my lip not to laugh. "Besides, it's not like you're so fucking normal. Who doesn't notice brains in their damn hair?"

"Someone who spends quite a bit of time decapitating things for a living."

"As if that's an excuse."

"Perhaps not, but it's definitely the reason."

Huffing, Lys kicks her legs out, muttering, "Most of us have fears, *Lizbet.*"

Little does she know that I do, too, but they center around not being able to save those stupid, stupid men who broke me so long ago.

And now around keeping her safe from the death and destruction my presence brings with it.

GHOST

DWYN

THE TINY TEQUILA BAR HIDES IN THE BACK OF A MICHELIN starred sushi restaurant in Nakameguro. The chef serves an excellent tasting menu, both in food and liquor. The atmosphere is calm and I need that after the job I did last week. I got what I needed from the giant servers, but I didn't leave as cleanly as I would have liked. My hacking skills aren't nearly as good as my girl or her teacher Razzie, but I'm not a novice. Unfortunately, their shit was a wee bit more serious than I could handle on my own.

C'est la vie.[1]

I pick up the papers in front of me, choosing one to rifle through. Using local rags like this for communication is very old school, but Arnaud was our mentor before his stupid advice. He always favored good tradecraft versus tech, which I assume is how Remy tracked him down to end his life. She knew all his tricks as well as the rest of us, including posting coded messages in papers most people don't pay attention to. It was a spy trick before any serial killers started using it, and whenever I end up in a new place, I check them daily out of habit.

Flipping through the ads with a sigh, I stop at the personals. This is where something will hide if indeed there's anything to find. My eyes scan them quickly and I toss it aside when I come up empty. I pick up another one, glancing at it and discarding it as quickly when I see nothing. "Damn it, you fuck knuckles. One of you has to be alive. I don't feel different, and I felt completely gutted when I thought she was dead."

The server comes over with my hamiguri clam ceviche and a highball filled with Clase Azul. I thank her, then take a long sip of the tequila with a sigh of appreciation. I'm calmer than usual because I spent hours in a climbing gym earlier, burning off as much restless energy as I could by challenging my skills. The last paper sits in front of me like it's mocking me and I blow out a breath. "Having no one to fuck with is the worst."

I mean that metaphorically, though since the train, I suppose it's literal, too.

"Alright. One more try, then I'll pretend I'm not ready to crawl out of my skin for the rest of the evening." An old guy at the next table stares at me as I talk to myself, and I spin the metal chopsticks between my fingers with a menacing leer. That makes him turn away quickly, and I return to glaring at the paper. "Here we go. No whammies."

Nakameguro Shimbun is thicker than the others, so I have to sort through until I find the part I'm looking for. There are a *lot* of ads looking for ex-pats of a very specific type, and I snicker at them as I run my fingers down the page. I'm cackling to myself by the time it jumps out at me—an ad looking for a companion to escape to a tropical jungle island. It wouldn't catch anyone's eyes, but the tiny clue stands out to me like a beacon. It's signed 'Rupert Coconut.'

I know exactly which motherfucker this is from and, of course, he's the first one I find.

Mauricio has always loved that damn song and when we were teens, he got into a shouting match with Remy over whether or not it's romantic. I can almost see them standing toe-to-toe, growling about lyrical poetry, irony, and feminism at the top of their lungs. My lips curve up at the visual of the younger version of our girl trembling with fury. She told him if she caught a man she was dating doing such a thing, she'd string him up like a marionette and give a puppet show before feeding him to the wildlife in our jungle of horrors. His response was less than apologetic and she punched him in the dick so hard he limped for a week.

"Still one of the best fucking things I've ever seen," I muse to myself as I pull out my phone. I open the dial pad and type in the numbers from the ad, hoping like hell I'm right. I mean, I suppose there could be some other asshole who thinks that's funny, but what are the odds?

"Riggs?"

"Murtaugh," I reply as joy spreads through me. A crash rings out and I hear the growl of irritation that's usually reserved for me and Coda. "Spot of trouble?"

"You have no idea." The line goes quiet for a moment, then he snarls in perfect Spanish.

That jackass is working; I'm going to throttle him.

"We're supposed to be lying low, you bossy asshole!" I've been so bored I damn near took up *Pokémon Go*, and he's fucking working in some gang or whatever. This time, *I* want to kill *him*, and the role reversal is striking.

"I know." Mo curses again, then I hear the distinct sound of a fist coming into contact with flesh. Whoever was misbehaving is now sporting a shiner, I'd bet. "It was an easy way out of the country."

He would have kicked any of our asses for something so off-book, but it won't do any good to taunt him until we're in person. "Whatever. Where?"

"Did you pull the Yokohama job?"

"Liked that, did you? It wasn't a job. I needed—"

"Their server power. *Mercatus?*"

I roll my eyes. "Yes, Captain Obvious. I saw it, too."

"Then you know." The noise behind him amps up again and he practically roars, "*Sal antes de que te despelleje vivo, idiotas!*[2]"

"Jeez, Mo-Mo. Gonna blow my eardrums out," I complain as I wince. "What's the play?"

Our leader is quiet for a moment, so I dig into my food. When he's done ridding himself of the distractions, he finally responds. "The *Forum* is a ploy. We have to know what their game is."

"Definitely. Anyone else?"

"No one yet. But you need to bid as one of your throwaways."

Fuck, I hate this kind of shit. I just want to steal shit and scale buildings.

"I hate politics, Mo."

"We don't have a choice, D. We're the last men standing right now. Until we know differently, you need to play along."

Throwing back the last of my tequila, I scratch my chin as I consider his words. "Okay. I'll put it in and follow my nose. What about you?"

"I'm staying here until I dig into the source that led me to the *Forum*. I'd followed protocol until that point, but when the pig said his boss had them storm the compound to capture *El Jefe* for a big event… I knew that meant the time for keeping my head in the sand was over."

I frown, fiddling with the chopsticks again as I ponder. "You think they're going to have an auction?"

"What else would they do at a *Forum?* They'll sell products, but also… things less savory than drugs or antiques. It's too big an event for the Kidnap/Ransom guys and traffickers to waste."

"I'll keep my ears open. Thieves are a chatty lot on the forums. Anything else?"

Mo sounds tired as he sighs. "Any sign of her?"

"Not a peep. But she'd end it herself before letting some slimy douchebag sell her. Our girl is stronger than that." The thought of someone putting Remy on a stage, be it for vengeance or worse, makes me grip the metal stick in my hand tightly. I ignore the surrounding whispers, unable to focus on anything but rage.

"Our girl?"

"Don't be dense, Mo-Mo. She's going to kick our asses all over the fucking room, but after that, you idiots will get to see what Jinxy and me already know. Then even Razzie will have to admit I'm a genius and I'll die a happy asshole."

"Somehow, I don't think that's how it's going to go, but you can dream." The sound of a door slamming over the line makes him snarl. "Shit. I have to go. These fucking losers can't be left alone for more than an hour before they fuck something up. Keep me informed."

He hangs up before I can answer, and I roll my eyes. *Always a dramatic sod, that one.* Dropping the burner in my water glass, I toss money on the table to cover my lunch and head out. I need to get to an electronics store to make use of their demo equipment.

It's NOT long before I'm standing in front of a laptop, ducking the salespeople as I navigate past the stupid operating system. They lock shit like this down to keep customers from doing gross or illegal stuff, but that won't deter me. It only takes a few minutes to get a hidden Tor browser running and log into the most notorious criminal marketplace in the world. Scrolling through the thieves'

partition, I look for the big announcement, making a face at the screen when I find it.

Why is every criminal who sits at the top of the heap a fucking cape wearing megalomaniac?

Everything about this post screams pissy little fuck with a fluffy cat, but I enter my bid under one of my extra aliases. I keep them to amuse myself—how Mo knew I did it is beyond me. Sometimes I take simple bullshit under one of them to keep myself busy and my mind quiet when I'm planning for bigger jobs. Sometimes I use them to piss off a client I've had bad experiences with. It's one big game to me when I'm not doing shit specifically for *Les Invisibles*.

I look around the store, pondering. The jackass running this shit-show will message me and I don't want to spend a lot of time in places like this. Plus, now I have to grab another phone. There's a massive crowd in here and employees scurry around, approaching the looky-loos or joining the ones that need tech support at the big wooden tables. It doesn't take long for me to figure out the ebb and flow, and I grin as I log out of the boards.

Walking around the edge of the store, I shed the jacket I wore in, leaving me in a black tee shirt and jeans. I pass by a table of people listening to a class being given by an animated guy with a headset mic on, pretending to listen as I look for my prey. Smirking, I head for the harried looking man watching the floor as he pretends to hang a box of tablet cases on pegs on the wall. Brushing past, I bump him with my shoulder, feigning embarrassment as I apologize profusely.

Once I'm out of his site line, I look at the employee ID in my palm with a satisfied grin. All I need to do is cause a distraction and I'm golden. Passing by the display of expensive, wireless earphones, I grab one of them and pretend to head for the counter to pay. I drop them into the bag of a customer who's leaving, then take my place at the back of the line. A jaunty tune plays in my mind and I whistle softly as I wait for the inevitable result of my low skill lifting.

An alarm goes off, lights flashing and sounds blaring at the door. The manager at the wall and the employees converge on the poor woman as she tries to explain herself. My eyes cut to the door behind the counter, making certain no one is paying attention before rounding the desk to head into the backroom. The lifted pass should get me into the cage and I'll grab what I need, then head out the back.

Dwyn O' Shanahan has a mission and nothing is going to stop him now.

---

1. That's life.
2. Get out before I skin you alive, idiots!

LOOKING AT ME

REMY

Luckily, the dumb girls get off without an incident, and neither of us draw the attention of the suspected operatives on the plane. Lys and I grab our bags, catching a cab at the stand out front to head into Manhattan. I have a small bolt hole in the Village and I want to drop off our stuff before we head to the Bronx. She watches as we drive over the Queensboro Bridge, humming under her breath. Our cabbie is quiet—something that will earn him a hefty tip if it continues—and I look at her curiously.

"What's wrong?"

She smiles faintly. "Nothing. I just haven't been here in a long time. I have a love/hate relationship with the Big Apple."

"Ex?" I ask, arching my brow. She hasn't mentioned being serious with anyone before, but that doesn't mean there's nothing in her past.

Shaking her head, she gives me a sad smile. "My aunt was killed on 9/11 when I was eight. She was working in one of the Towers."

I blink, not knowing what to say. How the hell does one even respond to something like that? I'm not nearly good enough at being a person to handle this. "I'm sorry, *Rosalyn.*"

The corners of her eyes crinkle as I emphasize her persona. "It's okay. I've had a long time to deal with it and, unlike *some* people, I actually went to a therapist without taking them out."

I never should have told her that, but that fucking Green Fairy betrayed me.

"Yes, well. Judge not and all that. You've got skeletons in your closet as well."

A smile replaces the sad look, and my friend nods. "You're right I do. I started taking climbing lessons afterward because I had it in my head that if I could have climbed the building like Spiderman, I could have saved her. Unfortunately for my parents, they didn't realize I'd be using to rob people blind one day rather than save damsels in distress."

"That's…kind of… a leap," I fumble.

"Well, they got killed in a drunk driving accident the next year and I ended up in foster care. So I got scrappy pretty quickly, and the skills I picked up came in handy. My life of crime wasn't far behind."

The cab is quiet for a few minutes as it sinks in. I'm uncertain how I feel now that I know her story. It's not as dramatic as the one I've been keeping to myself, but it's probably common amongst our brethren. Not the aunt, of course, but the tragic loss and journey into a… non-traditional career after time spent in foster care. "Do you regret it?"

Amazingly, I'm actually curious about that.

"Nope. I didn't choose this because I'm broken or some shit, Lizzie." She flashes me a wink and shrugs. "I chose it because I'm damn good at it and I make good money doing what I enjoy. How many people in the world can say that in the year of our goddess Britney, 2023?"

I snicker at her choice of epithets. "I can, but you can't use me as a yardstick, according to headshrinkers. The way I see the world is completely fucked by my childhood."

"I'll say," she snarks cheerfully. "But that's okay. You're teaching me to be more well-rounded, and I'm gonna instruct you on how to be less removed. Once we find your stupid boys, I'll bet they'll have shit to teach you, too."

Arching a brow, I smirk. "More likely the other way around if they survive my ire."

"Hallelujah, girl."

THE LOFT I renovated is tucked away from the major streets and avenues. Located in the meat-packing district, it's sparsely decorated, but extremely functional. When the cabbie drops us off, we pay him handsomely, knowing he'll remember the large tip more than our faces. Elysium tilts her head back, looking up at the ramshackle exterior of the building in confusion.

"A warehouse?"

Shaking my head, I motion for her to follow me up the small set of stairs to the steel door. "At one point, yes. I bought the damn place at an auction a few years after I left... my old life. I spent most of that year creating my network of places to crash or store everything I needed to stay breathing and on top of the game."

"But you don't have, like, a house? Or even an apartment?" Lys watches me go through the biometrics, then yank open the reinforced steel door.

Rolling my eyes as she rolls her case in, I follow with my own, flicking on the overhead lights as we enter. "Why bother? A good luxury hotel and tension relieving tryst after my work is complete is satisfactory and I don't have to clean up any messes."

"You're also tied to nothing and have zero pieces of the real you lying about."

I drop my bag on the detached island, then head over to flick on the power at the tricked out computing station against the back wall. "Ha ha. Should I be paying you by the hour for this, Doctor, or are we on some sort of quid pro quo Lechter barter system?"

"Okay, okay. I know it's been a hard two weeks for you, what with having to talk about shit rather than eat bugs and get tortured by a sadist in the desert."

This chick, I fucking swear. I would have killed anyone else just for the quiet.

"I still need a damn dentist while we're here. Don't let me forget," I reply. Lys grabs an armchair, pushing it from the middle of the room so she can sit close to the desk. Nothing I have is meant for more than one person to work at once—something made very clear to me by my friend every chance she gets. "Once we check this, we'll call a ride to my unit and load up on weapons. The crap we got past security won't convince this fancy rich dude we can handle his daughter at the big event."

"If we need anything specialized after the meeting, I have a contact. Rocko and Marco are twins who used to be some sort of special forces over here. They've got hooks into everything short of fight jets."

Turning my head slowly to look at her in surprise, I clear my throat. "Exactly whose kid do you think we're protecting, the Prime Minister? I don't think we'll need a rocket launcher, though it's nice to know we could find one without a lot of trouble."

"This is America, Remy. I could source a fucking tank if I had enough time."

We burst into laughter despite the ridiculousness of her claim. I don't doubt her—this country is full of whack-a-doos with military grade weaponry—but the idea of needing it in the middle of New York City is something out of a comic book movie. I'd prefer to *never* attract that many eyes to our work in a place like this; it could force me to dip into the shadows for years to negate their press.

"Here we go," I mutter as I point to the message on *Mercatus*. "We meet with the Admiral tomorrow at 1100 hours and if all goes well, he will send us to dinner with his princess by 2200. He's not fucking around with the schedule, which I appreciate. I'd like to finish this audition so we can move to the next."

"What's my story?"

My lips curve up. "You're the back-up regardless, but we don't know which identity to pick until we meet both of them. We need to make sure you're covered. If anyone figures out you're trailing me, I'd rather it hold up to scrutiny."

"Does that mean we're free to go have drinks tonight?"

"Lys… we can't get tanked before this meeting. I'm *not* meeting some crusty, bellowing, old military dude hungover, especially when I'm acting like a hitter. It will make my damn head explode."

Her smile is knowing, and that's when I realize she's going to win this conversation no matter what I do. "Just a few drinks in a place we might catch some useful gossip. Cross my heart."

"I'd better not have to dress up for this."

"I promise."

Hours later, I'm regretting my life choices as I swing around a pole on a high platform.

The girl I allowed to become my best friend is a wrecking ball with legs and I'm stuck up here grinding to club music as I look over the scene. If any of the guys could see me, they'd probably swallow their fucking tongues. I'm going by *Kiki Del Torro of Miami, Florida* and Lys is *Veronica Evans of Gatlinburg, Tennessee*—identities meant to put us a few years younger and a lot more naïve sounding. We're supposedly on a 'self-care' weekend trip to the city to de-stress from the pressures of our grad school program at some university.

It's not bad, as covers go, and no one has even looked at us oddly when Lys tells them. She believes someone who runs this club is deeply entrenched in one of the major trafficking circles, so we're here to get ourselves invited to the VIP lounge, where the gossip will be good. That's the only board where we have zero traction and I believe it's going to be a big moneymaker in the *Forum*. We need to get ears or eyes in there. If the guys are alive and not hiding, one of them might be a prisoner of one of the slimy gangs in that world.

I'll skin the first person I find out who touched any of them, but for now, I have to be invited to the table.

That thought skitters out of my head when I glimpse a group of slick looking men in designer clothes entering the club en masse. The crowd parts for them as they strut to the floor, and I grin to myself. A response like that means money and power—the two things that guarantee an invitation to the back rooms and high roller areas in a joint like this. I don't recognize the guy in the middle; he's hot in a dark, dangerous way, but the men gathered around him don't scream bodyguards. Their appearance and bearing are too rigid—no, these guys are soldiers. Maybe ex-military or law enforcement, but they're huge, dressed to the nines, and looking at their companion with respect.

"Ladies and gentlemen, we have our first crime lord," I murmur loud enough for my earpiece to pick up. I hear Lys laugh softly and continue. "Coming in the front, flanked by eight pros, and by the look, rich enough to not wear labels or obvious bling. This guy's a major player."

"I clocked a few small fish—male and female—sliding into the VIP from various entrances. One came out of the backroom, so I didn't see her face, but she had a sexy as hell guy with a braid who stayed close. This must be a meeting; too many suspicious VIPs for one night."

My expression pinches. Traffickers are secretive by nature, but a drunken club hook-up might loosen their tongues. That's why we came. Unfortunately, our plan is fucked if they're having a big wig meet-up back there. No one will want to let in random club bunnies if they're going to talk business. Only the biggest fish in the room will have all their groupies around as a display of power. The song changes and I climb the pole a little, wrapping my thighs around it tightly, so I can bend backwards in the most appealing pose possible as the group of sharks make their way across the floor.

I need to get Big Man's attention if I want an invitation to that damn room.

"Lys, stumble out near them. Act tipsy enough to be game to go somewhere with the group by drawing their attention to me. Whatever it takes to get them to watch. When they get stupid, tell them I'm your friend and we're here to party."

She snorts and I watch her toss back the shot on the bar in front of her. "Wasted club ho act, coming up."

Satisfied, I pull myself up again and close my eyes. The beat of the music flows through me as I twist, grind, and bend. It's not the first time I've done this—though not twenty feet in the air—so I know how to be convincing. Strippers are a great cover when you're hired to take out wicked folks; the clubs and parties they get hired for are rife with targets. It's an age-old truth that the more skin you have showing, the less careful people are because they decide with their libidos versus their brains. I'd like to say it's just men, but I've Mata Hari'd women plenty of times as well.

A scuffle on the floor reaches my ears, and I grin wickedly as my hips undulate. Draping myself over my left leg, I glance to the middle of the floor where my girl is now cozying up to the swarthy man surrounded by guards. His cadre looks less enthused by her histrionics, but the guy we need is lapping it up like a cat with cream. His lips bend to whisper in her ear and I know it's time to shine. Amping up my dance, I twirl around the pole, showing off my flexibility in an undeniable message. By the time the song finishes, I feel the platform lowering and I know our gambit worked.

All we have to do now is use this to ferret out information on what these slime balls are planning to sell.

BAD

MO

The cerveza is cold, but that doesn't make this place any less a dump.

El Jefe wasn't thrilled by the temper tantrum I threw when I was talking to Dwyn, so I convinced him I'd work harder to earn more than the fear of his men. I could give a fuck less about camaraderie, but it gave me an excuse to leave the compound. One of the least objectionable nephews advised me on which bar to pick, and I had him organize an outing for our team. I'm paying, but even these lushes won't run up enough to be worrisome. The owners wouldn't dare overcharge *The General* and risk pissing off *El Jefe*.

After I spoke to D, I wanted to get out to follow up on what the now dead invader relayed. My young employer is beyond paranoid and, unfortunately, he's proven right every couple of weeks. Taking the men out for a night on the town seemed like an apology to him, and he granted permission without blinking. Luckily, the men don't seem as concerned with 'bonding' as they do drinking themselves stupid and finding women. It gives me the opportunity to blend into the background as I nurse my drinks, watching and listening for soldiers from the other cartels.

It's been a bust so far, but I'm still hopeful. This place isn't loyal to any specific gang—Joaquin told me it's run by some British ex-merc who retired here a few years ago. I haven't seen the guy yet, but the men called him *Morder*, which is fucking weird. Who the hell gets nicknamed 'Chomp?' Shaking my head, I finish the end of this beer and hold up the bottle until the bartender nods at me.

A few beers won't hurt, though I'd much prefer scotch.

"*General*, the men are very grateful for your…" Joaquin searches for a moment and I stay quiet, allowing him to practice. "…your generosity."

"My pleasure," I reply with a shrug. "My temper is high, but I'm fair."

He nods eagerly, and I roll my eyes internally. Perhaps singling him out for advice was a bad plan. This kid is related to *El Jefe* and the last thing I need is him to think he's going to be my second-in-command. If he even whispers that desire to my boss, it will become reality and I do *not* need a puppy trailing me. I considered using one of the relatives as a plant close to my new boss when I first arrived, but most of them imbibe the product too often to be trusted. Drugs make people unpredictable and addiction makes them desperate. They will always choose the habit; it's simply the disease asserting itself.

"Indeed, you are, *General*! But you do not seem to be having a good time. Should I find you a woman? Many ladies would be *very* interested in entertaining you—possibly even together." Joaquin looks at me with a knowing smile, and it's hard not to wince.

Shaking my head, I look away as I reply. "No. I don't pay for sex —ever. If that's what's going on here, I'm going to be furious by the time we return to the compound."

"No, no! Never pay!"

His panicked response makes me narrow my eyes and I turn to him, my expression sharp. "That had better not mean the men are taking things they have not been granted permission to have."

The bartender sits the bottle in front of me with a smack, and I look up. This isn't the same man who was serving earlier; instead, it's a pale skinned, blue-eyed man with platinum spiky hair. He has sharp cheekbones, a muscled build, and the look of a predator. Joaquin's eyes widen and he babbles something before he damn near runs away. I watch, then turn back to look at the newcomer.

"Why are they terrified of you, *Chomp*?"

His lips curl up in a smirk and he shrugs. "Hard to say, mate. I don't stand for nonsense in my pub, including mercenaries playing at being in charge of a drug lord's army."

That was on the nose.

"I'm not playing at anything. You should know a job is a job." I shrug and look around, scanning the crowd. "Probably why you made this shithole neutral ground, though I don't know how you keep it that way."

"I have my ways of making a point." His grin widens, and there's something behind it that tells me his method involves a lot of blood. "You've been in the country a while and never let your shadow cross my doorstep. Why now?"

I take a sip of my beer, keeping my posture nonchalant. "Pissed off the boss by punishing his band of idiots too often. Morale booster."

The guy chuckles and shakes his head. "Teamwork was never my problem, nor authority. Used to work with a git who had issues with both before I retired. He's a real piece of work, but I keep my hat in the ring and he's at the top of the heap now. Perhaps you'll rise, too."

Maybe it doesn't matter that I haven't found any of that dipshit's compadres. The owner of this bar is around everyone and clearly knows the score. The rumor that he's an ex-mercenary is likely true, so I may pry intel out of him if I'm cautious. "Mmm. Not here; this is a temporary job. I don't want to spend the rest of my days defending coca leaves for spoiled brats."

Chomp laughs again, his eyes filled with amusement. "Then what is it you want, mate? I get the sense this is more social than you typically are. Tell me what you're in my bar to fish for and maybe I'll be inclined to help."

I arch a brow. "How much would that cost me?"

"Not a cent. I can smell a pro for miles and I'd like to spend my weekend with my girl, not putting this bloody place back together after you wreck it." He slings his bar towel over his shoulder. "You'd destroy the whole sodding room and likely not find what you wanted, anyway. I'm cutting out the part that will annoy me."

I don't trust him, but the offer seems fair, and he's spot on.

"Fine, but whatever bartender-patron confidentiality exists had better be good." He shrugs and winks, making me itch to punch something. "I'm looking for details about a big sale. A… guest… of the compound mentioned it and since activity on the internet there gets monitored closely, I'd prefer not to retrieve the information personally."

"That fucking *Forum*," he mutters angrily. "It's all over the dark web, including the neighborhood we share. If you ask me, it's bad news. Something doesn't smell right, even from here. But I know many of my former colleagues are bidding in various neighborhoods."

Feeling vindicated that I was correct, I swallow another sip of the beer before I speak. "Anyone know where or when yet?"

"Nope. That's a big red flag, too. Usually this shit takes months to assemble and by the time someone's advertising, they're ready to run the race. But this time, there's bidding, invitation to audition, auditions, and then acceptance to attend. Every single arm of *Mercatus* is involved. Makes me glad I retired."

"Why?"

"Because nothing that gathers that many criminals and scoundrels in one place ever ends well. Open Markets work because they're focused; this is chaos." He frowns as someone gestures for him at the end of the bar, flipping them off before he continues. "I wouldn't be caught in a casket at this shit, especially because the whispers say they have breathing assets for sale."

Breathing assets? They're selling captured operatives.

"That's a gamble, indeed. All the major players will send representatives to purchase those kinds of jewels."

"Yep." He pauses and studies me for a moment. "You realize your boss has bids in, right?"

My expression shifts to rage and I grip the bottle in my hand to keep from slamming my fist on the bar. "I did not."

"The child who would be king is promising he'll deliver an asset so valuable to everyone, from terrorists to hostile governments. Any idea what the fuck he's planning?"

"Obviously not."

I look around the room, finding Joaquin's eyes and nod. He looks disappointed, but heads out the door of the bar to find my driver. "Thanks for the tip."

"If you ask the little shit, he'll know you're more than what you say. Be cautious, mate."

I grin as I stick my hand out and shake the bartender's. "Don't worry. I have a feeling I won't have to ask. We don't have any prisoners at the moment, and the only person he knows who could steal someone important enough to sell is looking at you."

"*Vaya Con Dios*[1], then."

I nod at him, tossing a tip on the bar and heading into the crowd before he can protest. There's no doubt in my mind I'll get ordered to snatch the person *El Jefe* wants to sell, and I need to be ready for him to approach me.

First thing, I have to notify Dwyn as soon as I know where I'm going; it's time for us to reconnect.

WHEN JOAQUIN STOPS in front of the main house, I hop out, eager to get to my cabin. I don't have a destination for my brother yet, but I want to update him on what the odd bar owner shared. Dwyn will flip out when I tell him he can get out of his hole and into the fray. I smile to myself as we head up the stairs; I almost feel like my normal self.

"*Joaquín! El jefe quiere verlos a usted y al general inmediatamente[2].*"

The slight teen next to me cringes and I watch him react to the summons. He doesn't look like he's thrilled to be in his uncle's presence, nor does he want to be summoned to the big house. Taking pity on him, I look at the hulking form of one of *El Jefe's* house guards. His name is Luis and I'm pretty sure he's the one the maids are frightened of. No wonder Joaquin is shifting on his feet like he's expecting to be beaten.

"He doesn't need to come along. I'll speak with him alone," I bark as I stride forward. It takes everything in me not to roll my eyes at myself. I was just telling myself to stay the fuck out of this so I can slip away to deal with my missing brothers and Living Dead Girl, but now I'm protecting the squirt.

I've been working on easy shit for too long. My edge is fading.

"*No. El jefe quiere hablar con los dos.[3]*"

Fuck. Look what happens when I try to do something good. "Fine. Take us to him so we can get this over with. I'm tired and we have much to do tomorrow."

Luis grunts, turning on his heel to lead us inside. I cut my gaze to my young guide, noting how he's so tense he might take off into outer space. Most of *El Jefe*'s family love sucking up to him, and I expected the same from Joaquin. Even I can be wrong occasionally, I suppose, but this is more extreme than just mere dislike. There's bad blood between them, but the kid's still working here. We cross the living room, heading for the pool area out back, and I groan. This is the last place I want to meet with this jackass.

"Jefe, traje el general y el ratón para usted.[4]*"*

I blink at the nickname, eyeing Joaquin again. When it hits me, I groan. I know why he doesn't like his uncle and why he looks as though he'd prefer to swim in boiling oil rather than be here. It's a problem for later, but at least I know how to play this. "Good evening, *El Jefe.* What can I do for you?"

The slim man in the pile of cushions, women, coke dust, and cigar smoke gives me a slow grin. I've never seen him use his own shit, and I don't know when that changed. His lack of corruption made him more formidable; in fact, it's part of how he could take over this modern empire. Now he's suddenly filling his head with garbage in the same place as his wives and children? My expression tightens, but I don't let him see any other sign of my irritation.

"I have an assignment for you, General. You and my nephew are going to America to retrieve my investment."

---

1. go with God
2. Joaquin! The boss wants to see you and the general immediately
3. No. The boss wants to talk to both of you.
4. Boss, I brought the general and the mouse for you.

VILLAIN

REMY

The mark leads us past the velvet rope and enormous man guarding the door to the VIP lounge. He's chattering away with Lys as she giggles, but my eyes are flitting around the room, taking in the scene. It's a typical luxury room setting—big couches, dim lights, a full bar, hazy air, and the smell of sex and drugs. I couldn't care less what most of the inhabitants are doing, but I need to identify the dangers here before I can assess the situation properly.

In one corner, there's a group of sunglasses-wearing, tattooed men who resemble rappers. I don't know if that means they're *actual* musicians or if they're in another, more dangerous business. The man in the middle of their circle is a man in an Armani suit, with intricate braids and Prada shades. The women are fawning over him and he's sitting back with a glass of amber liquor as he watches the room. That's definitely the boss, no matter what their industry is. It's rowdy in their section, but nothing that concerns me—except his minions are packing heavy firepower. Even good tailoring doesn't hide the large weapons they've chosen, and I frown.

It's a tiny room for those kinds of guns.

As we wind through the lounge, I notice another set of guys who are, without a doubt, Sicilian crowded around the end of the bar. They keep shooting looks at the first group and I sigh internally. Rivals, I'd bet, and that makes this an even worse set-up. The Italians won't be carrying the same sort of weapons, but they'll be good at using what they have. If this goes sideways, they won't care who gets in the middle, either. Their concerns will be the damn lieutenant they've got with them and nothing else.

"Kiki, isn't this just the *coolest?!*"

My head whips to see my friend hanging on the Big Man's arm. Now that he's closer, I can see that he's Middle Eastern, and even hotter than he looked from afar. His gaze is disdainful, and I decide I'll let him live since he first saw me dancing on a pole. However, if he doesn't quit looking at me like I'm a lower life form, I may have to prune some royal family trees. I don't care what his damn net worth is, I won't allow that kind of disrespect. "Yeah, it's super chic. Your friend must be so connected."

The praise makes him sniff, appeased a little. His eyes roam up and down my mostly bare body and he flashes sparkling white teeth. "You're as smart as you are pretty, friend of Veronica."

As if he wasn't looking at me like I had a disease two seconds ago. Gross.

I give him a bright, falsely tipsy smile. "Thank you, Mister... uh, sorry! You didn't give me your name."

His laugh is dark, revealing the cruelty under his smooth outer appearance. "They call me *Il Tasso*, but you may call me Hamid."

It takes every single fiber of my being to stop myself from pulling my faithful wire out of the small slit inside the waistband of my booty shorts. By the time he figured out what I was doing, I could have myself wrapped around his back and the sharp titanium at his jugular. They might kill me afterward, but I could take him out.

"Now, Kiki, say thank you." Lys gives me a pretty smile, pushing her boobs against his suit-covered arm. "Hamid brought us to the most exclusive VIP room in town. He's such a gentleman."

The words clear the fog of rage from my brain and my hand drops to my hip instead of pulling my weapon. "Hell, yes, he did, girl! Hamid, we owe you *big time*."

My gushing makes him puff up, and he gives me a pleased nod as he gestures to the biggest couch. The spot looks like it's been kept unoccupied intentionally. It's situated to face the entire room, giving the people here a clear view of everything going on. Lys follows him, cuddling up next to him on the cushions, while I perch on the arm next to her. I haven't finished checking out the people here and if I don't distract myself from my anger, I'll do something unwise.

Like strangle the asshole who might have information on where Coda is.

A server walks up with a tray full of champagne flutes and I pluck one from it. I won't drink something I haven't seen poured, but I can pretend with the best of them. "Is this Dom or Cristal?"

Hamid gives me an amused look. "It's a 1907 Heidsieck. Don't toss it back like Cold Duck."

Smiling benignly, I bite the inside of my cheek to keep from snapping at the tool. Even if I was a club girl, it's unlikely I would ask which kind of expensive champagne is being served if I was that stupid. He obviously has a low opinion of women—something he shares with his headless ex-employees.

"Delicious!" Lys giggles.

I watch her for a moment after he turns, catching the move she uses fake drinking the shit. Knowing that this bottle probably cost about fifteen hundred dollars and it's being spit out is both amusing and sad. I'd enjoy it if they served it in a less ominous setting, but wasting this dick's money is satisfying, too. "Absolutely. It's going to go right to my head."

One of Hamid's goons snorts, drawing his attention to acting like a big man again. With their focus elsewhere, I'm able to go back to dissecting the rest of this motley crowd. There are two more distinct clusters of people, though one is small. The larger one is a Triad or Yakuza, but I'm not sure which. They have their backs to us, forming a shield around whoever is in charge of their gang, but I doubt there's not someone watching. My eyes flit to the last grouping, getting the sense it's actually the most dangerous.

After all, it's two people in a tank full of crocodiles and they don't seem concerned in the least.

The woman has sun-bronzed skin, a high blondish brown pony-tail, smoky eyes, and leather from head to toe. It's obvious she's strapped to the gills with steel, and no one said a word. Her companion is slumped in the chair with her, his body looking as though it's boneless. He has long platinum hair woven into intri-cate Viking braids and bright blue eyes that seem familiar. Every-thing about him says he's relaxed and content, but I get the sense that would change in a moment if his woman were to be threat-ened. I don't know who they are, but something about them reminds me of people I've seen before.

Shaking my head, I turn away and pretend to sip the stupidly expensive bubbly again. Lys meets my eyes as she drapes herself over *Il Tasso*'s arm, and I frown. If people don't start talking, this shit is going to be a bust. I'm not hanging about all night with this douchebag and his friends if it won't get us closer to our goal. I don't give a shit how damn good his party favors are. I'm about to mutter something only my friend can hear when our host stands, clapping his hands.

"Ladies and gentleman, I am honored by your presence. As you know, the major skill sets represented in the criminal community often look down upon our lines of business. However, we are about to attend a *Forum Romanum* for the first time in over a decade —an event where *our* products are poised to shine."

I arch a brow. Anything can sell well at something like this: art, people, jewels, live shows, real estate, bonds, vehicles, memorabilia… Hell, some disgusting old fucker bought a piece of the Pentagon wall at the last one. It made me sick to look at him, especially with his gleeful expression when he claimed it. I considered doing the world a service by rendering a 'freebie,' but the look on a few of the hitters' faces told me it wasn't necessary. Even good guys turned bad don't like evil that is callous.

Il Tasso smiles at his guests, looking both beneficent and psycho at the same time. "The physical items may fetch handsome prices, but none of them will come close to what we can demand for the things we have gathered over the years. Our offerings range from nubile flesh to workers, prisoners and captives, sacrifices and show pieces. This event will bring our profession into the spotlight we've never been allowed before."

"Exactly how do you intend to accomplish that?" The blond woman looks bored, her brown eyes flat as she crosses her legs. "Exotic animals? Yawn."

I watch them battle with their eyes, but Hamid chuckles and raises his hand. "Yes, The Blade has a point. We cannot bring the usual things like endangered tigers or rare birds. Drugs will not gain us the respect we want. Our stables must be full of the most alluring lots possible for the others to take us seriously. That's why we are meeting here tonight—to discuss what you're bringing from most common to your rarest product."

Now we're talking.

"Excuse me, *Il Tasso*. I hate to interrupt, but why should we share our secrets with everyone else? We don't even know when this will begin." That question comes from the Armani suit. He's taken off his sunglasses and I can see the suspicion on his face like someone drew it with a Sharpie.

"Because we are all criminals, Bull. If we know what the others are bringing, it will cause the ones with the least valuable offerings to up their game. I know well that we all have private collections where we keep some of our priceless conquests. This may be a good occasion to unload any we've grown tired of if they're still in resale condition."

Hamid gives each leader a smile that makes my bones chill and I reach down to squeeze Lys' arm. This motherfucker is using words like 'collection' and 'product,' but he means prisoners and slaves. It's not surprising the top tier operatives in other divisions want nothing to do with these pigs. The illustrious *Il Tasso* is suggesting his contemporaries clean out any people they've grown bored with torturing or assaulting for fuck knows how long by selling them to *new captors* for the cycle to begin again.

"And, of course, if you have merchandise too used to sell, we can use the death mongers to end them in a paid show. Everyone knows the Romans loved a good death match," he says with a loud laugh. The room is silent for a moment, then the laughter spreads. Before long, everyone is chortling and I feel the blank coldness of The Guillotine slipping over me unbidden.

These people deserve to lose their heads.

I frown, that thought disrupting the mental change. Since when I do I give a shit who deserves what? I'm paid to take people out and I do it; I don't judge whether they've earned that death.

"Fine, Badger. I will begin," the man behind the Asian gang says. His guards step back, revealing a tall, handsome man with a sneaky gleam in his eyes. "We will have ten lots of various ages from across Asia and the islands. All are unspoiled and there will be males and females. I also have a few high-end singles who can be purchased for public or private marriages. We have two very special items we acquired from private collectors—unsolved cases whose names will interest buyers. They are used, but in very good condition."

Lys has to be looking at me, but I continue to look bored as I pretend to drink the wine. We can't look as though we understand all the jargon or we'll meet the business end of someone's gun within minutes. None of the groups in here know *Il Tasso* picked us up on the floor and we're not part of his entourage. If they find out, it'll be a free-for-all.

"Your turn, Badger," the man he called Bull says. "Show us some goodwill since the Dragon revealed his hand."

Hamid looks at them all, his smile devious. "If you wish. Like the Dragon, I will have multiple lots of workers and free use product. My team has also trained quite a few brides and grooms that will appeal to those who appreciate partners who do not question the status quo. I also have a select number of offers for those with very specific tastes that will net quite the profit. But the jewels in my crown for this event do not belong to me—I am merely a middleman for their sale. I have a celebrity that will go for outrageous sums, several operatives from various agencies to auction to whoever hates them the most, and one very special lot that is in progress."

Celebrity.

My jaw clenches, but the look in my friend's eyes stops me from rising to murder this motherfucker. I have to remind myself that if I kill him, I won't be able to find Coda and someone will auction him, anyway. Once I have him back, I'm going to take Il Tasso apart slowly and make sure he feels every second—that's a promise.

The Guillotine never goes back on her word.

NIGHTMARE

REMY

"You look like a badass," Lys says as she watches me put the final touches on my new persona.

Her people skills kept me from slaughtering the entire VIP lounge last night, and we ditched Kiki and Veronica on the way home. NYC is amazing for dropping pieces in various dumpsters and cans as you walk the street, so I know they're gone for good. Today, I have to be *Dançarina do fogo* for my meeting with the Admiral. I'm dressed in tight black tactical pants, combat boots, and a tank top woven with Kevlar. The tailor lined my jacket with it as well, and I'm carrying more weapons than I've been able to in days. I hate it, but I have a holster underneath with a Sig—not that you can tell by how the get-up was designed.

Old military dudes won't take you seriously if you don't carry.

Looking in the mirror, I examine the sharp-winged liner, smoky eyes, dark lips, and black hair twisted into a bun at the nape of my neck. This crusty old fart is likely to balk at my gender, but I look professional and dangerous. I'd have no problem using the thin blade tucked in my back to gut someone, fancy tea room be damned. Finding out some cockwaffle playing at being a king has Coda Ramone—*my Coda Ramone*—locked up to sell like a prize bull at a county fair is pushing any semblance of 'normal' out of my brain.

"Remy, you can't let this throw you."

Whipping my head around, I look at my friend with a gaze so intense she shrinks a bit. "For *years*, I dreamed of their deaths at my hand. Betraying me to Arnaud, who then betrayed me to the High Legion… The things they would have done to me if I did not convince them I was dead are *unspeakable*, Elysium. I deal in death and torture as a career, but I've never done the things they did to Rinna when they caught her. I truly believed nothing could change the fury that seeped into my being at what they did."

She stops working on her wig, looking at me quietly as she waits.

"After I tracked down Arnaud, I believed I was still broken and wouldn't survive if I didn't deal with it. But… time marched on. I tried to fix myself, but all I learned is that I am perfectly suited for my profession without changing a thing. The anger at The Five went into a box from the past because I didn't need it anymore."

Lys frowns and murmurs, "Until Paris, right?"

I nod, leaning into the mirror to work on my eyebrows. "Yes. Deciding to save Coda threw my organized black and white world into colorful chaos. Then the fucking Douche started emailing me and the boxes popped open for the first time in over a decade. I found it ironic that I'd get paid to avenge myself with one of them, so I took the job, despite misgivings."

"Didn't go as planned, did it?" My friend grins, finally getting the red-haired bob on straight.

"Nope. I got invested in figuring out how Raz got a hit put out on him, and apparently, my ex-friends chased me cross- continent. We both know how my accidental meetings with Dwyn and Jinx went. I still can't believe I didn't—" I feel my cheeks get hot and I grumble. *"Les Invisibles* have brought in some really top tier surgeons since I died. It's embarrassing as hell."

She giggles, using a sponge to create a dusting of freckles across her nose and cheeks. "They didn't figure you out, either. I think that embarrassment is a shared venture, girl."

Mollified, I reach down to grab the titanium chopsticks and shove them into my bun. "True. Not to mention how much bone structure changes from teens to your thirties, I suppose. Anyway, once I understood I'd stumbled into some idiotic villain plot involving The Five, I didn't have time to sort out how I… felt… about it. Then shit went bananas, and now?"

"And now…"

"And now I'm filled with so much irrational fury that I consider leaving a bloodbath everywhere I go. The part of me that fuels The Guillotine is long past caring about anything but retribution. Not at *them*, but at the people who *dare* to take deaths that are mine, should I choose. I'm owed their pain, their sorrow, their regret, and even their lives if I wish it. I will allow no one on this planet to steal that right from me."

Her lips quirk as she looks at me via the mirror. "What about their love, Stabby Pants? Does that belong to you, too?"

I blanch, blinking at the mirror in panic. "What? No!"

"You fucked the *shit* out of two of them. Are you so dense that you think the other three will stand for that?" Lys lines her lips in nude, sighing as my facial features do awkward dances. "Nothing you've said to me is the reaction of someone who solely wants revenge. No, Remy, you want groveling, and then you want their souls. That won't happen if you kill them."

"Just because I'm a girl doesn't mean—"

"It has *nothing* to do with being a girl, and *everything* to do with being in love with them before you supposedly died. Shit like that doesn't go away and you've been transferring it to hate to get by."

This is way too much emotional shit for me to deal with before a meet.

"I… No, I don't!" We look at each again, and I can tell she's trying not to laugh at my flustered blurt. "Lys, we have to focus on this stupid job. Stay out of my head."

She shrugs, her smile knowing as she smacks her lips. "Fine. But you're being an idiot and I'm only stopping while we go chat up this old fool. I'm not scared of you anymore, Remy Arsine Benoit. You might be able to gut me with a butter knife, but I know your weakness."

This is why I don't allow people to live, if you're wondering—they get mouthy.

"You need to understand, missy, that I take my little girl's safety seriously." The silver-haired man gives me a stern look over the table, but it doesn't ruffle me. I'm sure he's scared the boxers off many a sailor in his day; however, until you've looked a man like The Commandant in the eye and lied, you don't know what intimidation is.

My former leader is tall, bald, imposing, and wears an eyepatch over an old injury that never healed correctly. He's every bit the sharp, no-nonsense dictator who rules with an iron fist. He doesn't speak until necessary and even then, it's not much. His eye is constantly taking in his surroundings, calculating the situation like a fucking robot. You can't read his expression, even if he's enraged, because his face is an indifferent mask.

That's a man who has a snowball's chance in hell of making me waiver—not this soft, old soldier.

"I appreciate that, Admiral. As the former head of NATO, you're uniquely positioned to have your family or acquaintances targeted for nefarious purposes." He harrumphs, but I cut him off before he can ramble on again. "However, my resume is packed with high-value targets such as your daughter. I've kept them safe for the duration of my assignment without fail. I may not look like the guard you envisioned, but I assure you, she is safe under my watch."

"Constance is headstrong, *Dançarina*. She will fight you tooth and nail—in fact, since puberty, she's made it a game to evade every detail she's ever had. It doesn't matter if they're male or female, green or experienced. My daughter does not understand the dangers that face her because of my former position. She puts herself in peril with an abandon only seen in youth, though by now, I'd hoped she would grow out of it."

My lips quirk up a little. That's every teen to early twenty-year-old in history, particularly ones with strict upbringings and constant surveillance. He's no different from a President or Mafia Don. They all have trouble keeping their children safe until they can either defend themselves or land somewhere safe enough to protect them. "Admiral, I have hunted people for a living. Someone in my profession doesn't only guard marks; we frequently accept positions on the other side of the coin. That's why you reached out to a less than legitimate source for this event, yes? You could have hired private security firms, including PMCs. Instead, you chose someone who operates in the shadows, like me."

He clears his throat, looking away for a moment, then stares me directly in the eyes. "I did. Not only because Constance is wily, but because the threats we've received are more than your normal stalker behavior. I believe she is in mortal danger from sources who are after more than state secrets. They want her for her value to me, perhaps in response to an operation I was part of many years ago. I've been involved with SEAL teams and incursions all over the world. The list is lengthy and most of it is classified, so I cannot provide you with options."

"That's not a problem. I operate under the assumption that everyone, even people your daughter has known for years, could be compromised until I know otherwise." I fold my hands on the table in front of me, looking at him confidently. "The world you are concerned about has people ranging from clowns to consummate professionals who will have planned every permutation and possibility in their scheme. We don't know which you are facing, so I will behave as though the highest threat is what she faces."

He nods sharply, his expression revealing slight relief. "Excellent. I shall call Constance over now that my concerns have been satisfied."

If only mine were.

"I need you to tell me why you're hiring me now and for this event. You may not be able to guide me towards specific threats, but you can inform what circumstances led you to change your usual tactics." Out of the corner of my eye, I see Lys sitting by a window with her hand in a thumbs up by her waist. She must see the girl coming, so this needs to be quick.

Once he's finished sending a text, the Admiral looks at me frankly. "This event is not a military or political one where the added security for my colleagues or higher-ranking officials makes me feel more secure. Instead, there will be event security and that of celebrities and influencers that I do not trust. Constance will wear something insane that has no room for personal weapons, though I'll have an alarm with a tracker placed in her jewelry."

My eyes narrow and I tilt my head. "Now the 'why,' sir. Yes, the event is less guarded, but I assume she's been at much less public spectacles without someone like me watching. What spooked you?"

"We received a package last week at our home. It's a guarded secret that is not accessible through normal methods. It would take a very skilled hacker who can break the Department of Defense encryption to find it." He sucks in a breath, looking at his hands, and I can see the father rather than the soldier. "It contained a freshly detached tongue. DNA tests revealed it was from Constance's roommate from college. She hadn't even been reported missing."

I pause, pursing my lips. A rich girl, likely from a connected family, doesn't disappear for days without an alarm being raised. That means the tongue was cut and sent very close together—a conclusion I'm sure the man in front of me made. "Why not the F.B.I.?"

"Because they have to follow procedure. You can do any and everything necessary to keep my daughter safe, even if it falls outside of the law."

I'll be damned; he's not fucking around.

"Understood. Constance will remain the priority regardless of other damage." He knows I'm saying I'll kill anyone who gets in my way without fail, and I know he's silently complicit in that agreement. "Is that her?"

Both of our gazes move to a gorgeous blond in her mid—twenties dressed like she just stepped off the runway. She glares at me as if I offended her ancestors, then talks into the phone pressed to her ear as she sits down. Her hand is up to keep me from talking and I arch a brow at her father. He has the grace to look sheepish, which I'd bet he's been doing her entire life.

Smirking, I reach over and snatch the phone, dumping it in the middle of the table. "My name is Hester Kiehl, and I'll be your protection for the gala. The first thing you should know is that unlike any other detail you've had in the past, I can and will knock you out to keep you safe. I will do whatever is required to prevent you from coming to harm and I don't give a rat's ass if you like it, princess. You're mine until Sunday morning, so get used to it."

Her fury is clear, but her father has to hide his pleased expression behind a cough.

We're off to a good start, then.

OUTLAWS AND OUTSIDERS

MO

OUR FLIGHT LANDS ON A PRIVATE STRIP IN WESTCHESTER COUNTY. *El Jefe* refused to allow Joaquin and I to fly in as normal passengers—something I believe would have raised less red flags. He certainly could purchase identities, but he bribed people and sent us to this damn private airstrip. I don't like being beholden to some random fucker the drug lord knows; if we have issues, he can dime us out in a flash. That would leave us stranded in the country until we found another route back.

Messy and I don't like it.

"Where are we headed first, General?"

Sighing, I lug the bags out of the hold, handing the kid his. I have very little, but he's too green to realize he shouldn't travel to a country illegally with more than what he can carry while running. It's not my place to teach him, but it affects me, so I growl, "Somewhere to ditch your ridiculous amount of shit, then we'll head to Manhattan to meet my contact."

His brow furrows. "*El Jefe* didn't say we were meeting anyone."

"That's because he doesn't know my contact. If that makes you uncomfortable, you can stay at the crash pad." I flick an annoyed glare at him, but I know I need to offer to let him opt out of defying his master.

"No. No, I want to come with you." He looks up at me with his chest puffed out and I bite back a groan.

I do not need a criminal duckling imprinting on me.

"Fine." I haul my duffle, striding over to the sleek black SUV waiting for us. I haven't been to New York for a couple of years, but I haven't forgotten how to get around. This thing likely has GPS and a tracker our friend in South America can watch, so we'll find another way into the city after we drop our stuff. I don't intend to stay on the outskirts, anyway; hopefully everything in that stupid suitcase he's got can be replaced. "Get in."

Hopping in, I turn the radio on, discouraging him from talking as we head out of the tiny airport. We have a small window before it's time to complete our objective, and I need to see Dwyn.

I need to know why we're here to kidnap an admiral's daughter.

AFTER A BRIEF PIT stop to get rid of the extra baggage, Joaquin and I take the train into the city. We get off at 125th Street in Harlem, then take the subway to Union Square and on to Bleecker Street. I'd prefer to take a less direct route, but we're pressed for time. I don't know how long we'll be able to evade the watchful gaze of our benefactor before our absence gets noted. The bar is tucked deep in the Village on a side street, so I wind around the crowds of tourists, college students, and workers quickly.

"When I'm meeting with the contact, you stay where I put you. Do not approach and do not draw attention to yourself. You shouldn't even look my way, to be honest."

"But…"

"No 'buts,' Joaquin. This contact is dangerous and not prone to playing nice with others." I have to fight to keep the grin off of my face because Dwyn is definitely both things. He wouldn't hurt the kid on sight, but he's also been living off grid for months with no one to help calm his crazy. My old friend is probably almost feral with no one to distract him from the nervous energy that rules his life.

He nods and I wind my way through the dense crowd of people in the crowd. This place is typically full, as it's a safe ground to meet those of different skill sets to discuss jobs. I've known the owner since we were young; he's one of the few *LI* operatives who weren't High Legion to be allowed to leave the island. My eyes light on the tall, rugged blond man with the look of a Viking behind the bar. His lips curl into a smirk and he tilts his head so slightly it's barely noticeable. I nod, moving in the direction he indicated to find my brother.

I'll have to be social with Tyr later.

Dwyn is in the back, his eyes on a group of people playing pool. His fingers twitch around his tequila and I know my guess about his ADHD was correct. My friend has a hard time controlling his impulsivity with people around to help, but alone, he's probably stolen half of Tokyo without leaving a trace. He'll never admit it; he knows the FUBAR protocol rules. But I guarantee the break-in at the tech firm is the least of what he's been doing since he escaped the blast.

"D," I say as I approach. I don't want to wig him out when he's on high alert. Like me, he may look engrossed in the pool game, but he's hyper aware of his surroundings, especially in this state.

He looks up, almost knocking his chair over, as he rushes forward to crush me in a hug. I blink, patting his back awkwardly as I try to process this response. He squeezes me again, then lets go to lead me over to his booth without a word.

Talk about hot and cold.

"Mo-Mo, this shit is so fucked," he murmurs, his gaze landing on mine. There's hurt in it and it occurs to me that for the first time in a long time, Dwyn is allowing himself to feel emotions that go deeper than surface level. "First, we find out she's not fucking dead, then some knobgobblers try to blow us all up, and then we have to split... but you're the only one I've found. I've been hunting as best I can without raising flags. I know; I know. I'm not *supposed* to, but fuck."

My eyes widen as he rambles on at the speed of light. I clear my throat when he pauses, my expression serious. "It's a lot to take in, and it's not over."

"Hell, no, it's not! I'm going to find the motherfucker who set that bomb and dismember them with a fucking spoon. I'll hand them from their feet and shock their balls with a generator. No, I'm going to *flay* them with a rusty pair of scissors. Wait, no, maybe I'll de-vein them while they're still alive. Yeah, all while they're alive... that's the ticket..."

"Dwyn." The one word stops his manic rant. "We'll make them pay when it's time. But for now, we have other issues. What did you find out about my target?"

The thief pouts, his knife sliding out of his sleeve so he can spin it on his palm. "Fine, ruin my fun, Mo-Mo. Nice to know you're still a stick in the mud."

I glare at him, my fists clenching on the table. "*Dwyn.*"

"Okay, okay." He holds up his free hand in surrender. "The girl is a socialite. She's an easy mark because she ditches her guards all the time. Everyone from dealers to gossip rags can get to her with ease. You shouldn't have to work hard to snatch her."

My brow arches and I frown. "What makes her valuable, outside of money?"

"Her dad's some ex-big wig admiral. Used to work at NATO, but it's been years. He might have intel that's old, but nothing that would get someone access to shit now." D shrugs, flicking the knife back and forth through his fingers like a psycho. "I suppose they could auction her for the money alone, but there are easier targets who would net more. Feels like your *boss* plans to sell her to bad guys for vengeance, not strategy."

Clasping my hands together, I think about that for a moment. It's conceivable a career Navy officer might have been involved in operations that touched *El Jefe*'s part of the world. His rank and the trajectory of his career tell me he was likely a SEAL himself, which means he'd be a natural to command covert incursions once he climbed the ladder. Central and South America have been CIA hotspots for decades—not to mention non-governmental operatives like those from *LI* or The Company. There might be a connection, however tenuous.

"She's collateral damage, then." D nods and I think about that. "I don't have a choice, though, Dwyn. I have to abduct her and hand her over to the contact waiting in the city. If I don't, we'll lose our way into the *Forum*."

He gives me a dark look. "Not if we tap our own accounts. We'll get invited on principle, even if we didn't bid. You know I'm right."

"Of course we will, you nit. But we can't risk anyone knowing we're alive. If Coda or Jinx or Raz are in trouble, letting the world know we're still kicking will put them on guard. We need them to be complacent and make mistakes. Even the most skilled snatchers relax when no one goes looking; if any of them are going up on the block, we have to be invisible until then."

"What about our girl?" His expression is fierce and I know he won't back down on this.

Sighing, I run my hand through my hair. "Fuck, D, I don't know. We'll be lucky if she doesn't kill us herself. The Remy we knew has been gone for years and The Guillotine isn't known for forgiveness."

"You've always been a hopeless dipshit with her," he growls. "Let me tell you something, Mauricio Battaglia. I let you fools convince me when we were kids, but this time, I won't get swayed. I've tasted heaven and I won't deny myself ever again. Remy Benoit can make me crawl through fucking glass naked on my hands and knees—and I'll do it. I'll dive in front of a bullet for her, grovel for her… hell, I'll even wear a goddamn ball gown if she asks. But I will *not* let go of that woman again. *Capito, idiota?*"

I'll be a pasta-slurping son of a bitch; he means it.

"I get it, D. Maybe I don't understand because, unlike you and Jinx, I haven't had a moment with her." I frown, waving my hand when he protests. "I don't mean sex, per se. You both interacted with her before and during, plus she left you clues to find her. There was some sort of connection and the rest of us only have her smart mouthed display at the zoo to go on. It was hot as fuck, but then someone tried to turn us into road ketchup."

Dwyn is quiet, but his knife spins on his palm like a top as he thinks about what I said. This is the best way he can control the hyperactivity when he's sitting; I know because I've had to hole up with the idiot before. The only one who comes close to that level of spiky, nerve-wracking vibes is Coda. The thought of our other friends makes my gut clench and I have to grit my teeth. I share D's lust for violence, especially if any of them have been harmed. But after we lost Remy, I took the reins as leader and I can't allow my emotions to rule me like the others do.

"Fine. I found cover for us to get into this shindig. I'm faking press creds and you're on security. The lack of thorough checks on the contracted staff was appalling, considering the guest list." He stops playing with his weapon and rests his palms on the table. "Your boss picked the least secure event the chick's been to all year. He must be connected up here."

In other words, he's got someone in law enforcement doing his dirty work.

"Good to know. I'll keep my eyes peeled for anyone who seems to watch too closely." I blink, remembering Joaquin suddenly. "I need another cover. Something simple. *El Jefe* sent a tag-a-long to make certain I followed his orders."

"But you're here."

I shrug and grin. "You fuckers aren't the only ones who can schmooze marks. I prefer to use my fists, but my tongue works fine."

His eyebrows bob. "That'll make our girl happy. Noted."

Groaning, I let out an exasperated breath. "Don't push, asshole. I'm not laying a finger on her—if she's alive—until we hash out the past. Sex makes things more complex, not less."

"Tell that to my dick. He's practically smitten."

"What a surprise."

KILLING BOYS

REMY

"Run it again."

My friend glares at me as she bats my hand away from my face. "You are a tyrant. Is it because you've got some weird, unknowable instinct about this job?"

Frowning, I put my hands on the arms of the chair and wrap my fingers around them. *I hate being this far out of control, even for a short time.* "Just because I'm letting you do my face doesn't mean you can boss me around. Run it again."

She sighs, blowing an annoyed breath through her lips like a raspberry before leaning in to shade the shadow along the waterline of my right eye. "*Fine.* You arrive at the Admiral's brownstone at twenty-one thirty. I'm supposed to trail behind you, but stay far enough back that I won't get seen."

"Yes. Go on."

Lys moves to my left eye before she continues. "Once the SUVs head for the venue, I stay on your tail until they pull away from the front door. You and the prissy princess head inside while I sneak in through the sub-basement. I get there via access in the restaurant next door; they have a loose back wall."

I blink eyes as she holds a cotton swab under the lashes she just coated in mascara. So far, her recitation is on point. But if I'm going to trust her to stay safe so I can focus, I need to hear it until I'm certain. "I'll be with her until she tries to ditch me, then I'll have to dash about until I find her again. What do you do after you get inside?"

Her groan is music to my ears. This is what Mo used to do to me when we were young.

"I take the underground access tunnels until I find the freight elevator. Take it to the ground floor, head down the hall and open the closet where you put the catering uniform. Put it on and then I can mingle while I watch your back."

I nod before she fusses with the raven wig, making sure she braided the long locks into a tight crown that's both beautiful and functional. "Exactly. You play your persona while you hand out cocktail weenies or whatever. I'll try to keep this brat from tarnishing my reputation and making her father lose his mind. Maybe we'll overhear something about the *Forum*, too, and that would be the icing on the cake. Simple enough, usually, but nothing has been easy since those idiots resurfaced."

Her lips curl, and she gives me a knowing look. "Open your mouth so I can work on your lips." I comply and she looks even happier. "Now you can't snark back at me. You can bitch and gripe all you like, but you made the choice to save that tool. Despite the risk and the past, your brain engaged and saved Coda Ramone. I don't care what you say; that means something, and he's not even the one you fucked!"

She's right; I can't fault her logic.

"I didn't know who they—"

"Stop. Talking."

Her voice is fierce, so I position myself for application again. Lys feathers a liner over the edges of my mouth, continuing her rant. "I know you didn't know who Jinx or Dwyn were when it happened. Though, honestly, there's a case to be made for people whose souls seem to call to one another, so they just come back together over and over. You probably don't believe in that because it's not fact based, but I do so shut it."

Blinking, I wait for her to pull back, then nod. "Okay. So if your touchy-feely shit is true, I was always going to collide with them again, no matter what I did."

"Absolutely," she says. "So, what's it going to take for you to forgive them?"

Fuck if I know. I've been asking myself that for months.

"I really don't know if I can, even if I'd like to. There's nothing that will change what happened; their explanations will only clarify the 'why' and 'how.' What's done is done—they chose wrong, and I almost died. Everything changed after that."

"Don't be dense, Remy. Of course, you can't fix the past. But it made you who you are now, and I think this Remy is better than the one who would have spent her life running from *LI*. You may have hidden behind an alias for privacy, but you could make a name for yourself. That wouldn't have happened if you and those stupid boys got off the island as teens."

"What you're not saying is we probably would have gotten killed within the first year, " I say wryly.

"Indubitably." She winks at me and steps back. "I think you're ready."

I'd better be. Failure is not in my vocabulary.

"I CANNOT BELIEVE my father hired some underworld goon to follow me…"

Constance has been yammering into her phone since we got into the SUV. She's dressed in a floaty, barely there gown and four-inch heels. Every inch of her looks polished, primped, and primed to make trouble for me. I don't know which vapid friend she's talking to, so I look through my dark glasses at her in the mirror as our escort drives. This shit is why I never wanted to work much in Mo's world—I can't be arsed to throw myself in the line of fire for people so self-absorbed that they refuse to protect themselves.

My charge is absolutely that type of job; I would have walked away if it wasn't for the connection to the Forum.

"Constance, you need to get off the damn phone. Your father wants to keep you safe and staying on the line of an active cell phone is asking for trouble."

She ignores me, and I draw in a steadying breath. The driver gives me a look that says he knows what I'm going through, so I guess Little Miss Society here gives all the employees shit. I don't care if it's only me, but knowing it isn't tells me a lot about how this evening will go. Constance will enter like the emperor without clothes. People will coo at her, then she'll attempt to get rid of me. No one will correct her, though they likely know she's being unsafe. After that, I'll spend the entire event chasing her to make sure I can do my job while she tells her friends how stupid I am.

This is probably how every single person who's tried to help her has gotten treated throughout her life. With her father absent and no mention of a mother, I assume this is her way of getting attention and taking control of her life. Unfortunately for her, I grew up in far less pleasant circumstances with much more controlling authority figures. I don't give a *fuck* what abandonment issues she has; she's a mission and I'll complete it even if I have to hogtie her to a fucking chair.

Turning in my seat, I grab the phone from her, pitching it out the window with a smirk. "Oops."

"My father will—"

"Probably give me a bonus for disconnecting you from that damn thing. Your friends will see you when we arrive. There's no need to chatter with them from end to end all damn day."

"Frigid bitch," she mutters.

My fingers itch as they clasp the lipstick sized wire in my pocket. It would break my rules, but I could convince myself this snot faced shit deserves to be put out of her misery. She obviously appreciates nothing and treats everyone as though they're below her. I could make the case for killing her and simply turning this job into surveillance, but it wouldn't give me the invite to the damn *Forum* without using one of my more well-known identities.

Goddamn it. Logic wins again.

I ignore her comment, pretending to be a mentally stable adult who doesn't slit people's throats for that kind of offense on the regular. No need for her to realize how close to home it strikes, given I have partaken of nothing other than self-pleasure for months. It's not like me, but I couldn't bring myself to chase the usual one-night stress relief with the guys out there. Gritting my jaw in irritation, I admit to myself that it didn't feel right to do so until I hash it out with The Five. It's yet another weird moral line invading my life that has never been a concern before.

Why do men ruin even the simple pleasures in life without trying?

"You can hate me all you want, Constance. My allegiance isn't to you or your whims; your father hired me to keep you safe at an event where your safety is in question. I'll do whatever it takes to succeed—regardless of whether it makes you bitter and catty. I don't want or need your approval."

There's a chuckle in the earpiece and I know Lys has been eavesdropping from her vehicle as she tails us. I haven't seen her which impresses me—but now I know she's definitely online and ready to roll. Satisfied with that knowledge and my takedown of the baby queen bee, I go back to mentally reviewing the layout of the event space in my head. The blueprints appear in my mind like a 3D hologram, turning and moving as I go over every corner, stairwell, and nook. I need to examine them in person as Constance wanders around, putting in facetime. I won't feel in control until I visually inspect each problem area and verify they won't be an issue.

"We're here."

I nod at the driver, glaring at my charge in the rearview mirror. "Stay put until I open your door. He won't unlock it until I give the signal, so you might as well pout now."

The socialite huffs as I exit the SUV, and when the door closes, I look up at the surrounding buildings. There aren't any telltale glints of barrels or binoculars, but I do a sweep around the entire length of it just in case. When I feel certain it's safe to allow her out, I wave at the driver, opening her door when he releases the locks. Constance steps out, all big sunglasses and blond hair as she looks around in the typical bored celebrity fashion. She finally moves out of the way after cameras whirr with enough pictures to last a lifetime and I close the car door, tapping the roof so our escort can go park.

"Let's go," I mutter at her. She's still posing and though I didn't see any dangers, I'm not a fan of the exposure in this red carpet nonsense the event runners have set up. "You're too accessible out here and—"

My voice cuts off when a small, weasely looking man breaks through the barriers and runs up the brat, shouting her name. Moving quickly, I grab his wrist, twisting it until he hits the ground with a howl of pain. Bending, I lean into his face and snarl, "Who the fuck are you, and do you have a death wish?"

"Oh, my god!" Constance wails as she stomps her foot. "Let him go, you psycho. That's Dante, my publicist."

Is this bitch fucking kidding me?

I don't let go; I merely turn my head to look at her like I'm Linda goddamn Blair in *The Exorcist*. "You knew he was meeting you here and didn't *tell* me? Are you out of your fucking *mind?*"

She sniffs and shrugs. "It's not my job to tell you shit."

Twisting the guy's wrist until I hear it snap, I give her a feral grin. "If you don't want your people to end up corpses, it actually *is*, little girl. Show me some ID, publicist, or this wrist won't be the last thing I break."

His eyes widen, and he whimpers, but complies. Fumbling with his free hand, he comes up with a wallet and I flip it open to confirm his name. I'm still uncertain he's what they say he is—I've seen plenty of industry people in my time and this guy does not look like one—but I nod. My grip on him releases and I rise, giving the girl I'm here to protect a cool look.

"You'd better think long and hard about how much you want to fight me on this. The people your father hired in the past are honorable—bound by ethics and oaths in their former careers that I neither subscribe to nor allow to guide me. In my line of work, amongst my peers, I act under our professional standards. I can assure you they are not pretty, but they are effective. It's not a joke when I say you will get someone killed if you don't stop playing around."

Constance studies me for a moment, gauging my honesty, then nods sharply. "Fine. He's my dealer and once we're done, he'll scram. I don't have any other surprise visitors, but I can't control who might know me and come into my personal space. I'm very popular."

Rolling my eyes, I mutter to myself internally about what her definition of popular likely entails. Rich brats like her attract bottom feeding sycophants all the time and I'm going to weed out which ones are possible threats when they attach themselves inside. "Take your nose candy and let's go. I want to get inside before anything else happens."

Or before I take you out myself and have to make excuses to your pathetic excuse for a parent.

MADNESS

CODA

The tension in this place has amped up exponentially.

While I've been allowed regular bathing and more robust meals, each time I'm outside of my room, I can feel the atmosphere getting more anticipatory. The guards remain faceless and silent, but in those exposed moments, I catch whispers from other areas and sounds I didn't hear before. I believe they've got more prisoners here now and they've had to expand their staff to cover the workload. More people shuffle about in neutral, bland clothing with masks, moving from place to place in the eerie quiet.

"Whoever this is has been planning this operation for a long time. They have money, influence, and resources," I mumble to myself as I pace back and forth. "They aren't concerned about reprisals if someone finds out an operative such as me got detained, and they don't give a shit what I can tell them—only that I'm in condition to be delivered to someone else."

That doesn't leave a lot of known groups to speculate on.

The Company has been in a negotiated detente with *LI* for several years. They operate opposite of us, but don't directly attack us unless we interfere with their jobs. There's a lot of competition for the bids on *Mercatus*, and operatives routinely snatch targets from one another, but no one looks to take the other side out. *Il Noche* refused a treaty, but they steer clear of the other two because their provenance and reach are bigger. I don't think either of them arranged a secret *Forum*; in fact, I think they'd announce it to the entire underworld if they were doing so. So would The Commandant—he's a consummate egomaniac and wouldn't allow anyone else to take the credit.

"Then who the *fuck* is this? Even before the damn bomb, there wasn't even a *whisper* of a new player on that level. This is batshit insane."

I can only imagine the leaders of the established organizations losing their shit in big, fancy rooms full of minions right now. Guys like Razzie are probably living on Monster and meth, so they can hack twenty-four-seven to locate the douchebags who fucked up the natural order in our darkened corners of the world. If they didn't trap me here, I'd probably be in interminable amounts of Zoom calls discussing our progress on locating the fucks.

Wait a tick… I think I found one positive thing about being kidnapped and held captive—no fucking meetings.

Chuckling to myself, I run my hand through my hair as I count backwards from a hundred. I need to engage the thinking part of my brain so I can continue puzzling out this shit. I feel the anxiety about the others rising and my blood pressure spiking as I head into a hyper period. That won't help me at all, and I have to stay focused. The minute I get an opening, I'm getting the hell out of here, and I can't do that if I'm not prepared.

Suddenly, I hear a noise outside my door. It's muffled, but it's definitely the sound of someone being led past my room. They're struggling and the jackholes are having trouble keeping them in line. I run to the door, peeking out the window to see what's going.

I don't want it to be anyone I know, but I also can't stand to not know.

I watch the thrashing person carefully, noting the red hair and pale skin of a guy that seems familiar. It's not one of The Five, nor it is Remy; I know that because these guards aren't trained for people with our skills. Any of them, even Raz, would have gotten out of the crowd of dipshits and made mayhem by now. This guy is putting up a good fight, but he's not a match for the ghouls who work here.

"I'll kill you all, you faceless arseholes! Wait until my agent hears about this. You're going to jail for the rest of all time. Let me go!"

My brows arches and I blink. *That's* where I know this dude from—he's the lead singer of an emerging punk band I looked into last year. I liked their sound and considered having them open for me on the next tour. Liam's a good-looking guy and he'd definitely fetch a good price in a trafficking auction. I guess the leader of this operation isn't simply accumulating operatives, but valuable, one-of-a-kind products for extremely wealthy bidders. People who would have to be kept in complete secrecy to prevent their presence from being reported—unless you killed them when you got done with them.

Oh, that's going to work out so poorly for these motherfuckers.

Mo and Remy's status are unknown, but if there's even a chance either of them figures out this shit is going on, it's going to be a bloodbath. I've never met two people who are more rigid about this line of work in my entire life, even as teens. I highly doubt Remy has changed her stance on it since she 'died,' and after seeing the rage in her at the zoo?

Someone's going to die slow and painful if she sets foot in that auction.

My lips curve and I pad over to my bed, flopping down on it to think about that little scenario. The girl I knew long ago grew up into a lethal, sexy as fuck killing machine and it's not a turnoff in the slightest. I'm a little jealous of Jinxy and Dwyn for getting the first taste, but I can wait in line. I never had an issue with sharing versus being a super, over-the-top controlling dickweasel.

That was Mo, and I guarantee it's part of why he was so eager to believe that snake oil salesman, Arnaud. We'd planned the escape for *months*, spinning every single variable until we were blue in the face. But that jackass came to us while Remy was out planting the explosives and Mo folded like a house of cards. Jinx was next, and I joined them when the evidence of discovery was clear, but D and Raz fought us hard.

It explains why Raz was so damn angry he put a gun to her head in that classroom.

"None of this matters if you end up a slave in someone's pleasure dungeon," I mutter to myself as I stack my hands behind my head. "Get serious about freeing yourself, Ramone. That's what she'd say, and she's right."

Time to stop muddling through and make shit happen before I lose the chance forever.

A LOUD BANG WAKES ME, and I sit up so quickly I almost fall off the cot.

Scrambling to the door, I crane my neck, trying to see where that noise came from. The angle is bad and I curse when I can't see the origin. It was close, and it's the most sound I've heard in a long time. I don't know if Liam was giving someone trouble again, or if this was a new person, but it was definitely the sound of a struggle. It only takes a moment for me to decide. I bang on my door, echoing the noise I heard.

"Hey, you royal fuckwads! Let us out of here. You want money? They'll pay a ransom."

I haven't tried this method yet because no one fucking talks, but what the hell can it hurt?

My door opens so quickly I almost lose my balance and a large goon in a weird mask looks at me. I assume he's making an angry face, but I can't see it, so I grin. "There you are, buddy. Look, I need to talk to whatever asshat is in charge here. You know who I am and I guarantee if this is about money, I can get you a sweet deal. There's no need for you to waste time on preparing me for some auction—"

The guys hauls off and decks me, ringing my bell pretty good. I'm out of practice with sparring, not entirely healed from detox, and they didn't start giving me real food until recently. Honestly, it's lucky I didn't drop like a sack of fucking potatoes. Good thing Mo loves to make a point with his fists and we all solve our disagreements with brawls. The muscle memory has to be what saved me from keeling over like a little bitch.

"Damn, man," I groan as I spit blood on the floor. "You'd think I called your mama fat. I offered to *pay* you; most people don't see that as a punch worthy offense."

My response doesn't phase the bulky sentry; he simply yanks me forward into the hallway without a word. Blinking as I half walk, half stumble along with the guard, I try to get a better look at the scenery. At the end of my hallway, there's a central area with molded metal picnic tables, but no one sitting at them. Corridors branch off the circular room in six directions, so I assume there's space for a damn lot of people if these fuckers choose to hold them.

Are they just a new trafficking ring making a big splash as they enter the scene?

"Sorry if you're not a dude. I can't tell with the mask and lumpy scrub shit you're wearing. I wouldn't know if you were Grimace, to be truthful. Even before you blurred my vision with your fist it wasn't obvious. Though, I don't *think* I remember your shape. I was pretty fucked up for the first month, though. Detox is a bitch, amirite?"

I'm babbling to see if I can even get a tiny response, but so far, nothing. Do they have these people on sedatives to dull their senses, too? That can't be it because it would fuck up their reaction time and this moron hit me within seconds. I growl a little, knowing this shit is *not* my gift, and if I could just keep myself level, I'd be able to put the pieces together better.

Wait. Keep myself together.

"Are you assholes drugging me again? What's the fucking point? Detox me from the fun stuff and let me rot while I almost die, then ignore me for two months, and now you're slipping mickeys in my food? What is your game?"

Beige Grimace doesn't answer. They simply drag me down a hall until we reach the room with the shower. The door opens and I'm handed off to a skinny pencil person who pulls me inside. Whatever they gave me isn't too strong because it's making me slower, but doesn't send me to outer space. The captor pushes me to the bathroom, handing me a new pile of scrubs, then clicks the door shut.

I don't get this place or these people at all. Nothing about how they behave is like normal kidnappers—not ransom snatchers, not pimps, not information extractors… no one does this crap. I think about Liam, tilting my head as I turn the hot water on. Is it possible this ring is only taking celebs? This could have nothing to do with *LI*, and I'm here simply because of my tight ass. That would be kind of a hoot, and I'd never hear the end from Mo, but it's also a hell of a lot safer.

"Who would put together a group focused on grabbing the most recognizable people in the world? Huge risk, huge reward—but also labor intensive and hard to maintain without drawing attention."

Mumbling to myself as I step in the spray and soap up, I let my brain wander to my brothers. Jinx would have tried talking his way out a while ago, but obviously, that's a dead end. Dwyn would have dismantled something to pick the lock and then made a break for it. Who knows what they would have done, but he would have been out of the cell within a day. Mo would have watched long enough to make a plan, then beat the shit out of a guard to make his play. Razzie… I'm not sure what he'd do without a connection to the internet. Maybe he'd convince them he could get them money if they gave him access? He definitely could, and it might have worked.

"But you had to spend an entire month getting healthy again because you're a fuck-up," I mutter. "You've been avoiding life since she died and now you're paying for it. That's why Jinxy and Dwyn got first crack; the universe knows you've been a screw up for a decade."

Oh, shit. I'm hitting the maudlin portion of chemical alteration.

I finish showering, dry off, and get my clothes on as quickly as I can. This isn't a new experience and I should definitely not be here mulling over my shortcomings alone.

I do stupid shit when I'm left to my own devices in this mood and Raz isn't here to talk me off the ledge.

PLAY DIRTY

REMY

For a moment, I'd thought I drilled it into Constance's head that she was endangering not only herself, but others. Unfortunately, I was wrong; the siren call of rebellion and entitlement was far too strong for the little shit to heed my warnings. The minute we stepped inside, she got surrounded by fawning toadies —male and female—and by the time I pushed through them, she disappeared.

Guess I know what her phone conversation centered on.

Striding through the crowds of glitterati like a hot knife through butter, my eyes scan the room for her blond head. My lips purse as I note nearly fifty blond heads with similar hairstyles and I grimace. What a lovely reunion for all these ex-sorority chicks to pretend they care about whatever the *cause célèbre* of the day is. This is going to suck; I knew I should have put a fucking tracker on her.

I close my eyes for a second, reconstructing the scene from our dazzling entry.

Constance stepped inside with me behind her to the right. A group of girls in slinky cocktail dresses approached first, air-kissing and squealing in that society woman manner. They were brunette in blue satin at the knee, raven in scarlet tea-length, silver in baby pink lace, and redhead in bright purple mini —all in towering heels. Men came from the left in a group as well—a pincer move they all probably perfected in high school. The guys were blond spikes with a vest in black, shaved head in all white unbuttoned, sandy in charcoal with a red tie, raven in midnight blue with bowtie, and green with dandy plaid and a vest. None of them seemed attached to my charge, just accompanying the girls. Once they converged, they all intermixed and surrounded her like a swarm. When the circle broke, she was gone, and they left with smirks.

"Since none of them were there to escort the petty princess, that means she's meeting someone or on the prowl. I need to move to higher ground and look for the peacocks. That's where she'll be."

A crackle in my ear turns to a chuckle. "Lose your beast already, Guillotine?"

"Do. Not. Say. That. On. An. Open. Line," I grit out in annoyance.

Working with another person is much harder than I would have expected. My jobs are typically smooth as cream, but Lys has been present for every quirk of fate in the past four and a half months, which I fucking hate. I don't like anyone knowing that I'm human and shit happens to me at the same rate as any other operative. I'm just excellent at pivoting to cover for it while still completing the job. Having Lys be a witness to that fact makes my ass twitch.

"Whatever, *Hester*. The point remains that your sneaky socialite has eluded you, and now you're ready to give her the old slice and dice."

She's not wrong.

"Just make your rounds while I find a perch and let me know if you see her."

Lys pauses for a second and I can almost *hear* the glee in her tone when she speaks. "Shall I mark her? I know you said it's silly, movie shit, but I brought it anyway."

Groaning in humiliation, I walk to the stairs with my hand brushing against my hair to hide the fact that I'm talking to myself. "Goddamn it, yes. You win. Hit her with the UV gel if you catch her."

I'm never going to live this down if a thief's UV marking trick is how I complete this clusterfuck.

The staircase winds along the back wall and as I climb it to get to the balcony, I notice this event has quite a few Hollywood types as well as socialites. It's not political, which explains the lack of heightened security the Admiral preferred, but it's filled with familiar faces from the media. The charity is something about children, but I didn't pay attention to it.

My experience in these circles as an assassin tells me the nonprofit world is filled with just as many thieves, abusers, and deviants as any other community. People simply don't look for them there and it makes the jobs where I get to take out the ugliest ones immensely satisfying. I may not have the same code as 'normies,' but my lines around what is not acceptable run as deep as ocean trenches. Too many of the assholes who attend shit like this run afoul of those rules and the rest of the sheep allow them to continue their evil for shitty reasons, like money and fame.

Focus, Remy. Find Constance and leave the rest for another avenger; there are plenty.

When I crest the top of the stairs, my eyes light on several things that make my innate sense of caution spike. I take a second to lean against the railing, sorting through what I saw to figure out what set me off. A platinum head moving through the people with purpose—familiar, but I can't place it from here. In a corner, a high ponytail and sleek black pantsuit with tan skin standing so she can see the entire room. Coming from the kitchen, a nervous looking Hispanic server who seemed like he did not know how to walk with a tray. At the bar, a man with a long braid, pretending not to pay attention to anything, but his posture was alert and ready.

This room is full of problems and I'm not sure if they're all mine.

"Lys, I need you to clock one of the waitstaff. He's about five foot five, Hispanic, small goatee, twenty-something, and has no clue what he's doing. No catering company allows untrained newbies at an event this fancy. This guy doesn't belong and we need to know what his game is."

"Got it, Boss," she sing-songs.

Sucking in a deep breath, I center myself so I can ignore her playful teasing and figure out this mess. This event was part of my task for the stupid *Forum* bid, so it stands to reason it might be part of others' as well. They may have assigned an operative to take my charge or another one of the sparkly rich folks for the auction. There might be thieves milling about looking to steal shit and possibly even assassins looking to take someone out. I haven't seen the usual high rollers, but that doesn't mean the small time bidders aren't sneaking about.

The possibility of a pack of my fellow criminals milling about with the rich dicks downstairs changes my approach. In fact, it means I need to secure Constance and get the hell out of here. Her father may be correct in assuming she's a target or he might be wrong, but having her flit about amid hungry low and mid-tier operatives looking to impress the mysterious *Forum* assmunch isn't the slightest bit appealing.

"See her yet?" I murmur as I continue to scan the crowd.

"Nope. The kid is in view, though. Looks like he's going to shake to pieces if anyone looks at him wrong. Definitely his first time on assignment."

Great. Hopefully, he's not armed.

"Some assholes are so stupid I want to raise the world's IQ by removing them from the average. Who sends someone that green to a place like this?" I shake my head, reaching into my pocket to feel the wire there. I'm itching to use it on the first person who pisses me off. It's been far too long since I've felt blood spray at my hand.

"You're quiet." Lys snorts, the humor in her voice fond. "You're imagining killing people again, aren't you? I can tell because you get this look on your face like you've had a secret orgasm and no one can tell."

I do? Fuck, I need to work on that shit.

"Stop watching me and look for the girl. She's not in the main room; I need to search the closed doors up here, so you sneak around the ones down there." Huffing, I spin on my heel and stomp down the hall. I'm not comfortable with someone reading me so well and I definitely don't enjoy knowing I have a recognizable 'killing someone fantasy' face. This is why I never 'people'; they see too much if you keep them around any length of time.

Yet, I grunt into the mic, "Thank you, Lys."

Her chuckle tells me everything I need to know—I'm completely fucked, and she's never going away.

Why does that feel like a victory?

SEARCHING the rooms up here only turned up a bunch of people fucking—none of them the one I wanted to find. I was fairly certain I might have walked in on some juicy gossip with some pairings, but I pay so little mind to famous people's shit that I wasn't sure. I'm only vaguely aware of who is married or dating or going to jail in any week; that is, unless someone hires me to get rid of their problem. Then my focus on their lives shifts so I can plan my approach. My lips curve when I realize I may have stumbled on future business while hunting down Constance. It makes this wild goose chase somewhat palatable.

"Check-in. Upstairs was a bust. What about you?"

I wait impatiently, trying not to be concerned when my friend doesn't answer right away. Turning at the end of the hall, I take the back stairs down as the seconds tick by. Finally, there's the sound of a huff and a door closing.

"Sorry. I had to get a stain off my shirt. Our clumsy plant spilled a tray full of those weird little soup mug things all over me. He damn near shit his pants when I yelled at him. But the catering manager sent me to clean off and I couldn't respond in front of the cunt while she bitched me out." I can hear the frustration in her tone, but something about her incident feels wrong to me.

"When did he run into you?" I round the corner at the bottom of the stairs, hoping to catch up to her in person.

"Right after I checked the first room downstairs. Why?"

My pace quickens as I push through the crowds, darting around people to get to the door where the staff enter the main room. "Something isn't right. I've seen a bunch of pros in the house, but this isn't the style of those people. It's far more devious and well-planned. I don't like the shiny newbie drawing your attention away from those rooms."

Lys looks at me as I stand in front of her with a perturbed expression on my face. "What's going on?"

I grimace, flicking my gaze to the surrounding people. "Nothing. Take me back to where you got souped."

We pass the kitchens, heading down a long corridor that gets fancier as we move further from the work area. My friend stops at the first door on the right, pointing. "I cleared this one and when I came out, the kid was hurrying down the hall and he crashed into me. It was red, like radish or tomato or some shit, so I didn't have a choice but to go clean it."

"Where did he go?" I ask as I stroll towards the next door cautiously. Leaning in, I listen at the door for voices before turning the knob slowly.

She shrugs. "I don't know. The minute I got up and yelled at him, the boss showed and sent him off with a growl, then herded me to the restroom."

"Hmm," I reply as I poke my head inside the room. My eyes widen as I note the disarray of the small study. There are books and pillows and papers everywhere—not the look I would expect from a place like this, even if it is a public party. There was a struggle in here, and I can't be sure if it was Constance or some other freaking mark.

This is bullshit; too many cooks spoil the broth and all that shit.

"Lys, someone was… taken… or killed… or something in here. We need to see what went on in the other rooms… *now*." I pin her with a dark gaze as she nods. "The Admiral is going to be pissed."

SOLDIERS

MO

All we have to do is get her out of here and we're home free.

The plan Dwyn and I came up with wasn't either of our usual styles, which ended up benefiting us. We put Joaquin on the serving staff instead of me, knowing his lack of finesse would draw attention from any pros in the building. The security on this thing was full of holes, but more important guests were bound to have their own hired muscle to watch over them. Knowing the guest list, most of them weren't at my skill level, and the only variable was the name attached to our target. So we operated more like our missing brothers rather than use our typical execution.

Years ago, Raz opened a small back door on our various skill boards on *Mercatus*. It allowed us to catch some of the communication between vendors and contractors besides ourselves, but it was spotty. It didn't always give us access to what we wanted, and we really only checked it when something felt amiss in our instructions. The benefit was knowing if vendors had double booked jobs to make certain they got what they wanted without fail. Unfortunately, the hit-or-miss nature of his hack was necessary to prevent anyone from discovering the code he planted, so it wasn't always helpful.

We scoured both boards under secondary aliases until we found a suspicious message hidden amongst the hitter requests that corresponded with the *Forum* assignments. They gave *Dançarina do fogo* a protection detail, and the coordinates matched up with the location of our target—Constance Braithewaite, daughter of Admiral Braithwaite. I'd never worked with her before, nor had I competed directly with this mid-tier operative for a job. She wasn't in my echelon and though I recognized the name; I had no reason to study her. Her rating was solid, though she wasn't a frequent contractor, so I reasoned she must have a steady source of income with some organization.

She'd be batting in the big leagues at this thing; I knew it would make the job much easier.

All of our quick preparation centered on my ability to assess the target and her detail from the moment they arrived, then transmit instructions to D and Joaquin. My cover was part of the press pool, so I didn't use an overly extensive disguise—people rarely look closely at the writhing band of bottom feeders snapping pictures as they come in. They smile and pose, but as long as you don't draw attention to yourself, no one gives the vultures a second look.

When the tall, muscled woman stepped out of the SUV and did a visual sweep, I stayed a row back, watching her carefully. *Dançarina do fogo* didn't disappoint: she checked the windows, roofs, and her surroundings in a careful circle. At the very least, I knew she was competent, though I couldn't tell exactly *how* competent behind her emotionless expression and sunglasses. The door to the SUV opened, and I chuckled as the socialite caused a ruckus when a shifty little fuck bum-rushed her. It wasn't surprising; these types of pampered morons rarely valued their own lives enough to be cautious, even when warned of danger.

I grinned behind the large camera rig as my competitor took down the little shit, whispering something to both of them that made the male go white. A familiar snap told me she'd broken his wrist and the flounce of her charge as they walked away was chuckle worthy. The guy hauled himself to his feet, and I knew it was my moment. I called out, pretending to be compassionate, but also hungry enough to offer him money for his tale of woe. It took a precious few moments to walk him over to the nondescript van I'd arrived in under the guise of calling paramedics while I interviewed him.

I didn't need *to snap his neck and stuff him in a huge dumpster, but I also didn't have time to worry about his fat mouth.*

That's when I jumped back into the van, using the equipment set up there to contact Joaquin to ensure he was fumbling around the party. He was supposed to make certain he distracted the blond bimbo by offering her blow—something extremely believable given his looks and the tendency of rich girls to behave exactly how one would expect. Once she was on the hook, he'd give her directions to meet him in one of the first-floor rooms beyond the kitchen to collect her nose candy.

Dwyn worried he'd fuck it up, but I knew my tag-a-long worked for his uncle and dealing was the one thing I could count on him to be experienced at. *El Jefe's* men sucked at doing anything remotely physical, but they absolutely knew how to spread the hold of his product in any environment. My only job now was watching the camera feeds Dwyn got us into and I hated it, but I also knew why the strategy was sound.

Even disguised, my build and size scream my profession and we didn't want to tip off Dançarina do fogo to our existence.

It took a lot of patience and caffeine to quell my itch to be in the mix; I've rarely been the one in the van and sitting there while my friend and the kid roamed the charity event was hard. It made me think about Raz, wondering where the fuck he was and if he was okay. Neither D nor I had heard a damn peep from any of the rest of The Five or the girl who had us by the balls months ago. Deep down, I hoped they were all just underground, burrowing in until the danger passed, but sometimes, fatalism would sneak in. Being stuck on camera duty made that bad feeling resurface and I damn near cracked my jaw, trying to push it away.

But my patience paid off when Joaquin muttered his signal on the comms, and Dwyn confirmed he was in place. We dressed my old friend to the nines, using one of the complex disguise kits he pulled from our personal storage vault. Using one of the *LI* ones would have tipped them to his survival and broken protocol, but luckily The Five have always been smart enough to have our stores in various major cities in case we were on the run. Perhaps creating these bolt holes was a product of the night Remy supposedly died—Arnaud had broken our trust so completely we never recovered from it—or maybe it was simply a survival instinct. But it had served us well over the years and this was one of those times.

I saw the red, spiky hair move through the crowd on screen and despite helping him apply everything, I barely recognized him. Not only was his look completely different, but he'd changed his posture, gait, and mannerisms in a way that was downright spooky. It occurred to me that when we all worked together, I was so busy running the missions that I didn't take time to appreciate how fucking talented my brothers actually were. I just got pissed when they went off-book—which was often—and then growled when shit went wrong.

Another thing our reincarnated ex-partner used to give me shit about.

So I continued watching him work the crowd like a pro, smiling a bit when I saw Jinx's influence on him. It was frustrating to know we hadn't heard from him, either, but six months wasn't up and our coming together was a huge breach of protocol. If we got made at the *Forum*, at least only the two of us would get the stick —and we were the two most used to it. D was always a wild card and I've always been the leader, so the crusty old fuck came after us more than anyone else. We're both prepared for his wrath if he finds out.

By the time he made his way to the hallway leading to the kitchens, I'd seen Joaquin peel off to use the staff entrance to wait for our partner. The wait after that was excruciating, because there were no cameras turned on down there. I tried to use the instructions D left to remotely turn them on, but it seemed like there was something blocking me. I almost left the van as the minutes ticked by, concerned he'd gotten caught or was in some sort of battle with *Dançarina*. But eventually, the red hair showed up on the outdoor feed with another dark one. They carried the blond woman into the alley, her head lolling as if she was drunk.

That meant the additive in her champagne worked—excellent.

Dwyn and Joaquin hustled her into the waiting black town car, giving me the heads up as they climbed inside.

My lips curve up as I watch them roll out of the alley and pull onto the street, passing my van. I'm surprised this worked—it was low tech, based on people skills rather than muscle, and included using a kid who barely knows more than street dealing. It should have blown up in our faces, but honestly? Maybe the simplicity is why it worked. I'll have to grill D when we meet at the safe house to await *El Jefe*'s directions for dropping this chick off.

Hopefully, it won't be long before he responds; D and I have shit to do.

"Yes, I understand. Yes, we can do that. Thank you. Joaquin was very helpful. Yes. I'll call when it's done."

Turning to my partners, I run a hand through my hair. I don't like this shit one bit and I know it shows. D and Joaquin drove the unconscious socialite back to our meeting spot without an issue.

The debrief was my concern and our instructions from *El Jefe* cemented my dislike of the situation. Pacing back and forth for a moment, I try to spin the pieces in my head, looking for the explanation for the rapidly evolving events happening in our world.

"You said there were other operatives in the main room?" I ask as I pin Dwyn with a serious look.

He snorts, flinging a knife at a piece of graffiti on the wall. It nails the smiley face between the eyes and he pumps his fist. "Yep. Various levels though some big ones, too. Pretty sure I saw that peacocking *Voleur* slithering around. There was a very professional-looking pair lurking in the corners I didn't know. But the woman had a stance like you and the guy moved like Company dudes. Of course, *Dançarina* was there and I'm pretty sure she had a cohort; she talked to herself more than people do if they're not security or headed for a rubber room."

Frowning, I look at the limp girl on the couch. *What the fuck is so special about her? Nothing.* My brows furrow as I look at Dwyn again. "Do you think this was their target or someone else?"

"The two pros disappeared before I went to the back and the first damn room I went in had a fucking mutilated corpse, so it's safe to say they didn't come for our nitwit. I lost track of *Voleur*, big surprise, but I didn't run into any dry husks. If it was him, he hadn't done his shit before Connie over there walked in my room and tried to fuck me for blow."

"She what?!" Joaquin asks in surprise.

I chuckle at his surprise. "Man, rich girls here will do anything to ease their boredom with life. It's not like where *El Jefe* lives."

"*Madre de Dios*[1]," he mutters as he crosses himself.

Dwyn gives me a look as if to ask where the hell this kid comes from and I shrug. It's likely he's never traveled more than a couple hours from home before this. "Well, buddy, welcome to America, I guess. The land of the free and home of the brainless."

"D," I say as I roll my eyes. "It's not like we're from some fucking utopia full of geniuses."

"We're not from anywhere, Mo-Mo, and that's how I like it. Now, where the hell do we unload this chick? I want to get her out of here, have some wings, and figure out when this damn *Forum* thing is. It's making my ass twitch to sit around here."

Everything makes his ass twitch.

---

1. Mother of god

RIOT

REMY

"Son of bitching, motherfucking, cocksucking…"

Having to admit to the pompous old fart that I lost his precious daughter was not the highlight of my career. Her own stupidity was part of the problem, but men like him cannot accept reasons without calling them excuses. The Admiral berated me for at least an hour before I took my leave; he only got that long because I truly felt like a failure, no matter what variables arose. However, I don't allow anyone to speak to me the way he did by the time I left —at least, not without taking their head as a trophy.

Unfortunately, I'll have to circle back for that vengeance after I've located my wayward charge.

"Why are you even bothering to look for her? She's a bubble-headed moron who didn't listen to you and made us lose our bid for the *Forum*. We need to go into one of the other sections and take a quick job, so you get the nod."

"Because she's stupid and selfish, but I don't like—"

A loud beep from one of the laptops set up around the room stops me in my tracks. That's a *Mercatus* message sound. We look at one another and scramble for the right computer quickly. Lys and I almost knock heads in eagerness and I laugh for the first time since we made our escape from the event. My friend grins and shrugs as she clicks the mouse, opening the screen so we can find out who is trying to contact us. The message screen pops up with an audio file and my gut takes an internal dive right for my feet. Lys arches a brow at me and I simply click 'play' on the file.

Greetings, Dançarina!

Despite your failure to complete this mission, we would like to extend you an invitation to participate in an event that will define a generation of criminals: the Forum Romanum of 2023.

Yes, it is unusual for someone who so spectacularly and utterly blew their assignment to be given such an honor, but this is a special circumstance. We chose you for this operation because you lacked the capability to execute it successfully.

Why, you might ask?

That is a fair question and one we owe you the answer to. It is not that we believe your work is not up to snuff; no, we believe you will be an excellent addition to the team we place you on at the event. However, we needed you to be a shield for the greater mission—allowing the girl to be taken by another asset for one of our vendors.

Sometimes, in order to make an omelet, you must crack some eggs, no?

Sadly, you were the egg we cracked and for that; I apologize. We could not inform you of the deception, or your performance would lack believability. Our client desperately wanted to strike out at the girl's father for some perceived slight by auctioning her off to the highest bidder. Given the Admiral's background and her looks, she'll fetch a good price regardless of what kind of deviant wants her, so we were happy to oblige a vendor in this manner.

Many of the tasks put to the applicants on the sections of Mercatus are similar—either to benefit us as the creators of the Forum or the vendors who will sell the most sought after products in history. All with a cut to us, of course. We cannot fund our future ventures without raking in donations from the rest of the community, whether they are aware of where their funds go or not.

This missive has gone on longer than I intended, but it is hard to run an empire this shrouded in secrecy, so you must bear with me, Dançarina.

We demand your presence in one week's time at four a.m. Our transports will take each sector of contractors to the location separately, using different routes and timetables to prevent anyone from tracking them. Your job will be one of utmost importance… you will assist with managing the cattle.

Keep them calm, prevent any value diminishing behavior, and use your strengths to ensure our lots are not damaged. You will have three other associates whom you will meet when the van arrives. If our cattle count rises, there will be additional operatives invited to join your team.

As a thank you for allowing us to tarnish your reputation slightly for the greater good, we are naming you head of the team—something which will elevate your Mercatus rating immensely once the event is over.

Do not be late and do not fail us in this endeavor, Dançarina.

We blew the last operative who failed their mission parameters to pieces in broad daylight despite a decade of experience in their field. I do not wish to do the same to you.

Omnes una manet nox[1], Dançarina.

I TURN to look at my friend, my expression tight with fury. "That ass-sucking little shit tried to blow me up, and now he's bragging about it. Not only that, but he attempted to take away *my* fucking closure with those jackasses who betrayed me."

Lys arches a brow as she watches me leap from my seat to stomp over to the pile of weapons on the counter. Picking up a set of knives, I spin them on my hands, not caring about nicks as I try to contain the tidal wave of anger flowing through me. Before she can stand, I fling one at the padded support beam, nailing a small dot on it with a snarl. The second knife flies immediately, embedding in another beam with precision. I walk over to yank them out and do it again, but I pause when my new bestie clears her throat.

"I get it. You're angry and your pride just took a hit. But we don't know who this asshole is and we do not know if any of your guys are in this damn auction or if they're all dead. We have to be smarter. You can kill whoever the fuck you want once we're in Remy. I'm on your side."

Her words make me want to scream because I know deep inside that she's right. However, the icy cold center of my soul wants to push this Remy aside and let the Guillotine go on a rampage. "But who the hell would I go on a rampage to kill? Fuck."

Lys walks over, plucking the knives out of my hand and tilting her head. "Exactly. Who are we taking out? We don't know. I think we need to go back to that fucking club and get the douchebag to invite us to the rumpus room again. I bet those dirtbags will have more info on the 'lots' our mysterious employer mentioned."

That's actually a good plan—if I can stay calm enough to keep my wire in my pocket and my fury pushed down into my feet.

It took a couple hours for me to calm myself so we could get ready for another night at The Neon Oasis. I handle failure poorly, and combined with the taunts from what I assume is my good friend Shadow Douche hiding behind a voice changer, I wasn't in the mood to let Lys primp me. The only thing I was in the mood for was blood and finding an underground fight club wouldn't get us any closer to the people we're hunting. Might have cooled me down faster to beat someone's ass, but the night is young.

Maybe I'll get lucky.

"Stop grinning with your damn teeth like that," Lys hisses as she sways next to me. "You look like a shark planning its next meal."

I shrug. It's accurate and I won't pretend otherwise. Tilting my head back, I let the long, blond ponytail brush my ass as I dance to the trance music playing in the early hours of the evening. The club isn't full yet, and the air doesn't stink with bodies and sweat like it will within a few hours. Right now, I'm hoping to get the attention of anyone who can open the gates to that upstairs room without having to go up on the pole again. I'm feeling a little too stabby to swing around the thing in mid-air.

"I'm here and I haven't punched anyone. That feels like a win," I reply as I jerk my chin at the bar. "I need a drink."

My friend pulls away from the guy she's dancing with, giving him a wave as she follows me to the bar. I hold up a fifty, getting immediate attention from the bartender, and within seconds of ordering, there are shots set up for us. Tossing mine back, I look around the dance floor for the boss man who brought us up last time. I don't see him, but when the crowd parts at the front door, I see someone I recognize: the suit and braids man.

"Shit. He didn't seem very interested last time, but maybe you can work your magic?" Lys arches her brow and I roll my eyes. "Fine, I'll help. But if I end up snapping some minion's neck for getting fresh, you have no one to blame but yourself, Elysium. You know what kind of mood I'm in."

She winks, laughing at my foul disposition. "I think you give yourself far too little credit, Guillotine. You survived thirteen years with that foul, psycho temper and didn't allow yourself to be caught. Don't blame me if being worried about those stupid boys has your panties in a knot and it's making you irrational."

If I didn't like her so damn much, I'd kill her just for being right all the fucking time.

"Fine," I mutter as I motion for the bartender to return. When he does, I slip him enough to get a full bottle and then motion for Lys to follow. I turn on the 'drunk girl' act as we head towards the man from the other night, clutching the open bottle of tequila like it's a health potion. She giggles as I pass it to her, tottering purposefully on the stupidly tall heels she wears. I pout and snatch it back—all right in the path of our mark on his way to the stairs for the VIP lounge.

"It's *my* turn," she says, wobbling as she grabs for the bottle. I keep it out of her reach, laughing and bouncing so the men approaching won't have a choice but to look at my chest. I feel their eyes as Lys and I tug the tequila back and forth, then finally the man in question steps into view.

"You lovely ladies seem to have a problem. Anything I can do to… help?"

You could take a nosedive off the Empire State Building and it'd benefit all of humanity.

But I keep that opinion to myself, batting my lashes as I look at the slimeball. "We only have one…*uno*… bottle of tequila and she's not sharing."

Lys presses up against his arm, pointing at me as she coos at the gangster. "No, *she's* not sharing. It's not nice."

His lips curve as he looks between us, then at his entourage. "I can certainly solve that for you, ladies. Would you like to join me in the VIP lounge? I'll have them bring us *all* bottles."

I've said it before and I'll say it again… if dicks had an off switch, men might actually have a chance at making good decisions.

"That would be amazing!" Lys squeals as she hugs his arm against her chest. "What do you think, Gigi?"

I have to force myself to smile like I'm not ready to eat someone alive—especially because the persona she picked is named *Gigi*. "I think that'd be super, Mimi!"

She frowns at the sarcasm in my tone, but the goons don't notice. They're too busy clearing the way for their boss to move through the crowd to the velvet rope and he's too busy holding his arm out for me. I take it, giving him a sultry look from under the thick, fake lashes Lys glued on tight enough to permanently attach the damn things. Tonight's look is definitely more blond ambition than sultry club chick, and despite feeling like my I.Q. has dropped a few points, I'll admit it's effective.

"G, we didn't ask this gentleman's name. Don't you think we should do that? We've been plain rude."

Nodding, I look over at her with the hint of a smirk on my face. She's getting damn good at this; I'm kind of impressed. "That's true, M. Pray tell, what *is* your name, kind sir?"

"They call me The Bull," he grunts as we approach the bouncer in front of the rope. "And you may do so as well."

Rolling my eyes wouldn't help our cause but come on— no one with a big cock needs to be called something like that.

"Ooooh. That sounds sexy," Lys coos at him, and I almost lose control this time. She's going to be the death of me if the men I'm trying to save aren't first.

"Maybe you'll get to see tonight, baby," the Bull replies with a shiny white grin. His face lights up at her preening, and I force myself to grin back at him.

I'm usually much better at this shit, but my impatience with finding out what the fuck is going on is waning. The Douche's taunts were aimed at *Dançarina*, but I felt them as deeply as if they'd been directed at me. This entire half a year of scheming hasn't turned up a solid lead except the man who will almost certainly upstairs holding court, and I haven't been able to question him yet, either. There's far too much outside of my control at the moment, and operating with a partner keeps me from finding a random asshole to vent my fury on.

The Guillotine feels trapped and I'm going to end up ceding control if I don't—

The moment we enter the lounge, my eyes dart around the room, assigning danger levels to every player in the space. What I didn't expect to see when we arrived in that glittering den of perversion were Dwyn O' Shanahan and Mauricio Battaglia—The Ghost and The Fist, betrayers of my youth, and wreckers of havoc in my life—standing in the middle of the room with a blindfolded blond girl. My gaze flicks to the short Hispanic kid with them, then to Dwyn's face as I let go of my escort. Something is off in the way they're standing and I can tell they're not here as themselves.

"Who're these guys?" I ask with a hiccup. "They look like buzz kills."

The Bull snorts, tugging us both to the corner he sat in before. "No one to worry about, baby. They've brought product for *Il Tasso* to auction off. Once he gets his people to cart it away, the party will begin."

Dwyn's eyes catch mine as I drop onto the sofa on one side of the garish moron. His brow arches for a brief second and I know he's made me. I don't know if Mo recognizes me as well because he's busy glaring at every single person in this room. He's not wrong; they're all filth, as far as I know, but it's also not very politic. That's his usual method, of course, so I know he never learned a damn thing from the shit I used to teach him when we were younger. Jinx and Coda would probably lose their minds at his bullshit.

Wait a minute. Where are the other clowns?

Looking at my friend, I tap my ear lightly to ask if she sees comms on either of them. She shakes her head and I lift the bottle to my mouth to hide my frown. No comms means definitely no Raz and likely no Jinx. These two must be on their own—maybe even tracking Coda like me. My anger at being outwitted on the protection detail fades when I realize I didn't lose to some rando snatch and grab fool; no, I lost to one of the best thieves and retrieval specialists on the planet. That's a lot less humiliating than what my recording said and—

My brain pauses again. That fucker also didn't say they gave me grace because The Ghost and The Fist trumped me. If it's really the Shadow Douche—which I'm certain of—he would have rubbed the top-tier folks in my face. So he doesn't know he has D or Mo working for him, either.

The pieces are coming together slowly, so I put the bottle on the table, giving the Bull a bright smile. "I'm going to the little girl's room. I'll be right back."

He nods, too busy feeling up Lys to pay nearly as much attention to me. I brush past the men in the middle of the room, shoving the earpiece I palmed into Dwyn's hand as I stumble past. His hand brushes my arm as I keep going and I have to bite my lip hard not to respond. I'm supposed to be drunk and fawning over that idiot trafficker; I can't stand to look at him and wonder where the hell the others are.

Slipping my hand into my pocket, I feel for the wire that helps me stay focused when I'm battling between emotions and turning it all off to function. When I get to the bathroom, it's empty, so I sit down on one of the toilets, opening and closing the wire as I stare at it.

Schink. Schink. Schink. Schink.

"You realize you didn't close the stall, right?"

I'm on my feet before the voice finishes, a knife in my other hand before I can blink. "Who the fuck are you?"

The brownish-blond woman with the high ponytail I saw here before and then at the charity event gives me a knowing smile. "They call me The Blade, but you knew that."

"How would I know that?" I ask with a pretty pout.

"Because you were here, the other night as some chick named Kiki and I saw you at that clusterfuck today pretending to be a protection detail. Gotta say, you're fucking fabulous at disguises. I wouldn't know if I weren't… you know. Who I am."

My eyes narrow, taking in her golden tan skin and tight black leather outfit. She's strapped to the gills with knives and daggers— hence the name, I suppose—and my attack position isn't bothering her in the slightest. In fact, she gives me her back to lean over the sink and reapply her dark wine colored lipstick. "Uh-huh. How is that I've never heard of you? Who do you work for and why are you talking to me?"

She snorts, then pops her lips. "I work for no one but myself in this profession. But you remind me of someone I like quite a bit. Maybe when she was a little greener, of course, but the resemblance is there, so it makes me feel generous. That's why I'm going to tell you that you should let your friends hand over that girl."

"Oh, for fuck's sake, I'm not—"

"You should. The Badger isn't the real player, and you'd rather catch the big guy, right? So let her go. They will not fuck her up before something as big as a *Forum* or she won't be worth anything. Let them do what they must and figure out how to work this out when you get to the big party. Trust me."

"Why in the hell should I do that?"

The Blade gives me a genuine smile, her blue eyes sparkling. "Because I promise myself and my spouses will clean up the dredges of this when it's over. It's sort of my thing."

What? Is she one of those nuts who thinks they're superheroes or some shit?"

"Don't look at me like that. I'm just a balancer of scales as a side-line. I only operate under my code, just like you, but I've found the family that supports me while I do it. You should try that." she turns to leave and I slip my wire back in my pocket, staring at the exit she went through.

"That's a lot easier said than done, Bathroom Prophet," I mutter. Shaking my head, I move to the mirror and check my face, looking into my eyes until I feel ready to go back out there.

It's showtime.

---

1. One night awaits us all.

MESSED UP

DWYN

I watch as my Jazzy, the girl who haunted my dreams for years after she supposedly died, comes out of the restroom. She perches on the couch at the arm of the dude who looks like he's trying to mimic Snoop Dogg. Her eyes wander around the room as she takes in the crowd. I remember that look; it's part faux disinterest and part calculated observation. The girl she used to be would file every minute detail in that big brain of hers, storing it for when she needed to shore up her cover or beat a retreat.

She knows us, but she's acting as though we're of no consequence at all.

It's a smart play, given the cover she's chosen. A party girl tagging along with a guy like that wouldn't give a shit who the other people in the room are or she wouldn't get invited back. I know that, but it makes my chest hurt to have her this close and yet so fucking far away. Gritting my jaw, I look at Mo, but he's focused on the staircase as he waits for our contact impatiently. He's so zeroed in on dropping this whiny girl off that he's not paying attention to the shit around him. Of course, he knows I am, even if his greenhorn pal isn't, so he isn't worried.

I'm ready to say something when the curvy woman who came out of the john before Remy sighs loudly. She looks around, crossing her arms over her chest as she faces the crowd.

"Where the hell is he? I don't have all night to stand around with you deviants."

Murmurs of agreement echo around us, and I frown, wondering what her game is. She's not afraid of this *Il Tasso* moron; that much is clear. But where she falls in the structure of the gathered traffickers, I don't know. The Five have always stayed away from this line of business; *Les Invisibles* has Lady Volkov's team to handle that. Mo and I did a little recon on the players before we set out for this meet, but I don't feel comfortable in the slightest.

The Bull looks over at her, sneering as he grips the leg of the chick opposite my girl. "Patience, Blade. He'll be here for the pickup, then we'll all discuss what progress we've made. The date and location for the *Forum* got sent out to the contractors earlier, so everything is on track."

"I'm aware of that, Bull. I, too, read my fucking email. What I don't do is stand around like a chump while a two-bit peon like Badger fucks around. I have more important tasks to complete prior to bringing my stable to the event."

He snorts, leaning back in his chair as if he's royalty. "I doubt that. You rarely take part in these events, and I doubt you have much to offer. Wait your turn."

Within seconds, the lounging man beside her is on his feet and in front of the smart mouthed asshole, a K-bar at his throat. "I'm sorry, mate. I must not have heard you correctly. Did you just insult my wife?"

Remy doesn't move a muscle. She simply sits on the arm of the sofa, her expression bland as the man who moved like a blur threatens The Bull. The other girl is still as well, and I tilt my head. They must be together. None of our girl's aliases are known for working with partners and this is as much a surprise as The

Flash over there coming for the dealer. But the world went topsy-turvy with that goddamn bomb in London, so who the hell knows what anyone is doing now? I can't say I'm disappointed to see her with someone who might watch her back.

"Darling, don't waste your anger on him. I prefer you save that growl for me," The Blade says with a smirk. "However, since I see that yet again, everyone but me has brought their entourage, so I must insist the rest of mine be allowed entrance to the meeting."

Her lethal spouse pulls away, spinning the blade on his hand faster than even I can, and he lopes back over to the intimidating woman with a sultry grin. "As you wish, wife."

The Bull looks shaken, and I'm fairly certain Mo's puppy dog pissed his pants, but everyone else just ignores the drama. When no one protests, the blond woman saunters closer, looking at Remy intently. "I want her to fetch my other operatives. A man with platinum hair and a red-haired woman—they'll be down-stairs somewhere and you won't miss them when you find them. I promise."

My eyes flick to Remy's, watching her as she rises from the spot, then she looks at the idiot she came with questioningly. "Is that kosher, baby?"

I'm going to wring his neck myself even though I know it's an act.

"I'm not sending some club slut to find anyone when we have a prisoner up here," the guy from the Triad finally speaks, his disdain clear in the tone of his voice.

Mo snorts, rolling his eyes at the group of men flanking the short, tattooed man in a three-piece suit. "Would it help if I send one of *my* men down with her? My boss is just as invested as you, and I don't need to get locked up tonight, either."

"Acceptable."

Mo nods at me, and I pretend to grumble in irritation. "Fine, I'll go with the bitch to bring your people back. Jesus Christ, save me from the pussy in this room."

My girl's eyes meet mine and for the briefest second, I think I see a sparkle before she strides past me. "Keep up, muscle man. I don't want to be gone long. The booze up here is *premium*."

Not nearly as top shelf as you, my little killer.

WE AREN'T DOWNSTAIRS for more than a minute when she turns to me and shoves me into the closest dark corner, her eyes flashing with emotion. I grin lazily, letting her take charge because I'm so fucking happy she's alive that my dick is practically doing backflips.

"What the fuck are you two *doing* here? Why do you have my failed assignment tied to a damn chair?" Her voice is a low hiss, and she's pressed tight to my form, her hands planted on either side of my head.

I pretend not to notice the sharp as hell wire stretched across my throat as I answer. "Your assignment? Jazzy, Remy, killer… whoever you are today… that girl is *Mo's* assignment from his current employer. We had to snatch her at some ball and they told us to bring her here."

Her eyes narrow and she studies my face as if looking for deceit, but all she finds is delight tinged with hunger. At least, I think it's what she finds because it's *definitely* what I feel. Wiggling my hips against hers, I bob my brows and she snorts disdainfully. "You are the only idiot on the planet who would steal my fucking ticket into that shitshow and then hope I'd fuck you as thanks."

Pouting a little, I shake my head. "Got it all wrong, baby. I'm so ecstatic you're alive that I'd fuck you on broadcast television if you'd let me. The stupid girl has zero to do with it."

Remy growls, the wire cutting into my skin a little as she slams her palms on the wall hard. "Don't tempt me, O' Shanahan. Why would Mo be working for a trafficker? We both know it isn't his style."

"Not yours, either, but here you are…" I sing song. Her glare hardens and I sigh. "Look, he's been in duck and cover for months like me. Our protocol says stay dark for six months if shit like London goes down. Sir Tight Ass took a job under one of his throw-aways for some dumbshit drug lord. He got sent here to retrieve the girl for his boss. I'm here because we stumbled into each other while looking into the insanity of *Mercatus*."

"Where's everyone else?" she asks as the wire slackens a bit.

I'm bleeding now, but I don't give a shit. Remy Benoit can bleed me all the fuck she wants if she's alive and pressed against me like she's trying to crawl into my body. "No clue. Neither of us have heard a peep from or about them. You?"

Giving me a long look, she finally lets go of one end of the weapon and flies back into its casing. "I've been chasing leads since Lys got me out of there. The closest I've gotten is the name of a mid-level player extracted from the guys who held me in their sandy hellhole for a month."

My eyes flash as I suss out what that likely meant and I snarl softly. "Held you for a month? Are you fucking insane—"

Her hand lifts from the wall, covering my mouth as she glares at me. "Don't ruin your good looks by trying to tell me how to take care of myself, Slick. I've been doing it for over ten years and I don't need a man spouting shit about how I run my business. Nothing happened at that place I didn't allow to happen and they're all dead now. Happy?"

No, I'm not. I want to dig those motherfuckers up and kill them again for even looking at her, but this will have to do.

"No. But I see your point." Sighing, I look at her, trying not to let her see what a goddamn sap I feel like when she's this close. She doesn't look like the Remy we knew or even the one we saw before the room went boom, but that doesn't matter. It's like I can feel her in my fucking *soul* again, and I'll be damned if I'm going to scare her away by acting like a tool. "What's the name?"

Her lips purse, and she looks away for a moment. "Be calm, asshole, because I'm barely able to keep myself together at the moment. If you go apeman, I cannot hold on to my temper up there. It will put us all in danger, and we won't find out if these asswipes have Coda. Do you understand?"

I don't like where this is going, but I nod. "Fine. What's the name?"

"*Il Tasso*," she says softly.

The douchebag who's making everyone up there wait? That's who she's been hunting since her Black Widow-style torture-cation?

"You have lost your mind," I growl. "Why are you letting him walk free instead of doing to him what his goons did to you?"

"Because he's not the one in charge, Dwyn!" She leans in closer, putting her nose against mine as she grits out, "There's a bigger problem than just the bomb or the *Forum* or the guys being M.I.A. It started after I scooped up Coda in Paris and it's been chasing me ever since. I can't torture his location out of this jackass but not figure out who the hell hired me to kill Raz!"

I blink at her, my jaw dropping open. *Did she just say…?*

"Yes. I said 'who hired me to kill Raz.' Now shut your pie hole."

Her response is so perfectly Remy that I can't think of anything else to do but kiss her. Our lips meet with a crush of desperation and before I know it, my hands are coasting over her curves eagerly. She lowers her hands, fisting my shirt before she flips us around so I'm pushing her into the hard surface of the club wall. I'm not even sure how she did it, but fuck me, it was hot as hell.

"We have to be quick," she mutters when our lips break.

I blink, looking at her with a crooked grin. "After four and a half months? Quick, I can fucking do, killer."

Her laugh is throaty as she wraps her thighs around mine, heat pouring from her as her mini skirt rides up. My palms run over her boobs, squeezing before I duck my head to bite her shoulder. Remy makes a dark sound and her hands drop to my waistband, undoing my belt without a second of hesitation. The minute they find my cock and stroke, I let out a relieved moan. My lips wander over her neck and I twist her nipples, tugging on the shields while she flicks my piercing mischievously.

"You know," I murmur by her ear. "This is the second time we're going to do this in a place where we can't really see anything. I'm going to get a complex."

"Don't be an idiot. You know you're hot, Slick. Now fuck me or we're going to get caught."

"Yes, ma'am." My hands slide down her torso to her waist, working the skirt up more so I can reach between us to find her pussy. There's nothing in my way and I groan, giving her a dark look when I realize she's commando under this shit. "Remy Benoit, you're a bad fucking influence."

"Dwyn O' Shanahan, I thought I told you to fuck me," she shoots back with a feral grin. "Otherwise, I'm going to find—"

Before she can finish her taunt, I drive into her, my cock sliding into her heat easily. Her lashes flutter as she moans and I press my lips to her ear again. "Hold on tight, killer."

Her nails dig into my shoulders as I thrust into her hard and fast, our breaths harsh pants as we slam into the wall. When she opens her eyes, I smirk at her, then take her lips in a hungry kiss.

Tongues twirl and teeth clash as our bodies crash together hard enough to bruise. I can't get enough of her and it feels like she can't get close enough to me to satisfy the emotions neither of us wants to put names to. When I feel my dick swelling, I drop one hand down to flick her clit, stroking her until she shudders against me. Her walls squeeze me harder and I up the pace, wanting to push her as far as I can in the little time we have.

One more twist of her piercing has her moaning into my mouth, and I let myself go, filling her as the orgasm slams into me as well. I pull away from her lips, looking into Remy's face as I brush the sweaty hairs from her cheeks. I know it's a wig but I can't help tucking the strands behind her ears as I look at her. My cock softens as the pinnacle fades, but I'm having trouble making myself move, even though I know we need to.

"We have to get back," she says, her voice breathy like an ingenue.

"Mmmhmm. Probably should visit the bathroom first, though. Made a mess."

Her eyes roll to the ceiling and she sighs. "Fuck, yeah, you did."

"What do we do now?" I ask as I finally pull out, letting her legs slide down to stand between me and the wall.

She snorts. "Other than wipe your cum off my legs, I say we go back upstairs and get ready for whatever Armageddon this damn *Forum* is going to bring. That work for you?"

I nod, tilting my head at her, watching as she straightens herself up. "Should I tell Mo?"

Her brow arches and she shrugs. "If you think he can handle it. If not, don't. I don't need either of you in my goddamn way."

"Why do you think that Blade chick sent you down here? Does she really have other people here or…?"

Remy tilts her head, her smile enigmatic as she shrugs at me. "No idea. For some reason, I think she's neutral. She's not on our side, but she's definitely not on the scumbag side. I admire a woman who plays her own game."

"Go clean up. I'll wait for you here and we can go back up after we do a quick sweep." She nods and I grab her arm before she heads off. "Just know if you touch that grubby asswipe you came up with, I'll chop his hands off and shove them up his ass before anyone in that room can stop me."

"Now you're just flirting with me," she replies with a wink.

I watch her saunter off towards the bathroom, running my hands through my hair as I try to compose myself.

That was not how I expected this night to go at all.

WHO I AM

REMY

It wasn't easy, but I kept myself from strangling that sleazy motherfucker when he finally showed. My tryst with Dwyn went unnoticed, despite returning with no extra minions for The Blade. She and her companion didn't seem surprised, but they both gave me amused looks when I returned to my place by The Bull. They were the only ones I worried about outing me, but their agenda didn't include me after *Il Tasso* arrived.

Lys fawned over our escort as needed, but I spent the rest of the night listening to the players chat while I pretended to drink myself silly. If Hamid realized we were the same girls as the night before, he didn't comment. He was focused more on taking delivery of Constance, then discussing what other 'merchandise' the sellers in the room were planning to transfer. It was clear he had a holding facility where he takes the people transferred to his care, but nothing he said gave away where it might be located.

When a bunch of scantily clad girls showed up to dance for the crowd, Lys and I slipped away. The meeting portion of the evening was over and talk of business was done, given The Blade and her companion disappeared right before we left. Dwyn caught my eyes as I pretended to totter to the stairs. His finger tapped his ear once, a devilish grin crossing his handsome features. I'd given him my comm, so I had to wait until we got downstairs to steal the other one from my favorite thief.

This morning, in the light of day, I wasn't as sure about using it as I was last night.

"They're not involved with the Shadow Douche. What's the problem?" Lys asks as she pulls on the joggers and zip-up hoodie. "We only have six days before this stupid free-for-all of doom, and you could use it for a booty call *every night*."

I roll my eyes at her as I lace up my sneakers. "No, I can't, and you know why."

Her pout is cute, but it's more about going for a run than my refusal to tap Dwyn every night. "I know no such thing, Remy Benoit."

Slipping my favorite lipstick wire in the pocket of my leggings, I give her a wry expression. "Let me count the ways, my friend. One, continued in person contact might lead the wrong people our way, which is a distraction we can't afford. Two, I can't keep fucking him without resolving shit. It will definitely cause trouble. Three, if he told Mo about it, I don't know if I can face knowing he hasn't tried to reach out."

"He's got the most to answer for, if you ask me. Make him beg," Lys says. She jumps to her feet, bouncing her toes as she pretends to jab at the air. "Give him one of those flying dick punches."

I blink, covering my mouth as I smother a laugh. She looks ridiculous, for one, but also, I'm not sure I can bring myself to damage the one useful part of him before I have a reason. *Remy, you've flipped your lid completely.* Shaking my head, I rise to my feet and head towards the door. "Come on, Rocky. Let's get some cardio in to burn off that energy, and then we'll see if the wily thief has any new info for us."

"Fine," she groans as she follows me out the door. "But if I pass out running laps around the fucking block in New York City, you'd better make sure I don't land in piss."

"Your odds are about eighty-twenty. Better watch your step," I mutter as I take off.

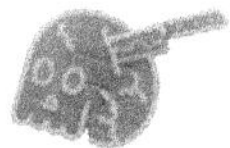

BY THE TIME we come back to the loft, there are multiple things inside making noise. I pant as I disengage the security system to let us in, smirking at Lys as she pantomimes dying on the floor in front of the door. She did fine, despite her dramatics, but I'm glad I decided we need to get more running in. I'm not sure what she'd do if she had to sprint through the jungle to survive, but I know it wouldn't be lasting for very long. The thought bothers the shit out of me, and I hold the door for her to stagger in before closing it behind us.

"You… barely made it." I accuse as I limp over to the tech area. "So much for convincing me you don't need training."

Lys flops on the couch, sprawling out like a starfish as she moans. "Remy, you added three fucking miles after we'd be running for two hours. You're not an assassin; you're a sadist!"

She's right on both accounts—mostly.

"When you're done being a drama llama, you can join me in being awesome," I retort as I sit in the big desk chair. I hurt, too, but not like her. I may have missed a few training days since I got back, but at least I'm headed back to my former fitness level. "There's a message on my 'Duchess' email. I haven't touched it since that damn party before the explosion."

"Are you going to open it? What if it tells people you're alive?"

Wrinkling my nose, I shake my head. "No one besides the guys knows I'm the Duchess. And unless the Douche made the connection between her and The Guillotine, no one expects me to be dead."

"Then why did we spend all the time getting into the *Forum* as nobodies?" Lys peels herself off the couch and hobbles over to join me. "Feels like we wasted a lot of time. The Duchess was sure to get an invitation."

"She did," I say softly as I point to the screen. "That's what the email is about."

"Jesus, Remy! We've been killing ourselves. What the hell was it for?"

Pausing as I gather my thoughts, I scratch my chin. "Truthfully, I wasn't sure if she would. If we hadn't developed other methods of getting in, we'd be screwed if we waited, and she wasn't on the list. But more than that, I wanted us to get invites to come in through the back door—figuratively—rather than enter as guests. This thing is bound to be held in some enormous fucking building in the middle of nowhere with layers on layers of security. There will be digital and physical things in place to keep unwanted visitors out."

"So?" My friend shrugs and gives me a confused look. "That's nothing either of us haven't faced before."

"Perhaps, but this is likely to be akin to breaking into Buckingham Palace. There will be way too many criminals, way too much loot, and too much to lose if we have to navigate breaking in and out." I tilt my head, running calculations in my head as I think about it. "However, The Duchess being invited adds a dimension to our approach we didn't have until now."

"Which is what? Putting a piece up for auction?"

An idea occurs to me and I go silent, unable to respond until my mind flashes through the variables. When I come back to reality, I grin broadly. "Yes, that's *exactly* what we'll do. I'll pull a piece out of storage and send it to be sold. Something that hasn't been seen in long enough that it will draw attention. But we'll still use the aliases to get onto the grounds as we planned before."

My friend sighs, pulling off her sneakers and wiggling her toes with a groan of pleasure. "Uh-huh. So what do you plan to sell off? A Monet? Etruscan statuary? Coins? And what the hell does selling it get you?"

"I have several paintings that even a *whisper* about being present at this thing will draw more attention than almost anything else being sold—except for the human collateral, of course." My lips curve up as I remember the night I established The Duchess with fondness. The normie world does not know who pulled off that heist, but in criminal circles, it won't be a surprise. It's about time someone started to upload that stuff. After all, it's been half a decade, and no one has even come close to solving the mystery.

"You know what? I'm going to let you surprise me. I feel I'm going to vomit when you tell me, and I'd prefer not to dry heave right now." I shrug and Lys grumbles. "What does selling them get us besides drooling fuckwits?"

"A place to leave a change of clothes, of course." I give her a smug look. "They won't open the crates until the owner is present. Before they go up for sale, they'll locate the owner, authenticate the items, then put them up for sale. Since we're all criminals, no one will chance opening the items and being accused of crooked shit if something is missing or damaged. Once we get into the facility as our other identities, we'll figure out where the dock is and sneak off to re-dress."

My friend gives me a wry look. "And who shall I go as, Mrs. Peacock? I got into the damn thing as Elysium."

I wave my hand. "I'll work you up as The Cat. No one's seen her face and The Duchess bringing her protégé won't get questioned."

"What are those boys going to do? There's no way they're going to back off now."

I sigh, leaning my head back against the chair. "That's the hard part. I'll have to use the earpiece to contact Dwyn. Otherwise, he or Mo could blow our damn cover."

"They *will* blow your cover if you don't." She looks at the boards, her brow furrowing for a moment. "What do you plan to do after you're changed into The Duchess? How is that going to help us get out of there with… whoever you find?"

I shrug, giving her a wicked grin. "I'm going to buy them."

She blinks, looking at me agape. "You're going to… buy… them?"

"Seems a hell of a lot easier than planning some elaborate escape, doesn't it? Sometimes, the simplest solution is the best one. I have more money than I could ever spend and the ability to make exponentially more, given my age. Dropping a couple million to save someone isn't a big deal."

Putting her hands over face, Lys tilts her head back, huffing an annoyed breath towards the ceiling. "You cannot seriously tell me you can afford to get in a bidding war with these rich assholes without batting a lash."

I think for a minute, then nod slowly. "I can and I will. I don't think it'd be prudent to go past a billion and a half, but then, D and Mo will be there. They'd probably chip in if we had to. I don't know what their finances look like now, but I can't imagine they'd be too far behind me."

"We're hunkered down in an abandoned building, Remy!"

"It's in a good location? Plus, why the hell do I need more than what we have here at the moment? There's a kitchen and places to sit and beds. I have computers and excellent security. What the hell is wrong with this loft?"

Her strangled growl confuses me, but I spin my chair around to look at my bestie honestly. "I like luxury after a job; it's why I stay in really nice suites for a bit before the next one. But I don't need more than what I use to work—and I'm damn good at my job. I don't review a file for less than five mil, Lys, and my price structure compensates me handsomely for tougher jobs and materials. Depending on what other jobs I take, I can clear eight figures in a quarter without trying."

"And we don't pay taxes because we're crooks," she says with a chuckle.

"No, I do in some places. My finances are labyrinthian mazes, but there are legitimate businesses I keep squared away, so I don't draw attention to myself. Shelf corps and real estate, that kind of shit."

"Does that mean you'll buy me a pony for Christmas?"

I blink, looking at her curiously. "If that's what you want and we don't die next week, sure."

She bursts into laughter and I watch, unsure what I said that was so funny. "You don't have to; I was only being silly."

"But do you *want* a pony?"

"I did as a kid. Who didn't?"

"Then I'll get you one." I kick off my shoes, wiggling my toes as I stretch. "We should RSVP to this thing, then I want to take a shower. We're ripe as hell."

"Remy, you don't have to get me a damn horse. You know that, right?"

"Yep. Now, type for me. Your whining has worn me out." I wink playfully as she elbows me out of the way to get closer to the keyboard.

She might have been joking, but The Guillotine keeps her promises.

If we make it to Christmas, that girl is waking up to a fucking horse if it kills me.

CHAMPIONS

REMY

"I think we've got all the possibilities covered," I murmured as I looked at the materials spread out across the walls of the old classroom. We picked this place because they abandoned it long before they brought us to the island. I may not have arrived the same year as the guys, but they only beat me by two years, max. Trusting their assessment wasn't easy, but we've yet to be proven wrong. Nothing has been touched when we weren't here; we'd know because a fate worse than death would have been meted out swiftly.

Les Invisibles didn't suffer traitors; they made certain everyone in residence knew what befell those who dared to cross those lines.

Mo studied the walls quietly, as was his typical behavior. His unease about the timing of our escape was a constant, so I meticulously plotted for every variable I could think of short of a zombie attack. I knew he still wasn't satisfied, but he got outvoted by the other boys. "What if they reschedule the induction for Volkov's team?"

"They won't. In the entire time we've been captive on this island of terrors, have they ever canceled an induction?" I looked at him in exasperation, frustrated that nothing I did made him happy. "They didn't even postpone the year that Legion member died during a mission the morning of the ceremony. That's not a plausible situation, Mo."

"Failure to plan—"

"Oh, stuff it, Mo-Mo. You've picked apart every one of her back-ups for months. There's nothing left to fuck this up. You're demanding she account for things that aren't ever going to happen."

I gave Dwyn a grateful look, and his grin made my chest tighten. It took years for me to befriend them all, but becoming a part of their group was almost immediate. Once I had the support of all the members of Team Five, they made sure no one else gave me a problem for being one of them. That shouldn't have been an issue, but they were all handsome as hell and the other girls hated how close I was to them. I went from invisible to unable to hide within weeks after they took me in fully.

"D's right, Mo. Remy has tested all the permutations repeatedly. We've even stressed tested them. This is ready." Raz looked at the tense boy with an earnest expression, and it was hard to keep from turning red.

The biggest secret in my life wasn't that I was being groomed to be a lethal assassin who operates outside the law for profit. No, the dark truth hidden in my soul was that I'd fallen for all of my team members one by one—an unfortunate circumstance that would end badly for me. Even escaping with them wouldn't change the fact that they saw me as a spoke on their wheel to be used as our missions saw fit. I was a friend they depended on in the field and someone they protected, but I'd never be like the girls they took for 'private tutoring.'

"You either trust me or you don't," I said belligerently.

My tone was more forceful than I intended, but thinking about the guys with the other females always made me cranky. They damn near terrified any male who came near me—which made losing my virginity a feat of epic plotting— but I was expected to endure whatever rude chippy they had along for the ride that week. I loved them too much to complain about it, other than when they were being dicks to innocent dudes who approached me. I had no intention of getting into some ridiculous fight with one of the few female survivors on this hellhole because they were availing themselves of the cocks I coveted.

Life is far more complex than petty grievances and I never had time for that kind of bullshit.

I wanted to be free.

Nothing on this planet would prevent me from achieving that goal, even the whims of my foolish heart.

"Remy, what do you need us to do?" Jinx gave me his dazzling smile and I almost forgot how to speak for a second.

"Uh…" I blinked and cleared my throat. "I need Mo to place the explosives. You and D are people wrangling. Raz will take the tech. Coda will be the temporary distraction at the ceremony. I'll make my way to the rendezvous point at the marina and check the supplies."

"I still don't like it."

"Relax, man," Coda crooned as he strummed his guitar across the room. "We've been working on this for a fucking year. It's solid."

Turning to face them all, I calm the thumping of my heart as I look at them. I can't ever have them, even if there was a moment in the jungle with Coda, but we can get away from this evil place. We can strike out on our own and make our own business together. I'll always have them as partners and my team; it will have to be enough.

"We're doing it tonight. Everyone needs to be ready. It's time for us to finally be free."

Gasping, I wake up and look around the loft with wide eyes. I haven't had dreams about the night I died for a couple of years. Somehow, I'd convinced myself I was past them, but obviously, I'm not. I scrub my hand over my face, hoping I didn't wake Lys. We have to be at the drop point for the fucking *Forum* in… I squint at the clock on my phone with a groan.

In two hours.

I press my lips together, looking up at the ceiling as my brain spins. Anxiety courses through my frame as I try to shake off the feeling of dread filling me. The last time I trusted an operation involving Mo and Dwyn, it literally blew up in my face and, ironically, so did my last meeting with The Five. My nose wrinkles as I fight the urge to doubt the entire situation—even as far back as the bomb.

Maybe it's too convenient that they all disappeared. Maybe the others are hiding, laughing at the girl dumb enough to fall for their shit twice.

"Maybe they're going to hand me over to that one-eyed sadist to ascend to their thrones," I whisper into the darkness.

Rolling off the bed, I pad into the living area, needing to move. I've never made wise decisions with these boys. Look at how I rushed to 'save' Coda despite it risking the cover I worked for over a decade to create. I ignored my gut with the fucking Shadow Douche and his job offer, then lied to myself about why I took it. My arms wrap around my torso, squeezing as I muddle through my paranoia.

"You've been acting like a silly teenage girl, Remy, not The Guillo-tine." Sucking in a deep breath, I walk over to the weapons table, my fingers itching to grasp something solid and trustworthy. I find a dagger first, closing my eyes as I savor the sensation of its pommel in my hand. Spinning on one foot, I launch at the target on the far wall, smiling faintly when it embeds in the center. "This is who you are."

"I disagree."

I whirl around, dropping into a defensive stance out of habit, but my muscles unclench when I see Lys leaning against the door frame. "Jesus fuck, if I hadn't thrown that before you spoke, you'd be a goddamn pincushion."

"That's why I waited until you were no longer armed." Her smile is crooked as she walks over the counter, running her fingers over the various weapons. "I didn't want to scare you, but I had to say something."

"Like what?"

"You're full of shit, Remy Benoit."

I arch a brow at her, picking up another knife and testing its heft. "Dangerous words when I'm barely awake and within reach of steel."

"Maybe, but someone has to tell you when you're being an asshole, even if it's to yourself." She grins as she picks up a switchblade, flicking it in and out before pointing it at me. "And you are *definitely* being a morose asshole right now."

I glare at her, tossing the knife in my hand at the target, then crossing my arms over my chest. "Defend your statement."

Lys rolls her eyes, but sighs. "Fine. I don't know the whole story about you and those guys on Death Island, but here's what I know. You crawled out of that hole and made a life for yourself. That took courage and good instincts. I'm sure a lot of what you had to do in order to build that legacy was ugly, but you don't regret it because you made the choices you had to. Your ability to thrive even in a nuclear wasteland is fucking amazing."

Shrugging, I look away. "I'm good at adapting; so what?"

"You don't just adapt. Look at how we met up for the first time in years and you realized I was an asset. After the mess at the party, you could have given me the kiss-off, but you didn't. It was obvious you did not know how to handle working with another person, but you've changed your approach to not only work with me successfully, but retrain me."

"I hate sloppy work. Whoever brought you in was a fucking lazy twat."

She snorts. "Maybe, but you didn't have to adopt me to fix it. Your instincts told you there was something worth saving and look at what we've done. We've infiltrated this bullshit event, found some of those stupid boys, and we're going to save people tomorrow. Even if it's *not* one of the missing Five, whatever we do to crash this shindig will prevent many people from being hurt."

I sigh deeply, irritated that she figured out I was planning on ruining the day of the traffickers, even if it didn't lead to Coda. The plan never left my head, but Lys knew I was going to fuck up their world, regardless. "I must be getting too predictable. You shouldn't know what I planned in secret."

"Remy, you hate that shit. You didn't have to say it out loud or write it down. I could see the hatred in your eyes when we went to that fucking club. Anyone who missed it simply wasn't paying attention. Besides, everyone has shit they won't tolerate. Yours is this."

She's right, but that doesn't mean I have to like it. I glance at the clock on the refrigerator, noting we've only lost a half hour on this touchy-feely nonsense. "Okay."

"Okay what?"

"Okay, you're right. I'm going to destroy those motherfuckers."

"And?"

She has to stick a fork in me, doesn't she?

"And I'm letting the past cloud my faith in my judgment with The Five," I grit out.

Her smile is smug as fuck as she walks over to the counter, flicking on the coffee machine. "Excellent. I'll make the coffee and you get the food out. We'll eat and go over this plan one more time, so you don't drive me fucking crazy on the drive."

Good fucking luck with that.

THE AIR IS chilly as groups of people stand in the middle of a field, eyeing one another in blatant suspicion. It's not unusual for criminals to behave like this when gathered in a non-neutral location, but since this pow-wow includes pros from the entire spectrum of skill sets, the tension is thick enough to cut with a knife.

Lys is standing with the thieves by a tall tree. They all look ready to bolt at a moment's notice, but her expression is calm. I like that about her, to be honest. She's very emotional about a fuck ton of things, but her approach to the job gets clinical and precise when the chips are down.

To my right, the squirrely ass members of the hackers' contingent are milling about playing with their phones and tablets. They aren't speaking to one another, but I highly doubt they aren't monitoring every single person in the area. Their skills aren't based on physical abilities, so they have to know what's going on around them if they come out of their damn Hobbit holes.

I'm amid the hitters, dressed in yet another well-crafted disguise, since *Dançerina* doesn't have a known face. The rest of the group is mostly male, though there's one square-jawed woman who seems to be of Nordic descent glaring at me like I offended her ancestors. Fuck if I know why, but my policy is to ignore bullshit until I'm forced to put a stop to it. It's not about pacifism as much as wasting my energy on shit that doesn't matter—and I firmly categorize people who form grudges with zero personal knowledge of the other person as irrelevant.

They made the last group grifters, though I don't recognize most of them based on this level. There might be a fixer or two in there, but they're a lot more rare than anyone lets on. They have to combine the talents of the grifter with that of a thief and a leader, with a dash of the most common criminal of all: a politician. Coda is the only one I know whose cover doesn't involve diplomacy or legislation, which makes him a unicorn both in his music career and his criminal undertaking.

That's why he'll net a fortune in this fucking auction and it's why I know in my gut he'll be here.

It doesn't matter if the buyers want sex, intel, or one of the most unique criminals in the underworld: Coda Ramone can do it all.

A LITTLE BIT DANGEROUS

REMY

"Out!"

My eyes narrow as the men wearing various ancient looking animal masks prod us towards a door at the opposite end of the building from where the grifters and thieves are headed. I'm not thrilled with Lys being that far away, but I'm even less happy about this fuck knuckle aiming a Mac-10 at my spinal column. I don't have the option of preventing either at the moment, but I turn to look at the one who touched me. He's wearing a gold ram with spiraling horns. I flip him off, glad his attire is unique enough to be memorable.

I'll come back for him later.

We're herded into a large waiting area with plastic benches and chairs. The masked minions gesture for us to take seats and, once all of us get settled, a voice comes over the speakers.

"Greetings, my chosen soldiers!

I am most humbled by your acceptance of this important duty for today's events. Your talents are many, but today, you will assist with herding and keeping our merchandise safe and secure. The assets will be in their dorms for much of the time, but they will need escorts to and from facilities, the dressing area, and to the auction block.

When they get purchased, we will require the buyers to declare intent publicly so we have evidence that will keep lips from getting loose in the future.

You will also be required to help ease that transition via subduing. It is not a main concern, as many sellers choose to pacify their lots prior to ascending the stage, but you must know what is expected of you, yes?"

The speech pattern reminds me of the Douche, just as the invitation audio did. However, broadcasting it over speakers means the fucker may not even be in the same country as this circus, much less the same building. Fury builds in my veins at the careful wording he's using for things like selling, public humiliation, beating or drugging the people being trafficked. I'll have to use the silly calm down shit Lys has been teaching me to bide my time. I have weapons, but not enough to take on this amount of muscle without risking capture.

Fuck this slime ball; I'm going to skin him strip by strip while he screams when I get my hands on him.

My hands clasp together as I glance around, memorizing every single brick in the white walls for when I need to get the hell out of here.

"Now my staff will show you to the main containment units. We will split you up, each taking a hallway to patrol and keep in good order.

Do not worry!

Those who are housed in your sections are unlikely to resist; they are mostly being kept docile by order of their current owners.

Off you go, my brethren!

Omnes una manet nox.[1]"

I suck in a breath as he intones that same fucking motto. There's no doubt in my mind the Shadow Douche is running this fucking show, though the voices in the messages may simply be one of his flunkies reading a script. Talented hackers like Raz can use audio files to filter out noise and unmask weird voice modulations, so this psycho probably has different people recording his bullshit all the time.

The muscle around me look at one another nervously and my lips curve. These people aren't used to megalomaniacal fuckheads. Most hitters get hired by cartels and mobs and idiots like *Tasso*, not the cackling lunatic seeking a suitcase nuke to bomb Disneyland. They don't know what to do with themselves now that they realize they've stepped in a giant pile of elephant poo up to their ankles.

But I do.

I stand, looking at the person in the hold hawk mask with a bored expression. "I need the can. Long ride from meet to here." The hawk shakes their head and I roll my eyes, sighing. "No worries. I can piss on the floor, but it's going to smell eventually."

One of the dudes behind me snorts, muttering something about brass balls, but I ignore it. This skill set thrives on the 'fuck you, I'll crack your spine' attitude. If I show anything less to these ignorant twats in masks, I'll be the brunt of jokes and shoulder checks for the rest of the event. The last thing I need is to lose my shit and castrate someone before I can verify if any of the missing members of The Five are being auctioned here.

"Fine." A burly minion with a goat mask grabs my arm, yanking me away from the front of the group.

Nope. That's not going to happen.

Turning into the man, I grip his forearm as I bring my knee up to slam into his gut. I stomp the instep of his outer foot and dart forward before he can react to headbutt him. The metal of the mask hurts like a bitch, but I spit on the floor as he drops, looking at the rest of the Animal Farm rejects with contempt. "Anyone else want to play or can I piss in peace?

My eyes coast over the other hitters, catching the glimmer of respect in their expressions and my chin goes up a notch. A fucker in a lion mask finally peels away from the huddled group of handlers, jerking his head towards a hallway while keeping well out of my reach. I smirk, watching every crack and crevice of the path to the bathroom carefully. When I walk inside, I scoff at the lion, muttering about listening to me remove my tampon and he scurries away.

I should really write a book on how to fuck up men and influence people.

Waiting until the footsteps fade, I open the door again and check for goons. It's empty, so I come out, heading further down the corridor away from the place they have the rest of my skill set. I pass several locked doors with no windows, but when I listen, I don't hear sounds of life. They must be storage or simply empty at the moment. Padding quietly deeper into the compound, I keep close to the walls until I reach a big open area that seems to be a loading and unloading bay.

Trucks, armored cars, vans, semis, and even a small plane are parked within the enormous structure and dozens of people in uniforms flit around on machinery. This must be where they take delivery of all the lots, then send it to specific areas to be held until it's time for sale. It's exactly what I needed to find, but I have no fucking clue where they're taking art. This entire area is an organized chaos and I'm not going to blend in with their bright jumpsuits in my black tactical shit.

A glint catches my eye and I squint a little as I crouch down. It's one of the stupid animal masks. If I can get to it, no one will question my clothing because these fuckers are higher on the totem pole than dock workers. At least, I assume they are since they're dealing with talent and assets, not just boxes. The trick will be getting over to the owl face before someone sees me and then using it to find out where my goddamn crates are.

One step at a time, Remy.

I watch the people moving for another moment, clocking the patterns of movement before I mark a path. When the big forklift rolls by again, I dart out, diving behind a stack of pallets before it passes. Next, I crouch low, creeping along the back wall until I reach the end of the stacks. I have to pause while several groups of workers carry smaller crates towards a door on the far side, but once they're gone, I scramble to a wall where the mask is sitting by a keypad. I'm adjusting it over my face when someone calls out behind me.

"Oi, you! Come over here and open the door for the prisoners."

With a quick inhale, I let go of Remy and The Guillotine washes over me. Turning to face the loud foreman with a clipboard, I nod, my eyes devoid of emotion as I walk over to grab the end of a chain he's holding onto. If I hadn't slipped into my work mindset, my stomach would have roiled at the state of the ten dirty, scared girls attached to the chain like animals. They're chattering in another language—Mandarin, I believe—but I pretend not to understand as I yank the end to get them moving.

Another trail of girls is being led to a doorway nearby, so I walk towards that line of Hispanic teens quickly. There's a minion with a boar mask at the entrance and he looks at me for a moment, then shrugs. "Triad delivery. Eight in line, condition low, probably used. I'll take them in."

Imagining my wire slicing through his carotid is satisfying, but I can't do it right now.

"Got it," I mutter back. Once he takes the chain, I find the workers steering the sealed crates and boxes that appear to be art. I follow them carefully, avoiding the people with clipboards so I don't get distracted again. Time is running short and I don't know if the idiots who took me to the bathroom have discovered my absence yet.

My lips curve when I see a jumpsuit-clad worker struggling to steer a large crate on wheels into a much smaller doorway. By the size, I'd guess it's a sculpture and probably irreplaceable, but this guy is trying to jam it through the frame like Ross with the fucking couch. Hurrying over, I hold up my hand, tilting the box and helping the guy turn and rock it until he's able to get it through the doorway. His expression is terrified when he gets a good look at my mask and he takes off the second we're in the damn storage room.

I guess Hawk Mask is a dick.

No matter, though, because now I'm surrounded by artwork packed in large crates and containers—one of which is definitely mine. I get to work, moving around the room quickly until I find the large wooden crate with the fake shipping information from The Duchess. Grabbing a crowbar from a nearby table, I pry it open to see the three perfectly sized inner crates where the Vermeer and two Rembrandts are wrapped and packed in layers of protective cushioning.

What I want is behind them, so I carefully slide one of the canvas crates out, leaning it against the outer wall so I can squeeze inside to remove the mounds of straw, packing, and rapid fill bags that surround my priceless artwork. My grin is wicked as I find the bottom end of the air-filled pouches, the last five of which contain the clothing and accessories I need to become The Duchess. I leave Lys' items tucked down in the material; she'll have to get it on her own.

Looking around, I find a smaller crate open, the vase inside looking a lot like one I know is missing from the British Museum. This will do, I think. I stuff the bags into the wooden box, put the lid on, and carry it out of the storage room. As I make my way towards the large hallway on the opposite side of the warehouse area, I keep my head up and the air of confidence in place. I need to get past the crowd of worker bees here and into the main section of the complex, then I can change.

"Hey! Where are you going with that box?"

Whipping around, I give the burly guy with a clipboard a dark look through my mask, hoping he's never questioned the person who typically wears it. "The boss wants this to show a client. Special, private viewing."

He eyes me for a minute, then finally nods. "S'posed to radio down for that shit."

"Would you like to tell him that yourself?" I ask, hoping I'm right about how scared the peons in this organization are of its leaders.

"No, no. Uh, yeah. Go that way and uh, carry on."

It never fails; assholes like the Douche always run their shit on fear and ignorance.

Now, I just need to get changed and mingle with the honored guests until it's time. Hopefully, I won't have to wait very long. Shutting down the real Remy and allowing The Guillotine to take charge means I won't have the patience to leave witnesses if someone pisses me off.

---

1. One night awaits us all.

DEAD MAN WALKING

MO

I hate this plan almost as much as I hated the plan on the island.

However, I learned my damn lesson about underestimating our former team member when she showed up very much alive and kicking thirteen years later. We'd attended her fucking funeral, mourned her for years, and never healed—all the while she was busy proving her plan would work even with a fuck ton of unexpected variables thrown in.

Hell, I can't even be mad about it because I'm the one who made everything go sideways. My inability to let her lead without being a controlling asshole got her killed—or should have. Whatever, it's still my goddamn fault. Oddly enough, she doesn't seem to give a shit about that at the moment. In fact, all Remy Benoit is focused on is finding the missing members of The Five.

I'm not sure if it's so she can kill us herself, yell at us until we grovel, or fuck us, but that's her only concern.

After we got back to the crash pad, Dwyn sent Joaquin on an errand and recanted his evening with the glee of a kid in a candy store. The two of them have always been mischievous and down-right dangerous when they worked together. The addition of sex whenever and wherever they feel like adds another migraine inducing dimension that I can't even fathom. If we find Coda, I might actually slam my head against the wall so the pain will keep me sane.

Jinx and Raz were always better at wrangling the two of them. Not knowing if they're alive, dead, or captive is making my skin feel too tight. I felt the same about D until I spotted him, and Coda until Remy said she had a lead. She wouldn't bullshit me if she thought he was dead, so I'm trying to just believe her without a mountain of proof to verify her claim.

It's hard as fuck and that's part of why I hate this goddamn plan.

D and I are using the invitation sent to *El Jefe*. Joaquin convinced him it was too dangerous to come to the States with his enemies watching so closely. It impressed me that he got through the call without pissing his pants, so as a reward, he's posing as his cousin's lackey as he joins us at the *Forum*. We're all dressed in tuxedos and satin eye masks as the plane touches down on the small airstrip. The blindfolds were required of everyone on this flight and all the others, bringing customers to this weird location somewhere upstate. The flight wasn't long, but they kept the windows latched, the Wi-Fi off and they blocked all cellular signals the second we entered the private jet.

I look over at Dwyn as I raise my mask, chuckling as he makes faces while he sings inside his head. He's got Airpods in, of course, but I can only imagine what it sounds like in his mind while he jams out. I've always wondered how he can simply exist before a mission or job without obsessively going over the plan a million times. It's astounding to watch him bounce in his seat to some pop music, crunching on a biscotto without a care in the world.

"Dude, stop staring at me. You can ask a million times, but I'm not going to kiss you."

I take it back; he can do this shit because he's a fucking idiot.

"I'd rather lick a faucet in a gas station bathroom in Vegas, you fuckwit." Even Joaquin flinches at that, and I'm pretty sure he doesn't have a clue just how gross that would be.

"Keep tragically lying to yourself, Mo-Mo. Our girl jumped me like I was a vibrating blue alien and you are *jealous as fuck.* Admit it and maybe I'll help you find the right words to earn your way back into her deliciously sexy graces."

I blink, looking at him in confusion. "A… blue.. alien?"

"It's a book series, *General.*" Dwyn lifts his mask and we both look at him. My tag-a-long drug dealer turns bright red under his olive skin. "What? We have TikTok in Colombia."

Dwyn bursts out laughing, clutching his sides as he reaches over to fist bump with the young lieutenant. I raise my hands, rubbing my temples as I try to rid my brain of thoughts about dirty faucets and vibrating aliens. I need to focus on the upcoming event and fuck if I know how when I'm sitting with Heckle & Jeckle over here.

"Perhaps you two could tell me what the plan is again."

"Uhhhh…" Dwyn looks around, his eyes sweeping over the mostly sleeping people in the surrounding seats. "I dunno how good an idea that is. Too many…" He points to his ears and I roll my eyes.

As if that was some sort of undecipherable code. For fuck's sake.

"We get inside and examine the goods. Watch for her to arrive and monitor the bids. D has the link to her friend, but she's flying solo. I hate it, but she doesn't know how thoroughly they will search her when she wins. Once she has what she wants, we all meet and scram."

The resident psycho gives me a knowing look. "Do you really think that will be the end of this?"

"Nope," I say with a sigh. "You know how she used to be about this shit. I'd be prepared for her to add her own special brand of 'fuck you' to the equation."

Joaquin leans in, his mask raised as he looks at us in confusion. "What does that mean?"

I shrug, shaking my head. "No idea, J. But I advise keeping your eyes open and your ass ready to run."

ONCE THEY HERDED us all off of the plane, they took us inside, allowing us to remove the masks to see a lavish waiting room. I've been at high-powered events before, but the amount of theater involved in this one is insane. The person running it is obviously a complete egomaniac and can't help but try to impress everyone with his over-the-top accommodations. It's not working, but that's because their guests are simply used to being catered to, even the ones who aren't vapid rich people.

My eyes flit to the group on the far side of the room, noting colleagues like *Ape Regina* and *Alqatu* milling about with their inner circles. There are CEOs, heirs, minor royalty from across the globe, and celebrities pretending not to know one another. Various socialites and well-known diplomats are in attendance and it disgusts me to see at least a few legislators and justices from several countries.

Avarice has no national identity, only an insatiable thirst.

When a man in tails enters from the inner doorway, the room goes quiet. He's tall, with a thin mustache and a regal bearing that is born of being raised in the profession he's employed in. A real English butler standing before the gathering of elites and billion-aires isn't unusual, but this one knows he's holding the keys to a wonderland of dark desires for everyone here.

"Ladies, gentlemen, honored guests, and Your Majesties, it is my sincerest honor to welcome you to the twenty-twenty-three *Forum Romanum*. You will step inside one at a time, receive your assigned paddles and bid cards, then you are free to examine the merchandise as you see fit. There is an open bar and servers will pass rare and exotic delights for you to nibble on as you browse. Please form a line in front of me with the dignity of your exalted positions."

I look at Dwyn, baffled by this development. This isn't how the underworld auctions are run; no, it's more like a private auction at Sotheby's than the normal procedures. Remy isn't in the room with us, nor is her little thief friend, and it makes me nervous as hell that something has happened.

"Relax, Mo-Mo. The chick would have tapped the link if shit went off the rails."

I wish I shared his confidence, but this is fucking weird.

"Is this normal?" Joaquin asks me quietly.

Shaking my head, I lead my companions to the line, making certain we aren't near the front or the back. I'm not fond of the attention you get from being in either position, and I want to remain as inconspicuous as possible. "No. This is… I don't know what this is."

"*El Jefe* would not like being here. You were right to have me convince him to stay at home. We are very exposed and they are funneling us like cattle. Dangerous for those who have enemies."

"No shit," Dwyn grumbles. "Luckily, *Benjamin Norquist* and *Rafael de Palma* don't have ties to anyone but your uncle. That should keep people away on principle—drug lords aren't the most hospitable sorts."

I tune them out as we move towards the front of the line. Something about the way this event is set-up makes the hairs on the back of my neck stand up. It's not just my operational awareness;

there's more to it than a big ass money pit for everyone to dive into. Bottlenecking the crowd, secret transport, and masked staff members working the entryway? Everything about this is tweaking my internal tripwires—I just don't know what part to focus on to work out what the bigger picture is.

"Next?" The person at the table is wearing all black and an ancient looking gold cat mask that covers their face. I frown at them, but pull the invitation and letter of approval from *El Jefe*. The cat rifles through a stack of papers, marking off a line on one, then returns the documents to me. A bid card and a paddle appear, both emblazoned with the number two hundred and sixty-seven on them. "You may enter with your party. Browse, imbibe, and enjoy our bacchanalian delights."

Jesus Christ, this dipshit is full of himself.

Nodding, I walk through the heavy door, Dwyn and Joaquin trailing behind me. The first thing I see is an enormous warehouse that's been converted to a lavish show room full of miniature stages in long rows and columns. Signs hang on the ceiling right as we come in, pointing us towards goods, services, or exotic delights. It doesn't take a genius to figure out the last one is where the living merchandise will be, so I jerk my head in that direction.

We follow the arrows until we reach a partition that stretches from one end of the warehouse to the other. Heavy velvet curtains block our view and three fucking giants I recognize guard the entrance. These assholes are from my skill set and they're here to make certain no one without the means to purchase from this area gets in. Holding up my bid card, I wait for it to be scanned. When his device gives the green light, the gorilla-like jackass grunts and nods at one of the others. He pulls the curtain back and the three of us step inside the dark area carefully.

"Holy shit, Mo," Dwyn whispers as he looks at the first stage. "Do you know who that is?"

"The fucking British girl they never found," I growl under my breath. "She's a goddamn teenager now and look what the hell they have her wearing."

This shit is going to make me lose it.

Before I lose my grip, a woman steps in front of me. She's got long, wavy red hair and a pinup body poured into a bright purple satin dress. Her eyes are a deep blue, matching the extremely expensive looking sapphire and platinum cat-eye pendant dangling from her neck. She gives me a sultry smile, then winks at my companions. "Hey, there sailors. Don't go rocking the boat just yet. It's not time for the party."

"Who the fuck are you?" Dwyn asks. "Are we supposed to know you?"

The redhead shrugs, tilting her head as she gives us an amused look. "Perhaps not, but I know someone we have in common. She'll be coming through that curtain… ah!"

D and I whirl around at her words, turning just in time to see Remy glide in with all the grace of her moniker. She's clad in a black satin gown that reminds of Audrey Hepburn, right down to the pearls at her neck and wrists. Her hair is honey colored tonight, piled on top of her head in a sleek up-do that's adorned with a small tiara. My lips curve as I watch her walk in, wondering where in the hell she's got all her weapons stashed in a dress that is so revealing.

I'd enjoy searching for—no. No, that's not happening anytime soon.

"Well, I'll be a beer-battered biscuit," Dwyn drawls playfully. "Our girl is looking *smoking* tonight."

"Not our girl," I mutter as I remember the weird woman and turn back to face her—but she's gone. "Where the fuck did she run off to? And who was she?"

"Hell if I know. The people here are weird. Let's just follow Jazzy from a distance." He pauses and looks at me sternly. "And don't fly off the damn handle. This is all fucked and we know it, but we can't save everyone. Our priority tonight is our girl and our brothers—if they're even here."

Fuck, I hate when he's right.

BIG BAD WOLF

REMY

The minute I walk into the closed off area, my eyes are drawn to Mo and Dwyn like magnets. They look fucking fantastic and my body reacts like I didn't just fuck the shit out of D in that club recently. Of course, before this damn clusterfuck, I was having sex a lot more often, so this dry spell brought on by my intense focus is affecting me more than I'd like to admit. However, I can't let hormones distract me when my mission tonight is this important.

Especially not as The Duchess.

My chin raises as they allow me entrance and I move through the crowd without so much as a glance their way. I know they'll follow; it's the plan. But a little part of me wishes I could see their reaction to the disguise we put together for this affair. I'm not lacking in self-esteem; I simply want to know they're suffering at my hands, even minimally. The wounds from my past and my current thirst for remuneration demands tribute despite the battle going on in my heart.

I don't look at every exhibit for fear of losing my cool. The call for valuable merchandise in *Mercatus* was enough to tip me off, but I also heard the discussions in the club when Lys and I were there. Hearing the casual discussion of selling unwilling people for nefarious purposes was bad enough; seeing the toll being owned and used takes on those people will stoke a fire I can't yet unleash. So I keep my eyes directly ahead, moving toward the far end where the most valuable lots will be showcased.

The distance is farther than I would have expected, and I know it means there is an inordinate amount of people being sold to the disgusting customers in attendance. Gritting my teeth as I pretend not to hear leering men and snooty women discuss purchasing slaves and servants like it's absolutely normal, I continue down the aisle with one purpose in mind: find out if any of The Five is being auctioned.

When I reach the last stage, it's empty, but there's a crowd standing in front of it practically licking their chops. If the look on the faces of the deviants waiting is any sign, this is the spot where I might strike gold. The lots right before it contained captured spies and soldiers from both sides of the law, including the erstwhile Constance. She was blindfolded, but she looked as though they had kept her clean but sedated. I should have been more concerned about her, but despite my Duchess outside, I'm still The Guillotine on the inside... so I'm not worried about her in the slightest.

The only thing I want is what's owed to me—the chance for closure with those who betrayed me.

I will permit no one to take that from me, no matter what the cost. My eyes drift over the crowd as we wait for the big reveal, and I arch a brow when I see the spiky platinum locks of the killer I've met once before. His curvaceous redhead is standing next to him, and before I know it, she catches my gaze. Her lips quirk and she leans in to kiss his sharp jaw before she saunters over to me.

"We meet again," she practically purrs. "Bidding on something you lost, I take it?"

My eyes narrow and I nod. "Yes. Someone at this event—or more than one someone—is about to die, I assume?"

She laughs throatily, her shoulder rising and falling carelessly. "Perhaps. My husband and I are here as observers more than contractors. It's my primary and our wife that have skin in this game."

Frowning, I try to untangle that sentence, but I don't quite get there. "Huh?"

"You may have met our bronzed spouse—she goes by The Blade when she's working?"

That gets my attention. It also explains why the woman was so interested in me at the club. Apparently, I just attract psychos. "I didn't know she was… your… wife?"

"Mine and his. My primary mate rarely accompanies her on jobs; when he moved into my home, he retired from the life of an operative. However, much like me, he cannot say 'no' to the woman he loves. Our husband is no different with us, I suppose."

"That's… a lot of information to take in at once," I reply lamely. "You're… all married? And to… *Le Voleur?*"

The redhead laughs again, her eyes twinkling as she nods. "He *hates* that name, you know. Says it's far too Lestat de Lioncourt for him. I like to call him that when I'm trying to piss him off; it makes for *excellent* make-up sex."

I blink at her again, unsure how the hell I'm supposed to be reacting. "Angry sex is pretty hot."

Yeah, way to be smooth, Remy.

"It is! But you don't have to worry, Guillotine. We're not here at the behest of our employers, nor are we going to purchase your rock god. I have more than enough alpha male bullshit to juggle between my spouses and my family. I simply enjoy finding another female in our profession who is smart, capable, and loyal."

How the fuck does she know I'm any of those things?

I give her a confused look, and she winks at me. "Don't overthink it. I have many things at my disposal. You haven't even dreamed of what I can access, and I'm not talking about Company tech. Just know they don't control me or my spouses, and you have allies should you need. All you have to do is ask."

"How would I get a hold of you?"

"You know how to whistle, don't you?" With that, she turns on her heel, walking back to the man in the bespoke tuxedo holding a glass of what I hope to hell is red wine.

I'm not sure what fucking vase I broke in another life, but I'm well over my limit for weird shit happening to me for a while.

I shake my head to clear it, intending to turn around and look for the guys, but right at that moment, the lights on the small stage go dark.

It's showtime.

"LADIES AND GENTLEMAN. The final lot in our special auction is so tempting that we require you to be screened before we give you access to bid. Please approach one of the staff members holding bid card readers if you wish to participate. They will verify you can cover the starting bid and after that, we will show you a live feed of the asset in question. The tablet we give you will allow you to bid at the auction for thirty minutes. It will close with the high bid and we will escort the winner to claim their prize. If the winner cannot authenticate their intentions, we will open the bids again after we have dealt with the loser."

That's the second time they've used that terminology and I don't like it one bit. What the hell does it mean to authenticate their intent? I originally thought they meant verify the payment once purchased, but that doesn't seem likely in this context. They're checking our bank accounts before we're even allowed to view their most valuable product. Outside of confirming an instant bank transfer, there's nothing to 'authenticate' after that.

A short man in a tux walks up to me, holding out the bid card scanner with a bland smile. "Are you bidding, Duchess?"

My lips curve and I pretend to consider it, hoping my coy act will make the avid eyes around me discount my desire to win. "Oh, I suppose so. Is the prize really worth all this fuss?"

"I believe you will be pleased, Miss." I wave my card over the device and the light turns green. "Here is your tablet. Hold on to it and in a few short moments, the video auction will begin. Follow that group just ahead to the viewing area."

Shit. They're pulling us away from the others so no one too poor to play along sees what they have to sell.

I nod at the staffer, taking my thin tablet before I look over my shoulder. Dwyn and Mo look unhappy when they see the line of people in front of me who are moving to enter another space with their handhelds. The kid Mo seems to have adopted pokes his arm, whispering something to him that gets a vehement head shake. I'm not sure why they've suddenly invited this cartel crony into the circle, but I doubt it's because he's a brilliant tactician.

Lys hasn't appeared yet and I tap my ear, hoping Dwyn is watching something besides my ass as I head for the line to get into the viewing area. I can't wait for her or the guys to devise a plan; I'm going 'old school Remy.'

That means solo and only worried about the target I'm here to deal with.

THE TABLETS COME ALIVE NOT long after we're ushered into the small, nondescript room. My heart lurches into my throat when I see Coda sitting in a chair in a barren cell. He looks a little underweight, at least, from what I've seen in the media before everything went to hell and what I felt lugging his ass around Paris. His eyes are dull, like he might be drugged, and his fingers are tapping on his knees rhythmically. He's been locked up for all this time without a guitar. Hell, he might have even gone through detox in that cell.

No wonder he looks like his soul has left his fucking body.

Anger wells up within me and I have to clench my hands around the device carefully before I snap it in half. Coda Ramone may have betrayed me as a kid, but I've never wished shit like this on him or any of them. Maybe a bad case of crabs in the early years, but not the despair I see etched on his face. They have disconnected him from his life, his family, his escape, and his music—they're lucky he didn't snap something and cut his wrists. According to the news, it wouldn't be the first time he'd tried over the years.

Though, I thought perhaps they used that as an excuse to cover for mission injuries. Seeing his expression on this video, I'm not sure I was right. I think Coda is more broken than anyone realized, and this imprisonment has made it worse. It makes the fire inside of me turn to unforgiving ice.

All I have to do is win this fucking auction and I can burn this goddamn place to the ground.

The video goes on for a little longer, then it finally cuts to the bid screen. I don't flinch at the opening bid of ten million. It's a drop in the bucket for someone who looks, sings, and parties like Coda. My eyes track every raise, topping it within a half second as people attempt to snipe the rock star out from under one another. The bids escalate, getting faster and more aggressive as the timer counts down the minutes at the top of the screen. I'm winning most of the time, but there's another bidder who seems intent on outbidding me.

My eyes cut to the side briefly, trying to figure out who is riding my ass this closely. If I can scare them, they might back off. Clicking the button to raise to eighteen, I watch to see which people jump on the next level. I finally catch the old bat, hoping to snipe me when we hit twenty-five. I reach into my bodice, pulling out the small throwing knife tucked between my boobs. Pinching it, I wait until I've answered her next counter, then fling the knife hard at her chair.

It embeds in the back of the chair with a solid 'thwack,' distracting the woman as she turns to see what happened. Her face turns deathly pale when she sees the weapon, and she looks around for the culprit. When she gets to me, I wink at her, practically daring her to report me. She swallows hard and returns to her chair, but the rapid one-up bids stop.

Take that, you sick old witch.

Before long, the timer winds down and I only have to raise a few more times as the last minute sniping assholes try to wiggle in at the last second. The auction closes at forty, which is respectable, but not as high as I thought my ex-friend would go for. Inflation really is fucking shit up for everyone, I suppose.

"Bidder two hundred sixty-seven, please step forward and follow your steward to the authentication room."

Rising from my seat, I ignore the rest of the people in the room as I walk to the stage. I won't do them the courtesy of acknowledging their existence after I spent the past half hour keeping Coda out of their dirty hands.

"This way, Duchess. Your prize awaits authentication, and then we can discuss transportation."

RIVER

CODA

They've got me in front of a fucking camera, streaming for all of their buyers to see.

It was obvious this was coming; the noises outside my cell increased over the past couple days, including some new additions who were far less quiet than me. Females, young ones, crying and sniffling as they passed and one girl who was so obnoxious as she screeched about her father that I almost stopped feeling sorry for her.

Almost.

But when they took me to the shower area and gave me clothes that resembled my normal attire, I knew the day of reckoning was upon me. I've bided my time because I know jack shit about this place and escaping with no information and no plan would not help me. My best chance at getting away was definitely either in-transit to a new location or once I got to the buyer's hideaway. They kept me in good condition, so I was less concerned about being sold for my *LI* knowledge than to a pervert—something that boded well for my ability to run.

Those people are far less capable with security, even if they've paid experts to design their dungeons.

So I remained compliant, pretending to take the meds they gave me, and finished my food like a good little prisoner. But my mind is clear now and my strength is coming back. I'm ready to plan my escape once I know what I'm up against, I just have to survive this fucking auction without losing my shit. That's easier said than done, depending on what they ask of me with this damn camera on. It hasn't been invasive yet, but I don't know how far they'll go to entice their buyers.

Time drags as I stare into the lens as the goons in animal masks encourage me to do from the sidelines. My hyperactivity flares, so I press my fingertips to my thighs, playing piano exercises on them to get some of the restlessness out. I can't let them see how badly I need to move; I don't want someone to sedate me for transport. So I clench my jaw and force a cocky grin on my face as I play through scales on the sides of my legs.

You just need to last long enough to get out of this place, Coda. You can do it.

Oddly, the voice sounds like Remy—the new one, not the one we thought was dead. I've dreamed of her every night since I was conscious enough to remember it. Well, her and my brothers, plus revenge on the fucks who have me in a goddamned prison cell. Sometimes it's all of us beating the living fuck out of my faceless captors and that's my favorite non-naked version.

Thinking of the sultry badass who stood up to us at the damn zoo makes my cock twitch, and I curse D and Jinxy in my mind. Those fuckers got a taste of her without even apologizing because they *happened* on her in disguise. It's not fucking fair, and I still want to punch them for it. She might have saved my drunk ass in Paris, but I didn't even get a chance to grope her! Of all the outrageous bullshit that's gone on since that night, not being able to feel her up is one of the most egregious things.

That's right… I said it. Not squeezing her perfect ass is worse than this stupid prison.

"The auction is now *closed*. Bidder two hundred sixty-seven, please step forward and follow your steward to the authentication room."

Shit. Authentication room? What the fuck is that?

Cursing my brain for running off on its own while the stupid timer counted down, I watch the Bear and the Tiger mask flick the camera off. They undo the hidden restraints on the chair and haul me to my feet.

"Well, it's been lovely, gents, but looks like our time together is at an end," I snark, hoping to get a reaction out of them. If they're inclined to be dicks, they might clue me into what the hell goes on in this room I'm being dragged to.

A grunt is the only sound the Bear makes and the Tiger snorts. That doesn't help at all.

"Guess I'll have to find out what's coming when I get there, eh? You guys are no fun at all."

MY EYES POP open when they lead me to a room primarily filled with a giant king size bed.

Oh, fuck…. literally.

"Are we having a sleepover? I haven't done that since I was a kid, but I guess if that's your thing…"

The Bear grunts, shoving me toward the bed roughly. His partner comes over and yanks me up, positioning me at the end of the bed upright. I'm not restrained, but I guess that's the point. These motherfuckers expect me to service whoever bought me in the middle of this damn thing and… I look, catching the blink of a light in the corner.

They're taping it. Son of a bitch.

"I guess that's what 'authentication' means, huh? If your buyer grows a fucking conscience, you've got them on tape forcing someone to have sex, so they can't share this with law enforcement. You're sick; who works for people who think this is okay?"

Neither of my captors respond. They leave me fuming in my spot, closing the door behind them. My eyes skate around the room, looking for something, anything that could ward off whatever pervert is coming for me. There's nothing but the bed—not other furniture, toys, or even lube.

Not good. Not fucking good at all.

Swallowing hard, I close my eyes. Sexual abuse wasn't as big a threat on the island for guys as it was for girls, but most of them got desensitized to it quickly. We had classes teaching us to use our bodies as lures and weapons—embarrassing, but part of the curriculum. Chicks like Remy mastered the art of pretending to seduce their captors and targets without even thinking about it. And I'd be lying if I said I'd never done it myself, but… this is different.

This doesn't give me a choice and I want to fucking smash something.

Getting through it will require going somewhere else in my head, just like we do during torture. You find a happy place, and let go of yourself, disconnecting from reality to hide in the shelter of your memory. It won't keep you from being damaged, but it sure as hell helps you survive until it's over. At least, that's what I remember from CapRes training. I haven't had to do it since they inducted us because my skill set doesn't get down and dirty like that.

I take a deep breath, closing my eyes and letting my mind float away, preparing for the worst when the door opens.

"This way, Madame. Your purchase awaits. Once you are authenticated, we will return with toiletries. You will be given the choice of retiring to the luxury suites or being transported to your vehicles afterward."

My eyes are still closed, but I can't help being relieved it's a woman. I'm not opposed to hot guys at all, but the lack of lubricant worried me. If this is inescapable, I didn't want to be in some makeshift infirmary afterwards. That would be the final nail in the humiliation coffin.

"I'll take my leave now, Madame. Enjoy and thank you for attending our premier event." The door closes behind the guy, leaving us in silence.

I can't take it anymore.

It takes enormous willpower, but I finally pry my eyes open only to have my jaw drop in shock. The smug grin of the woman dressed like a classic film beauty gives the disguise away. Her eyes, hair, and bearing are completely different, but after the zoo, I can never mistake that look again. The elegant, regally dressed buyer is none other than Remy Arsine Benoit and she looks so pleased with herself that it's making my words stick in my throat.

"What, no relieved greeting? Not even a curse? I'm disappointed, Coda."

Blinking, I rise to my feet, striding over to her and yanking her against my chest. Our lips crash together violently, painful but hungry as the fear in my gut escapes. I've spent months trying not to be afraid, but having her in my arms at this moment is unleashing every emotion I've locked away—maybe for years. I bite her lower lip hard, suckling on it as she groans against my mouth.

"That's more like it, cowboy. I like being greeted as though you'll die if you don't get to touch me. It's one of my standard rules." Pulling back, I arch a brow at her, and she shrugs, her lips curving up. "Okay, I made that up just now. Sounded good, though, didn't it?"

"It sounds as if you plan on keeping me around," I croak.

Her eyes dance and she snorts. "Remains to be seen. However, I did not know about this authentication bullshit when I decided to purchase you. That memo didn't make the rounds."

"Holy shit, you found them? They're alive?" A sliver of hope blooms in my chest and I put my hands on either side of her face, holding it as I look for the truth.

"Yep. Stumbled on to them—or they stumbled into *my* undercover operation like clod-footed himbos, I should say. Lys and I were tracking leads that would have gotten us to your jailer when this fucking *Forum* shit started. Luckily, I had time to heal before I had to hop into a bunch of fancy gowns and shit. Nothing worse than having to wear all that Dermablend, right?"

I look at her suspiciously. "What would have needed to be covered up?"

That makes her pause for a moment, then she shakes her head. "Later. We need to get out of here, and despite my dislike of the situation, I'm pretty sure there's only one road out."

"Fuck," I mutter. Of course I want her; I've always wanted her. Our fucking kiss that night is part of why Mo lost his shit and sided with Arnaud. But with some pervs recording? That's not at all what I want for the first time I slide inside the girl I've never gotten over. "This sucks."

"Good to know it's such a chore," she shoots back, yanking herself away and stalking towards the door. "I could just—"

Moving more quickly than I have since I got here, I slam her into the door and press my lips to her ear. "That's not what I meant, Spitfire. I meant I prefer not to fuck you for the first time on camera, but we don't have a choice."

"Oh." Her body relaxes against mine and I chuckle softly. "Then fucking say that, asshole. Don't make me think you're going to chicken out like you did last time."

Ouch. Low blow, Remy.

Spinning her around, I lean in to look into her eyes. I plant my arm on either side of her face, hoping to block what I'm saying from prying eyes. "I will *never* choose anyone over you again. Not Mo, not anyone. Do you understand? Nod if you understand."

Her eyes are suspicious, but she nods slowly as I place my lips against hers, our breaths mingling. "And even if it takes me the rest of my goddamn life, I'll make you believe that. But for now, we're going to need to do this quick and dirty. Can you do that, Spitfire?"

"The question is can you, cowboy? Because I happen to *enjoy* being slammed into shit. See for yourself."

Her smirk makes my dick jump again, and I curse under my breath about the lack of time and privacy. Angling my body to block some of her, I lift my hands and reach around to the back of the dress. It's far too contoured to lift it and she'll have to step out of it even for a quickie. The thought of those fuckers seeing her in lingerie makes me snarl, but I pull the zipper down with practiced ease.

"I really should be more angry about how easy that was for you," she mutters as I bend to slide it down her body. I wink up at her before letting her balance on my shoulder to step out of the material.

That's when I pay attention to the shit she has one under the damn thing: a full set of pinup style lingerie complete with sheer black stockings and garters.

"This is bullshit," I grumble as my hand glides up her thighs to settle on her waist. "I demand a redo of this outfit or I'm going to pout for a month. Just letting you know."

"I wouldn't expect any less from a self-centered rock star," she retorts. "Now stop gawking and fuck me so we can get the hell out of here. You haven't forgotten how, right?"

Nope.

I undo the jeans quickly, shoving them down to let my cock spring free. They left boxers, but I didn't bother and when her hand wraps around me, I thank whatever deity gave me the idea to skip them. Grabbing her hips hard, I lift her legs on either side of mine, squeezing as she strokes my eager dick.

"I love when they're pierced, you know. Jinx and D are," she mutters.

"For fuck's sake, woman, focus," I mutter as I push her into the door for balance. "If you must know, we all went together on a drunken lark."

"I cannot think of a better sentence in the English language right now," she breathes as she lets go of me to grind her hips against mine. "It's like my birthday and Christmas wrapped in one. If I did that shit, of course."

Reaching down, I rip the scrap of lace covering her pussy and delve into her heat. She's got steel, too, and for a second, I have to hold still before I do something embarrassing. The slickness I find makes me groan, and I press my forehead against her. "Ready?"

"Mostly. But do it now," she pants softly. "I don't want to wait."

Pulling my fingers away from her, I grip her thighs again and adjust, driving into her hard. The sound that rips from her throat will haunt my dreams for the rest of my life, I fucking swear. I stay still for a moment, clamping down on my self-control, but she squeezes my cock and I lose the battle. Hips piston into her, smacking our bodies together hard and making the door rattle in the frame. I dip my head, kissing her hungrily as I fuck her faster, racing towards a finish I never thought I'd get to see.

When we break to breathe, she growls softly and unwinds one of her arms from my neck. Her hand goes straight to her pussy, and I know she's working her clit while I hold us up.

"Dirty girl," I rumble against her ear. "That's something I'll want to watch later."

"You'll have to be a very good boy first," she shoots back, and I grin wickedly.

Remy was made for us—- and Mo can fuck right off if he thinks I'm ever letting her go.

"Promises, promises," I say as my thrusts speed up. "Right now, it's your turn to be the good girl and come for me. "

IMMORTALS

REMY

THE BASTARDS BARELY GAVE CODA TIME TO ZIP HIS DAMN PANTS before they pounded on the door. My lip curled as I imagined someone standing outside of it listening and I sent a thanks to the universe that he had insisted on removing my bra. I tucked my wire in one cup and a curved blade is hiding under the other breast. I move forward a little, lifting my weight off the wood, but my eyes meet the rocker's, hoping he understands why I don't want to let the camera get a visual of my back without my dress on.

He grins when it hits him, pulling the door open slightly to snatch a bag from whoever is there. Closing it with a click, Coda steps back from me, his eyes still hot as they roam over me. I know he means it, but he's also putting on a show for the feed. Walking over to the bed, he dumps the contents on it, picking up the black pants first. I'd wonder how the hell they knew what size to send, but they look like what the masked guards are wearing. They must have a stock of them on-site.

I catch them when he tosses them my way, carefully stepping in and fastening them over the remnants of my lacy undergarments.

He tosses me a black tee next and I yank it over my head, wanting to get my back covered as quickly as possible. I've got stilettos strapped to the garters on the back of my thighs and two small switchblades clipped to the belt just under where my dress stopped in the small of my back. Keeping that information to ourselves is paramount, especially since we have no idea where they're taking us after this.

"You ready, Spitfire?" he asks, his voice gravelly. I cock a brow, gesturing at the boots still on the bed. He chuckles and walks over with them in hand. "Come now. I've seen you kick a bear's ass *without* shoes. Are you worried about these fools?"

"No," I snort. "But I also prefer not to tear my feet up on unknown shit if I have a choice. That bear thing wasn't voluntary and you know it."

"True. You had to save Razzie from himself." He pauses, then tilts his head. "There's really no trace of the others yet?"

"Not a single word. Hell, it took me months to get something solid on you and not for lack of trying. I probably would have found Mo eventually because he was working. Dwyn's good at burrowing, so he would have taken longer. Jinx always left crumbs—at least when I knew him—so that's concerning. Raz could hole up for eternity, and we wouldn't find him if he didn't want us to. I mean, unless that's changed." I give him an uncomfortable look, shrugging as I make sure my hair is on tight.

"That's pretty spot on. I'm normally easiest because of my cover and Jinx is next. We're in the spotlight more than the others." Coda comes closer, leaning in to press his lips to my temple. "I have faith in you, Remy. When we were younger, I let doubt creep in, but now… I know you're going to save us—all of us."

If only sweet words could make it so.

"FOLLOW ME, Duchess. As requested, we have the plane standing by. I sent a steward for your associates since you informed us you have business with them in the city. You'll be required to wear masks as before until you land, but then you and your purchase will be free to enjoy your new arrangement."

I make a face at the butler as he walks Coda and I through the corridors towards a large hangar. My 'merchandise' is busy smirking at every single person we pass, and it takes a lot of effort not to roll my eyes. He's lapping up the attention—something he's always been good at—and I'd prefer they ignore us. Something about this arrangement feels much too easy, and I don't know what it is. It seems like we're being cut loose with little preamble.

Of course, the payment went through, so unless they know who we are, perhaps it really is this simple.

"Thank you. I am very grateful to you for assisting me with gathering my next team. Allowing them to fly back with me is very convenient and your service is impeccable," I reply as we head into the open area. I didn't catch this guy's name, but I hate knowing he's working for such assholes. I'd bet he'd be a perfect 'Alfred' to someone's Batman rather than working for the fucking Penguin.

When we reach the steps to the plane, I let go of Coda's hand to hold the rail as I ascend. He waits for me to get to the top and I grin to myself. His manners aren't half-bad for a reprobate; maybe we're actually fooling these tools. I wait for him to join me, making my way to the cabin. Sitting on the cushy couch and chairs are Lys, Dwyn, and Mo.

Okay, I'm going to be cautiously happy because no one is tied up.

"Get over here, you son of a bitch!" Dwyn yells. Coda rushes over, punching him on the arm as he drops into a seat between him and Mo.

"I told you we'd get there," Lys says to me when I sit on the couch next to her. "It just took time."

Shaking my head, I look around the cabin, still feeling off. "You did, but we're short two. We haven't won yet."

A static-y voice mumbles something over the speakers and I click my belt on as the plane moves. I turn my chair, but the windows are covered.

Mo rolls his eyes as he shrugs. "They did it on the way here, too. Your mask is in the pocket. We have to put them on or they'll stop."

"Yeah, some asshole day trader tried it on the way in and they wouldn't taxi until it was back," Dwyn adds.

I don't like this.; I have a bad feeling.

But once everyone puts them on, the plane moves again and I hear a hangar door opening. It's too late to do anything about my weird gut feeling without making ourselves bigger targets, so I grip the arms of the seats as the speed ramps up along the runway. Before long, we're in the air and I settle back into my chair. There's so much I want to say to the men in front of me, but I just don't know who's listening.

I frown when it occurs to me we're short another person. Mo and Dwyn had one of his boss' toadies with them when I saw them in the auction block. He's not here. "Where's… uh… your friend?"

Mo stays silent, looking at me as if he can see through and doesn't like what he's found. Dwyn, however, leans forward and looks at me with mischief written all over his face. "Joaquin will meet us in the city, Duchess. He's driving the items *El Jefe* bought to a secondary airstrip where they will be smuggled out of the country."

That seems… odd.

"Ah. I remember now. You mentioned your associate might be late to the meeting with our client," I reply carefully. I'm making this up on the fly, but what else am I supposed to do? They've obviously got something up their sleeves and I can't read their damn minds.

Lys gives me a wink and I frown. *Is she in on this, too?*

"Good to see you're well," Mo says as he looks at Coda. His voice is gruff and I can tell he's holding back whatever he wants to say, but it's obvious he was worried. Maybe the stone faced muscle man has learned to express… something? His eyes flick to me, the gaze intense and I look away.

Probably not.

We're all quiet for a while after that, absorbed in thoughts that we can't voice out loud. It doesn't bother me, but I watch Coda and Dwyn fidget in their seats, fighting the urge to move and chatter. I swallow hard when a lump forms in the back of my throat. I didn't know I'd missed camaraderie or even company until I adopted Lys by mistake and having these idiots sitting across from me like they used to is making me even more squishy inside.

Grunting, I tilt my chair back, closing my eyes. Maybe some rest would help. This has been an emotional day and I don't do emotions we—My thoughts stop when the intercom crackles then a voice I recognize instantly fills the room.

"Greetings, Duchess!

Or should I say… Guillotine?

I applaud your absolutely ingenious strategy of forming two well-known identities in vastly different skill sets!
It *makes so much more sense that you've evaded both hunters and law enforcement for years. You were not only a woman, but also multi-skilled.*

Truly, you're to be commended for your resourcefulness and cunning.

Unfortunately for you and your compatriots on this flight, my admiration only goes so far. You defied my orders to eliminate the hacker and after I responded in kind to your betrayal; you had the gall not to die. I could have forgiven that impertinence in the right circumstances, Guillotine, really, I could have.

But you spent your time hunting down this pathetic rockstar rather than complete the job I graciously offered you.

Alas, fool me once, shame on you. Fool me twice—well, I don't allow that.

You might think I set this entire event up to get even with you, but I assure you, I did not. I simply followed the clues you left in the desert to that cretin, Il Tasso, and his ilk. When I realized he had something you desired, I arranged this Forum to lure you while also expanding my reach and filling my coffers.

Win-win-win, as they say.

It might seem silly to give you all this information, but I enjoyed our previous talks. I wanted to explain why I'm doing what I am and let you know I'm truly saddened that we cannot work together for the glorious future we discussed.

I simply cannot abide such insubordination and if I did, I'd lose control of the army of loyal followers I'm amassing. So take comfort in knowing your death will ignite a spark that will fuel the fire our world so desperately needs to cleanse the forest.

Goodbye, Guillotine.

Enjoy your final moments, as deliverance is upon you."

My head whips around when I hear a sound near the cockpit. A hawk masked man clad in black looks at us and I can *feel* the smirk as he opens the door to the plane, leaping out without a word.

"Fuck," Mo says as the wind tears through cabin. "We have to get out of here."

"How?" Dwyn shouts. "We're in the air, man."

I look at the guys and my friend, my gut churning as I worry about someone other than me for the first time in a situation like this. My mind goes blank, The Guillotine taking over as I rise from my seat. Ignoring their bickering and shouts, I walk to the back of the cabin, looking in the closets typically used by air staff. There are several packs stuffed in the last one and I yank them out. The pilot took the one by the cockpit, but there are four here. Someone will have to share, but hopefully, it will get us to the ground without being too damaged.

"Everyone shut up!" I growl as I look at them and toss the bags in the middle of the floor. "Lys needs to share with someone. She's small, so Mo can take her. Let's move."

My words sink in and before I know it, Mo is talking with my friend as they head for the open door. My eyes find Coda's and he gives me a lop-sided grin. Everyone straps into their chutes, preparing to jump despite the odds being fucking terrible.

"Time to go," Mo says. His arms around Lys as he simply falls out the door without even looking down. I can hear her screaming as they go and I nod at Coda.

He jumps next, but Dwyn insists on me going next. I leap out, watching for him to follow. When he's almost even with me, I open my mouth to yell, but nothing comes out when the plane we just jumped from explodes.

"Could people stop trying to *blow me up* for *one fucking day*??!" I shout in fury.

Dwyn shrugs, reaching behind his shoulder to pull on the release, then his eyes widen. I blink when his face falls, ice filling my veins as I realize what's happening.

"You'd better not be getting ready to tell me that parachute is a knapsack, asshole." Coda glares as he drifts past us and I suck in a breath.

"Hold on to me, D."

"That won't work. I'm too—"

"Just do it. Whatever happens, we're all together."

Which won't matter a damn bit if we're dead, but that's okay.

I've come back to life before.

Preorder Wicked (Book Three of Villains & Vixens) here!

REVIEWS, PRINT, AND MERCHANDISE

If you have enjoyed this book, please leave reviews! It helps other
readers find my work,
which helps me as an indie author.

Thank you!

**Reviews are appreciated
on the following platforms:**

Amazon
Goodreads
Bookbub
StoryGraph
TikTok
Instagram
Facebook

To purchase print copies or merchandise, go to The Worlds of
Cassandra Featherstone

WORLD GUIDE & PRONUNCIATIONS (NOT DONE)

PEOPLE

Remy Arsine Benoit (Reh MEE ARseeuhn Beh NWAH) FMC who survived a death trap and has been living under aliases for the past thirteen years

Aliases: The Duchess, The Guillotine

Nicknames: Pinky, Jazz, Shooter, Blue Raspberry Girl, Smurfette, Bluey, Feral Girl

Scents: Night blooming Cereus, Rose, woodsy notes, peach, apricot, vanilla, musk, amber

Identifying Marks: UV The Six tattoo, various ink all over her body to cover that, nipple piercings, clit and labia piercings, earrings, septum, tongue piercing, all can be taken out.

Coda Ramone (COHduh Ruhmoan) 'emo cowboy' rock star, fixer, and member of The Five; supposedly did stuff with goats;

Aliases: Jazz Man, The Cowboy

Nicknames: Emo Boy

Scents: Orange, Grapefruit, Pepper, Pelargonium, Flint,Vetiver, Cedar, Patchouli, Benzoin

Identifying Marks: UV tattoo of The Six, various tattoos all over body

Dwyn O' Shanahan (DW in OH ShahniHahN) master thief, ADHD, thrill seeker and member of The Five; has hyper-spatial synesthesia;

Aliases: The Ghost, The Creeper

Nicknames: D, Slick, Dwynnie

Scents: Coal, English Rose, Oak, Black Currant, gunpowder, Wildflowers, Violet Leaf, Oakmoss, Herbal Notes

Identifying Marks: tattoos, the UV tattoo of The Six, magic cross

Raz Miranda (RahZ Mihranduh) hacker, lover of Jinx, and member of The Five

Aliases: L'Araña

Nicknames: Razzie, Professor Pokemon, Van Boy

Scents: Bitter Orange, Bergamot, Black Pepper, Fir, gunpowder, Tobacco, Cognac

Identifying Marks: tattoos, UV tattoo of The Six

Mauricio Battaglia (Mahr EE che OH Buh TAHG LEEuh) Mo (MOH) leader, mercenary, and member of The Five

Aliases: The Fist of Salmanaca

Nicknames: Mo; Mo-Mo, Capitán, Señor Grumpypants, Ironman,

Scents: Nutmeg, Gasoline, Bitter Orange, Black Pepper, gunpowder, Jasmine, Hyacinth, Leather,, Sandalwood, Teak Wood, Marigold, Mastic

Identifying Marks: UV tattoo of The Six; various tattoos; has teeth ahrpened to wolf's fangs by *LI*

Jinx Monroe (Jihncks MOHN roh) grifter, lover of Jinx, and member of The Five

Aliases: The Chameleon, *El Mata,* Alharba'

Nicknames: Jinxy; J; Casanova

Scents: Labdanum, Cognac, Opoponax, Myrrh, Leather, Patchouli, gunpowder, , Cedar, Wormwood, White Tobacco, Celery, Musk

Identifying Marks: UV tattoo of The Six; tongue piercing

Elysium (EE lees ee um) Lys (LiSS) a lower level thief Remy worked with in the past who is now her BFF; loves 80s and 90s cartoons; makes Remy watch TV and movies to get pop culture educated

Aliases:

Nicknames: Lys, Morgana.

Scents: vanilla, almond, fruity, nutty, powdery,woody, white floral, balsamic

Identifying Marks: tattoos, wild hair.

Ape Regina (ahPAY Reh GEE nuh) master thief/grfiter who takes credit for her ex-partners' wrok

Le Voleur de Sangre (luh VOH-lair deh SAHNg) assassin, employed by The Company, leaves his victims drained of blood, and mate of *Reina Pantera*

Reine Pantera (ray-nuh Pan-tear-uh) redheaded assassin, thief, and more; employed by The Company, mate of *Le Voleur,* aka little Tailfeather

Alqatu (ahL Cat oo) famous thief at Prague Castle event

Professor Arnaud (ar-Noh) the *Les invisibles* master forger and professor who convinced the guys to betray Remy as a teen; now dead

The Cobra (coh-bruh) mobster Remy kills at beginning of Blood-thirsty

Shadow Douche (sahd-OH Doosh) voice-only villain who hires Remy to kill Raz; seeming mastermind of somehting much bigger

The Commandant (com-ehn-dahnt) eyepatch wearing vicious leader of *Les Invisibles*

Charice (share-ees) Coda's long-suffering agent

Tomáš (tohmahss) concierge at Mandarin Oriental in Prague

High Legion- a group of the highest members of *Les Invisibles*, includes The Commandant

The Company- one of the large criminal organizations, competitor with *Les Invisibles*

El Guapo (L gwap-oh) famous hacker at Prague Castle

Horseman (whore-s-man) famous assassin at Prague Castle

Lady Volkov (lay-dee vohl-kahv) member of the High Legion; her teams compete with The Five

Trái dúa (tchai-zoa) female operative who leads Lady Volkov's team

The Raptor (rap-tore) member of the High Legion; untrustworthy;

Brannigan (bran-ih-gain) CEO Remy entices for human trafficking at the Prague Castle; marked for death later in her mind

The Syndicate- the third largest criminal organization

Nachte- leader of goons in Sex Machines Museum

Il Noche- another large criminal organization

The Collective- group robbing the old Nazi's house in London

An Taibhse (anh tau-shuh) elite thief at Baron's villa

Umbra Vulpes (uhm-bruh vuhl-peyz) elite thief at Baron's villa

Dmitry Laska (dim-mee-tree lah-skee) elite thief at Baron's villa

The Blade (blay-d) assassin and thief, free lance, mate of mysterious long haired man

Joaquin (Wakeen) newphew of *El Jefe* who escapes with Mo to get out of the cartel

Morder "Chomp" (MORE dair) ex-Company assassin who lives in jungle of Columbia, owns bar where ne'er do-wells meet

Tyr (Teer)

Il Tasso (eel Tahsoh) mid-level criminal who has Reny put in the Somalian prison

LOCATIONS

Mangust's Compound- desert in Somalia

Hotel- Beledywn, Somalia

Safe House- Paris, France

Rainforest Compound- Colombia

Loft/Warehouse- New York City

Prison/Institution- Unknown

Lair of Masks- Unknown

Yokohama Industries- Tokyo

National Museum- Paris, France

The Bitter End- bar in Colombia

The Plaza Hotel- New York City

Crash Spot- Westchester County

The Neon Oasis- criminal club in NYC

Les Invisibles Compound- mysterious island off the coast of Argentina where orphans are taken to be trained for the criminal life

Chez Arc En Ciel- club where Remy performs and kills The Cobra for a job

l'Academie des Invisibles- school where the criminals are trained on the island

Hôtel de Crillion- Remy's hotel in Paris when she kills The Cobra

Reverse Cowgirl- bar in Paris where Remy saves Coda

Hotel Rossi- hotel in Berlin when Remy arrives

Postadion- location Remy chooses for meet; gets blown up by thermobarmic drone bomb

Mandarin Oriental Hotel Prague- hotel Remy stays in when she gets to Prague

Sex Machines Museum- place Remy goes for a meet for the Douche

Omega Six and Alpha Nine- storage units The Five use and Remy hides hers near

Mercatus- online forum for criminals and those in need of services to match for jobs on the dark web

Prague Castle- location of large fancy party for *Mercatus* merchants and buyers;

TERMS USED IN V&V WORLD

Open Market- large scale event for thieves and grifters in the criminal world only held occasionally when something big is getting ready to happen; the party at Prague Castle is assumed to be one

Dead Man's Wedding- grift run by The Five at the Prague Castle

HVTs- high value targets

Kansas City Shuffle- grift Jinx uses at Open Market

Mummy's Tiara- another grift Jinx uses at Open Market

Deus ex machina- specialized Open Market for hitters and assassins

Zero Days- Open Markets for hackers only

Commedia dell'Arte- Open Market free-for-alls

Chernobyl- The Five's code words for a meltdown and to get off fast

Boom boom dudes- bombers by trade

Edward Albee- grift used at the Baron's villa

Columbian necktie- a form of execution or post-mortem mutilation in which the victim's tongue is pulled through a deep cut beneath the jaw and left dangling on the neck

CapRes training- training where the trainees are made to suffer actual capture and rendition techniques in order to learn to survive them without giving up their organizations

LIST OF REMY'S ALIASES

Arabella Montaigne- Paris club, French girl in chorus of burlesque

Naomi Sue Blanchard- sorority girl from Texas in bar in Paris

Hannah- librarian from Brooklyn on train to Alsace

Harley Manneheim- emo girl Chicago native disguise Remy chooses in Berlin after she ditches Kate

Lizbet Hurst- Frankfirt Germanu disguise Remy chooses in Berlin

Kate Archer- pink haired Australiian disguise Remy chooses in Berlin; it gets worn out of the storage unit

Melanie Hannibal- Londoner disguise used in the German train station after the bomb

Starla Jaanse- Dutch investigative reporter disguise used when getting off the train in Prague

Irina Petrovich- disguise from Moscow Remy uses in Prague

Elysia Fromme- disguise Remy uses for the Open Market at Prague Castle

Stella Buonotti- disguise used by Remy in Prague that features the blue hair of the orginal book cover

Callista Roman- disguise out of Chicago Remy uses in Prgaue after the Sex Museums fiasco, liquor distributor

GET A SECRET BONUS SCENE!

For another secret bonus scene that follows *Veiled Flame, click the link below, sign up for my newsletter, and get your freebie.*

Get your bonus scene here!

SNEAK PEEK: VEILED FLAME

LOSER

Kat

The little blue icon on my app has been glaring at me all day, but I'm too damn nervous to open it. Everyone at Woodlawn High has been buzzing all day with their notifications and the squeals of joy and moans of despair were too much for me to take. My anxiety is through the roof—this is the moment I've been waiting for since middle school, but I can't seem to force myself to bite the billet and check.

Maybe it's because I don't have the support system most of my classmates have?

That's probably true, given I've always been a loner and I don't fit into any specific 'caste' here. It's hard to make friends when you get shuffled from foster home to foster home over the years. I've rarely stayed anywhere long enough to make a friend, much less a group of them.

I'm not delinquent or anything—the families I've been placed with just return me like a pair of pants that doesn't fit after a year or so. The caseworkers click their tongues sympathetically and hunt down a new placement, but I've never been given a reason *why* people don't want me around. One lady said I must be born under a bad sign and hell if I knew what that meant other than I'm not good enough to keep around.

It would be different, almost understandable, if I misbehaved or got bad grades. But I don't—I'm always in the top five percent of my class and I do everything I'm asked. I don't even lord my smarts over the other kids or adults. Being presentable and unassuming was something I adapted long ago to improve my probability of staying in a home long term.

Unfortunately, it never worked and though I should be a shoo-in for scholarships and acceptances galore, I can't bring myself to be rejected yet again.

So I wait for the last bell of the day, slinging my bag over my shoulder and trudging home to the latest in my temporary housing. I can't even contemplate looking at the possible heartache waiting for me in the college application system WHS insisted we use. The fear is too great and despite knowing I'll be on my own for good at the end of this year, I'm unable to risk the pain.

I hate being this way.

My court mandated therapist says it's some sort of attachment disorder that's common in foster kids, but I think that's bullshit. The problem isn't *me* not forming attachments; it's asshole adults not forming one to me. Being left at a safe haven in a fucking basket as a baby wasn't because *I* did anything wrong—again, fucking adults couldn't handle their commitments.

As usual, I arrive home to an empty house. There are two other kids who live here—Bryce and Blake—but they're at football practice. Of course, the Jamesons *love* them; they get to strut around at games because their strays are the stars of the team. I'm not mistreated, but I'm definitely an afterthought. Both of my 'parents' are still at work, so I drop my bag on the couch and head for the kitchen to get a snack:

Don't get me wrong. I *could* have been placed in far worse homes than any of the seven I've been in since elementary school. None of the ex-fosters starved, beat, molested, or abused me. They were all decent folks with jobs and houses that weren't hellholes, but they never liked me.

I have no idea why. I tried to be everything they wanted.

But when the end of each school year came, I was handed in like a textbook and off I went to some group home until the next contestant stepped up. It baffled everyone, not just me, but that's what happened every single time.

Sighing, I pull some fruit out of the fridge and grab a soda. I have homework to do and if I want to have time to work on my stories, I'll need to get it done before the house is full of people at dinner time. Bryce and Blake will have gotten messages about their applications, too, and I'd bet my pinkie toe those idiots got into some big sports school. Brett and Allison will be oozing happiness for them and I don't know if I'll be able to keep food down if I have to admit my failure when they ask.

Being eighteen sucks ass.

After I grab my books and tablet, I head down to the den. I have to give my current parents credit; they set up a very nice workspace for us to study in the converted basement. By the time they took me in, the Jamesons created a cozy room down here where the three of us could relax and do our work for school without being interrupted. It might have been more for the boys than me, but I appreciated it all the same. Desks, a couch, big chairs, and bookshelves fill the space, making it almost seem like our mini-library. They even put a small fridge for drinks and snacks in case we had to be up late to cram.

It's my favorite place in the entire house and I spend most of my time here.

I sink into the huge armchair, putting my drink and snack on the side table. It only takes a few minutes to arrange myself in the soft cushions and I pause to tug my headphones out of my pocket. Music always soothes my jagged edges and I need it to stay focused on the bullshit AP Calculus I need to keep my average up in. My course load is heavy, but I applied to tough colleges. I wouldn't have a chance to get in, especially on a scholarship, if I wasn't taking equally challenging classes in comparison to all the prep school kids.

As always, the sounds of Vivaldi carry me away as I scrawl equations on my screen and before long, thoughts of the blue notification completely fade away.

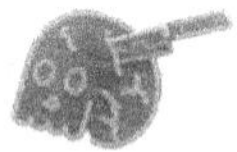

"Kat!"

The shouts barely register as I continue working on the problem set, gnawing on my lower lip in concentration.

"Jesus fuck, where is she? I could eat a hippo!"

"Kat!"

Thumping followed by what could pass for a stampede of elephants jerks me out of my math filled trance when Bryce and Blake come down the stairs. They smell as bad as the aforementioned pachyderm's cage, so they must have rushed home right after practice. The blond twins glare at me as if I'm the offending element despite being sweaty and covered in dirt and grass stains.

This doesn't bode well.

Usually, they're tired and hungry after practices so I'm used to cranky ass boys, but tonight, there's a light to their faces. That had to mean they've gotten their letters and dinner will be a gush fest in honor of their perfection. I'm going to need all of my strength to fake smile and nod as Brett and Allison fawn over them.

I don't begrudge them their success—not really. They work hard and play even harder on the field. It's not their fault they're the American dream teens and I'm the nerdy basement troll no one wants. But it's awfully hard living in the shadow of their bright light, especially when I'm no less intelligent or talented.

"I'm finishing the AP Calc, guys. What do you want?"

They roll their eyes at me before Blake scoffs. "It's not due until Monday. You're so hyper."

Duh. I take anxiety meds, douchebag; of course I'm 'hyper.'

"I can only be who I am, Blake." That earns me a snort from Bryce and I know it's because he thinks that's the problem. "Is dinner ready?"

"Almost. Get upstairs and set the table so we can shower—Brett's orders." Blake grins smugly.

The two of them seem to always arrange it so chores get passed to me for some half-assed reason and this is no exception. Sighing, I put my stuff aside, fully intending to hide down here after the dinner mess is cleaned up. Likely by me, but like I said, I could definitely live in worse foster homes so I let it go. Doing some chores isn't worth risking the group home for the last few months of my high school career.

They take off running up the stairs and I wait for them to disappear before I follow suit. My phone is tucked in my pocket and I feel like it's a stone of shame I have to bear. I know once the adults make over the twins' success, they will remember me, and I'll be forced to find out what disappointment lies in wait for me. The dread weighs on me, but I head into the sunny kitchen and pick up the pre-prepared pile of plates, silverware, and napkins on the counter.

Allison looks up from the stove and gives me a half-smile, nodding as I take the dishes into the dining room. Like I said, no one is mean or horrid, they just seem…obligated. After a while, it makes it hard to waste time trying to be bright and sunny. Being reserved makes it a hell of a lot easier not to feel rebuffed when they don't pay attention to you regardless.

"Make sure you include champagne glasses for your dad and I!" she calls from the other room.

The twins definitely got acceptance somewhere big. Brett must have gotten the bubbly on the way home.

Once I set the table, I return to help Allison bring out the roast and sides. I'm a little amazed at her efficiency when it comes to getting the housework done while working full time, but I suppose it's something people with real parents get taught as they grow up. My home life has been so fractured that I haven't learned how to cook more than very basic shit from YouTube videos. That may be a problem after graduation, but I've never felt comfortable enough to ask Allison if she'd teach me. I'm sure she would try, but it doesn't feel right.

"How was school, Kat?"

I look over my shoulder, seeing Brett in the entry to the dining room. He's already changed from work and smiling, but I see the distraction in his eyes. He's waiting for the boys to come down. "It was fine. I've got a Calc test at the end of the week. I'll be studying a lot to get ready."

"Good, good. No matter what happens with applications, keeping your grades up will ensure no one pulls any offers," he says.

Those words aren't for me. They are for the two wet haired boys who just appeared behind him.

"Kat's too much of a geek to ever let her grades slip, Dad," Blake says as he pushes past his brother and drops into his usual chair at the table. "Grab me a Powerade since you're in the kitchen, mouse!"

Both Brett and Bryce stare at me and I turn around, heading to the fridge despite the fact that I was *not* closer than the other twin. Out of habit, I take two of the drinks and a soda for myself. I've been here long enough to know Bryce will send me back to get him one as well. It would feel like typical sibling stuff, but for some reason, I just *know* they do it to fuck with me. I have no idea why I feel that way, but trusting my gut has been the one thing that helped me get through all the upheaval in my life over the years. It's a good gauge for knowing when I'll get booted or if people are being earnest in their reactions.

The therapist says that's some sort of trauma induced early trigger warning shit, by the way.

After I hand out the drinks, I sit down on my side of the table and we wait for Allison to come out. Brett is at his seat at the far end of the table and the twins are punching each other as they look at something on their phones. I know where this is all going but I drop my gaze to the table, swallowing the coppery taste of fear as it courses through my body.

I'm going to be exposed and there's nothing I can do to stop it.

Read the first three episodes free on Kindle Vella: https://www.amazon.com/kindle-vella/story/B0BSTMB1X3

SNEAK PEEK:
COME OUT & PREY

JUST A GIRL

Delores

Sighing, I look around my bedroom at the posters and decorations covering my walls. My obsession with pop music, musical theater, and high school rom-coms sickens my parents. They would prefer me to be into heavy metal and horror movies like the other kids my age.

Being the only child in a family as prominent as mine is difficult when you don't fit the mold. My parents—like their parents and all my friends' parents—are apex predators. Preds rule our world, and the division between us and prey is so severe that we regulate them to a completely different echelon of society. Prey shifters are weak and beneath our lofty abilities. The ruling class of elite predator families stretches back generations, and they've evolved into a bunch of assholes who only care about succession and greed.

My animal has not manifested yet, but it will soon enough. Luckily for me, none of my friends have manifested their inner animals, either. I'm part of the in-crowd at school, and my boyfriend, Todd, is the most popular guy in my class. While he and I aren't officially engaged yet, we've talked about it enough that I know it's only a matter of time before he puts a ring on my finger. I should be on top of the world, but I can't help but feel like my life just doesn't fit me the way it's supposed to.

Every teenager wishes their life was different, but I dream of becoming an entirely different person. Not inside, mind, because I'm pretty comfortable with who I am. I don't want to be part of this legacy, this society, or even this family. They are all focused on competing to be the richest, the deadliest, or the most powerful, and I want no part of it.

I walked over to my closet and pulled out the outfit that I had chosen for my tour of Apex Academy. My mother hired her personal designers to create a custom school uniform for today and expects me to present the 'appropriate' image of the sole heir to a Council seat.

I hate having to pretend to be like them because I'm nothing like them.

Regardless, I pull on the short, pink pleated skirt, three quarter length sleeve blouse, knee socks, and Mary Janes that comprise the uniform for my exclusive private high school. Since I'm using a 'college visit' day to tour the Academy, I'm expected to represent Shifter Secondary as well.

Shifter Secondary is the most exclusive high school for unmanifested shifter teens on the East Coast. Unfortunately for me, it was not my parents' first choice for my education. They hoped I'd follow in their footsteps by choosing to force my animal to emerge early. If I had done that, I could have attended *Apex Academy Lower School.*

I didn't have the stomach to use my body in that manner at fourteen.

Their heirs followed my lead, which made my mother and father furious and their hoity-toity council colleagues angry. My closest friends, the Heathers, also refused to force their animals to emerge, as did Todd and his friends. That was the first time the adults in our circle decided I was a bad influence. After that, I had to toe the line at every turn, ensuring that I followed all the strict rules and regulations that govern the heirs to council seats.

Everywhere I went, I had to dress in a manner befitting the next Drew to sit at the table. They forced me to take dance lessons, piano lessons, diction lessons, and other more humiliating tutorials to prepare for the day that I became a true predator. In our society, teenagers have no say in how we prepare for our animals to emerge.

Your parents make all the decisions, choose your friends, choose your mates, and decide every detail of your life down to what you eat every single day. At least, that's how it is in my family, because my mother is from the old world.

She came over from Slovenia when she was incredibly young and met my father on the society fundraiser circuit. Her idea of preparing her daughter for the future involves lessons in makeup, clothing, jewelry, and on how to keep your mate satisfied. Lucille is completely unconcerned about whether I end up happy, only that I attend to my council seat and my husband's *needs*.

Once I get dressed, I grab my vintage Vuitton bag and peek at the mirror for a last check before I head downstairs. I tuck my perfectly highlighted blonde tresses behind my ears, and the smokey eye and winged liner are on point with this year's fashion trends. I apply a quick swipe of cherry red lip gloss and open my mouth, inspecting my teeth to make sure they are pearly white. Even though once I develop threatening incisors or sharp fangs, something will inevitably cover them in blood, my parents want my smile to look like a toothpaste commercial.

It's all such utter bullshit.

I take a deep breath and turn on my heel, heading for the door. I can already hear my parents yelling in a Scotch and vodka induced rage in the drawing room. It's only eleven thirty in the morning, for Hera's sake.

Lucille and Bruno don't fuck around with cocktail hour. They are nicely sauced by ten a.m. every day, without exception. I can't remember a time when my parents didn't get drunk off their asses at an event or party, much less in our 'home'. They liquor up and fight until they part for the day, and then start again once they arrive home from their daily commitments.

I brace for the barrage of criticism my mother will subject me to when I cross the threshold. Closing my eyes, I whisper words of encouragement to myself via lyrics to some of my favorite songs, desperately trying to hype myself up before she can tear me down.

"Delores! I hear you breathing at the top of the stairs, darling. Come down this instant and let your father and I inspect your presentation."

My mother's purr *sounds* friendly, but believe me, it's not. I roll my eyes as I make my way down the stairs, knowing my mother won't hesitate to send one of the staff if I don't acquiesce to her command. Most of their staff would gleefully jizz themselves with being chosen to drag me downstairs for inspection.

At this time of day, the only servant in the drawing room will be Matilda—my ex-nanny turned personal assistant—and that request would test her loyalties. As the only person in my household who has my back, I don't want to put her in that position, so I answer. "Yes, Lucille. I'm on my way."

I'm not allowed to refer to her as 'mother' because it makes her feel old. 'Lucille' is always what I've called the woman who supposedly gave birth to me. I'd be tempted to disbelieve we shared any DNA at all if it weren't for our similar bone structure. She's about as nurturing as a rattlesnake, and if it weren't for Matilda, I might have died as a child. If the kitchen staff whispers are accurate, I have to accept that my mother neglected to feed me much of the time.

"You coddle her far too much, Lucille," my father growls. "As the heir to our family seat, Delores will come without being instructed to do so. We will not tolerate her insolence after her animal emerges. She will behave as I command or suffer the consequences."

The last of Bruno's rant echoes off the marble walls of the foyer as I step onto the hideously expensive, endangered teak floor. Schooling my features into the mask of indifference I wear whenever I have to deal with them, I enter their den of drunken fights with my spine steeled for an emotional assault.

"I apologize for my tardiness, Father. I only wished to perfect the image I will present during my tour of Apex Academy. I realize it is imperative I impress the Headmistress and her staff."

The humanoid features of his face shift seamlessly, and the hungry crocodile inside of him gives me a toothy smirk. "You will impress them, daughter, or so help me… I'll send you to Bloodstone Isle."

My stomach drops like a stone as I barely suppress a shiver.

Bloodstone Isle is a reformatory school. It's surrounded by spells and enchantments to prevent students from escaping—a feat that has only happened once in its one thousand years of existence. The most feared cat group in the shifter world—the Khan ambush—runs the school, and they're rumored to consume errant students when the Council allows it.

It's the threat both rich and poor shifter parents used to keep their children in line. Wealthy parents like mine use it as a method of controlling any heirs that refuse to conform to the rigid structure of our society. Predators don't value the lives of those who are weak, and they label heirs who refuse to take their rightful place at the top of the food chain weak. Everyone knows Bloodstone is full of criminals, miscreants, and psychos, and even they don't seem to survive.

Bloodstone is a death sentence—pure and simple.

"Y-yes, Father. I understand," I croak out. As if the pressure of touring my new school isn't enough, now I worry the Dean will relay something to my parents that gets me shipped off to Death Island.

"Bruno, darling, if you scare her, she'll frown. That causes wrinkles. Delores, chin up and smile for us."

Swallowing the lump in my throat, I flash my mother my brightest smile. Her blood-red lips curve, and her leopard fangs burst free as she all but purrs. "I will not have you sullying the family name, Delores. It's bad enough that your education gave you ideas about your value beyond breeding stock. You will take the seat on the Council when it is time, but the husband we select will control the business—as nature intended. Do you hear me?"

My eyes narrow briefly, and for what is possibly the millionth time this week alone, I nod at my mother to appease her temper. "Yes, Lucille."

"Excellent!" The leopard fades as she claps her hands. "Matilda!"

The tiny woman steps up, her eyes wide behind her glasses. She's a pred, but the smaller size of hawk shifters puts her in the servant class. I believe she genuinely lives in fear of one or both of my parents deciding to eat her. "Yes, madam?"

"Fetch Bruiser. He will accompany Delores to the academy for her tour. Tell him to take the Escalade—it won't do for her to arrive in a tiny car—it will draw attention to her extra weight. We must make an impression."

Matilda nods, and I feel the fear radiating from her, and I don't blame her. Bruiser is one of my parents' bodyguards and our frequent chauffeur. He's a Komodo dragon shifter and the house staff are terrified of him. It's hard not to be, given that he prefers to play with his food, then eat it after it's dead. The kitchen crew believes he 'handled' the gardener that looked too long at my mother when I was ten. He disappeared without a trace.

Once Matilda scurries away, I watch my parents drink and bicker about their plans for the day. Bruno is going golfing with a congressman, and Lucille is going to the spa. We all know that both outings will include stops at the homes of their current pieces of ass for a quickie, but no one talks about it. The appearance of the loving couple has to be maintained, although neither of them has slept in the same room since I was a baby.

They don't give a damn about fidelity; I learned that at an early age. Children often discover things they shouldn't because of adults discount their ability to understand the conversations happening around them.

I stopped keeping track of who they're boning long ago, because I'd need an assistant to keep the affairs straight.

While my parents' marriage is a sham, I remind myself that my boyfriend, Todd, isn't like them. Yes, his parents only own half the live entertainment industry, but my father allows me to see Todd. The other parents will force the Heathers to accept an arranged betrothal, and I'm grateful I'm lucky enough to have found the perfect match on my own as my high school sweetheart.

"Delores, Bruiser is ready to escort you to Apex. He's pulling the car around now," the hawk shifter says softly.

Snapping out of my reverie, I smile at the trembling woman. Bruiser must have scared the living hell out of her. For no other reason than it amused him, I'm sure. He's as much a brute as his name implies, and I don't look forward to riding alone to the academy with him.

Something about that shifter gives me the creeps…

SNEAK PEEK: HOME TO THE HOLLOW

CHAPTER 1- ROAD TO THE HOLLOW

Jolene

"I'm sorry; could you repeat that?"

Looking at the agent in front of me in disbelief, I lean forward as if changing my position will alter the words that came out of his mouth. He grimaces, clearly unused to relaying this news to prospective trainees. After a moment of silence that feels oppressive, he clears his throat. I wait, unwilling to make his job easier.

"Miss… Whitley," he begins, pulling at the knot on his tie as he stands. He walks around the mahogany desk, coming to lean against the corner diagonal to me.

The crisp navy suit is standard government official, and the Harvard stripe on his tie tells me all I need to know about his upbringing. This guy grew up with a silver spoon in his mouth and rose up the ranks in the F.B.I. by playing politics. Handling a situation like mine is probably not his typical task, and I wonder why they chose him for this duty. I meet his gaze steadily, having learned the tricks of his trade from years of dealing with CEOs and officials with significantly more status than him.

He sighs, clearly disappointed that I'm not a blubbering mess. His wife—I can see the ring on his hand—is probably a sorority belle from UV that lets him run roughshod over her to secure her position as trophy wife. This man has aims much higher than his current position in the DOJ, and he's less than thrilled to be here speaking with me.

"Miss Whitley. As I said, I cannot release the information used to make hiring decisions. You can make a FOIA request, if you so choose, but I was told that because of the circumstances of your childhood, that request is likely to remain classified."

"Circumstances of my… I grew up in a small town in the Midwest, not Beirut! My parents were teachers, for the love of God. They have awarded me three degrees, and I developed a career consulting with governments and CEOs of multi-national corporations! I have *never* failed a background check, Agent Grant. This is outrageous."

Crossing his arms over his chest, he sighs again, running a hand over his slicked back hair. "I cannot speak to that. I can only relay the information that we have denied your application, and that re-applying during another session will not change the results. You simply cannot work for the F.B.I. or any other agency under the Department of Justice."

I stand, infuriated beyond all reason. My eyes flash with anger as I stare him down. "This is *not* over, Agent Grant. I am *more* than qualified. There is not one blemish on my record. I deserve to be here. I will fight this decision tooth and nail—I have aimed all of my education and training at working within the behavioral unit of this agency."

Shaking his head, he pushes off the desk and drops back into the luxurious chair. "You can do what you wish, Miss Whitley, but the answer will remain the same. I suggest you focus your considerable talents and effort on finding another career path—one that is actually open to you."

My face is a mask of shock, but I quickly school it, picking up my purse and turning on my heel to stalk out of his office. I wasn't lying; I intend to fight this to the fucking Supreme Court if necessary. I've been working towards being a member of the profiling team since I left teaching, and I have every confidence that I can prove that I'm not only qualified, but in no way a security risk.

How *dare* they turn down my application and refuse to give me a reason? That can't be legal! It's a government position; they have to release the records if I request them. But the agent seemed to believe that I'd run into a brick wall with such a request, so there's something going on. Did I piss off some diplomat while I was in Europe and not realize it? Is someone pulling the strings to destroy my career?

I look around and realize that I've exited the building and I'm standing in the elevator to the parking structure. I was so angry that I made my way back to my car completely on autopilot. I check my pocket and realize that I even signed out and returned the visitors' badge. Taking a deep breath, I close my eyes.

It's been a long time since I was so angry that I had a functioning black out. The last time was when my parents got killed and because of my assignment, I couldn't come home for their funeral. The time before that was the last day I worked in a school. Both times, I lost time like this—I was functioning like a regular person to everyone around me, but when I came to, I had no idea what I'd done during that period. It usually lasts for weeks, but this time, it was only about fifteen minutes.

Clicking the remote to my car, I climb in and rest my forehead on the steering wheel. Each time this happened in the past, I spent months piecing together what happened while I was out. Through careful interrogation and immaculate people skills, I could recreate every minute of the lost time and record it in the journal I've been keeping since childhood. The school therapist always made me show her the journals to prove that I recovered my memories from the episodes.

Andromeda Bane was *not* a woman to be trifled with and even the kids and teens at the schools knew it.

I sigh. I haven't thought of her for a long time. The image of her powerful features and kind eyes fills my mind, and I reach up to wipe a tear from the corner of my eye. She clearly brooked no shit, but she was always available when I needed her. Her name was a threat and a prayer at Whistler's Hollow Formative and Finishing Schools. Those of us who grew up under her care defended her to the others—the ones who landed in her office because of intentional misbehavior rather than diagnoses.

My head lifts, and I sniffle, my heart crushed at what may be the end of my dreams. Perhaps it is time that I go home and face the place where my parents died. I haven't been there since I moved back to the States because I can't bear to see my childhood home without my parents in it. When they died, I used a state-side attorney to settle their affairs and hired a service to come in and air the house out every couple of months. I couldn't bear to sell it, although I never intended to return to the Hollow. It took my parents, and I never wanted to see it again.

But without the F.B.I. training, there's nothing for me in Richmond. I moved here when I came home from Europe so that I'd be in proximity to my dream, and if that truly is impossible, there's no reason for me to stay. Most of my belongings are still in storage despite living here for two years. I needed little creature comforts to work at the college while I finished my doctorate in Clinical Psychology online. I've been a nomad for so long that I haven't taken the time to develop relationships or put down roots here—even my lease is month-to-month.

It occurs to me I've been sitting in my car in the lot for a long time. If anyone walked by, they'd think that I've lost my marbles. I need to get home, make myself a drink, and think about this.

I never thought I'd be considering moving back to Whistler's Hollow.

Unfortunately, the past is no longer in the past.

Get the mini-omnibus of Road, Return & Roused here!

ABOUT CASSANDRA FEATHERSTONE

Cassandra Featherstone has chan-neled her lifelong passion for writing into a flourishing career, a journey that started when she first grasped a pencil as a gifted child with ADHD.

Her debut novel, born during the solitude of COVID lockdown in March 2020, draws on a tapestry of personal encounters and insights that resonate deeply with her readers.

An international bestseller, Cassandra has topped Amazon charts in categories such as LGBT Anthologies, LGBTQ+ Mystery, and Bisexual Romance, among others. Her works navigate the complexities of bullying, PTSD, body dysmorphia, mental health struggles, personal reinvention, and the empowerment of claiming one's own space. Importantly, Cassandra offers a thoughtful and respectful portrayal of LGBTQIA+ relationships, subtly reflecting her own connection with the community through her narratives.

Her literary repertoire spans sci-fi fantasy, urban fantasy, paranormal, and comedic genres in academy whychoose settings, with a strong commitment to portraying consensual, safe, and accurately depicted BDSM and kink lifestyles. Her books are an invitation to explore transformative stories that are both inclusive and engaging.

Often affectionately called 'The Muppet' for her wacky theater kid personality, she resides in the Midwest with her tech-savvy husband, their creatively inclined college student, a literary-minded dog, and four scheming cats.

READ MORE AT CASSANDRA'S WEBSITE OR HER FACEBOOK PAGE. SIGN UP FOR EXCLUSIVE CONTENT AND UPDATES HERE.

FIND HER ON ANY OF THE SOCIAL MEDIA BELOW AS SHE *LOVES* TO CHAT AND *NEVER* SLEEPS!

ALSO BY CASSANDRA FEATHERSTONE

THE MISFIT PROTECTION PROGRAM SERIES

Road to the Hollow

Return to the Hollow

Home to the Hollow

Rejected in the Hollow

Revealed in the Hollow

Healing in the Hollow

Revenge in the Hollow

AUDIO OF THE MISFIT PROTECTION PROGRAM SERIES

Road to the Hollow

APEX ACADEMY CAPERS

Come Out and Prey

Let Us Prey

In Prey We Trust

Oh Holy Spite (3.5 novella)

Eat. Prey. Love.

Prey It By Ear

AUDIO OF THE APEX ACADEMY CAPERS SERIES

Come Out & Prey

Let Us Prey

In Prey We Trust

TRANSLATIONS OF THE APEX ACADEMY CAPERS SERIES

Come Out & Prey (German)

Let Us Prey (German)

In Prey Trust (German)

DISCORDIA UNIVERSITY

Veiled Flame (Book One)

Quiet Burn (Book Two)

Zero Spark (Book Three)

SECRETS OF STATE U

Blood on the Ice (Book One)

Suspicions on the Stage (Book Two)

Ç

Hell on Wheels (Book One)

Jammer in the Box (Book Two)

F.E.A.R. ACADEMY

Failed State (Book One)

Title TBA (Book Two)

VILLAINS & VIXENS

Bloodthirsty (Book One)

Ruthless (Book Two)

Wicked (Book Three)

Agents of the Ouroboros

Rise of the Resistance

F.E.A.R. Academy

ANTHOLOGIES

Unwritten

Shifters Unleashed

Jingle My Balls

Love is in the Air

Silent Night

Snowed In

All Hallows Eve

www.ingramcontent.com/pod-product-compliance
Lightning Source LLC
Chambersburg PA
CBHW070656010826
48975CB00014B/1442